PRAISE FOR

ALWAYS NEVER MEANT TO BE

"WHITTIER DEFTLY CREATES MORAL ambiguity in the characters' actions... This engrossing, plot-driven novel will keep readers glued to the pages. Similarly, as the duo scouts movie locations, traveling from popular tourist haunts like Pike's Place Market to lesser-known scenic parks, the author creates a love letter to Seattle, such that readers might find themselves planning a trip... The ultimate outcome is neither predictable nor trite. An engaging, thought-provoking love story."

— *Kirkus Reviews*

MAGICAL SEATTLE SERIES

ALWAYS NEVER MEANT TO BE

a love story

AJ WHITTIER

To Amy for reading this thing again and again. And to Maliah for making me write it in the first place (and also for reading it again and again). I literally couldn't have done it without either of you.

CONTENT NOTES

THIS IS <u>NOT</u> A Romance. I start with this because I don't want my Romance-reading girlies to be disappointed. I love Romance. I read Romance and I write Romance. This is <u>not</u> a Romance.

This is a love story. It has many of the same hallmarks as a Romance, with two gorgeous, flawed people falling head over heels, with lots of laughter and tears along the way. It has joy, magic, tons of music, and the wonders of Seattle. But it also has a bittersweet pang that is beautiful, healing, and a teeny, tiny bit of a gut punch. Or maybe a big gut punch, depending on your mood when you read it.

Sometimes this kind of story just feels good. I have always adored bittersweet love stories and I decided it was time I wrote one of my own. If you relish that delicious, upside down, ugh-why-is-this-so-good-but-also-so-upsetting feeling, you might just love this story. I hope you will. I know it makes me very happy. I'm weird like that.

However, at the end of the day – and the end of the book – this is not a Romance. This is a story that features a Hopeful Ever After, but not a traditional Happily Ever After. I hope you'll fall for Sarah and Joe just as I have, and long for them to make it work even as you know it's impossible. I cherish this story so much and it would be a great honor to have you go on this wonderful, often funny, sometimes sad, and ultimately uplifting journey with me.

But if you're someone who only likes Romance, with all that entails – including most importantly, the traditional HEA – this book is not for you. I'm writing lots of other books that I hope will delight you, but you probably want to skip this one!

I also want to acknowledge that this book deals with a variety of topics that may be upsetting for some readers. Chief among these is internalized fatphobia. The main character Sarah wrestles with her weight and feelings of low self-worth, which I have attempted to reflect honestly on the page. But she is also on a journey to overcome those feelings, and that is a beautiful thing!

This book also includes infidelity (although the main characters are never unfaithful to each other), alcohol use, mentions of divorce, and brief references to an ill child and another who is in a car accident (but ultimately okay). If any of these topics are troubling or problematic for you, please read with care.

TWO BABIES, OR HOW IT STARTED
(MARCH, 1983)

ONCE UPON A TIME, there was a mother and a father. And another mother and another father. Of course, none of them were technically mothers or fathers yet, but they soon would be. Because two babies were about to be born.

The girl announced her arrival first in the afternoon, but decided to take her time, not sure she was ready to face the world yet. Several hours in, as her mother hobbled down the Pittsburgh Memorial Hospital corridor trying to coax her little one out, the doctor said, "Don't worry, she'll come out when she's ready."

To which her mother wailed, "Well, whatever she's waiting for, I wish she would hurry up!"

And as she spoke, the mother-to-be of a rather more eager little boy was wheeled around the corner toward her room. The two mothers locked eyes as they breathed through their respective contractions before the nurse placed the boy's mother in the room right next door to the girl's mother.

The boy on his way seemed in a better mood than the girl. He gave his mother little fuss and readied himself for his entrance as quickly as could reasonably be expected. And now, miraculously, the girl finally seemed to be getting ready, too. At last.

The next few hours passed in a whirlwind. And then it happened.

The date was Sunday, March 20th, and the time was 11:38 PM, the precise moment of the Vernal Equinox in Pittsburgh, Pennsylvania. The very instant when the earth straightened out for a fleeting moment and sat itself squarely at a 0° tilt on its axis. Which is to say, no tilt at all, neither toward nor away from the sun. A moment of perfect balance.

There were 10,749 babies born around the world that day. Of those, only two were born that same magical minute when the earth rested at zero. It was surely just a coincidence that those two were born in Pittsburgh, in the same hospital, in rooms right next to each other. That those two special babies took their very first breaths at the exact same instant. That they exercised their lungs in their first moments of life so loudly, so ferociously, that their little ears heard each other, as if they were crying out not just to be alive, but to be heard—and found—by each other. Mere happenstance. What else could it be?

Two perfect babies entered the world at exactly the same moment. Two babies cried out and two babies heard. And Fate smiled.

The tiny girl with the faintest wisp of blonde hair had ten fingers, ten toes, and the most beautiful, scrunchiest little face her parents had ever seen. She cried loudly at first, her inner turmoil on magnificent display, but fell instantly asleep against her mother's chest.

In the next room, a chubby boy with a surprisingly dense shock of dark hair slept in his proud papa's arms. It was no surprise his son was a big boy, dad being a bit of a giant himself. He considered it a good omen. "Our son is going to do big things!"

Eventually, as the mothers grew weak from exhaustion, the fathers agreed to go home and let them sleep.

The girl's mother whispered, "Sleep well, my sweet Sarah," and kissed her tiny forehead before handing her to the nurse, but in the nurse's arms, the newborn cried, restless, unsettled, desperate for the comfort denied her. The nurse popped a pink cap on the baby's head, then led the girl's father down the hall to the nursery. The girl howled and her father worried something was wrong, but the nurse assured him this was normal. She'd soon settle back in to sleep. He watched as the tiniest, most precious gift in his life was laid carefully into a bed and swaddled tightly for comfort. Still the girl howled.

Next door, the boy got his own cap in a dapper shade of sky blue before his father carried him to the nursery. In his father's arms, the boy was calm, quiet, entirely at peace, just as he had been with his mother. At the door to the nursery, the father passed his son, his sun, to the nurse with a quiet, almost inaudible, "G'night, Joseph. Joey. Joe."

But as the nurse took him, the boy began to cry, then to scream. The nurse smiled at the father reassuringly and whispered, "He'll be fine," as she pushed through the door.

Two fathers stood outside a hospital nursery, watching the room within. One stared at his tiny girl in her pink hat, still wailing out for some small comfort to help her rest, her face fiery red, her eyes sealed shut, swaddled, but utterly unsoothed. The other watched as the nurse prepared his son to put him down for the night, his face as red and angry now as the girl's while they screamed and cried and called to each other once again.

Two fathers watched with rapt attention, each terrified his child's shrieks were a certain sign something must be terribly wrong. Each unwilling to leave until they knew all was well. And then they saw it.

The nurse carried the screaming boy toward the howling girl, and as she walked the boy past the girl's bed, the babies stopped crying at precisely the same instant. The nurse lovingly settled the boy into the bed next to the girl, and the two fathers relaxed at last, relieved that their babies would be just fine.

Two babies, a boy and a girl, now peacefully side by side, gurgled quietly a moment, listened, and then fell asleep. Perfectly happy to spend their first night in this big, scary world together. For now they knew they would be just fine.

At least for a while.

PART ONE

FATE

IN POINT OF FACT, Fate has often used food as the instrument of Her designs, a primary tool by which to shape lives and fit pieces together in a cosmic puzzle whose picture can only be seen from the divine height of stars beyond stars. Right along with shooting stars and newborn babies. No belief required, thank you very much. In fact, the less folks believe, the more She enjoys the challenge. And food is as good a place as any to begin.

CHAPTER ONE

SPACE NOODLES AND SEATTLE CHOCOLATES

THE ONLY THING THAT comes to mind when the garage door grinds open is, *Here we go again.* Another night going through the motions. Another night trying to believe it can be like it used to be. Before Sarah turned invisible.

It's already eight o'clock, but despite her plaintively growling stomach, Sarah patiently waited until Ben texted he was finally coming home to start boiling the pasta and robotically chopping the salad veggies. A default subroutine to run and complete as expected, night after night, on cue. Though she has altered the program a little in recent months, adding the onion she loves back into the mix. She used to skip the onion, worried about her breath in intimate encounters, but such concerns are irrelevant these days, so she adds extra.

She manufactures a cheerful "welcome home" smile and silently engages in her most sacred daily ritual, hoping for the best as Ben trudges in and drops his laptop bag on the island. He knocks his chunky glasses crooked pulling off his coat. "Hi, hon," he says, but before she can respond, he's carrying his jacket to the mudroom.

The bitter truth strikes Sarah once again. For years, one delightful rom-com after another had made the case that middle-aged women with perfect kitchens always got happy endings. Maybe they'd have some unexpected complications, sexy shenanigans, and unfortunate miscommunications along the way, but happy endings were assured. And the large, bright space with Carrera marble backsplash, waterfall quartz countertops, and glitzy chandelier was everything she wanted when they finished the renovation three years ago. It was supposed to be the finishing touch on an already nearly perfect life, even if she wasn't much of a cook. Fulfilling career, happy marriage, great sex life, dream kitchen.

Well, at least she's still got the kitchen.

Sarah restores her smile as Ben returns. "Hey. Dinner's almost ready."

"Wow, you're eating late."

She freezes, draining pasta still hanging over the sink. *You're... eating late? You're?*

"Of course. I was waiting for you," she says, preparing herself for what comes next.

"Oh, I grabbed something at the office. Didn't I tell you?" Ben speaks absentmindedly as he scans his texts.

Why does she keep thinking it will be different? Sarah squeezes the handles of the pasta drainer tighter. "Must have slipped your mind."

After spending all weekend working instead of with her, or even in the same house, the very least he could do is have dinner with her. No, scratch that. The least he could do is tell her he isn't coming home for dinner. Again.

Ben offers a perfunctory peck to the side of her head. "Sorry. It's this client. There's so much going on I can't think straight." Then he walks off as if that's the end of it. And so it is, whether she likes it or not. She probably wouldn't have the courage to call him on it anyway. She doesn't have the courage for much these days.

She considers dumping the whole pot of spaghetti in the sink in a fit of rage. That'll show him. Except he's already carried his laptop to his office and won't reemerge for hours, so the message would be as wasted as the pasta. She clenches her eyes shut, compressing her feelings, reshaping her anger into something more comfortable – rejection. Then she goes with option two, eating the whole thing herself.

After dinner, she attempts to watch TV, but the pasta makes her too sleepy to focus, so she texts Gabi to fill her in. Gabi replies within 60 seconds.

Again?!?!? Wtf! I think there are some boxing gloves Max left in the garage somewhere. Want me to fight him for your honor? Gabi's loyalties have never been in doubt.

Tempting. But why do you still have anything of Max's? Sarah mutes the TV and flips channels while Gabi types.

He didn't ask and I didn't offer.

Sarah shakes her head in dismay. *GET RID OF THEM!*

But then how would I defend your honor?

Sarah giggles. Best of all possible friends, Gabi has kept Sarah afloat the last couple years. Sarah might still be adrift, but at least she isn't drowning, and that's mostly thanks to Gabi. Sarah announces her intention to go to bed, weathers Gabi's "old lady" mockery for a few texts, then pockets her phone. Before she can switch off the TV, however, she stops at the sight of the one person she can never click off, Joseph Robert Parker.

She hadn't been paying attention to what movie was playing until he came onscreen, but her heart pings and her insides pulse as she unmutes. At the deep rumble of his voice, she feels the familiar, entirely ridiculous twinge between her legs. How can he still have this effect on her after all this time? Ever since the first instant she laid eyes on him almost twenty years ago, her sights have locked on him like a missile targeting system. Every single time. Not just because he's handsome. She could name a dozen other hunky actors who provide equally good eye candy. And not just because he's talented, though serious acting chops are a prerequisite for someone to make her list of favorites. But Joe has always had something special.

Admittedly, she's never been able to pinpoint that "something" for anyone, including herself, but she sure as hell feels it. It rings out and vibrates within her like an enormous cathedral bell clanging across the entire city while she foolishly, yet inevitably climbs the bell tower, reaches out, and places her hand directly on it. And like a divine tuning fork forged by God Himself, since the moment she was first struck, she still resonates at the same pitch and frequency every time she sees Joe. She *feels* him.

He's been on her TV a lot the last couple years, of course. Especially when everything first went to hell, he was her constant streaming companion. After her job at Synergy fell apart, Sarah fell apart, too. And it seemed only Joseph Robert Parker could put the pieces back together. With her job gone, her husband newly absent, and her hope on the fritz, Joe's movies and shows were the one thing she could count on. When everything was wrong, he was right. When everything felt bad, Joe felt not just okay, but downright good. Eventually, Gabi intervened when she realized just how bad Sarah had gotten and dragged her out of the subbasement of her depression – if not fully out into the world, at least to the daylight basement where she could glimpse sun now and then. But it was Joe who kept her going until then, a few blissful hours at a time.

Sarah has seen this movie naturally. She's watched his entire body of work at least three times in the past two years, but she plops on the couch anyway. It's a small part and his last scene is coming up. She'll wait until it's over, then go to bed.

***

Sarah readies herself for bed with her soothing nightly ritual of expensive skincare, her one reassurance that she hasn't completely given up on herself. But her calm is quickly dashed when she makes the mistake of opening her laptop in bed and surfing to the jobs site for new offerings. She shouldn't do these things so close to bedtime, but she's been avoiding it lately and it's too early to sleep, so she forces herself. Normally, she checks in a couple times a week, ostensibly searching for a job, but willing to settle for a direction. None has emerged. Then again, she's not even sure where to look. Most recently she was "chief operating officer for a large brand marketing company." So operations? Marketing? Executive positions? All of the above? Nothing really feels right anymore.

She slams the laptop shut and tosses it onto the window seat, taking her frustrations out on the innocent machine. She has to figure this out somehow. She can't be jobless and aimless forever. Or living alone in her marriage, as far as that goes. God, she misses what they used to be so fucking much. Ben's right downstairs, but he may as well be on the moon. For approximately the seven hundredth day in a row, Sarah wonders how she let herself fall into this pit of despair. What happened to the smart, confident professional who rose to the top of her company? To the scrappy, can-do fighter who could turn every challenge into an opportunity? To the woman who knew how to seize the day and have fun?

When five minutes staring at the wall yield no discernible results, she heads down for a glass of water, then pops her head into the office to check on Ben. He nearly jumps through the ceiling when she speaks. "Gonna be working long?"

It's a silly question. Of course, he is. He's always working. Or at least he's always at the office or buried in this room doing *something*. What he's doing, she's never really sure, but it's certainly not *her* these days. She pushes down the worry. Still, under the circumstances, the question is more of a pleasantry than anything else. Something to pass the interminable time. But to her surprise, he replies, "Not too much longer, I think."

The answer so shocks her she almost doesn't reply. "So should I wait up?" She does her best to inflect her voice with optimism and a hint of promise, but not so much as to open herself up to disappointment.

"Oh, I'm sure you must be tired," he says without looking at her.

At nine o'clock? Why's he sure she'd be tired? Other than her perpetual exhaustion with life, that is. That and the fact that she's already in her nightshirt with the sleeping cat on it. Okay, that might be reason enough. But she could make an effort, with a little incentive. "Actually, I'm not."

Ben taps away at his keyboard, but flicks her a quick glance and half smile before looking back to his monitor. "Great, see you soon."

As Sarah climbs the stairs, she considers her options. In truth, she is tired. Tired of hoping. Tired of trying. After all this time, surely she should know better. Still, if Ben is coming to bed early, she can try one more time. She walks into her closet and pulls off her cat shirt, then slides on a silky, strappy pink nightie that Ben has always loved. The halter straps hold her heavy breasts in place just so, showing her ample cleavage to best advantage, while the babydoll skirt flows gracefully over the rolls she'd rather forget. It is, quite literally, the best she can do. And in better times, it would be more than enough. Hell, in better times, he'd pull it off her body before she hit the bed. Tonight, she'll just drape herself across the bed and see where the night takes her.

Two hours later, she's still wide awake reading her self-help book on gratitude, waiting on Ben and working through a meditation in the book to remind herself how fortunate she is. In theory, she's living the good life. So good she's riddled with shame for feeling so empty anyway. With so many people struggling in the world, she has no right to complain, but the void doesn't care about any of that.

Maybe it's too hard to stay hungry when she has so much. At least financial need would be some kind of incentive, albeit an unwelcome one, to kick her into motion. Why overcome her fears – of rejection, of failure, even of success – when she can just sink into them like her cozy reading chair? But comfort has its price. As it is, she slips away a little more each day and fears one day soon she might be gone, lost at sea forever.

Ben breezes through, his short cropped brown locks mussed from stress fidgeting, with a pleasant, but disinterested "You're still up" as he shuts the door to the bathroom for his nightlies. He's the clueless captain of a passing ship who waves a friendly hello at the castaway dying of thirst – and just keeps sailing. Not even a hint of recognition or interest in the nightie, let alone what lies beneath it. She's an idiot to keep trying. To keep dreaming that he'll come back to her. Be the sweet, attentive, ravenous Ben he used to be.

Then again, she can't really blame him. She's not very interested in herself anymore either. Sarah glares at the romance novel on her bedside table, abandoned because it was too depressing, then switches off her light.

***

Sarah pushes past the large oak door to her bedroom and kicks her shoes across the hardwood before planting herself by the window. She smirks as she sings her "hello" into the phone, clearly pleased with herself. Her latest text was too big a tease for Gabi to resist long.

"Space Noodles and Seattle Chocolates? Is this a decoder ring situation?" Gabi's snark drips through the line.

"For your host gift. They're perfect." Sarah gazes out at the well-manicured, tree-lined street below. The cushy window seat is her favorite place to while away the lonely hours.

"Space Noodles? I feel like you're making this up."

"They're little noodles shaped like the Space Needle," Sarah explains. "I would have thought the name gave them away."

"Noodles shaped like the Space Needle? Crikey!"

Gabi, the notorious word collector, is at it again. Sarah snickers at her latest linguistic acquisition, bursting in like a foreign stranger. "Crikey? What, are you Aussie now?"

"I'm trying it out," Gabi says. "It's that or huzzah."

"Those are really the choices?"

"Anyway, these Space Noodle things sound janky as hell."

"Trust me, Space Noodles and Seattle Chocolates are perfect." Sarah hears the skepticism implicit in Gabi's silence and continues. "They represent Seattle, they don't break or spill, and they're fun. Who doesn't like pasta and chocolate?"

"Hmm," Gabi mumbles noncommittally while fiddling with something on her end of the line. "Think I need to wash my dress before packing it? What if it shrinks?"

Gabi wore the new dress in question to work that day to show it off. She looked stunning in the bright white, which set off her warm brown skin beautifully, even in the dingy fluorescent light of the food bank office. "Did you spill anything on it?"

"What am I? Four?"

"Pack it. So, what else do you have left to do?"

"Just need to do laundry, pick up my dry cleaning, find my passport, get a new suitcase, stop my mail, book my train, research my itinerary, and pack," Gabi pauses. "And, of course, get a host gift."

"Oh, is that all?" Sarah shudders. "Thank goodness you didn't wait until the last minute." How can she not even have a suitcase yet? Sarah might be a mess, but she's invariably a well-prepared mess. "Why don't I get the host gift for you?" It's the least she can do after Gabi has almost singlehandedly kept her afloat the last two years.

"They got 'em at the airport?"

"Yes, but—"

Gabi cuts her off. "Great, I'll get them before I board."

"You'll never have time."

"I'll make time," Gabi snaps.

"You can't show up in Amsterdam empty-handed." A young girl toddles down the street, stomping in puddles as she goes. Sarah smiles as she watches the little one, all rosy cheeks and blonde curls, not unlike Sarah's when her hair was shorter.

Gabi lassos her back. "So how long does it take to get to the airport again?"

"I'll get them," Sarah says.

"You're not driving all the way to the airport for gifts I can get myself when I'm there," Gabi says.

"They do have them other places. I'll go downtown." Sarah trains her eyes as far down the street as she can. "I need to get out anyway. I can't spend another day cooped up in this house wondering if I'll be eating alone again tonight."

As Sarah wraps up her conversation, the girl outside takes a tumble and gets soaked. Sarah watches with a pang as the girl's momentary distress quickly turns to giggles at an approaching dog. She never minds the screams and shrieks that waft through her windows, no matter how loud or persistent, because they're always followed by the easy laughter of little people still unscarred and unscared by the world. She envies their untamed spirits.

Ever since the Synergy debacle, Sarah's own spirit has taken a hit. More than tamed, she's downright crushed. She's been unmoored, incapable of docking anywhere new. There are no doubt plenty of suitable ports for her, if only she could find them. But she can barely remember what dry land even looks like now. What would she find if she finally came into shore? Is there a better, happier Sarah waiting on some distant land? One with a job and an identity of her own, who remembers how to live and connect? Wouldn't that be nice? But for now, she remains at sea, adrift on a vast ocean of both opportunity and regret.

Maybe she's just waiting for someone to throw her one of those tethered life preservers and guide her back to land. *Pull me in,* she thinks.

There was a time when Ben would have been the one to pull her in. Not her savior, but her partner who loved her for all she once was. Now he's just that clueless captain waving at the castaway. Or maybe he's sailing in a completely different ocean.

But if not Ben, then who?

CHAPTER TWO

CALIFORNIA DREAMING

THE POOL LOOKS DAMN good right now. The sun, the warm water, the strangely alluring scent of chlorine. The escape. Maybe if Joe could swim hard enough, he could swim away the ache that seems to be his constant companion these days. Instead, he considers hurling his phone into the pool after that call with his agent.

Melanie steps onto the patio, polished and perfect as always. Nails freshly done, not a single red hair out of place, and styled to within an inch of her life. A composition of carefully assembled perfection. AI couldn't have done better. She crosses her arms, waiting. Joe glances at her, then back at the pool and says, "Working title, 'Battle of the Pixies.' Jesus."

"They'll come up with something better," she says.

"Not the point."

"Clark says it's a good gig. A summer release."

Joe bites his upper lip in frustration. When his wife and his agent start tag teaming him, it's never a good sign. The script must be terrible. "When did you talk to Clark?"

"He wanted me to get you on board with it. You've gotten so picky."

Joe should probably be grateful for the offer. To be working at all, even in crap like "Battle of the Pixies," is a hard-earned privilege after all these years. "I just want to do something I can be proud of."

"Maybe you can be proud of this."

"A dozen scenes playing another clueless dad making model airplanes while his kids accidentally unleash a pixie war around him? Not interested."

"Clark says it's good money," she says. That's always the bottom line for Melanie. Artistic standards or professional pride be damned.

Sure, Joe used to take every job he was offered. He had to when the gigs were sparse, the kids were hungry, and they almost lost the house. But now? Okay, maybe they'll never be rich. But they're solidly middle class with college funds, a paid off house, and money in the bank. When does he get to say no?

"Of course it's good money. That's the only way they can get anyone to do that crap."

"It's good money, Joe."

"But at what cost?"

Melanie's foot taps an irritated rhythm. "You haven't even read it."

"I don't have to read it to know it's shit." He kicks the pink flamingo floaty gently across the pool.

"At least read it."

The two of them make a hell of a team, Melanie and Clark. The pressure from both sides could crush coal into a diamond. He can't be too angry at Clark, however. Clark has stood by him in the lean times and fat, and never given up on him. And at least he's helping Joe get his own movie made, too. That counts for a lot.

But Melanie? Why can't she see how much it matters to him that he actually feel good about his work? It's not like they're desperate. At least she's stopped nudging him to give it all up for a day job since he finally started making a steady living. Even so, her attitude could never really be mistaken for actual support. He expels an exasperated breath and looks down. "I told Clark he could send it to me."

"Thank you," she says before unfolding her arms and walking inside.

Joe kneels by the pool and runs his fingers through the water, the flecks of blue shimmering and twitching around his hand. Every glimmer a shooting star, another wish lost. Or maybe a wish he can recapture if he tries hard enough. And if Fate is very, very kind.

He heads inside, grabs his messenger bag, and drops it onto the kitchen counter to confirm he's got everything. Charger, headphones, sunglasses, laptop.

He stares at a hard copy of his screenplay, debating whether to bring it. He probably won't need it – and he's got it on the laptop – but he might bring it anyway. Better safe than sorry. Besides, having it around makes it feel more real, the emblem of all his years sacrificing and fighting the powers-that-be to get it made. In two more months, God willing, they'll begin principal photography – with him in the lead, despite the naysayers. His script. His movie. His way. Finally.

Nathan sits on the sofa in the family room, game controller cemented to his hands, embroiled in a ferocious fight to the death with an army of orcs and trolls. Melanie walks into the kitchen carrying her purse and a jacket. Avery, Mel's teenage carbon copy except for dark auburn hair where her mother's is a chemically assisted fiery red, trails behind, face buried in her phone.

Thumbs tapping furiously, Avery asks, "Why can't I drive myself?"

"Because I need to go to the grocery store while you're at rehearsal," Melanie says.

"Why can't I take Daddy's car?"

"Because he's driving himself to the airport." Melanie notices the script on the countertop and frowns. "You sure you don't mind driving yourself?"

It isn't a real question. She has no intention of driving him, but Joe goes through the motions anyway. He shakes his head. "It's fine. Parking won't cost that much for a few days."

"Don't they usually send a car?" Avery says.

Joe marvels at how Avery can maintain two separate conversations at the same time, one in the room and one at the end of her thumbs. "I'm paying this time, so nobody's sending a car."

Avery nods, but isn't interested enough to follow-up on why he's paying for himself. "Will you be back for my concert Friday night?"

"Your final senior concert? I wouldn't miss it."

"You've missed lots of concerts, Daddy." Avery's eyes are glued to her phone, but Joe winces at the wounded child whine in her voice.

"Never by choice, honey. Only when I was shooting. You know that."

"Isn't that where you're going?"

"No, we're scouting locations in Seattle." Joe catches Melanie's expression, pursed lips, jaw set. She really can't even pretend to be happy about Joe making his dream come true, can she? Not when it doesn't come with a big paycheck. Not when he's put his own money into the project. She squints at the bright sunshine and pulls out her sunglasses to avoid his gaze.

"Oh," Avery registers, "for *your* movie." She glances up at her father, a flicker of focus and a grudging smile of teen approbation. "That's cool, Dad." She grows red at the eye contact and returns to her phone. "I'm proud of you," she says without looking up again.

Joe gazes at his daughter in dumb surprise and glee. "Thank you, honey!" Then to Nathan, "You hear that, Nate? Your sister's proud of me."

Nathan, fully immersed in the essential work of separating trolls from their limbs, issues an oblivious grunt, a Pavlovian response to hearing his name.

Avery peeks up from her phone long enough to spot her father still grinning and rolls her eyes. "Don't make a whole thing of it, jeez." Moment over. "But I thought you were shooting that sci-fi movie?"

"I leave next week for that one. I'll be gone a couple weeks for that, but this is a quick trip."

"So you'll be there Friday?" she asks again.

"I promise."

Melanie checks her phone. "Let's go."

Avery pockets her phone and runs to her father. She wraps her arms around him and gives him a peck on the cheek. "Bye, Daddy. Love you."

"Love you, too, baby. See you Friday."

"Now!" Melanie calls from the door, then by rote, "Bye, hon. Safe trip." She disappears, with Avery behind her before Joe can say a word in response. No hug. No kiss. No "I love you." Not even eye contact. Just a dull ache in the hole where such things should go.

Joe's eyes fall on the script, his talisman against any further setbacks or last-minute snafus on his last chance to prove himself as a leading man. If it works, doors could open to the real, meaty roles he took for granted back in his student days. But if it flops or falls apart? A lifetime of secondary detectives, sexy neighbors, and bumbling dads. If he's lucky. Maybe he'll always make a living, but it's not the dream. Nowhere close. He runs a thumb over one of the brads binding the pages together, then slides the script into his bag, which he sets by his suitcase.

He watches Nathan playing his game, his gangly legs stretched across the ottoman and hanging off the other side. If Avery is Melanie's mini-me, then Nathan is Joe's doppelgänger. Still two inches shorter than Joe's 6'3" frame, but at just sixteen, he still has time to catch up. Joe plops onto the couch next to him. "I'm about to head out, Nate."

Nathan, who's busy skewering a troll through the eyes, had seemed oblivious to everything around him, but somehow picks up where Avery left off. "You'll be at my track meet Saturday?"

"With a bullhorn, buddy." Joe slaps Nathan's leg as he speaks.

"Please don't."

Joe musses Nathan's hair, distracting him from his game. Nathan yanks away and keeps his eyes locked as he slays an orc. "By the way, if you've got a meet Saturday, shouldn't you be out running or something instead of sitting on this couch?"

"We ran earlier. Now I'm practicing hand-eye coordination."

"Well, *Eye*'ve got to *hand* it to you, you're pretty good." Joe elbows Nathan. "See what I did there?"

Nathan groans, "Don't quit your day job."

Joe chuckles. "Speaking of which, I better get on the road." Nathan shows no sign of stopping his game, so Joe gets up, walks behind the couch, and kisses his son on the head. "I love you, Nate."

"Love you, too," Nathan says as his knight drinks a potion and doubles in size. Joe watches a moment longer, double taps the back of the couch, and heads for the door. He grabs his Dodgers cap from the island and puts it on before picking up his bags.

As Joe opens the door, Nathan calls out, "Dad!" He pauses the game and dashes over to hug his father. "I'm proud of you, too."

This moment means everything. He's doing this movie for them, after all. Joe squeezes Nathan tightly, savoring the gift his son is giving him. "Thanks, buddy."

***

Joe sips his beer in 2C while other passengers bump past him to their seats. He splurged on first class in deference to his long legs. Normally it's a luxury reserved for trips paid for by production companies, but the differential wasn't so bad on the short hop from LA to Seattle and he decided to celebrate this momentous occasion by treating himself. He's also splurged on a suite at the hotel. What Melanie doesn't know won't hurt her.

Joe stares at his phone, debating whether to call or text Mel. He opts for a text. *Boarded. Leaving soon.* He thinks a moment longer, then adds *Love you* before hitting send.

He watches the message pop from send to sent, wondering if the words are true. Does he love her? After twenty years together, the answer has to be yes. Of course. As a co-parent, certainly. And he wants her to be happy. That's love, isn't it?

Melanie texts back, *Safe travels.*

The three dots flash, disappear, then after a moment, reappear. Finally, a kissy face emoji pops in. What might seem flirtatious in another context now reads as a passive aggressive evasion to Joe. At least *he* can still say the words.

He clicks over to his locations manager Luke. *On the plane. Will text when I land. How's Seattle?* Joe waits, but no dots appear. He checks the time, then adds, *You probably haven't landed yet. I'll get in too late to meet tonight, but will check in with you when I arrive. Could you send the locations list?*

He tucks his phone in the seat pocket and pulls out Stephen Fry's latest book on Greek mythology. He'd planned to read all the way to Seattle, but now, with his dream looming, his mind wanders off the page to the vicissitudes of Fate in his own life. To all the things that could still go wrong.

***

Joe peers anxiously out the window of his Uber, awaiting his first glimpses of the city. If actual Seattle doesn't match the well-researched, but hypothetical Seattle in his script, he might be in trouble. After all, he fought to shoot on location here. It would be cheaper to shoot in Vancouver, a frequent stand-in with all the industry infrastructure and well-scouted locations already in place. But Joe is determined the film should feel authentic. He doesn't want fake Seattle with stock footage of the Space Needle. Now both he and the city have to deliver.

Thank goodness Luke agreed to squeak this in under the wire, one of his last projects before his paternity leave. Given the shooting schedule, there's not much wiggle room timewise for the preliminary locations scout, but Joe pats the messenger bag where his script is tucked. His precious talisman. Everything's fine. As the locations manager, Luke will be on top of everything. Joe just decided to tag along at the last minute because this is *his* baby. But his baby is in safe hands with Luke.

Any lingering doubts disappear when the city rises into view. As they drive past the industrial part of town with a bustling seaport in the distance,

Joe casts his eyes forward to not one, but two side-by-side stadiums, and then to the glowing city skyline beyond them. Seattle can't match the grandeur of Manhattan or the scale of many other larger cities he's visited. But the vast expanse of twinkling lights and the endless construction cranes poking their beaks out at every opening announce a city undeniably vibrant and alive.

Within minutes, Joe rolls into his hotel with satisfaction. The grand art deco lobby feels swanky enough to mark an occasion of such magnitude. When he reaches his suite, he snaps a few photos for posterity, then calls Luke. "Hey, brother, I'm at my hotel. Call me back."

Joe unpacks and waits for a return call that doesn't come. It's getting late. He calls again and follows with a text, but no reply. The name of Luke's less swanky nearby hotel escapes Joe, so he can't call the room. He has no choice but to wait. He shouldn't worry – they already have plans to meet in the morning – but it's strange. He expected to confirm, plus Joe wants the list of locations to review before bed.

He paces awhile, but shakes it off and goes to brush his teeth. Luke's a pro, more than capable of handling the job without Joe's interference. Everything's fine. He checks his phone one more time, sets his alarm, and climbs into bed.

Ten minutes later, as his brain begins to drift at last, a text from Luke buzzes in.

Blanca's in labor. Talk later. Sorry.

"Shit," Joe mumbles at his phone. He says a little prayer for Luke, Blanca, and the baby arriving two weeks early.

But then his thoughts turn. To the wasted trip. How can he scout locations without his locations manager? He's just the tag-along. And to where this setback could lead. The entire production schedule depends on the initial scouting trip happening with enough time for next steps – team visits to the best spots, budgeting, negotiations, confirmations – before the shoot begins. One delay leads to another, then the shoot is postponed, and then it's over before it's begun. Films are killed every day due to delays. Especially small indies with shaky financing. Dread knots in Joe's stomach.

After three failed series and a couple other indies no one saw, everything's riding on this. His reputation, his own money, maybe even his career. If this thing unravels, his dream is over. He'll be relegated forever to the minor leagues. And now the window is closing.

CHAPTER THREE

FATE WINKS

SARAH STARES DOWN AT her too tight jeans as she attempts to button them. They fit perfectly when she left Synergy, or more accurately when Synergy left her. She tries hard to embrace her curves. She was always chubby as a kid and she never lost her freshman fifteen. Not to mention the "senior ten" she picked up during her parents' divorce. And she'd added a few more here and there over the years, too. But she'd always been healthy and looked good. So she'd always felt good, too. Until now.

Somehow the twenty she's packed on since she took her hiatus from life nag at her like never before. The curves that always felt sexy before have mutated into proof of her failings and shame. Probably because Ben doesn't even look at her anymore, let alone see or want her. Every time his eyes glide over her like a piece of furniture, she withers a little more. She feels like a comfy chair from his bachelor days, one he's glad he still has, but never bothers to sit in anymore.

So, her growing insecurities flare as she tugs the zipper slowly upward and the fat compresses behind the denim. She pops on her favorite shapeless, button-down and the bulge above her jeans disappears under the waves of white cotton. She tosses on a lightweight tan cardigan and hopes she passes for easy, coastal chic. A semi-faithful reproduction of the old Sarah, so the casual observer won't know.

In the spirit of recapturing the past, she grabs her phone and calls Ben. Voicemail. "Hey, just wanted to let you know I'm headed downtown today to pick up some things for Gabi. Let me know if you need anything while I'm out and about." Sarah stands a little taller at her momentary show of normalcy. He won't call back, of course. He'll be too busy with work and whatever else fills his every waking hour. But at least she tried.

From the side of her bed, she scans the mess in her closet. That's another thing she should try, cleaning up that chaos. And the shoes scattered around the floor. And the products and trinkets strewn across the top of the dresser. Maybe tomorrow. But on the way to the door, she trips on her own damn shoes and stumbles headlong into the dresser, sending a framed photo of her and Ben tumbling down on top of her. With a quick self-inventory, she finds nothing seriously hurt beyond her pride. She flips onto her back, rubs her tender head, and examines the photo. They used to be so good. She misses the days when they talked about everything and actually spent time together. Back then, he couldn't get enough of her – the cute-nerdy-smart guy and the curvy overachiever just felt right. Then something changed and Ben checked out. Right when she needed him most. He's just not there anymore. But look how happy they were in this photo.

Sarah makes her way downstairs deep in thought. Was this how it was for her parents before they divorced? She has no idea, of course, because they completely hid it from her until it was all over but the paperwork. The news shredded her senior year of college into a million disillusioned pieces. A seismic event that prompted the tailspin of all tailspins and caused her to lose all faith in love for nearly a decade. If it hadn't been for Gabi, she shudders to think where she would have ended up.

At the time, she couldn't begin to understand how two people who had seemed so good together could just end. How everything she once considered bedrock could be ripped away forever. How the things she cared about most could one day evaporate into thin air. But now, as she contemplates yet another failed attempt to rekindle the flame last night, it's starting to make sense.

Sarah clicks on the family room television and pours her coffee. She leans on the kitchen island and blinks sleepily, considering the possibility of resting her head on the cool quartz countertop and taking a short nap before going out. She's only been up an hour, but she's already tired. One meaningless day after another has a way of doing that.

She grabs the remote and switches to one of the morning shows. Black coffee over the mindless chatter of smiling anchors throwing softballs to A-listers usually offers the path of least resistance into her days. She Googles the precise location of her target souvenir shop, then pops the address into Waze. Traffic's bad. Yeesh, really bad. She'd planned on getting out early to get her errand over with so she could go back to bed and read the rest of the day, but maybe she'll wait a bit longer.

There's no rush, after all. It's not like anyone's waiting for her.

***

Joe takes his time heading out since he has no particular schedule anymore. He sits over his room service enjoying his view of the Puget Sound. The Seattle Wheel pokes out by the waterfront, and in the distance, the Space Needle. It's overcast, but beautiful nonetheless. His brief internet search leaves him no clearer on a plan than before, so he loiters and watches a ferry sail in from an island across the way.

When he finally descends to the lobby, he asks the concierge for a map of Seattle. She hands him something chock-full of colorful, disproportionately sized icons of all the popular downtown tourist destinations. But which are actually worth his time? He puffs out a breath and thanks her.

Luke calls as Joe steps into the sunlight. He's jubilant. Mother and baby are well. Joe bubbles with excitement, genuinely delighted and relieved for his friend, his own woes a distant worry for at least sixty seconds.

"I'm just sorry I can't make it up there. I know this really screws up the timeline," Luke says.

"Don't give it another thought. Family's all that matters," Joe says without hesitation. "I'll figure something out."

Will he though? His magnanimity wears thin as he remembers just how fully screwed he actually is. The schedule's already tight, and if Luke's offline with a newborn for the next few weeks, they won't have time to start from scratch when he's back. It really is falling apart after all.

But even as he frets, Joe's eyes glide diagonally across the street and land on a tall, heavy-set woman with wild blonde waves catching the wind. Hope sparks unexpectedly where darkness descended only moments ago.

***

Waiting at the red light, something faintly familiar strikes Sarah. An ancient, deeply buried memory she can't access, but can't erase either. The air crackles and buzzes around her. She hears and feels a hum.

Crossing the road, she searches for the street equipment that must be making the noise, but finds nothing. It's her. She feels the vibration within, like a swarm of stingless bees dancing happily around her insides.

At the next corner, she turns and hits the crosswalk button before something jolts her eyes from the green walking man to the figure standing across the street from her. It's not a voluntary action. It's a physical force – an undiscovered law of physics at work. An invisible tether has just yanked on her and pulled her in... to him.

And there he is. Not on TV or a movie screen. Not in a magazine or online photo. But standing right there, by the hotel entrance across the street. A glorious mirage rising from the desert. She nearly jumps out of her skin when she spots him. To anyone else, he would likely be unrecognizable, hidden under a Dodgers cap, dark shades, and a thick beard. But to Sarah, he's unmistakable, even from a distance.

Joseph Robert Parker.

And he's looking right at her.

***

A lightning bolt of something foreign and jarring rips through him. Even before she saw him, he knew beyond a shadow of doubt that this woman – a complete stranger – was coming toward him. To him. For him.

He should turn and walk away right now. Go back inside. Hide. Anything to avoid this encounter. He's mastered the art and science of avoiding the inevitable temptations that even his minor celebrity status, paired with his very good genes, have brought him. He's a family man first. He always walks away. Always. But he can't move. Or breathe. A force larger than him rivets him to the spot.

Now, as she approaches, the magnetic pull is so strong he has to grab the wall to brace himself. When their eyes lock, he's struck by an intense spark of recognition, though he's never seen her before.

More than a spark, it's a light. She's certainly attractive – stunning even – but more than that, she's glowing. It must be a trick of the sun. He slides his fingers under his sunglasses and rubs his eyes, but when he pulls his shades off, she glows even more brightly. He can't look away. He wishes Luke well and hangs up the phone just as she reaches his side of the street.

He doesn't wait for her to arrive. He takes the last few steps toward her.

They smile at each other.

"Hi."

"Hi."

Chapter Four

Beginning

Sarah and Joe stand face to face for the first time, eyes locked, strangely silent, bemused smiles affixed to each of their faces. They should feel uncomfortable in the silence, but neither does. A veil of kismet enshrouds them.

For a split second – or is it hours? – Sarah's mind stills, the constant whir of her over-busy, overburdened psyche inexplicably at rest. Joe's spirit is equally calm, serene even, but his mind is working overtime processing something oblique and impossible. It's a speeding train, rushing headlong toward an unknown destination he can't yet see, but senses is just around the bend. If only he can reach it.

Finally, someone pushes out of the hotel behind Joe and breaks the spell. Sarah's the first to remember herself and goes hot with humiliation. She imagines quietly stepping into a giant crater and allowing the earth to close up around her. A slightly less horrific fate than the embarrassment of staring in bizarre silence into the eyes of Joseph Robert Parker. She pulls herself together as best she can and attempts actual words.

"The…This is…um…" *This is mortifying, is what this is.* "I, uh… you…" *Dear God!* The word salad is worse than silence. This moment will go down in infamy. The back of her neck tingles with anxiety. Sarah takes a deep breath and reaches once more for coherent thought. "Sorry." *Breathe.* "I'm an idiot." *Calm.* "But *you're* Joseph Robert Parker."

Joe shakes his head lightly, as if shaking off a cartoon anvil, and remembers his role in this familiar play. "Yes... hello." Both relieved and disappointed, he realizes she's just a fan. Whatever he thought, whomever he mistook her for, it's evaporating before his eyes. Almost. He extends his hand. "And you are?"

"Sarah Abbott." She does her best to suppress the tremor in her voice when her skin sparks at his touch. Despite her own height, he towers over her. A magnificent giant.

"Nice to meet you, Sarah Abbott."

Her breath comes in giddy gasps as she sneaks glimpses while avoiding his eyes, determined not to stare again. "I'm sorry to bother you. But I'm a big fan of your work." She cringes at herself. She's always hated thinking of herself as his fan. It's irrational obviously. What else could she be? But the word "fan" makes her feel like a screaming preteen or a sad cat lady.

Never mind that he was the one and only place where hope and healing felt possible after Synergy. He was an elite recovery center for broken-hearted, sad girls. But the word "fan" always sounds so trivial, like just another rock among the multitudes on an endless stone beach. Small, insignificant, no more special or important than a million other tiny gray stones rolling in and out with the tide, never noticed or mattering to anyone. And although she never even imagined meeting him – let alone mattering – something has always felt wrong about lumping herself in with the nameless, faceless masses.

Yet standing right in front of him, her one unimaginable chance to impress, the most gleaming sentiment she can manage is "I'm a big fan of your work." Scholars will study her erudition and wit for generations to come.

"That's nice to hear," he says.

"Sorry, what?" She sees him smiling warmly, but the words can't permeate her fog.

"That you're a fan of my work. That's very nice. Thank you."

"Right. Sorry. I don't know what's wrong with me. Must be the shock of meeting Joseph Robert Parker." She announces his name like an SNL emcee, then washes crimson at her own cheesiness.

Joe's discomfort escapes in a chuckle. "Call me Joe." He hadn't a clue why, but he dropped his guard entirely when Sarah first approached, without a second thought. Without so much as a glimmer of the defensiveness that typically marks every fan interaction. He simply, instinctively, trusted her – as if he were meant to. But as the conversation takes on the familiar shape of any other awkward fan encounter, his wall returns. "Please," he adds.

Well aware how lucky he is to have such moments now and then, Joe seldom begrudges his fans their own moments with him. And he's strangely charmed by Sarah's panic despite himself, but everyone in the business learns early to be careful. He readies himself for the too curious questions, planning how to escape the conversation without saying too much about why he's in town. He smiles graciously and awaits the inevitable request for a selfie.

"Anyway, I don't want to take up too much of your time," Sarah says. "I'm sure you must be busy."

"Oh, uhh...," Joe replies. His mind trips over options to say more, but nothing comes. She's rendered him speechless. He's supposed to be the cool one in these encounters.

Sarah sets her shoulders and nods definitively. "Thank you so much for letting me say hello." Most fans cling until he gently removes them and glides away himself. But not this woman, whose newly rigid posture transmits her determination to walk away from this interaction with her dignity intact. "It's such a pleasure to meet you. Enjoy Seattle."

Stunned, Joe murmurs, "Pleasure to meet you, too," as Sarah marches past and down the block. It's never that quick and easy. Yet, there she goes. Down the street. Away from him. But this isn't right. The ever-lingering ache inside him transmutes into a growing chasm with each step she takes farther away. This isn't how it's supposed to be. The magnet is too strong. It's pulling him apart as she goes.

A voice calls out. "Hey, do you happen to know where I might find a souvenir shop?" Joe's shocked to realize the voice is his.

***

His cool restored, Joe holds the door for Sarah. "So why are you going to a souvenir shop?"

"It's an errand for a friend. Long story," Sarah says, eyeing the foodstuffs by the register.

"Sounds like you're a good friend."

"I'm a friend with time on my hands anyway."

Joe nods, not one to pry. He plays his cards close with strangers, too. They each scan the shop, Sarah scouting her noodles and chocolates, Joe seeking inspiration. Every inch overflows with the usual suspects – magnets, keyrings, sweatshirts, postcards, cityscapes, and Space Needle everything. Plus a few not-so-usual items like a wall full of pricey glass art.

"Beautiful, aren't they?" Sarah says.

"They certainly are."

"Chihuly founded a glass school here back in the 70s. Made Seattle one of the world's foremost glass art meccas."

"Tour guide by trade?"

"Strictly amateur," she laughs. "I'm a font of useless Seattle information. Ask me anything."

"Perfect Seattle gift for my kids?"

"How old?"

"Avery's 18 and Nathan's 16."

Sarah balks. "Teenagers? That's pro level, sorry," she says with an amused grimace. After a moment, she peels off when she spots her goodies near the front while Joe meanders toward the back. When she returns, it's with bagged noodles and chocolates in hand. "Any luck?"

"Not yet."

"Well, let's see..." As they make their way down the aisle, Sarah shakes a snow globe of the Seattle waterfront with a moving ferry and shows Joe the result.

He smiles. "Cute. But maybe I should wait until I see it myself. Seems wrong to get a souvenir of a place I haven't been."

She points to a wooden box with a black and red fish in the traditional Northwest Coast Indigenous style printed on it. "Smoked sockeye salmon?" she offers with a smirk. "Kids love that, right?"

"Absolutely," he says slyly. "Unfortunately, that's what I got them for Christmas."

Sarah snaps her fingers in faux disappointment. A few steps later, she picks up a plush pillow in the shape of the Space Needle, which for some reason has a giant troll hanging from the top like King Kong. She clutches it to her chest for a quick cuddle, then holds it proudly up to Joe. Joe chuckles and shakes his head. When they fall silent, she finally asks the inevitable question, "So what are you doing in Seattle? If it's okay to ask."

Joe's first instinct in these conversations is to evade and extricate as quickly as possible, not to give too much away. It's always safest to keep your distance. But to Joe's surprise, he unfurls the whole story without hesitation. He takes one look at her open expression and curious, deep brown eyes and he wants to tell her. About his movie, about Luke's baby, and about how his entire Seattle plan has imploded. "I was just the ride-along, you know? So now I'm stuck. I know the types of locations in the script, obviously, but no specifics."

"Locations like what?"

"There are a couple of houses, which I know he's narrowed down. And some jazz clubs that we were supposed to tour Thursday with a guide." Joe purses his lips. "I suppose I could still do that. But beyond that, we need scenic nature locations, a record store, and some iconic Seattle stuff. And I haven't got a clue where to start with any of that."

"Hmm."

He holds up his map half-heartedly. "I've got this map?" He unfolds it. "See, it's got a little Pike Place Market on it here. And a little Space Needle there. And some sort of, I don't know, orange spikey thing next to it."

Sarah smirks. "That's Chihuly glass. For the Museum."

"Of course it is," Joe chuckles. "And this colorful blob?" Joe's pulse quickens as she leans in to take a closer look.

"The Museum of Pop."

"Alright. Good. This is progress. I should have you as my interpreter." He grins and lifts his eyes from the map to her face as he speaks. Their eyes lock for a charged instant before she clears her throat and steps gently back.

Sarah offers a ceremonial bow. "Happy to be of service."

Joe charges onward. "Well, if you have any suggestions about where to go first, or at all for that matter, I'm open. There's a lot to choose from."

"I mean, Pike Place Market is right down the street. That's a no-brainer," Sarah says pointing at the map. "Then you could hop on the Monorail over to Seattle Center." Joe absorbs as best he can without the requisite geographical knowledge, but in truth, he's lost. It must show because suddenly Sarah blurts out, "I could take you if you want." The words gush out in a torrent as if she's said them too quickly to stop herself.

"Take me?" His ears ring with alarm. *Here we go.* They always want more than he's willing to give. "Oh, I couldn't ask you to do that." But Sarah doesn't cling. Hell, she practically ran away from him twenty minutes ago. Which is so disarming he finds himself repeatedly saying things he would normally never say. He told her his plans for Seattle? He told her about his kids?

"I can at least take you to the tourist sites. Easy peasy," she chirps before tapping her phone awake and beginning to scroll. "And I can probably scrape together a few other spots if it's helpful."

Of course it would be helpful. How else is he going to figure this stuff out? It's so damn tempting to say yes. But she's a complete stranger. A beautiful stranger. He can't possibly accept, as his once again racing pulse reminds him. "That's incredibly nice of you. But I'm sure you've got other things to do."

"I really don't," Sarah confesses half to herself. But when she glimpses Joe's frozen smile and deer-in-the-headlights eyes, a red streak shoots up her chest and finishes at her cheeks. "I mean, I'm sorry, that was a ridiculous idea. You don't know me. I could be a Lifetime movie waiting to happen. Totally get it."

"To be fair, you don't know me either," Joe says jovially. "I could be a monster in real life."

"Good point. Better safe than sorry." Her still rosy cheeks broadcast her embarrassment. "Don't know what I was thinking."

Joe scrambles to reassure her. "It's a kind offer..."

"No worries. You've been extremely gracious, but I've got my chocolates and noodles, so I'm gonna leave you to your day. Good luck with everything. I will definitely watch your movie when it comes out. Great meeting you." She shakes her head definitively. "Totally not a monster."

Joe clasps her hand with both of his, holding onto her a moment longer. "It was lovely meeting you, Sarah. Thank you for helping me find this place."

Sarah offers a weak smile, a tiny wave, and bolts. A strange tug in Joe's chest pulls him several steps toward the door as she goes, but he anchors himself and sighs down at his map. When he looks up, she's gone. Out the window he watches with a pang as she pumps the crosswalk button like she's running for her life.

He reviews his options for the day, reassuring himself he's made the right decision. He obviously couldn't take her up on her offer. So what can he do? Go home and rebook the trip? A waste of money and time. Wander around like a lost tourist? Spend half a day trying to find a paid guide to help him? He could call the team to discuss options, but that'll waste a whole day just trying to reach them all.

Outside, Sarah's rushing across the street. She never even asked for a picture. She never asked him for anything. Not even his time. In a flash, he's out the door and for the second time in under an hour, he pulls her back to him.

"Sarah!" She stops on the other side of the street. "Can I take you up on that offer?"

She yells back, "Seriously?" Suddenly she's glowing again. "I guess I better add some time on my parking!"

CHAPTER FIVE

SEATTLE RAIN

THEY START AS SARAH proposed, with a quick walk down to Pike Place Market. She warns it may be too crowded and too expensive to shoot there on an indie budget, but he may as well see it. One glance and he knows she's right.

The crowds are insane and moving through them is like a full contact sport, but Sarah deftly navigates the terrain like an Everest Sherpa safely guiding her charge to the peak. She takes him past the endless crafts, produce, meats, and flowers on a hyper-speed tour of the key destinations: the golden piggy bank, the guys who throw fish, the gum wall, the giant boot, happily hidden in the quieter lower level, and the mini-donuts.

"You gotta try these," she says.

They watch a machine drizzle little loops of dough into hot oil that transforms those same gooey loops into donuts before their eyes. When they get their order, half a dozen mixed powdered and cinnamon, Sarah thrusts the oily paper bag toward Joe. He grins at the tantalizing prospect, pulls out a powdered donut, and pops half of it in his mouth in one bite.

He lets out a little moan of pleasure. "They're still warm."

"Of course."

"That's damn good."

"Right?" she says, devouring one herself.

They simultaneously point at each other and realize they're both covered in powdered sugar. Sarah's mind flashes to a favorite episode of River's

Run when Joe's character wiped a spot of whipped cream off his girlfriend's face. A cliché that always works – on TV anyway.

Sarah self-consciously brushes her own face clean as Joe does the same. They chuckle at the scene but avert their eyes. Sarah imagines an undercurrent of something heavy and deep, but also lighter than air flowing through the moment and rumbling in her gut. Something more than momentary sheepishness lingering between them. She rolls her eyes at herself and shakes it off. "Ready?"

On their way out, Sarah points out the original Starbucks with its line out the door and a one-man-band busker named TJ something who Sarah notes has been playing Pike Place for over 20 years. But TJ is packing up his equipment because the sky is growing ominous with dark clouds. "Rain's coming," she says as she glances at him before quickly turning away again. It feels too dangerous to look him in the eye. "Let's see if we can get to the Monorail before it hits."

As they labor up the steep hill to the Monorail, Sarah relaxes. The distraction of the climb takes her mind off the constant flutters in her stomach. And as it turns out, talking to Joe is much easier when she doesn't actually have to look at him. So easy it's alarming. So natural, it's unnatural. As long as she doesn't look at him.

A mist falls. Then the mist becomes a sprinkle. "Now this is one thing I'm worried about filming here," Joe says. "The rain."

Sarah scoffs. "This isn't rain."

"You're not helping," he chuckles. "Rain on location means delays, cost overruns. We can't afford that."

"You're shooting July into August, right? You have nothing to worry about. It'll be glorious then. Now the smoke on the other hand..."

The sprinkle upgrades to a light drizzle.

"Uh-oh," Joe grunts.

"What's the matter, California boy? Can't handle a little rain?"

"Maybe we should get some umbrellas."

"Seattleites who use umbrellas get mocked mercilessly." The rain increases to a full downpour. Sarah relents. "Fine. C'mon."

They duck into a doorway to hide from the rain. Constrained by the tight quarters, they're a little too close, but they assume elevator positions and attempt to wait it out, ignoring the electricity between them. Proximity doesn't count in an elevator, after all. You just have to wait for your floor.

Sarah clocks Joe's furrowed brow. He's worried. "This kind of heavy rain is rare here. It should pass quickly," she says.

"At least now I can say I've been in Seattle rain."

Someone tries to push out the door from the store, but Sarah's blocking them. She does the elevator shuffle, stepping gingerly to her right, closer to Joe, to get behind the door so it can open while still maintaining a modicum of personal space. But when the guy inside the shop can finally get out, he shoves the door into Sarah, and Sarah into Joe.

A frisson of tension flashes at the unexpected intimacy thrust upon them. Sarah's rain-chilled body instantly warms at the contact. Her breath catches as his earthy scent of leather – and oak maybe – washes over her. His body's gone rigid. He's pulled his arms tight in front of him as a barrier, his mouth pressed tightly closed. She dares gaze up to his face, to his eyes. Those amazing crystal blues have brought her so much joy over the years, but now all she sees is panic. He's horrified at actual physical contact with her. Not that she expected him to take her in his arms or anything. But to recoil from a simple, inadvertent shove? Humiliating.

Sarah resumes her original position as soon as the door closes. The flutters have returned. "Sorry."

"No, it's fine," says his mouth, while his face says *holy hell get me out of here!*

Sarah tries to shake the moment. "This really doesn't happen often. And the summers are beautiful. You'll see."

Joe looks through the door behind him to the souvenir shop inside. "I'm getting an umbrella. Want one?"

Sarah shakes her head with a polite smile. "You go on. I'll wait here." She could use a minute to regroup anyway. Get herself on steady ground again. Before she gets carried away with her own fantasies.

When Joe emerges, the rain's back to a light, but steady sprinkle. He pops open a bright blue umbrella with large, white stylized block letters on two adjacent panels that read, "My dad went to Seattle and all I got was this lousy umbrella." Sarah walks stubbornly next to him in the rain, her hair wet and frizzier by the moment.

"How you doin' there?" Joe says.

"Fine, thanks," she grumbles. Admitting the truth now would be as humiliating as that unexpected doorway collision that sent her reeling only moments ago.

"Me, too. Nice and comfy and dry under my umbrella," he taunts.

The light mist picks up again. Now she's getting soaked. She grits her teeth and folds her arms against her body.

"Okay, this is ridiculous! Get under here." He grabs her arm and pulls her under the umbrella. Once again, they're thrust together, huddled close to stay dry. But notably, he doesn't seem horrified this time. "Is everyone in Seattle as stubborn as you are?"

"Maybe," she smirks, "but they'll never admit it."

***

They hop on the Monorail and Sarah pushes Joe to a west-facing seat for view of the Sound at cross streets. It sparkles in spots where sunrays break through the clouds.

She fills him in about their destination, Seattle Center, an aggregation of many of the city's most celebrated cultural institutions. She notes that it was built for the space age 1962 World's Fair, which is why half the campus looks like an episode of "The Jetsons." As they approach, she directs Joe's attention to the front of the train for his first view of the Space Needle nobly towering overhead, presiding over the city, and the moment they roll through the MoPop building before pulling into the station. She leads him off the platform and down the ramp to emerge in front of the Chihuly bar.

Joe pauses to do a full 360 of pictures. When he finishes, Sarah leads them away from the Space Needle, explaining they'll do a full circuit and finish where they started. Joe continues to take pictures as they stroll, capturing as much as possible to share with the team later.

Between shots, he broaches a topic he's been cautiously avoiding. "So... is this a day off for you?" He struggles to land on the right words, keenly aware of the potential minefields in asking, but he needs to know more about her. He has the distinct impression she doesn't work, but she's so dynamic and clever, he can't imagine why not. Unless she's got kiddos at home, of course. Which, for some reason, he hopes isn't the case. "Or...?"

"I'm currently between gigs," she says tensely. "For quite a while now, actually."

"By choice?" The air changes around them as she turns from him and casts her eyes across campus. She's practically a stranger and it's none of his business. He's not normally one to pry, but something spurs him past polite conversation with Sarah. She's quickly become an impossible riddle, and he needs clues.

"That's a complicated question."

"I'm okay with complicated answers."

"Ah, but no time. Too much to see." She pulls the folded umbrella from his hand and waves it in the air like a tour guide. "Follow me," she shouts in an obvious attempt to redirect him. Interesting.

He scrunches his face in thought, then smiles. "Nah, you'll tell me. I can wait."

CHAPTER SIX

HANDS

SEATTLE CENTER'S FOOD COURT, The Armory, pulses with life as locals grabbing lunch and tourists recovering their strength stretch out like tentacles from the tables at the center to each of the upscale eateries around the perimeter. Wood-fired pizza, a trendy diner, meat pies, vegan bowls, BBQ, a candy store, a local taco institution, and more. The space echoes with the din of hundreds of voices bouncing around the giant hangar of concrete and steel, a strangely comforting wall of sound where every word feels private despite the surrounding throngs.

Sarah's still reeling from Joe's comment before they walked in. Why is he so interested in her? There's literally nothing interesting about her compared to his life. And the way he was so sure she'd tell him. Like he already knew her. Like she mattered. Her stomach does a gentle somersault as her tension evaporates. She suppresses a smile, her insides now roiling with delight and confusion. Why did it make her feel so giddy to hear him say that?

Sarah scans the space reviewing lunch options. "What are your feelings on falafel?"

"Falafel is my life," Joe deadpans. "Obviously."

At the counter, Joe insists on paying and thanks the guy graciously. Sarah watches him drop a generous tip in the cup after the guy walks away. Most people tip on their cards or wait to be seen by the server when they drop their cash tips, eager to be acknowledged for their generosity, but that doesn't seem to enter the equation for Joe. He's generous without the need for recognition. She smiles at the quiet revelation.

Joe leans across the counter, interested to watch the falafel being made. Sarah's gaze catches on his hands crossed on the countertop. His beautiful hands. The large and strong hands of a giant, but sinewy, not clunky or clumsy. His long fingers taper to perfectly kept nails, clean and manicured, but masculine. Hands Rodin might have sculpted.

Suddenly, Sarah is someplace else, an intense sense memory stirring. Those hands bring it back like it was yesterday. His hands, impossibly, that reached for her through the stars and saved her long before the Synergy mess. A dream that literally changed her life more than a decade ago. That dream she'd let drift into the recesses of her mind, but could never truly forget – and it all started with Joe's hands. This is definitely not the time to think about *that*. About how a dream of Joe once saved her, just in time, from a terrible match – and freed her up to find something so much better with Ben not long after. This is neither the time nor place to unpack the thoughts now racing through her head, but Sarah's mind slips and slides anyway between this moment and that long buried memory. Her reverie is only broken by Joe chivalrously lifting both trays from the counter and saying, "Ready?"

Sarah takes a seat at a small round table and to her surprise, Joe plants himself in the chair adjacent rather than across. He eagerly unwraps his sandwich and moans his approval with his first bite. He offers a vigorous thumbs up with his free hand and takes his time chewing, putting on quite a show. When he swallows, he takes a swig of water and asks, "So how do you fill your days when you're not playing tour guide to lost actors?"

Sarah chokes out a dismissive laugh. What *does* she do with her days? "Don't ask. It's too pathetic."

Joe gives her an encouraging upward nod. "Come on."

"Read. Go to movies." She's practically apologizing. "Putter around tidying things. I'm an excellent putterer. And I go to yoga three times a week, believe it or not."

"Why wouldn't I believe it?"

"I thought it might help me lose weight." She gestures at herself in self-flagellating dismay. "It didn't." A surge of shame pulses through Sarah as she admits her failings, but there's no use denying it. It's not like he can't see. And somehow, she instinctively trusts him. Remembering that dream must have really done a job on her. "But at least it shuts my brain up for a while. And I have gotten stronger."

He studies her, no hint of judgment or condescension in his expression or voice. Rather, almost, admiration? "That's great."

"And I volunteer."

"Where?"

Sarah picks at her sandwich and takes a small bite, but the powdered sugar incident has her too self-conscious to eat much. "The Renton Foodbank."

"Renton, is that where you live?" he mumbles through another mouthful of falafel.

"No, I live in Bellevue. But my friend Gabi runs it. She got me involved."

"Are these places far from here?"

"They're all suburbs. Bellevue's the biggest. It's another little city across the water."

"Which water? There's a lot of water around here."

"Lake Washington. It's the biggest lake in the area. Okay, look." She scoots over to his side so she's next to him and holds up her right hand in the air, flat in front of him. "This is Lake Washington."

"Your hand?"

"Yes." She points to the side of her thumb. "This is Seattle. We're here." She slides her pointer straight across her knuckles to the side of her pinkie. "And this is Bellevue, where I live."

"Okay. And Renton?"

"Renton, where the food bank is...." She slides her finger from her Bellevue pinkie all the way down to her wrist bone. "Renton is down here."

"That looks far."

She points back to her thumb, "Maybe from here. But it's not so bad from Bellevue." She motions again from her pinkie to her wrist and taps her wrist as she continues. "And it gives me something productive to do."

Staring at her own wrist where she's still pointing, Sarah goes hot with a sudden awareness of how close their bodies are. She throws a sidelong glance at Joe, which he catches and throws back with a half-smile. Then she clocks a quick shift in his focus, from her wrist to her... wedding ring? She drops both hands and beats a hasty retreat to her original spot.

Joe clears his throat. "So, what do you do at the foodbank?"

Sarah shoves another bite in her mouth to quell her inner churning. "At first, I was sorting food shipments, stocking the shelves like a store. Very hands on." She gestures broadly with her hands by way of illustration, then catches herself. She tucks them under the table. "Which was nice because I got to know the clients. Makes the work more meaningful."

"I'll bet." He gazes at her intently – like she's unfurling tales of service in the Peace Corps, not schlepping cartons of applesauce. He couldn't possibly be interested in any of this, but she's too nervous to stop herself.

"But then they lost their office manager, so I offered to help during their transition. It was supposed to be temporary, but nine months later I'm still doing it."

"They should hire you."

"They've tried. But it wouldn't be fair to them. It's not what I want to do long term." Sarah shrugs and takes a bite of her sandwich before tossing it down on the paper.

Joe's brows rise expectantly. "What do you want to do?"

"Not a clue," she chuckles miserably. "But for now, at least it gets me out of the house."

"How often do you go?"

"Every Monday and Friday. Bookends to the week. Or the weekend, I suppose." She lets a grim smile escape. "I never know whether I'm coming or going, so it could go either way."

Joe gulps down some water, then takes a piece of ice in his mouth and crunches it. "So, you're married?"

Sarah jars at the suddenness of the question. "Yes, yeah, I am. His name is Ben." Joe's strangely inscrutable as he gulps more ice and wordlessly waits for her to continue. "We've been married for eight years. Together eleven." A flicker of something resembling disappointment crosses his face, but it comes and goes so quickly it must be her imagination.

"But no kids?" he asks. Sarah shakes her head. "Wasn't for you or...?"

She grabs her falafel wrapper and slowly shreds it. Thinking of Ben, of her home life, of her non-life, is putting a real damper on this otherwise delightful fantasy she's clearly whipped up in her mind – because it couldn't possibly be real. "I don't want to bore you with the gory details."

"Sorry, I shouldn't pry," he says with a tiny nose crinkle that nearly melts her. She gives a shrug to which he replies, "But I'm interested in you." For a moment, the world goes still and Sarah loses her capacity to speak. Why on earth would he be interested in her? They eat quietly, enjoying their falafel and company, before Joe picks up where he left off. "And so you know, you can tell me whatever you want. I won't be bored."

"Trust me, my life, compared to yours, is very pedestrian."

"Honestly, it's a nice change," he says. "When you spend all your time talking about the industry, schmoozing, hustling for jobs, it's pretty isolating from normal life."

"What about at home?"

Joe parses his words carefully. "Home is... complicated. Don't get me wrong, I love my family more than life itself. But..."

"Home is complicated. Believe me, I get it." A pang of guilt slices through her.

"And when you're in the business, you never know what people want," he confides. "It's hard to let new people in, so you never get to have real conversations. Plus, they usually just want to tell you how great you are. At least to your face."

Sarah folds in on herself. "Oh God, I'm one of those people!"

"You're not. I could tell right away."

Sarah shields her eyes with her hand, hiding from her shame. "How?"

"You didn't want anything from me." Joe gently pulls Sarah's hand from her face with his own warm hand. "Hey, seriously. I didn't mean you, I promise." His sunshine smile breaks across his face. "You're not like anyone I've met."

His words are as unsettling as they are thrilling. What can he possibly mean? He's not like anyone she's met, obviously. But she's no one to him. Joe takes a final bite of his sandwich and Sarah allows herself a good look at him for the first time since they met that morning. Even buried under that beard, with his dark waves subdued under a baseball cap, he's still so handsome it almost hurts. It seems impossible she's sitting next to him, like this must be another mad dream that's come along, once again, right when she most needs it to save her from herself.

She summons the courage to say what she's really thinking. "Well, to be fair... I do get something out of this. I get to spend the day with a movie star."

"Not a movie star," he corrects. "Just an actor."

"Alright. I get to spend the day with a handsome actor. Still pretty good."

"Handsome?" he echoes.

She ignores him. *As if he doesn't know.* "I'm still surprised you said yes, honestly. I don't think I would have – in your shoes."

"Well, *to be fair*," he parrots with a twinkle, "I was desperate."

CHAPTER SEVEN

SIMPLE JOYS

AFTER LUNCH, THEY RESUME their tour of Seattle Center. Joe snaps pictures all around as they stroll past the mural amphitheater to the Pacific Science Center, with its strange spacey white arcs, mod 60s water features, and dinosaurs for some reason, then double back past the arena to the International Fountain.

It sits in the basin of a large cement bowl rimmed with bench seating at least 200' wide for people to stroll around, and if they dare, descend toward the spouts. The shining silver dome is covered in nozzles that shoot water in unpredictable directions and heights, synchronized with a musical soundtrack.

Two small children dodge the random sprays, undeterred by the chill in the air and blithely unaware of how miserable they'll be if they actually get wet. "Great, right?" Sarah says. "The water cannons shoot as high as 120' in the air. It's *very* exciting. Especially in the summertime. The fountain is packed, all these kids screaming as they get soaked." Her face lights up. "Acting like they don't want it, but you know they do."

Joe smiles at her enthusiasm. "You like kids," he observes.

"Of course."

Joe raises his brows at her expectantly. He wants the story and somehow, after three hours together, they've already found a wordless shorthand.

Sarah rolls her eyes and gives in. "We got married on the late side. I was 34. I had a new job at the time, and it was pretty demanding. Both our jobs were demanding actually. We never really decided we didn't want kids. We just, kind of, never got around to it."

"But you could still…"

"Technically, sure. But…" she shrugs. "Sometimes Fate has other plans for us."

Joe eyes the spouts of water thoughtfully and mutters mostly to himself, "Indeed it does."

"What about you? You have two?"

"Avery and Nathan. Avery's going to Stanford this fall."

"Impressive! You must be so proud."

"I am. They're easily the best thing I've ever done." He beams. "I love being their dad. I wouldn't trade it for anything."

"Got pictures?"

"Always." Joe pulls out his phone and flips through a few photos. Vacation pictures from a recent family trip to the beach. The whole family in bathing suits and sunglasses, on a boat, sipping fruity drinks. His wife is in a hot pink and yellow bikini, her body tan and toned, boobs sky high, the ideal California body. Joe's perfect counterpart.

"They're beautiful kids," she says as she leans in to see better.

"Thanks." He nods appreciatively.

"Your wife is beautiful, too,"

Joe smiles, but slips his phone back into his pocket without a word as the water cannons explode in a triumphant, final flourish.

They spend the next half hour meandering through the nooks and crannies of the Seattle Center campus before landing in front of the Museum of Pop. But Joe looks down instead of up, fixated on a bright orange, circular design painted on the ground. "Oooh, a labyrinth," he proclaims giddily.

"Yep," she agrees, equal parts amused and perplexed by his glee.

"We've got to do it!"

"We do?" Sarah has walked across this life-size, dayglo labyrinth at least a dozen times and never even considered walking it.

Joe holds his arms out in a helpless, sorry-no-choice gesture and backs into the entrance, daring Sarah to follow. He hooks his index finger towards himself, pulling her in.

Sarah smiles and follows as Joe takes on the task in earnest. He walks slowly, Sarah trailing behind. He chatters away about why he loves labyrinths and how they have a nice stone one behind his church, and about how he's always loved the story of the Minotaur, and all the Greek myths, which is something he got from his father who has a thing for the classics.

When they round a curve into the second quadrant, Joe falls under the meditative spell of the twists and turns. Sarah, who's just been listening anyway, shares the silence. She's only a few feet behind Joe, but it's enough that they cross each other smiling again and again, like a roller coaster line where you zig-zag past the same people an infinite number of times in a purgatory of double-backs until at last you somehow, miraculously, reach your destination.

After a few more back-and-forths, Joe speaks again. "I think one of the things I love most about Greek mythology is how the gods are always interfering, whether humans want them to or not. Like, Fate and Destiny always have a hand in things. You know?"

"Hmm," Sarah says noncommittally.

Joe stares carefully down at the path as he continues, speaking slowly, "What about you...? Do you believe in Fate?"

"As a literary device?" she chuckles. "Absolutely."

Joe nods his head and continues wordlessly. They remain mute through the third quadrant, each lost in their own thoughts, as intended. At what they thought was the end of the third section, the path unexpectedly winds back to the second, then back to the first, taking them both by surprise.

"Wait a minute here!" Joe exclaims with a laugh. "I thought we were nearly done."

"What trickery is this?"

"We better pick it up."

They wend their way finally into the fourth quadrant and speedwalk the final leg. Their excitement grows as the destination draws near and Joe's giddiness returns. "Almost there!"

Faster and faster Joe coils round the last curves, Sarah speeding up to keep pace. In the final approach, he sprints to the center, throws his arms in the air, and cheers. Sarah attempts to do the same, but rushes headlong into the center as Joe spins around to face her and nearly crashes into him. They hoot and high five each other.

"That was awesome," he says.

"Yeah, it was," Sarah cheerfully agrees with more joy and ease than she's felt in... months? Years?

They take a moment to breathe in the full, silly triumph of the labyrinth before Joe points up at MoPop, a misshapen blob of a structure. He takes in the oddity, all curves and unnatural waves of metal gathered like fabric, coated in a cheerful, multicolored mirrored shell that nearly makes up for the discomfiting shape of the thing. "So what's this again?"

After a brief explanation and quick visit to the ticket counter, they stand at the heart of the museum. Sarah shakes her head in dismay at a giant, funnel shaped tower of guitars of every color and style, plus a few keyboards and drums thrown in for good measure. It extends up to the next level with the other exhibits encircling it like satellites in orbit. "We really don't have time for this. It's almost two o'clock," she says.

Joe rebuffs her. "You can't expect me to stand outside a music museum and not go in."

"It's not a music museum *per se*."

He assumes his best courtroom prosecutor persona. "Did you or did you not tell me the building was inspired by Jimi Hendrix's guitar?"

"That's what I heard," Sarah confesses.

"And are we or are we not standing in front of a two-story high guitar tornado?" He didn't guest star on all those legal procedurals for nothing.

"We are."

"I rest my case."

Sarah raises her hands in surrender. "It's your dime. Spend it how you want. But can we at least keep it moving?"

"Atta girl!" he grins.

They reluctantly skip the movie costume displays, but do a quick pass through a seemingly endless array of exhibits about Seattle music legends – Nirvana and the Foo Fighters, Pearl Jam, Heart, Soundgarden, Alice in Chains, Queensrÿche, and of course, Jimi. And the newer generation – Brandi Carlile, Sleater-Kinney, the Head and the Heart, and the list goes on.

Joe leans in to read a placard about Quincy Jones. "You know, the music scene is why I set my movie here."

"Will you tell me about it?"

"Of course," he says, implicit trust in his tone. "But first..." He holds up the museum map and taps it with a gleam in his eye. "We play."

Chapter Eight

Strolling and Trolling

The driving tour starts with a flash visit to the wonderfully strange downtown library with its neon yellow escalators, strange sci-fi movie red floor, and the dizzying 10th floor overlook. An extraordinary location that the average tour guide, or visiting location scout, would likely miss.

Back in the car, their stories weave together as they drive. Sarah tells him about the sights, Joe takes photos and tells her about his movie.

"Hammering Man, Seattle Art Museum," she says pointing to a two-story high moving sculpture.

Snap. "It's about a guy, Sean – that's me – whose jazz musician father dies," Joe says.

"Pioneer Square. Seattle's oldest historical neighborhood. Dates back to the Gold Rush."

Snap, snap, snap. "Sean comes to Seattle, where his dad played as a young musician, to spread his ashes and discover the town his father loved so much."

"The Seattle Spheres."

Snap, snap. "He was really close to his dad, but when he gets here, he finds out his dad had another kid, a daughter who grew up here. And he has to reconcile with that before he can move on and finally spread his father's ashes," Joe finishes.

"That sounds powerful."

"I hope so," he says with a hint of uncertainty. "Feels like it could be a turning point for me. If I can pull it off."

"Doubting yourself?"

"I'm just glad it's getting made, honestly. Nobody wanted me in the lead. They wanted an A-lister chasing credibility between blockbusters."

"But you're doing it." She beams with pride she has no legitimate claim to.

Joe lights up at her approbation. "Damn right, I am!"

Sarah's heart does a disorienting somersault at his burst of joy. She grasps for a quick follow-up to stop herself lingering too long in the moment. "And you're producing, too. Even more impressive."

"You're impressed with me?"

Supersonic flutters catch a high-speed train from Sarah's heart to her stomach, which lurches uneasily. She can't quite read his tone. Is it actual surprise? Cockiness? Mockery? She would almost interpret it as flirtation if she didn't know better. But men like Joe don't flirt with women like Sarah. Then again, maybe he flirts with everyone. That's probably just what actors do.

"Well, I'm not *not* impressed," she equivocates. "Hey look, we're here!" Discernible relief tinges her voice.

She pulls into a street spot by Kerry Park, an itty-bitty parklet in Queen Anne that offers the most spectacular view of the city. A view that most visitors never see. They hop out to see the view, but Sarah instantly fills with regret.

It's the perfect backdrop, she reminds herself, and she couldn't very well *not* show it to Joe. She brings every out-of-town guest here. He's not special. And with the weather cleared up, they can see past the Space Needle, Puget Sound, and the Seattle Wheel, all the way to Mount Rainier. It truly is a glorious view.

But as they stroll up to the best vantage point, no less than three different couples are posing for selfies, and a photographer is taking what appear to be engagement photos of yet another couple purposefully mooning at each other. A pit grows in Sarah's stomach because suddenly, the whole place feels alarmingly romantic and weird. Like she's brought him to Makeout Point. What will Joe think? What would Ben think?

"Wow, it's like a convention," she says with horror, eyeing the 100% paired off population. "Sorry, no one told me it was couples' day at the park."

Joe laughs and photographs the view. Sarah hangs back a safe distance, making sure Joe knows she didn't mean anything by bringing him to Lovers Lane Seattle. She notices a couple kissing and groans quietly. If she could teleport away from this embarrassment, she would. Instead, she inches behind the sculpture that stands at the center of the park.

When he's done, Joe scans the others, then tracks Sarah and beckons her. "Let's do a selfie."

Sarah feels the heat of a blush at even the thought of posing next to Joe. Here. Around all these... couples. "What? No! You don't want me in your picture."

"Clearly, I do. Come here."

She trudges over, dragging a leaden ball of anxiety in tow, and pastes on a smile to camouflage her several battalions of conflicted feelings fighting for dominion. And as Joe wraps his arm around her for the photo, make that a legion.

Her insides vibrate when Joe pulls her in. He stoops to bring his head next to hers and holds his phone out with the other hand. "Ready? Say cheese!"

Sarah inadvertently glances at Joe the moment he snaps the picture. "Wait, I think I blinked."

"Okay, let's do it again." He gives her a little extra squeeze to loosen her up, which has the exact opposite effect, but she appreciates the effort.

She takes a deep breath to relax, and to her surprise a small giggle escapes on her exhale. This moment is such a dream. This whole day is impossible. And though she's denied her feelings all day, acting as if it were perfectly normal to spend a day with Joseph Robert Parker, suddenly the dam breaks and the joy erupts on her face as he clicks the button.

They take a quick look. The second is clearly the keeper. They're both looking in the camera, eyes wide with delighted, open smiles on their faces. "Give me your number. I'll text it to you."

Sarah complies, then adds, "You can delete the first photo."

"I will do no such thing, thank you very much. I require a full and comprehensive record of the day."

Sarah wants to object, but is interrupted by her phone buzzing, first with the photo, and immediately after with a reply text from her brother-in-law Alec, her local music expert. "Aha! We've got record stores. And one of them is in Fremont." She gives her fist a small celebratory pump in the air.

"What does that mean?"

"That means we're going to see the troll!"

***

The Fremont Troll is a massive, terrible beast of concrete and steel who sits beneath the Aurora Bridge waiting to prey on passing cars. At eighteen feet high from his chest to the top of his head, he is formidable, truly a sight to behold. And feared. One eye is obscured by his long cement troll locks, but his other eye glints with metal and malevolence as he clasps an actual Volkswagen Beetle under the long, bony fingers of one of his enormous hands. The troll is famously hungry for cars.

Joe gawks at the troll in wonder while he photographs it. "This guy's great."

"Yeah, he's popular around these parts," Sarah says.

"Do me a favor. Hop up there for a picture. It will help with scale."

Sarah freezes. "I'm not... that's not... I'm not a climber. But I can stand in front of it?"

"That's no fun."

"Then you can climb it," Sarah offers, "and I'll take your picture."

Joe presses his lips together and shakes his head in mock disappointment, but hands her his phone and begins to climb. When he reaches the troll's left shoulder, he strikes a pose and Sarah takes the shot. But he doesn't climb down when she's done. Instead, he calls to her. "You know, it's a nice view up here. You should come check it out."

"I'm good down here."

Joe holds out his hand by way of invitation, charm and challenge sparking in his eyes as he wills her forward. He jerks his head back in a "c'mon" motion and stares at her until she has no choice but to start climbing. She makes her way around the side and up the back of the concrete structure, but pauses when she reaches the last large step to mount the troll's shoulder, unsure how to proceed.

Joe reaches out his hand from above. She hesitates. Her pulse races, though she can't decipher the source. Is it the climb? Or the hand? She takes Joe's hand and finds the answer as a spark of electricity shoots straight from her fingertips to her heart. With one hearty tug, he lifts her straight up, and for a glimmering instant, Sarah feels light as a feather in more ways than one. When she reaches the top, he pulls her into him like a gravitational force and they stand close on the shoulder of a giant.

Lightheaded and dizzy, Sarah visibly swoons. Joe clutches her, one hand on her arm, the other at her back to steady her. "You okay?"

She trembles as she gazes up at his limpid pools of high-holy-hell-why-does-he-look-like-that? She forces herself to pull it together with a couple deep breaths. "I'm fine."

"Here, trade places with me," Joe says. Before Sarah can object or even understand what's happening, he's gripping her by both arms and sliding her to the right while he slides his own body closely behind her to the left. A hot thrill radiates inward from each arm where he makes contact. The two charges meet in the middle at her heart, and travel directly down - all the way down – as he moves her away from the troll's outer shoulder to the more protected spot by his head. She reaches out a hand and braces herself against the troll's hair as she gasps.

"Better?" he says. Sarah nods breathlessly, unable to speak. "I'm sorry. I shouldn't have forced you. Are you afraid of heights?" He's still holding her.

"The height would be fine if it didn't require climbing to get to it. And it's a little..." She darts her eyes frantically, allowing an alleged fear of heights to camouflage the real source of her palpitations. "Tight up here."

Joe drops his hands and steps back the smidge the space will allow. "But you made it. And I knew you could! See, you have to trust yourself."

If only he knew. Except, maybe he does. The way he asks questions and really listens to the answers. After less than a day, it's like he's shining a floodlight into her soul. Like he sees everything. Maybe too much. They look at each other a hair too long, each of them deciding what to say next.

"Oh, here." Sarah pulls Joe's phone out of her pocket and hands it to him. It rings as he takes it. It's Melanie.

"I better take this."

As he taps the button to answer, Sarah motions a "should I go?" move, but he shakes his head no.

"Hey, hon. How are you?"

Sarah hears the word "hon" and freezes.

"Yeah, we're finding some great stuff." Joe puts up a "one minute" finger, but Sarah's heart sinks. She sits down on the troll's shoulder and slides carefully down, tuning out his conversation, out of both politeness and self-preservation.

She had no illusions anything was going on, of course. Joe's happily married, after all. And despite their problems, she would never do anything to hurt Ben. Besides, even if they were both free, the noble, beautiful lion doesn't mate with the squat, chubby badger.

Still, it was nice to escape for a little while. To pretend it was just the two of them and this crazy, crazy day was actually her life. And, alright fine, maybe she did have *some* illusions. Not that anything real was happening.

That wasn't a possibility. But at least for a day, she was tasting the sweetness of dreams instead of the bitter pill of hopelessness she'd been swallowing nightly with her entirely superfluous birth control pill.

So what if it was all in her imagination? At least she was having fun for once. For the first time in longer than she could remember, she was living her life in color. In glowing yellow escalators and crystal blue eyes and the bright orange twists and turns of a labyrinth that only Joe could lead her through.

But now, as she stands on the ground watching Joe talk to his wife, still aggressively tuning out his words, Sarah drifts back out to sea and reminds herself this will all be over before she knows it. Life will simply go back to the way it was, so she shouldn't get too attached.

Fantasies can be dangerous.

CHAPTER NINE

MUSIC OF THE HEART

AFTER A QUICK STOP at a Fremont record shop that's cheerful, but too poppy and sterile to work, they head for West Seattle. Sarah tells Joe about Ben's sister Wendy and brother-in-law Alec, the sound engineer and vinyl collector who gave her the list of shops. Then about their two beautiful daughters, Lexi and Emma, who Sarah babysits sometimes.

Joe's stomach curdles slightly at the information, which interests him more than it should. A layered soup of feelings bubbles in his gut. First the sweetness of imagining her with family, happy and surrounded by love – something he already wants for her after less than a day. But the sweetness is chased by something bitter. An irrational shot of envy of the people who get to spend a lifetime with her.

And to finish, the strangest sensation of all. Almost imperceptible. A subtle, but undeniable note of both sweet and sour at once. Relief. Relief that the family she describes is someone else's. That the children she loves aren't her own. Why this should matter he doesn't understand, but it does. And none of it makes any sense.

After over eight straight hours of nonstop talking, Joe and Sarah fall into companionable silence on the drive. Not talked out, merely content to marinate peacefully in the low-grade energy field forming around them. Music plays and Sarah quietly hums along. Her voice is lovely. They'd sung together in the pop museum's sound lab, of course, but that had been the oafish screeching of two people goofing off. This is the first hint of her real voice. "Don't hold back on my account," he says.

"Hm?" she replies, distracted by a lane change.

"Feel free to sing. I like it."

Sarah blushes. "Oh, no! Sorry."

Joe shakes his head in a double take. "You're sorry I like it?"

Before Sarah can respond, her phone rings through the Bluetooth. She instinctively hits the answer button on her steering wheel before she can stop herself. Ben's voice booms over the car speakers, "Hi, hon, sorry I missed your call."

"That's okay," Sarah calls out. "Wait, hold on," she adds, panic rising in her voice. In a fluster, she clutches around for the phone, scrabbles to get control of it, then clicks the button to switch the call back to her phone, which she holds up to her ear. "Sorry about that."

When she'd called Ben outside the record shop, to check in about dinner before trekking down to West Seattle, she'd almost seemed as if she'd wanted Joe to hear her message. She was all, "Hi, Sweetie!" and "I've had such a crazy day!" and "Love you!" in a voice too loudly singsong to be missed, though she had turned her back to Joe.

The message was clear. *Everything's fine. Everything's normal.* Like she was trying hard to convince someone of something, but why and for whom were less clear.

Yet now, she couldn't get her husband off speaker fast enough. Somebody wasn't supposed to hear something. But the who and the why are no more clear this time.

Ben's voice echoes in Joe's ears, erasing his abstraction and making him suddenly very concrete. So concrete he may as well be sitting in the car with them. Clearly, Sarah would rather Joe not listen in this time, but he has no choice in the matter now, sitting all of twelve inches away from her. The road noise drowns out Ben's words, but Joe can't help but listen to Sarah.

"Yeah, I wanted to see... oh, okay... Hong Kong? Okay. What time is it there now?... 9:15 in the morning? Wow. Today or tomorrow?... Huh.

Okay, well, sure. I hope the call goes well... So, I was going to tell you... No, don't worry. I can tell you later... Okay... Bye."

Sarah fumbles to set the phone down. Joe watches, uncertain what to say, or whether to say anything. Sarah grips the wheel with both hands as she pushes out a slow breath. She seems both tense and relieved simultaneously, as if she got something she wanted, but at some cost. The cost of exposure, of Joe's witness. Based on her end of the conversation, he assumes they'll carry on to the record store now, and he's delighted at the prospect. But it feels unkind to ask, and she's not offering anything up.

The moment is laden and thick. Finally, he breaks the silence. "So, I hate to ask, but I do have a question."

"What's that?" Her voice is tight as a drum.

Joe pauses dramatically, takes a deep breath, and says, "Don't you have a hands-free law in this state?"

Sarah bursts out laughing, her tension expelled in one boisterous blast.

***

The rush hour drive to West Seattle is brutal, as every other driver can attest. But Joe and Sarah barely notice. They arrive an hour later in the highest of spirits, the music and company turning the minutes into cherry blossoms blowing gently away – sweet, beautiful, and far too fleeting.

Easy Street Records is iconic. Overflowing from top to bottom with new and used CDs and vinyl, the store is rough, scuffed, and worn in all the right ways with the perfect amount of grunge to feel the history of great artists pulsing through the bones of the place. The shop bustles with customers and a crowded café, and Joe does his best to sneak photos without bothering anyone. "Now, this is what I'm talkin' about!" Joe announces with a grin.

Loud modern rock plays, but Joe gets the sense it could as easily be Johnny Cash or 80s hip hop. When Sarah tells him everyone from Lou

Reed to Elvis Costello to Brandi Carlile has played in-store, and that Pearl Jam released a live album recorded there, it clinches what Joe could already feel – this is a store for music lovers. This is a store for Joe.

"Want to look around?" Sarah asks. Joe enthusiastically nods as he sneaks a few more shots before tucking his phone away. They roam the displays, perusing different racks, but loosely tethered by instinct, never straying too far from each other. Joe finds a David Bowie rack and flips through it.

The music changes. At first Joe doesn't notice, but then the song breaks through his concentration. The sweetest sadness presses in at the old-timey rendition of "You Are My Sunshine" sung with a twangy folk vocal accompanied by a banjo. It's the song that always transports him. That will always bring her back. He listens, staring blankly into space, an album poised in his unmoving hand.

Sarah speeds to his side. "Are you okay?"

Joe blinks himself back to the present and smiles at her. "Yeah, I'm fine."

"What is it?"

Joe pauses, unsure how much to say. "It's this song. It always makes me think of my mom."

"This song?" Sarah listens to identify it. "So good memories, then?"

"Yeah," he says after a moment of consideration. Joe goes on to tell her about his mom, Iris, who had the most beautiful voice in the church choir. His favorite reason to attend church every Sunday. "She sang to me every night before bed from when I was a baby," he explains. "And we used to sing together as I was growing up. I would sit next to her at the piano as she played, then when I took up the guitar, I played and we'd sing while she made dinner." He pauses as his feelings bubble up to his throat and smiles at a memory he keeps to himself.

For his part, Joe's love of his mother and music became inseparable. He loved music in its own right, yes, and he loved to sing. But singing with her was the greatest expression of love he could imagine. It felt transcendent.

He didn't have that word for it back then, of course, but he knew the feeling. The feeling that singing with someone he loved with all his heart would bond them together forever.

They stroll back to the car, absorbed in their own thoughts until Sarah blurts out, "Thank you for telling me about your mom."

It was easy to tell her. It felt natural. Talking to Sarah is the easiest thing in the world. He can't understand any of it, but after a single day with this woman, he's willing to tell her just about anything. It's both exhilarating and terrifying. But when she acknowledges the significance of the story, she presses on a raw nerve in his heart. It doesn't hurt exactly, but it does send a powerful wave of emotion flooding through his system. He freezes, momentarily incapacitated by his vulnerability.

"I mean it," she adds. "I'm honored."

Joe's eyes prickle with the telltale twinge in his nose. If he says even a word, the tears will come. He fidgets with the phone in his pocket, clicking the on/off button repeatedly, an emergency meditative focal point.

Sarah pivots at Joe's silence. "Sorry. Did I say something I shouldn't?"

Joe centers himself with a breath and looks her square in the eye. "Not at all."

Sarah checks the time and changes the subject. "It's after 7:30, and I know you're probably starving. But if we hurry, and you don't mind waiting a little longer to eat, we might make it back downtown while there's enough light for some pictures of the Great Wheel."

Joe nods, more grateful than he can say.

***

Post-rush hour, they make good time back from West Seattle and arrive at the waterfront before sunset. Joe gets as many pictures as he can in every direction – of the pier, Miner's Landing, and the Great Wheel, which lights up as they approach. The large Ferris wheel glows in shades of blue, teal, and purple, which will be all the more impressive after the sun goes down. The line isn't long, so Joe suggests they go for a ride.

"Really?" Alarm pitches Sarah's voice an octave too high.

Joe shakes his head. "It's your town. Why am I always having to talk you into things?"

Sarah shrugs her acquiescence. She's learned quickly that resistance is futile when it comes to Joe. They hop into the line and it moves fast. They expect a gondola to themselves since it's not crowded, so Joe chooses the city view as they climb in and Sarah plants herself on the water view side. But right behind them, the staffer dude sends in a family of three, parents with a son of about seven, to share their gondola. Sarah jumps up and moves over to Joe's bench - a safe, appropriate distance apart, naturally – so the family can take the bench across from them.

"This is fun," Joe says. Sarah agrees, but says no more, silenced by the presence of their gondola mates.

They ride up slowly, halting each minute while another gondola is loaded, their own glass enclosed gondola shifting lightly, either from the wind or from the vibrations of the loading and unloading. Sarah grows tense with the rocking, but does her best to relax. When they get about halfway up to the top, she starts pointing out notable landmarks. The two stadiums, Smith Tower, the ferry to Bainbridge Island, Pike Place Market, the Space Needle.

Across the way, the boy whines. Sarah's commentary has made him realize he's on the wrong side. All he can easily see is the water, which is totally boring. He wants to see the city. His parents shush him and eye Sarah and Joe apologetically, but Joe jumps up. "Do you want to switch?"

Sarah panics as the car shakes. "Joe, I don't think we're supposed to stand up."

"No, it's fine," he says, then to the family. "Here, trade with us. We're happy to take the water view."

"Are you sure?" the mother says.

"Of course," Joe responds jovially. And so the five of them carefully take turns crossing the gondola to switch places. The father moves over next to Sarah bringing his son with him ever so slowly, then Joe sits in his place. When the three of them are seated, the mother gets up and makes her way for Sarah's seat.

Cautious as they are, the gondola rocks with each step and Sarah's pulse races. She braces herself against the window as the mother approaches, realizing she'll have to move to finish this transaction. Her hand reaches for something to hold, but finds no purchase. There are only the glass doors and she dares not touch those.

Joe stretches out his hand. Sarah takes it, and he squeezes reassuringly. She grips it tightly, stands, and inches her way across the gondola, crossing paths with the mother as she goes. The rocking continues, but Joe has her. She's safe. He pulls her in, and when she lands on the bench, she's right beside him, still desperately clutching his hand.

"You made it," he says.

"I'm not so sure," she gasps in response, still breathless with anxiety.

"You *are* afraid of heights."

"It's not the height. It's the shaking."

Joe drops Sarah's hand and wraps his arm around her instead, giving her a quick, friendly hug. "Well, don't worry. I've got you." He pulls his arm back and smiles warmly at her, doing his best to allay her fear.

It works. Instantaneously, Sarah's fear is replaced with a different pre-occupation, the giant, still smoldering scorch mark now stretching across her back and onto her left arm, in the precise shape and position where Joe's arm and hand just were.

The sunset view of the water and islands is spectacular. Joe and Sarah ride in silence as they take in the glorious streaks of pink, orange, yellow, and ever darker shades of blue as the sun gracefully descends over the Puget Sound.

As beautiful as it is, Sarah's still rattled by the occasional rocking and hums to herself to soothe her nerves. The family across the way takes no note, now happily chattering about their view of the city, what they did that day, and what's on the docket for tomorrow. She hums low and quiet, a subconscious response to her anxiety, but Joe hears. And Joe listens.

She's singing, "You Are My Sunshine." Of all songs. No doubt picked up from the music store. Her voice lilts gently into his mind first, then his heart, leading him back in time. He gazes at the sunset, drifting with the tune, wandering back to the day everything changed for him.

Sarah catches the faraway look in Joe's eyes. "You in there?"

Joe shifts his gaze from the sunset to Sarah, his thoughts trailing slowly behind. "Yeah."

"What is it?"

Joe considers a moment. "'You Are My Sunshine,'" he says. Sarah gives him a confused look, so he clarifies. "You were just singing it."

"I was singing? Sorry."

"Please stop apologizing. Especially for that."

She can't help herself. "Sorry." She shrugs with an apologetic half-giggle.

"It's just…" Joe looks first to the family, who are too embroiled in their own conversation to notice anything he says. Then he peers into Sarah's eyes for something, a safe harbor for his words, then continues in a low voice. "I sang that to my mother right before she died."

"Oh, Joe."

"It was a couple years ago. She had cancer, had been fighting it for years, and was finally done. My dad called me home and I sat with her for three days. She never smoked, but the cancer made it to her lungs, so she couldn't really even speak. She was on oxygen, in and out of consciousness."

"I'm so sorry. That must have been so hard."

"Hospice care came every day, and the rest of the time, I just sat and sang to her. Like she always sang to me. Sometimes she'd smile when she heard me singing, even before she opened her eyes." He pauses to glance at Sarah who wipes a tear away. He takes a deep breath and goes on. "She had such a beautiful voice. To see her silenced like that broke my heart. Then on the last day, she reached for me and I just knew it was coming. So I started singing that song."

"'You Are My Sunshine,'" Sarah says.

"Yeah. And somehow, she joined in. Her voice was raspy and thin, and she couldn't finish the song, but it was her. She was there."

Sarah says nothing, giving Joe the space he needs. Joe drifts back to the moment that would stay in his heart forever. Music was the cement that sealed them together forever. He's found other ways to show his love, of course, adapting his heart to the unique shape of each relationship, whether romantic, familial, or platonic. Those he loves never doubt it. Although he's never felt that eternal bond with anyone else, music remains Joe's first and most powerful love language.

"It was a miracle." He nods his certainty. "Then she promised she'd always be there, and I told her I loved her. And Dad and I held her, and then she was gone."

Sarah opens her mouth, as if to speak, but nothing comes. Joe smiles wistfully at her, then turns back to the water as the last sliver of sun disappears on the horizon.

"I've never told anyone that. Not even Mel. She wouldn't have understood what it meant to me. Not really." He breaks off, searching for an explanation of what he's just said, a way to defend Melanie from the accusation he's just cast. He continues thoughtfully, "Music just doesn't connect for her in the same way. So, Dad was there, but other than that..." He trails off, glances at Sarah, and shakes his head before looking back to the view.

Sarah watches Joe carefully, searching for the right word or action. She studies his hand, desperate to take it, to comfort him, to hold him, but that's too intimate. A quick hand to help someone along, as he has offered her, is very different. It's not her place. It's not her hand to take.

But she can't do nothing, so she reaches out and touches his forearm. His jacket provides a vital protective layer and she rests her hand there, giving a gentle squeeze that says what needs to be said.

Joe's eyes remain fixed on the fading colors of the sky, but he reaches his other hand across and squeezes hers in thanks before releasing a deep exhale. As if he's freeing a breath he's been holding for years. They remain like that, in silence, for the rest of the ride.

***

They saunter along the pier, now glowing brighter than daylight with LCDs and neon of every color. Joe bites into a piece of fish from a basket of fish and chips as Sarah scoops a spoonful of clam chowder from a paper bowl.

"You sure that's enough for you? You've barely eaten today," he says.

"I've been feasting on life," she deadpans.

Joe smirks as he thrusts his basket toward her. "At least have some fries." They're crispy, golden, and still steaming hot.

Sarah devours the intoxicating fried food aroma. "If you insist. I'll have one fry." She bites into it and the salty, greasy goodness melts her insides. "Maybe two." She smirks, reaching for two more.

"Sarah, I want to thank you for today. I can't even tell you what you've done for me."

"Just today?" she says. Joe looks at her noncommittally, so she continues, "Are you done with me already? Wham, bam, thank you ma'am?"

Joe's face darkens with horror. "What? No! I would never—"

"I'm kidding," she says with a grin. "But you said you needed pretty, outdoorsy scenery, right? Don't you want the nature tour tomorrow?"

He recovers his cheer. "Absolutely I do! I just didn't want to assume."

"Because I have so many better things to do with my time?"

Joe stifles a laugh. "Great then. We're on. Whatever you want, I'm all yours."

All hers? Dangerous words. A dangerous idea. "You may regret that."

"No chance," he says, so low and rumbly it reaches Sarah's stomach like a sonic boom.

They eat and walk quietly, their hot food combatting the chill of the waterfront breeze, until Sarah breaks the silence. "I have a question. You can totally say no, but... could I read your script?"

Joe lights up. "You want to read my script?"

"Of course."

"Then, of course you can read it," he says without hesitation. "I should warn you, though. It's not quite right."

"Meaning?"

"It's hard to explain. Everyone else seems happy with it, but I know it needs something. A more emotional trigger for Sean's breakthrough. Something intense and visceral. I'm hoping I'll find some inspiration while I'm here."

"Like what exactly?"

"For example, if we had the budget, I'd make it a giant parade. Or fireworks. But we don't have that kind of money. So maybe something in nature? Not just pretty scenery, but like something that actually *happens* here? Seattle's version of Old Faithful maybe? Something that produces a strong sensory response."

"Maybe we could get Mount Rainer to blow," she offers cheerfully.

"Maybe non-lethal?"

"Oh, non-lethal is a requirement?" She grins as she drops her bowl in the trash. "I'll think on it."

***

Sarah waits in the lobby while Joe collects the screenplay from his room. He holds the script and contemplates how readily he agreed to let her read it, without a flicker of hesitation. In any other situation, with any other person, he *would* have hesitated. Even if they were in the industry, let alone a random fan. But with Sarah, the yes came as naturally as everything else does with her. Somehow, with her, it's always a yes. Still, with the benefit of distance and a moment to think, he forces himself to pause. If this script is his talisman against mishaps, is it wise to hand it off? Then again, maybe it's already done its job. Didn't Sarah show up at the precise moment everything was falling apart? They had seen so much today, some of it would have to work.

Not that Joe's superstitious about most things. Other than wearing his Dodgers cap 24/7 during the World Series. He's more of a God and Fate guy than a sucker for miscellaneous superstitions, but after so many years of struggle, he doesn't like taking chances.

Still, if Sarah is the good luck the script has brought him, then surely it can't hurt to give it to her to read. He clutches the script close and carries it to the lobby, where Sarah pops off the couch when he emerges from the elevator. Joe gives a little bow as he hands it over. "Here you go, Madame."

She accepts it with a lighthearted, but earnest flourish of ceremony. As she does, Joe senses the script conferring its power on Sarah. Somehow, she has become as integral to the film's success as the screenplay itself.

Sarah clasps the script lovingly, greedily, protectively against her chest. "I'll guard it with my life." And Joe knows she will. She pauses, reluctant to leave, but the time has come. "See you tomorrow then. Say 9:00? Pick you up out front?"

"Looking forward to it."

"Me, too." They linger a moment longer. Sarah runs her fingers over the script title and Joe's name. "Triple threat Joseph Robert Parker," she says, half to herself. She smiles, gives a small wave, and leaves. Joe watches her until she's out of sight.

CHAPTER TEN

LITTLE LIES

SARAH CURLS INTO HER bedroom armchair to read the script. Ben still isn't home from his late-night call to Hong Kong, which suits her fine because she can read undisturbed. It's her first screenplay and she's not accustomed to the leanness of the description or the spareness of the form. But the dialogue's crisp and she's surprised how vividly she can imagine the scenes unfolding, especially with Joe playing Sean. He'll be amazing.

She's torn through the script and already cried twice when she hears Ben coming in from the garage. She curses, desperate to finish before he interrupts. As he mills around downstairs, she imagines him working his way through his normal routine. Hanging his coat, getting a glass of water, pulling out his laptop at the kitchen island or heading to his office. Though at this time of night, he might forgo the laptop and focus on his phone. She frantically flips the pages, reading as quickly as possible without losing the dramatic tension. Only a few more pages.

She hears him climbing the stairs and prays he'll detour, but within moments, he walks in. She stiffens. "Hey, hon," he says moving toward the bathroom. "How was your day?"

"Good," she chirps on autopilot, but before she can say more, he's turned on the water in the bathroom. And when the water goes on, the ears go off.

"Good," he calls from the bathroom. He brushes his teeth and steps out long enough to toss his shirt in the hamper, toothbrush still in his mouth. He disappears again, closing the door behind him.

Sarah returns to the script and pushes through, hoping the badly timed disruption won't ruin the ending for her. In the final pages, Sean spreads his father's ashes at the waterside, surrounded by trees. Sarah envisions the scene so clearly it launches a pinball in her head, bouncing around and lighting up at all the locations where it might come to life.

Knowing Joe needed scenic nature locations, she'd already mapped out a good bunch of parks to visit, but the script has given her a clearer vision. She's no longer just a tour guide. She's discovering the woodsy refuge where Sean's parents will first kiss. The lonely spot where Sean will hurl his father's watch angrily into the water. The peaceful retreat where Sean will finally kneel, spread his father's ashes, and watch them drift slowly away from shore.

"Whatcha reading?" Ben asks emerging from the bathroom.

Sarah realizes her mistake. She hadn't meant for Ben to see the script, but she'd been so determined to get through it before he came in that she completely forgot to stash it. Not that she has anything to hide. She hasn't done anything wrong and there's no crime in reading a screenplay. It all just feels so complicated to explain, and she'd wanted to keep things simple. "Yeah, I wanted to tell you about this," she says,

She doesn't want to tell him, of course. There's a part of her that wants to keep the whole day to herself, a precious private gift from the gods that's far too special to share with anyone else. Least of all Ben.

If she could ever tell anyone, it would be Gabi. But this day. How can Sarah begin to explain it to anyone? She can't even explain it to herself. Still, she can't keep it secret. She has nothing to hide, but the very act of hiding it would become something to hide. So, she swallows hard, screws up her courage, and says, "Something crazy happened today."

She braces herself, struggling to find a way to say she spent the whole day with a gorgeous actor without making Ben jealous. If he even cares enough to get jealous anymore. There was a time when he did certainly, but now? Still, spending the day with another man who happens to be a hunky celebrity might be enough to make anyone jealous out of sheer principle.

But after all, it's not like anything happened. Possibly the lightest of flirtation, the way any actor flirts with his fans to keep them happy, but he'd been a perfect gentleman. It had all been completely innocent.

"I went downtown today, to get that stuff for Gabi," she says. "You know, for her trip?"

"Oh right," Ben replies, staring at his phone.

Her heart races as she prepares to go on. But why? Nothing happened. And never would. Never could. Even aside from the fact that they were both married, an obvious deal-breaker, she's seen enough celebrity red carpets to know that Hollywood hunks want women as impressive as they are. Joe's own photos prove that. So whatever little flights of fantasy she's taken during the day, she's well aware they're no more than that. "And I ran into this actor," Sarah continues as she climbs into bed. "I don't know if you know him by name or not. I'm sure you've seen him. Joseph Robert Parker?" She knows perfectly well Ben has seen him. If Ben paid even the slightest bit of attention during the worst of Sarah's spiral, he must have seen Joe onscreen nonstop.

Ben looks up thoughtfully a quick moment, then shrugs. "You met this guy? That's cool." Back to his phone.

"Well, yeah, but there's more." She pauses, seeking the right words. "So, I guess they're making a movie here later this year."

"Oh cool," Ben says with the same dull inflection he'd use if she announced she was clipping her toenails.

"And they planned this trip to scout locations, but I guess the location guy had a family emergency or something. And he was the one who had the locations list."

"Well, I hope they got it figured out," Ben says absently.

Sarah's eyes land on the far corner of the ceiling where she spots a lone string of cobweb bisecting the angle. She stares at it while speaking. "Well, yeah, they did…" *They???* "So, the funny thing is, you know, I was down there anyway and didn't have anything else to do, and… long story short, I kind of ended up playing tour guide all day."

Ben finally focuses on Sarah. "Like you took them around town yourself?"

There it is again. First *they*, now *them*. She has to say something. She shrugs. "Crazy, right?"

"Where did you go?"

"All over. Pike Place, Seattle Center, Kerry Park, the library, the Fremont Troll." *Say something. Say it now!*

"Wow! You really were a tour guide," Ben says, astonished. "I'm not surprised. You're always the best host when we have company in town. Hey, maybe this will be the start of a new career."

Sarah forces a chuckle. "Actually, I did say I'd do it again tomorrow too."

Ben's mouth hangs open a moment like he's going to say something more, but instead he presses his hand to his stomach and holds up his other hand to say "hold on." Then he scurries off to the bathroom, leaving Sarah to stew.

The weight of the omission crushes her into the bed, a piano on her chest, so heavy she might never get back up. What has she done? And why? In truth, it's worse than omission. She used the word herself. "They." Only once, but the damage was done.

She grabs her phone for distraction, but soon realizes no amount of social media scrolling will subdue her. She considers texting Gabi, but when she opens her text messages, she spots the message from an unknown 310 number, and remembers who and what it must be. She taps once and there it is. The picture of her and Joe, faces pressed together, happy as two very happy clams.

***

Joe sits at his desk taking notes on his photos as he scrolls. He gets to the Kerry Park shots and marvels once again at the view. Then he comes to the selfies with Sarah and quickly swipes to the second shot. He stares at it a long while and smiles. It's been quite a day.

Out of curiosity, he swipes back to the first picture, the one Sarah asked him to delete because she'd blinked. But when he examines it more closely, she's not blinking at all. She's looking at him. Her lips are gently upturned. She's containing a smile fighting to come out and her eyes are fixed on him with a look that shoots through every inch of his body.

Of course, a single frame of any moment in time can be misleading. He thinks of the many occasions when a badly timed pause button has made news anchors appear to reenact "The Exorcist" while reporting the good news story of the day. Indeed, he's had enough awkward pictures of himself published over the years to know any random shot can suggest something very different than the reality.

The expression on Sarah's face doesn't read like a fluke, however. It reads like truth. But he's probably imagining it.

Joe flips back to the second photo, the one where they're both smiling into the camera, and he studies himself. He looks happy. He's hard to see under the ball cap and thick beard, but the size of his smile is a dead giveaway. He scrutinizes himself a moment longer and runs his fingers through his beard.

***

Sarah clicks away from the photo when Ben comes back. He climbs into bed, says goodnight, and rolls over to go to sleep. The topic of the day literally flushed away. Sarah stares blankly at her phone, then goes to her browser and searches Joe's name.

For all her devotion, she's never done this before. She's only ever read interviews and stories that crossed her path organically, on her web browser or via social media. Those she's devoured for nearly twenty years, ever since she was first transfixed by him in an otherwise mediocre HBO film. She'd missed his name, but never forgot him. Then one day, a few years later, she stopped at the grocery and there he was on the cover of Entertainment Weekly. Joseph Robert Parker, the sexy star of a hotly anticipated new nighttime soap about the world of high finance, "Safe as Houses." Sarah did a happy dance.

There were other shows along the way, and movies, and she watched them all, of course. But she had perhaps too studiously avoided directly looking him up online. As if that particular rabbit hole might be too dangerous. Or maybe she simply didn't want to feel like some nerdy fangirl. Whatever the reason, she never did it. Until now.

She flips through a few pictures, then clicks his Wikipedia page. She reads the brief intro – "best known for his starring roles on television as Reid Bentley on 'Safe as Houses,' Garrett Barnes in 'River's Run,' and Dr. Simon Galloway on 'Doc Hope.'" Sarah grieves the brevity of all three. Both "Safe as Houses" and "River's Run" lasted only a season. "Doc Hope" made it two, but even that ended five years ago. On the bright side, he's popping up in more movies these days – though mostly supporting roles despite his irrefutable hotness – but she misses her regular appointments with Joe in the lead.

She scrolls next to the basic statistics box and a chill blasts through her. She blinks several times, waiting for the words to sort themselves into something sensible.

Born: *March 20, 1983*
Pittsburgh, Pennsylvania, U.S.
Education: *Carnegie Mellon University*
Years Active: *2005-Present*
Spouse(s): *Melanie Parker*
Children: *2*

Sarah stares at the top three lines in disbelief. They were both born in Pittsburgh. *On the same day.*

She flirts with calling it Fate – how could it be otherwise? Except she doesn't believe in Fate. Still, such a strange coincidence is remarkable, even to Sarah. She chokes back a laugh of astonishment and delight, then chases it with something darker and fearful. With anyone else, it would be a ridiculously fun discovery. With Joe, it somehow knocks her off her axis and onto a new one. The alignment confuses and unnerves her.

And Carnegie Mellon is barely a mile from the University of Pittsburgh where she went. Same bars, same shops, same parties. They had to be there at the same time.

She attempts to read the rest of the profile, but her concentration is shattered. She switches off her phone and the light.

In the darkness, she stares at the dim shadows on the ceiling and the even murkier shadows in her mind. A memory stirs.

CHAPTER ELEVEN

NEW YEAR'S EVE (DECEMBER, 2004)

THE EMOTIONAL SHRAPNEL OF Sarah's parents' divorce embedded itself into every aspect of her senior year. They were her foundation, her family, her safe place. Her certainty in an uncertain world, simply sucked out of existence without so much as a word of warning. Her trust obliterated. Her faith in love and marriage fallen like the dead leaves covering the ground all over campus.

Her relationship with Tyler, her boyfriend since sophomore year, took the first hit when she spun out. With her concentration gone, her coursework quickly followed. Sarah packed on ten pounds and waited to self-destruct, which she would have done if Gabi hadn't had the sheer audacity to force her out of her funk and out on the town.

Gabi was Sarah's rock, standing steadfastly by her side to pick up every broken piece as Sarah shattered like crystal. She held Sarah as she wept over her parents, wailed over her doomed academic career, and sobbed over her breakup with the only boy she'd ever loved. And when Sarah was finally ready, Gabi helped her put the pieces back together.

By New Year's Eve, Gabi was determined that Sarah get back out there. "They're calling this 'the party to end all parties.'" Apparently, everyone who was anyone, or who wanted to be someone, would be at this party. However, Sarah remained unconvinced, so Gabi pulled out the big guns. "Please, babe. It'll be epic." Gabi always had a word, and "epic" had been a favorite, but she'd retired it by sophomore year. Yet, here it was again, like a bad penny.

"Epic, you say? I don't think anything's been epic in two years."

"See! We have to go!"

Sarah rolled her eyes. "Well, I mean, if it's going to be epic..."

The girls dressed up, slathered on more make-up than Sarah had ever worn in her life (even on Halloween), bought themselves some festive New Year crowns, and marched into the den of iniquity. As it turned out, it was a typical Greek bacchanalia. Huge crowds, free-flowing booze and other substances, and music pulsing at a volume and vibration so intense she could barely hear her own thoughts. In short, a carbon copy of every other frat party she'd ever attended. Until the fight broke out.

Sarah had a headache and begged Gabi to go. Gabi had hoped to hold out for a midnight kiss, but she didn't have the heart to let Sarah suffer, and she hadn't met a single guy she'd actually want to kiss anyway. They pushed outside to head home, moments before the midnight countdown.

As they stepped into the fresh air, Sarah felt a jolt go through her as the air all around snapped and buzzed to life. At first she thought it was just the shock of the cold air combined with the relief of escaping that sweaty, living boom box, but the sensation continued as they reached the sidewalk by the street.

"10... 9... 8...," the countdown began. Everyone in the house and yard shouted in unison. Sarah paused and looked back at the house, searching for some explanation of the strange buzzing she both heard and felt. She found none. She asked Gabi, but Gabi had no idea what she was talking about.

"You okay?" Gabi asked.

"Yeah, I...." Sarah couldn't understand what was happening.

"7... 6..."

"We should get you home."

"Yeah," Sarah agreed, but she stayed planted in her spot. Maybe it was her headache, but she'd never had a headache like this before.

"5... 4..."

And it didn't actually hurt anymore. It just... hummed. She looked around again and coming down the sidewalk from the other direction was a group of guys headed to the party. Her eyes fell instinctively, insistently on one dark-haired guy who towered over the rest.

"3... 2... 1..."

It was dark and she could barely see him, but the vibration got stronger and Sarah grew dizzy as he approached. Then he glanced her way and stopped in his tracks.

"Happy New Year!" rang out a chorus of drunken voices.

For a split second that stretched into eternity, they gawked at each other from a distance, mouths agape. As the world around them erupted in laughter, spontaneous kisses, and blowing horns, the two strangers stood transfixed, each barely an apparition in the darkness. The concussive explosion of merriment momentarily silenced by something much bigger. They each took a step toward the other.

The door of the frat house burst open, and two guys fell through it punching each other like a couple of cowboys plowing through saloon doors after one is caught cheating at poker. Half a dozen more guys piled out behind them, taking sides and entering into what instantly became a full blown rumble. The spell broken by the erupting violence, all eyes inevitably turned to the brawl. Horrified, Gabi grabbed Sarah and rushed her away before the cops came or the violence spread. Sarah looked back with a palpable sense of regret, but was too confused to resist.

The next morning, Sarah nursed a mild hangover and tried to make sense of the night before. Something had happened, but what? She'd felt so strange, but the feeling passed the further they got from the party and was long gone by the time they reached their apartment. The physical sensation passed, but not the bone deep instinct that the guy she locked eyes with was *someone*. She barely slept as her mind looped round and round about him. That guy she couldn't even see properly, yet couldn't stop thinking about.

The fight became the talk of campus for weeks. In the end, seven guys got expelled, three more got suspended, and the frat was shut down indefinitely. So, it was the party to end all parties after all. At least for that frat. But despite all that, Sarah never forgot the party for a very different reason.

Chapter Twelve

Holding Back

In her closet, Sarah pushes to the back of her drawer, past the simple cotton hipsters she's worn exclusively for the past two years and runs her fingers across her more delicate, special undies. The ones with lace and silk and pretty colors and designs, the kind that come with matching bras. Before she can select anything, she's interrupted by a call she can't ignore. She completely forgot about yoga with Gabi.

"Where were you?" Gabi demands when Sarah picks up.

"Oh my gosh, sorry! Something came up," Sarah says as she walks out of the closet and plops on the side of the bed.

"What comes up at seven in the morning?"

Sarah stares at herself in the full-length mirror next to the closet. "I'm just getting ready."

"Ready for what? What's going on?" Gabi needles, her intrigue radar beeping too loudly to ignore.

"It's a long story." Sarah watches her reflection as she traces her jawline with her fingertips. Is it her imagination, or does she look different today? Better.

"I've got time. Wait, no, I don't. Crikey, I'm late."

Sarah chuckles. "Crikey's sticking then?"

"Quit dodging. What are you doing that's worth bailing on me?"

"I'll tell you later, I promise." She will tell her. But it's too big a story to tell in Cliff's Notes. Gabi will demand every detail.

"Oooh, you're sketchy as hell. Tell me now."

She doesn't have time for this any more than Gabi does. "I promise I'll tell you everything tomorrow. Gotta go. Love you!" Gabi grumbles her displeasure, but Sarah moves quickly to hang up before Gabi can object or demand more information.

She returns to the fancy undies. Would any of them even still fit? One way to find out. She pulls out a silky light blue pair with embroidered yellow and green flowers and sheer matching bra. She slips them on, and to her delight, they fit. A tad snug, but for once, the bulge of her curves looks sexy and womanly to her, so she fights off her demons and goes with it.

No one will see them, of course. Including Ben, if the past year is any indication. But putting them on makes her feel pretty, and for the first time in a long time, she wants to feel pretty. Caring about such things – caring about much of anything – is an unfamiliar sensation these days. But she welcomes it.

She strolls through her large closet with more care and attention than any time in recent memory. She takes her time trying on options and checking them in the mirror. She dismisses the ones she doesn't like, but eschews the self-loathing that usually accompanies such exercises, instead opting simply to focus on finding something that feels good. What a difference a day makes.

***

Sarah's leaning on the passenger door when Joe walks out. She feels him coming and braces herself, but when she sees him, dear God!

No cap, no sunglasses, and no beard! His square jaw revealed, Sarah suddenly feels like she's staring at a TAG Heuer model, all rugged angularity that transforms the mere act of donning a fitted Henley and faded jeans into a work of art. How he can be anything less than the biggest star in the world looking like that is beyond her. Seeing him like that through the remove of a TV screen was one thing, but in person, he's almost blinding. The slight dampening effect of the beard and hat had contained his handsomeness in a way that made it manageable enough for Sarah, like acoustic curtains on a stage stopping the sounds of her heart from bouncing all over the walls and ceiling in an endless, uncontrollable ricochet.

But now, with this version of Handsome Joe unleashed, complete with his perfectly tousled dark waves topping his artfully chiseled jawline, she doubts she'll be able to string two words together all day. Does he have any clue what an impact shaving that beard has?

"Good morning," he says. The light from his smile radiates out and turns her knees to jelly. Apparently, she's been wearing dark sunglasses for the last 24 hours and has now removed them. Everything is brighter and more vivid. She didn't know that was possible after yesterday, but the proof stands before her, as tall and blinding as a lighthouse.

"Hi," she manages to get out. She points to his face and summons the words, "You shaved."

"Yeah." Joe runs his hand over his face, and Sarah quivers at the thought of doing the same. "It felt like the right time."

Sarah tries to conjure the Joe of yesterday to her mind, the one she could actually talk to, in an attempt to form a cohesive thought. "But aren't you afraid of being recognized?"

He shrugs. "That doesn't happen very often. I usually figure better safe than sorry, but we're not going to be in crowded places today, right?"

She can't stop staring. "Right."

"And I still have these if I need them." He waves the baseball cap and sunglasses in his hand. Then he adds, "You look really nice, by the way."

Sarah flusters and dashes away to her side of the car in a flurry of hems and haws and "oh, no, um, no's." But suddenly, she's glad she took the time to blow out her hair into silky, soft waves today instead of yesterday's wild frizz. Joe laughs and climbs into the car.

She relaxes slightly once they're settled in the car and she no longer has to look directly at Joe. She grabs a piece of paper from the backseat and hands it to him, studiously avoiding eye contact as she does.

"I brought you this," she says. "It's a list of all the places we went yesterday, in order, and a tentative list of places I'm planning for today, though that could still change."

"This is incredible."

"I also included links to most of these places, so you or whoever can find them more easily. If you want to," she says.

"I want to."

"I'll send it digitally when we're done, but I figured I'd wait until the end of the day in case anything changes."

"You're amazing." Sarah glimpses her crimson cheeks in the mirror as Joe quickly adds, "I mean, it's incredibly generous of you to do all this for a perfect stranger."

"You're not exactly a perfect stranger. You're Joseph Robert Parker." The words are a reminder to herself more than anything. *This isn't real. This is a crazy daydream that will all be over soon. Don't get too attached.*

Joe catches her eye in a flicker from the road and says, "I'm just Joe, Sarah."

"Right," she replies, aiming for easy airiness as she pulls onto the freeway. "By the way, Just Joe, I read your script."

"And?"

Sarah detects a genuine note of anxiety as he winces in nervous anticipation. "I loved it."

"Really?"

"Yeah, really. It made me cry more than once. It's beautiful."

He lights up. "Thank you!"

"Thank you for letting me read it." She's moved by how sincere he seems, to think her opinion matters at all. She allows the emotional dust to settle while changing lanes. "And I have good news/bad news."

"Okay?"

"The good news is, I've had an idea about something that *might* work for that scene. You know, the trigger for Sean's breakdown."

"That's great news! What is it?"

"I want to keep it a surprise, if that's okay," Sarah says. "It would be hard to describe and do it justice, but I think it could work. It's pretty special and definitely visceral. You just have to see it. I don't want to overpromise, but maybe?"

Joe peruses the list in his hand. "Is there a hint on this list?"

She shakes her head. "It's not on there yet."

"Hmm," he grumbles. "Fine. What's the bad news?"

"Well, it doesn't happen until sunset. So that's another long day, I'm afraid."

He grins. "I'm still waiting for the bad news."

Sarah barely holds back her own grin by pursing her lips, settling on a tight-lipped, reluctant smile as she flips on the radio for a much-needed distraction.

Joe gazes out the window while Sarah hums along quietly for half a song before he says, "I'm so happy you liked it."

He nearly asks about the giant brick building floating above the city like a medieval castle on a hill, but he'd rather listen to Sarah. She hums along with each song so naturally, so absent-mindedly, the music simply emanates from her, each of her breaths made up of melodies and harmonies instead of oxygen and carbon dioxide.

Joe listens intently, and contentedly, but he wants more. He wants to hear her real voice. "You know you don't have to hold back on my account, right?"

"What?"

"Singing. Why are you holding back?"

Sarah balks. "I'm not holding back. What do you mean?"

"Are you kidding? You're always holding back. Holding back is very big with you."

Sarah's mouth gapes wide with amused indignation. "How dare you? After one day? You don't know me well enough to say that."

"Yeah," Joe says proudly. "I really do."

His words hang in the air, silencing Sarah, his meaning unclear. Even to him. The moment has suddenly taken on a larger significance, which he didn't intend. Unless he did. But he reads her vulnerability in the silence and backs off, refocusing on the question at hand. "Come on. Sing out, Sarah!" he shouts.

"Was that a 'Gypsy' reference?"

"You know 'Gypsy'?"

"Of course, I know 'Gypsy,'" she announces with equal parts pride and offense. "What kind of philistine do you think I am? I'm surprised you do though."

"I was a musical theater major." He beams proudly that he's been able to surprise her with something she didn't know.

"But you never sing publicly. I've never seen you sing."

"I used to, back when I did theater. But once I landed in LA, my career took a different direction. There wasn't any call for it."

"Well, good news. Musicals are back, baby. You should get yourself a musical. I want to hear you sing."

"I'll sing right now," he says, then looks at her pointedly. "If you will." He turns up the radio.

Although Sarah was humming along moments earlier, she shakes her head. "I don't know this song."

Joe squints suspiciously. "Fine. We'll find something you do know." He clicks through her programmed channels, a couple modern rock and pop channels where she continues to shake her head, then a classical station and NPR. Finally, he lands on a 90s channel where the Backstreet Boys are playing. "Now I know you know this," he says firmly.

Sarah frowns, but he's got her and they both know it. "Backstreet's back," he says matter-of-factly. He gives her a wry smile and dares her to deny it.

She can't. "Alright," she says, bobbing her head to what is clearly an irresistible beat to any 90s kid. She starts with a few timid yeee-ahs, but by the end of the song, they are both car dancing and singing full out.

Backstreet is followed by TLC, Bell Biv DeVoe, and Alanis Morissette, by which time Sarah is so fully lost in the music she misses every Mercer Island exit for the park. She cringes with embarrassment, but Joe keeps singing Smash Mouth at her by way of reassurance. By the time they loop back and finally pull into the parking lot, they've knocked out three more 90s classics, spirits soaring even higher than their voices.

When the unmistakable opening notes of Sixpence None The Richer's "Kiss Me" play, however, Sarah shuffles uncomfortably. Before anyone can sing the first line, she grabs the volume button and turns it down. "Sorry," she says.

"Something wrong?"

"I just want to concentrate while I'm parking. There are a lot of people walking around here. A lot of dogs."

Joe thinks about the song that was playing, that is still playing so low he can barely hear it if he strains. *Kiss Me.*

"A lot of dogs," he says as he studies her. "Yeah."

***

The path into the park opens onto a grand vista of a verdant hillside dipping downward in front of them with enormous evergreen trees at the bottom, made miniature by the distance, and Lake Washington beyond. A flagpole stands in the middle of the hill with the flag gently blowing in the breeze. The sun is bright, the grass is green, and the water and sky blue. A perfect day in a perfect park.

As they stroll, Sarah points out an amphitheater to the left that might work for his outdoor concert scene. He snaps photos as they go. On the right they pass an enclosed dog park and stop to watch several dogs chase balls in and out of the lake, soaking everyone in a six-foot radius each time they emerge. Joe watches Sarah as much as the dogs. She sparkles at the scene.

"I should get a dog," she muses as they resume their walk. "At least it would give me something to do. Get me out of the house."

They reach the end of the path and settle on a bench overlooking a small beach. "Yeah, a dog could be good, sure," Joe says noncommittally. "Or maybe – and I'm just spitballing here – maybe a job?" he digs with a provocative smirk.

The good-natured jab lands soundly, but she can't muster anger at this man who somehow sees her so clearly, so quickly. Sarah's mouth gapes open again, genuinely indignant this time, but the familiarity also sends a thrill down her spine. "You, sir, take liberties."

"Do I?" He squints at her. "I don't usually," he says with a slow, low drawl.

A bowling ball hits her chest and rolls down her body. "You barely know me!"

Joe purses his lips, raises a brow, and tilts his head at her. They each wait a tick to see if the other will admit the truth out loud, but they don't. Instead Joe throws his hands up in fake surrender and shrugs. "Get a pittie. Sweetest dogs in the world."

Sarah harrumphs her displeasure. She watches a speedboat zoom past while Joe stays fixed on her. "Come on, Sarah. Why does a woman who could do anything in the world—" She balks, but he continues, "—choose not to do anything?"

"I didn't ch—" She stops herself and sighs. "It's a long story."

"I'm a captive audience."

"It's also fairly tragic."

"More tragic than my dying mother?"

Touché. Sarah studies Joe's expression. Expectant, patient, safe. She turns back to the water, takes a deep breath, and begins.

Chapter Thirteen

Revelations

"I used to work for a company called Synergy," Sarah says. "Actually, I kind of ran it."

"You ran it?" An impressed smile twerks his lips upward.

"It was built by Polly and Chuck over thirty years. It was their company, but they were getting close to retirement and they'd made me COO, so I had been doing more and more as they phased out. I think they thought – I thought – everyone thought I'd take over as CEO one day."

"What kind of company was it?"

"We were the biggest brand marketing company in the region." Joe looks at her blankly. "You know, pens with logos, branded foam footballs, keyrings. All that swag you get at conventions."

Joe points at his Dodgers cap and nods. "Gotcha. So what happened?"

A mother with two youngsters rolls up. They let their little corgi off the leash and the kids screech as they chase it. Joe jerks his head toward the path behind them and he and Sarah return to their walk.

Away from the noise, Sarah resumes her story. "I really loved it. Polly and Chuck were good people. They treated everyone like family. As the company grew over the years, it got really big, but they always brought people on with intention. No matter how well the company did, it didn't matter if the people weren't well cared for. They brought me up through the ranks and put their trust in me."

"Sounds like they were good mentors," Joe says.

"More than that." Sarah winces and walks silently, building her strength to tell the rest. "I wasn't very close with my parents for a long time. They split up when I was in college and I was angry, and it's a whole long story. We're better now, but they're still far away, and the point is, Polly and Chuck became like surrogate parents. They helped me through a lot, and it was their partnership, seeing how strong they were together, that finally restored my faith in love and the possibility of marriage. And then…"

When Sarah pauses, Joe chimes in. "Don't tell me they got divorced."

"Worse. One of their daughters had a baby with a congenital heart defect. Little Mabel they called her. She was their fifth grandchild, but she was so sick. And the medical bills were just starting. And suddenly Polly and Chuck's priorities changed."

They dip down the hill to a path by the water and run into a guy walking his golden retriever. Sarah coos and scratches the smiling pup until its helicopter tail threatens to lift it from the ground. She walks away smiling, content to walk in silence, leaving the story behind with the dog. Joe watches her, observes her careful avoidance, then finally presses. "Sarah, come on. What happened?"

Sarah looks up at the sky, then down, before saying, "They decided to sell the company, move to Boston, and take care of Little Mabel and the rest of the family."

"Damn. And you couldn't maybe…?"

"Not even close," Sarah says. "The sale price was well into the eight digits, way out my league. They consulted with me and worked hard to make a deal that would protect their employees, but in the end, our biggest national competitor bought it. They made a lot of promises about keeping jobs and maintaining the regional spirit, but none of it was true. They slowly tapered operations, doing round after round of layoffs. They gave nice severance packages, but money doesn't ease the pain of betrayal, the loss of friendships, or the fear of an unknown future."

"So you were laid off?" Joe asks.

"Not exactly. I stayed on as long as I could, hoping I could protect everyone else, but I couldn't. Then they offered me a role at HQ in Normal, Illinois, but we weren't interested in moving, so they gave me one year severance and a two-year non-compete. And that was it."

When Sarah doesn't say more, Joe nudges her. "Why do I feel like that's not really it?"

Sarah attempts to skip a stone across the water and gives a defeated laugh when it sinks on impact. "I watched the company I loved get stripped for parts. I watched people I loved get sent packing, despite my best efforts. I couldn't do a damn thing."

Joe sees the anguish on Sarah's face and how her failure weighs on her. He sees how each departure tore a piece from her soul while simultaneously adding a new weight to her shoulders, an increasingly fragile frame carrying an ever-growing burden. A stick figure Atlas shrugging under the weight of a world she couldn't save.

"It's not your fault. You did everything you could."

"It wasn't enough, though. I wasn't enough."

Joe catches Sarah's arm so she'll look at him. "You are enough, Sarah."

By the time Sarah finishes her story, they've made their way across much of the park to the wood and concrete piers extending like electronic circuits in strange geometric patterns over the water.

"I don't blame them," she says. "Polly and Chuck. How could they do anything different?"

"But it still hurts," Joe says, a low current of compassion laced through his voice that rattles Sarah. "It still feels like an abandonment."

She nods wordlessly. Polly and Chuck loved her, she knew that. But if even such good people with whom she had such a close, trusting relationship could leave, how could she have faith in anything? It was her parents' divorce all over again. It's simply never been in Sarah's DNA to do things half-hearted, to invest herself in anything without caring deeply. Yet, how can she invest herself only to lose everything again? If nothing that matters lasts, why bother?

She watches a fisherman cast his line at the end of one of the piers. "Anyway, I guess I kind of gave up after that. I don't know what's wrong with me."

"You're too hard on yourself," Joe says.

She continues as if she hasn't heard him. "I think Ben thinks I'm crazy. He definitely doesn't get me anymore. Hell, I don't even get me these days."

"You're not crazy."

Sarah looks briefly away from the fisherman to challenge Joe. "Sure about that?"

Joe shakes his head. "You just had your heart broken."

Sarah turns away again, avoiding the insight along with his eyes. The water laps on the bottom of the pier as it rocks gently beneath their feet.

Joe goes on, "You had your heart broken and nobody realized it. So nobody helped you heal it."

***

Sarah and Joe hike single file along a narrow trail, Sarah in the lead, crunching through an inexhaustible bed of dried pine needles. The trail wends through a densely forested area in a thin line along the edge of the lake. It would be dangerously romantic if the confines of the path didn't necessitate continual forward motion to stay ahead of the next set of hikers sure to follow shortly.

A few minutes down the trail they hear voices ahead of them. Hikers approaching from the opposite direction. Within seconds, the others are in view. A hiker collision is imminent, but Sarah and Joe have come too far to go back now. Water to one side, steep bank of trees to the other, they scout around for a wider section of path, but find none.

Joe looks behind him and spots a tiny, flat patch between two trees, just off the path, barely big enough for two. He grabs Sarah's arm and pulls her back toward him onto the patch, pulling her in close so the group of three can squeeze past. With Joe's hand on her arm, the heat of his chest against her back, and his breath in her hair, Sarah stiffens to avoid melting.

Three women in workout clothes pass by, thanking Joe and Sarah and chattering away as they go. When they clear the path, relief washes over Sarah, but she finds herself standing where she is a moment too long. Finally, she steps back onto the path, conscious of the crunching needles beneath her feet. Before she can go any further, Joe speaks. "Sarah."

She stops, terrified by the tone of his voice. There is too much intimacy, too much tenderness. What could he possibly have to say to her to say her name like that?

"Sarah, look at me."

Staring forward, Sarah straightens her back, squares her shoulders, and raises her jaw before turning slowly around with what she hopes is an easy smile painted on her face.

"You're going to be okay," he says.

The words shoot right through her, a bullet of kindness and hope that shocks her as much as any made of lead. That he would still be thinking about her story, about her, both touches and unsettles her. Her eyes fill. He's hit a nerve too raw, a nerve she's never willingly left exposed for exactly this reason. Yet, he's gone directly to it.

She trembles and wipes her tears. "I'm a long way from okay."

Another tear falls and Joe reaches out to catch it. It's tender and kind. And yes, intimate, but not inappropriate. A healer's touch.

"You're closer than you think."

***

On the walk back to the car, Sarah freezes and sucks in a sharp breath. The blood drains from her extremities. "Oh my God!"

"What is it?" Joe asks scanning the horizon for threats.

"My... my..." She can't get the words out. "My... Wendy," she finally mumbles.

"Your Wendy? You're not making any sense," he says.

Sarah's eyes fix in the distance. She points discreetly toward the park entrance and the woman, child, and dog strolling in.

Joe tracks her line of sight. "Them? Is that Wendy?"

Before Sarah can answer, a child's voice rings through the park, clear as a bell. "Aunt Sarah!"

"Aunt Sarah," Joe repeats as the little girl runs toward them. "Come on," he says, gently leading Sarah forward like a zombie.

With the forward motion, Sarah finally recovers herself and slides on a bright smile for her niece just as the six-year-old rams into her. "Hey, sweetie," she says as she scoops the girl into her arms with difficulty. "Ugh, you're getting too big for this!"

Joe looks at the little girl and says, "Are you Wendy?"

But the woman now standing in front of them answers, "No, I am." Wendy looks Joe up and down with assessing eyes. Sarah leans over to her for a hug and a distraction.

"This little cutie," Sarah explains as the girl giggles, "is Emma."

"Hi, Emma," Joe says with a deferential nod of his head.

"And this is Wendy. My sister-in-law. Ben's sister." She catches Joe's eyes for a moment and spots what she hopes is a glimmer of understanding.

"Hello," Wendy says. The normally bubbly and warm Wendy's face is closed off and suspicious, not like her at all.

"Wendy, this is, um, Joe."

"And that's Harold," Emma announces, pointing down at the leashed basset hound sniffing Joe's feet.

"Yes, we can't forget Harold, can we?" Sarah says as she stoops to set down Emma and scratch the pooch behind his ears. "Hello, Harold. How are you, sir?"

Sarah feebly hopes that all the familial niceties will camouflage her panic as Wendy continues to stare at Joe. It's not the stare of someone enamored of his good looks, which would be perfectly understandable given the relative perfection of the broad-shouldered giant standing next to her. But no. There are daggers in Wendy's eyes.

Sarah fumbles toward normal conversation. She strokes Emma's hair and pushes a brown curl behind her ear. "So why aren't you in school, young lady?"

"Instructional day," Wendy says coldly. She shoots Sarah a pointed look. "And why aren't you in school?"

Sarah has to clear this up. She's already waited too long to just get it out there. Her mouth goes dry. "Sorry, I should have explained. Joe is, um... making a movie." She's blowing this badly. Suddenly her conversation with Ben last night flashes through her head. "They." That's the pronoun she'd used. And now, here she stands with Joe, who is very clearly just Joe. Joe who knows nothing of Sarah's misguided lie.

Wendy gives Joe heavy side-eye before asking, "What does that mean?"

Sarah's heart races as she tries to think of an answer, but Joe answers smoothly, "We're shooting a film in Seattle later this summer. This was supposed to be our location scouting trip, but the locations manager had a family emergency. So Sarah was nice enough to step in."

Wendy's posture relaxes a little, but she's still suspicious. "So, how did that happen?" Before Joe can answer, she looks at Sarah. "Sarah?"

"Gosh, it's a crazy story," Sarah sputters. She glances at Joe, hoping her panic isn't all over her face, but he's looking down at his phone. Most unhelpful. "I went downtown yesterday on an errand for Gabi. You know Gabi." Ugh. Of course, she knows Gabi. Gabi's family. "And—"

Joe looks up from his phone. "Sarah, sorry to interrupt. I just got a text from Naomi."

"N-Naomi?" Sarah stutters.

"She said they got turned around and went the wrong way on the freeway. They're not going to make it here."

"Oh... they're not?" Sarah slows her breath and tries to let her brain catch up to whatever's happening right now.

"Who's Naomi?" Wendy says. Her eyes widen, her interest supplanting her suspicion. Almost. The power of the word "they."

"Naomi is, um—" Sarah casts her eyes to Joe. "Remind me, what does Naomi do again?"

"Naomi is the line producer," he says. "There were too many of us to fit in one car, so we split up. Lucky me, I got the local." He hitches a thumb toward Sarah. "The rest of them obviously don't know where they're going. Speaking of which, she asked if we could just meet them at the next site." Then to Wendy, "Sarah's been real a rock star."

Wendy's scowl fades as her shoulders drop, and a smile finally creeps onto her face. "Wow, that's so cool. How fun! Hear that, Emma? Aunt Sarah's helping make a movie."

Sarah shrugs modestly. "Oh, not really."

"I like movies," Emma says as she twists the hem of Sarah's shirt in her fingers.

"I know you do!" Sarah replies. "You're my favorite movie bud, huh? Hey, maybe if Mommy says yes, you and me and Lexi can go to the movies Sunday. What do you say?"

"That's a great idea." Wendy smiles, anticipating an afternoon of mommy-daddy time.

"Yay!" Emma cheers.

"Yay," Sarah repeats.

Harold bays at a passing dog and tugs at his leash. "Well, we better get to the dog park before Harold loses it," Wendy says.

"Okay, I'll see you Sunday, sweetie," Sarah says before smothering Emma in kisses. "I love you."

"I love you!" Emma giggles under the barrage of kisses before Wendy lures her away.

Once Sarah and Joe are safely out of range, Sarah exhales a heavy breath. She looks at Joe. "Thank you." Joe just smiles. "I just feel so silly," she goes on. "I don't know why I panicked like that. And I feel bad that I made you lie."

"Hey, Sarah, you didn't make me do anything. I understand optics. Sometimes a little spin is just part of the job. It's okay. You know you're not doing anything wrong, right?"

Sarah's heart flutters with gratitude. "But then, why did you step in?"

He gives her a weary look that suggests a long, complicated backstory and says, "Like I said, optics."

***

After a drive just long enough to bounce from boy bands to grunge bands, they pull up to a local sandwich shop. Joe presses his hand lightly on Sarah's back as he escorts her in. She thrills at his touch even as she reminds herself he's just being a gentleman.

Over lunch, they fall into conversation about his career for the first time. He tells her about the endless auditions and rejections, the joy of the successes, and the inevitable heartbreak each time his big break came to a premature end. "Ironically, 'Safe as Houses' just about broke me both spiritually and financially."

"I loved that show," Sarah coos wistfully.

"So did everyone when it premiered. But it was the wrong show at the wrong time. Between the writers' strike, which cut us down to fourteen episodes that first season, and the global financial crisis the next year, no one was in the mood to watch sexy stockbrokers doing evil things anymore." Joe's TV stardom was over as quickly as it started. "And unfortunately, we bought a house under the promise of a long run." He pinches the bridge of his nose as if to pinch back the memory. Or the pain. "You can imagine how well that worked out." Then he recounts the staggering array of guest spots that kept him barely afloat financially, but nearly killed his spirit more than once.

Sarah sees it all as clearly as a movie, Joe's biopic, and she's awash with every emotion as she listens. Hope, longing, joy, heartbreak, desperation, gratitude. She feels if she's taken every step of the journey by his side.

"I wanted to be a superstar, you know? The next George Clooney. A debonair heartthrob with the taste and integrity to do only excellent work. But it turns out most of us don't get the luxury of choice." He grimaces, then adds with a rueful laugh. "Most actors have to take every job we can get and hope they don't suck."

"Seems like you're working a lot these days," she says.

"I'm making a decent living. At last. I get to drop in and out of the red carpet life now and then. I even met Clooney. That's not too bad, I guess."

"Still want to be a superstar?"

"Not really, to be honest. I've seen up close what that kind of fame does to people's lives." He leans into the table and looks at her seriously. "But I want the work. You know? The good roles. I want them so damn bad I can taste it." Sarah gives a tiny nod of understanding. "I just want so much more." He holds her gaze a moment longer, and she forces herself not to break first. Finally, he falls back in his chair, sips his soda, and adds, "But at least I'm working. My kids are healthy and happy. I'm lucky."

Sarah muses over what Joe has said, and slightly more over what he didn't say. Over who he didn't mention. "But you still have dreams."

"Yeah. I still have dreams."

"Like what?"

His brows knit together. "You know, that's the first time anyone's asked me that in a long, long time."

"You and Melanie don't talk about stuff like that?"

"Not really. No."

"Well, I imagine she just knows," Sarah says. A noble effort to patch over the marred surface she's accidentally exposed. "She probably knows your dreams as well as you do after all this time."

"Yeah. You're probably right." Joe nods, reassuring himself, then takes a sip of soda. "But it's nice to be asked." He smiles again, but turns grim as he disappears into his thoughts.

Sarah attempts to restore the sunshine. "So, those dreams?"

He perks up. "Well, yeah, like getting this movie made, for one thing. I've got a lot riding on this. I can't believe it's actually going to happen."

"I can," she says proudly.

A flicker of eye contact hints at a conversation resting beneath the surface. Teasing and truths inching them ever closer. Joe's eyes twinkle with the threat of a tenderness that frightens Sarah. "You know, I've been terrified for months that this whole thing would still fall apart on me. I thought that was happening yesterday." The corners of his mouth curl up. "But somehow, I'm not so worried anymore. Now I feel like it's all going to be okay." When Sarah smiles mutely, unsure what to say, he points out the window. "What's that?" She looks away, and he steals a chip from her tray.

"Hey, that's mine," she balks noisily as Joe crunches down. Sarah issues another loud grunt of disgust, but secretly delights at the casual intimacy. Joe steals a few more chips before returning to his sandwich while she drains her soda, reflecting on her next words. "So, I have a confession to make." Joe's gaze lifts from his sandwich. "I Googled you last night."

Joe brightens, amused at the prospect. "You did? Did you find anything good? Am I secretly dating Jennifer Aniston or anything? Because that would be great for my career."

"I didn't find any mention of Jen, no."

"Damn. I keep hoping. What did you find?"

Sarah pulls the lid off her soda and stirs the straw in the ice before speaking, "Well, I did find something pretty incredible. Actually."

Joe leans in. "Yeah?" He waits a moment, then prods, "You're holding back again. What is it?"

Sarah takes a deep breath. "Apparently you were born in Pittsburgh."

"This is not news," he laughs.

"Well, it was to me," Sarah says steadily. "Because I was born in Pittsburgh, too."

"No kidding!"

"On March 20th."

"What?!" Joe drops his sandwich.

"1983."

"The same day?" he says. Sarah nods. "What hospital were you born in? What time?"

"I don't know."

She answers too quickly. Joe eyes her with suspicion, but goes on. "What do you suppose it means? Something that crazy, it has to mean something, right?"

"I think it's just a crazy coincidence." And even if it's not, she couldn't possibly share the wild notions taking hold in her brain.

"That's more than coincidence. That right there is Fate." His nose crinkles in delighted astonishment at this even deeper connection than either of them could have guessed.

Sarah slurps the remnants of melted ice and swallows hard. "There's more."

"How can there possibly be more?" Joe asks, still tickled by the discovery.

"I went to Pitt," Sarah says without elaboration.

None is needed. "I went to Carnegie Mellon."

"I know." Sarah braces herself for the possibility that the most puzzling, most elusive memory of her life, the guy she never met at a New Year's Eve party and never forgot, might be confirmed as more than a figment of her imagination.

Joe's face breaks wide with wonder at the possibilities. "We could have seen each other. Been to the same bars." Sarah shrugs as Joe gestures around them. "Eaten at the same restaurants."

"We could have."

"We probably went to the same parties—" Joe stops short. His face clouds over and his brow furrows. He zeroes in on Sarah, saying nothing, as his eyes search for something both inside and out.

Sarah studies his expression in return. She can almost see the gears turning. She imagines him playing one of those memory matching games with the little picture cards, trying to find the match for the girl in the New Year's crown. Counting down to the truth. If this is real. If it was really him.

5...

Anxiety tingles at the back of her neck. If he finds the match, it was real, and what would that mean?

4...

And if he doesn't, then all of this is nothing but her imagination. Which, of course, it has to be.

3...

If all of this is real, it's terrifying. If it's not, it's heartbreaking. Either way, she's not prepared to deal with it.

2...

Joe looks at her intently, a new light in his eyes. His face relaxes into a bemused smile as if he's just solved a lifelong mystery. As if he's just matched the girl in the New Year's Crown.

1...

Joe opens his mouth to speak, to say words Sarah's not ready to hear. "It was you...," he mumbles almost to himself.

Sarah jumps up before he can continue. "I'm gonna get a refill," she announces. "Want anything?" She doesn't wait for him to answer.

Chapter Fourteen

Angel in the Marble

THEY SPEND THE AFTERNOON traversing town, driving long treks from one magical locale to the next, singing together and laughing at their own ridiculousness. Their youths in perfect musical harmony, they excavate the full 90s repertoire. Britney Spears, Counting Crows, Green Day. Joe applauds Sarah's soulful solo turn harmonizing with En Vogue, which only this morning would have stopped her cold. But not now. She keeps singing.

They break their songfests with leisurely strolls through one lush, green waterfront park after another, each with its own character and charm. Joe takes photos of each, in case the first doesn't work out, but the city teems with beauty and any of the options will work. He already has what he needs, but admitting that might cut the day short, so he says nothing.

Singing with Sarah carves Joe out in a way he hasn't felt in years, maybe decades. Maybe ever. Something new and precious is making space within him and fitting itself exactly to that space. The carving out is not without pain. The pain of removing unused but still attached pieces of himself to make room. The pain of custom shaping a space he knows will be left empty again at some point, leaving only a hole where once there was music. But it feels as essential as breathing now and fills him with an indescribable joy, despite the pain.

Michelangelo said every block of stone had a statue in it, and it was the sculptor's job to release it. "I saw the angel in the marble and carved until I set it free," he said about his sculpture of David. Joe always liked that idea.

That the most extraordinary beauty could be hidden inside all along, just waiting to be discovered.

Now, as he sings with Sarah, he sees the truth of it in himself. That Sarah was somehow always there, undiscovered and waiting. Or perhaps in his case, the inverse was true, that the hole was always there, temporarily stuffed full of misplaced affections and unnamed longings, simply waiting to be revealed and filled at last with something real. Something that fits. Something fleeting perhaps. But also eternal.

***

Somewhere on the east side of the lake, they stroll through what must be the fifth park of the day. Joe envisions Sarah's hand map of the area, now burned in his brain. Seattle was her thumb. Bellevue, where she lives, was her pinkie joint. And Renton, where she volunteers "every Monday and Friday," was her wrist bone. Based on his tenuous sense of direction, he imagines they are now somewhere near the top of her pinkie.

Their energy flags, but not their spirits. The park sits high above Lake Washington. Nestled within a wooded overlook, they lean against a stone wall between them and a steep drop-off to the water. Sarah gazes across to the hillsides and distant Seattle skyline. Joe does the same until he catches sight of Sarah's hands on the wall, pink with the chill of the air and the stone. His eyes rivet to the hand next to him, suddenly so desperate to take it that he must summon herculean strength to resist.

But where his hand resists, his mind does not. He imagines lifting his hand to her, sliding his fingers over her soft skin and between her fingers, heating her cold hand with his warm one. His hand completely at rest with hers. Then ambling through the park, still hand in hand, no longer needing to speak. Saying everything through their fingertips. Her thumb and forefinger sandwiched between his own, caressing the back of her hand, saying all the things he knows he cannot say aloud.

Stop.

But no, he sees it again. The moment he places his hand on hers. This time he sees Sarah freeze. Inhale slowly. Look up at him. She gazes into his eyes and releases a slow, tender smile. A smile of surrender. And yes. He leans in to kiss her and her hand clasps his tightly as their lips touch. He sees it all. Feels it.

Stop.

He presses his eyes shut to block out the image. This can't happen. He knows this can't happen. But... what if it could?

He shoves his hands in his pockets and suggests they walk some more. Perhaps movement and changing scenery will help. Although Sarah's hand is no longer in sight, it's still so close. The air particles shift between their hands as they swing mere inches apart. It would be so easy to reach down and clasp it. Would she take his hand if he offered it? He'd offered her a hand of assistance before, which she'd gladly accepted. But now? For no other reason than simple desire? Would she push him away? Would she run?

They wander along a path with a manicured grassy field on one side and the forested area leading to the water on the other. Dog owners chat while their collie and lab chase each other around the green. He tries to concentrate on the dogs, but the light in Sarah's eyes as she watches nearly blinds him and the dogs disappear.

How can she be that girl from New Year's Eve all those years ago? The same girl who glowed in the streetlight while he stared like an idiot. The same girl who silenced the noisiest night of the year with one look, and then disappeared before he could even get her name. The same woman who shares both his birthdate and birthplace and now takes his breath away with her mere existence. This has to be Fate.

Sarah laughs as the dogs tumble over each other. He taps his best acting skills to laugh along like everything is normal. He can't do it. Instead, he pulls out his phone and fakes an emergency. "You know, I just remembered there's something I need to take care of. Would you excuse me a minute?"

Sarah startles. "Of course. Everything okay?"

"Fine. Just need a minute."

She nods, confused but accommodating. Joe nods back reassuringly and dashes off. He heads back to the overlook in the woods, making sure he is a safe distance away, well out of earshot. He's not out of sight, but partially obscured by the trees. Sarah half-watches the dogs, but mostly watches him, concerned. He waves and grabs a seat on the bench to seem more natural.

He hunches over and fights the urge to hyperventilate. It's a familiar sensation, like the moments before a life-changing audition, the results of which could make or break him. When it feels like his whole future rides on the choices he's about to make.

Aware of Sarah's eyes, he pulls out his phone, clicks off the ringer, and starts a fake conversation. "What are you doing?" he says in a low, fierce voice to himself. "What the fuck are you doing? This can't happen. You know this can't happen. She's married. You're married. This can't happen." He scrubs his face vigorously and takes a few breaths, blowing each out hard like he's lifting an incredibly heavy weight. In fact, he is. "Wake up. Seriously. Wake the fuck up!"

He pulls the phone away from his face, then switches it on for real. He thinks of calling Melanie. He stares at her name and number, considering the call – just a friendly hello to connect – imagining how the conversation would go. What he would say to her. What she would say back. How anything they might say would help. But it wouldn't.

Instead, he calls Avery. She picks up surprisingly quickly. "Hi, Dad."

Joe heaves a sigh of relief at her voice. "Hi, sweetheart. How's your day going?"

"Ah, you know."

"I don't. That's why I asked," he nudges. "How did your calculus test go?"

"Tests don't matter anymore. I already got in."

"Tests still matter."

"Fine. I got an A."

"That's my girl!"

Avery pauses a moment, distracted. "Dad, Olivia's texting like crazy. She's all salty about something." Well, he got 15-20 seconds of focused attention. Not bad.

"Okay, I won't keep you long. I just wanted to hear your voice. Is your brother around?"

"He's at practice."

"Oh, right. Will you tell him I called?"

Avery has switched to speaker, and Joe waits through the telltale delays as she texts and talks at the same time. "Sure," she says.

"And tell him I love him."

"There is literally a zero out of zero chance I'm doing that."

"Avery." There's an unmissable edge in Joe's voice, an edge Avery knows too well.

She lets out a guttural moan like she's being asked to clean the camp toilet. "Fine. I'll tell him. But I refuse to be nice about it."

"As if I would ever ask you to debase yourself with anything as low as being nice to your brother."

"You know I'll be gone soon. You won't have me to be your messenger boy anymore," Avery snarks. "Then you'll have to be *my* messenger boy."

"Promises, promises. Okay, kiddo, I'll let you go. Just one more thing."

"Yes?" she grumbles.

"I love you."

He can almost hear the eye roll, but she softens. "I love you, too, daddy."

Joe hangs up and takes a deep breath to center himself. He's back on solid ground. This is all a harmless flight of fancy. Yes, Sarah is beautiful and kind. And she listens and sees him. Talking with her is easier than breathing. And singing with her frees him in a way he couldn't have imagined before today. But Fate or not, it's not real. It can't be. Avery's real. Nathan's real. His commitment to them, that's real. And, for better or worse –

admittedly, mostly worse these days – his commitment to Melanie is real, too.

Then again, what did Avery say? She'd be gone soon. It's true. She's leaving in a few months. And Nathan is right behind her. Joe would do anything for those kids. He already has. But they'll both be gone before he knows it. Maybe Joe's turn is finally coming. But not yet.

Joe slaps his knees a couple of times to confirm he's back in his body and heads back to Sarah. He's himself again.

Everything is fine.

***

On the way to their final stop of the night, the mystery destination, they settle on a low-key satellite station playing singer-songwriters and acoustic versions of big hits, all suitably mellow to coast into the evening. They sing less now, happily exhausted and content mostly to listen and occasionally hum along.

They drive along the lake for the view until Sarah notices the time and cuts over to the freeway. Can't miss dusk, wherever they're going. The gentle hum of the tires on the road lulls Joe into a pleasant stupor. He's just conscious enough to know he's falling asleep, something he would normally never let happen outside family road trips. But he's so relaxed now, so drained from a day of emotions too intense to name, he allows himself to drift off.

In his dream, the angel in the marble appears. A figure he assumes is Michelangelo chips away at a giant block of white stone. After a few strikes, the angel bursts forward. Only it isn't Michelangelo's David. It's a woman, magnificent and blinding. He can't see her face, nor her body really. She's more like a brilliant light blasting out of a vaguely human silhouette, but she's unmistakably a woman. And she's singing.

She sings quietly, almost to herself, her light getting brighter and brighter until...

Joe wakes slowly, briefly disoriented, no idea how long he's been sleeping, but entirely at ease. Before he opens his eyes, Sarah's voice floats into his consciousness. She's singing low and quiet with the radio. He pries his eyes open. "Hi," he says with a heavy-lidded smile.

"Did I wake you? Sorry. It's one of my favorite songs. I couldn't resist."

Joe blinks himself awake and checks the display. "Del Amitri?"

"Scottish band."

"Okay if I start it over?" he says as he hits rewind and turns it up. The moment the song restarts, Joe is seized with the melancholy guitar and the raw, yet strangely soothing vocal. A deceptively simple love song, the lyrics drip with longing, sadness, and devotion. "Tell Her This," the words of a man in love and incapable of expressing it. The kind of song that wrenches your heart from your chest if you let it. He smiles and announces he likes it after the first verse, then goes quiet to listen to both the singer and Sarah.

He stares blankly at the glovebox, sinking deeper until the music strikes a chord too powerful to resist and the lyrics hit too close to home. A heartfelt promise to be by her side when she needs him. An unconscious impulse jolts Joe's gaze to Sarah for a moment too long as the music swells to aching proportions before he catches himself and looks away. This feeling is too dangerous to indulge even a second longer.

He fixes his eyes in the distance to avoid another misguided glance. His heart beats louder, synchronizing itself to the song. He feels he might suffocate. And that he's breathing for the first time. He gnaws on his upper lip, fighting the truth this band he's never heard of is now singing to him, as if they've transcribed the lyrics directly from his heart.

He dares not look, nor let her see him looking. But when his raspy surrogate sings about longing to kiss her, Joe casts an involuntary sidelong glance before he can stop himself. He squeezes his eyes shut and turns away from her until the song strums to its mournful ending, discreetly wiping away a tear when he finally opens them.

"You okay?" Sarah asks.

"Fine. Got some sleep in my eyes. That's all."

"It's a good song, right?"

He takes her in, beaming with pride, eager for him to love the song as much as she does. Blissfully unaware the song has just disassembled his heart and left him to put it back together. "Beautiful," he says.

***

The crows swoop past them in dramatic flourishes claiming their territory and proclaiming their preeminence. Joe and Sarah watch from a long walkway overlooking sixty acres of wetlands, a nighttime haven for sleeping crows. The sun is fading and everywhere they turn, crows dart around in ominous trajectories, oblivious to their observers, yet threatening nonetheless. Cawing their warnings and arrivals.

"Just wait. They're not here yet," Sarah says.

"You mean there are more?"

Sarah smiles and raises her brows in teasing temptation. There are already so many of them. Joe gives silent thanks for the roof covering the overlook, understanding at last why Sarah made him bring the umbrella for the walk back to the car. Sarah watches the sky with animated anticipation and Joe follows suit.

"After we're done here," he says, "I'd like to buy you dinner. If it's not too late for you."

"You don't have to do that."

"I know I don't have to. I want to." A hair too insistent, he checks himself and adds, "It's literally the least I can do after all you've done for me."

"You've already bought me three meals."

"A couple sandwiches and a cup of soup?" She shrugs, so he goes on, "Is this your way of saying you don't want to have dinner with me?"

She continues looking out at the birds, but offers a reluctantly delighted smile. "No."

"No, you don't want to? Or no, that's not your way of saying you don't want to," he laughs.

"No. That's not my way of saying I don't want to."

"So, say you *wanted* to have dinner with me. How would you say that?"

Sarah looks him in the eye, suppressing her laughter. "Joe, I would like to have dinner with you."

"Good."

Turning back to the wetlands, they barely contain their grins, now more absorbed in their thoughts than the wildlife show.

The cacophony surrounding them grows, the sound a swelling intrusion. The cantankerous, but easily discernible individual caws of hundreds of crows, one after another, has been replaced by a deafening wall of sound. As if on cue, as the sun reaches for the horizon, thousands upon thousands of crows fly in from every direction.

The sky grows dark. Too dark, too quickly. The mass of crows blot out the light above. Tens of thousands of them swooping in all at once, screaming bloody murder. Not just a murder of crows. A massacre.

Joe stares dumbfounded as Sarah smirks in satisfaction. Finally, Joe snaps out of his trance and remembers to pull out his phone. He clicks on the camera, snaps a couple photos, then switches to video. He records the crows as he speaks. "This is incredible," he yells over the noise.

"I know!" she yells back.

"I've got goosebumps!"

"Me, too," she says.

He pans the camera from the wetlands to Sarah, the crows behind her swerving and diving around in a menacing backdrop. She shows him her arm and without thinking he brushes his fingers over her bumpy skin.

"Boy, you weren't kidding!" he says gleefully.

As she laughs, he catches her wiping a tear, still on camera. He switches it off.

***

Sarah's skin burns from Joe's touch and her eyes fill instantly. Already on a razor's edge as their time together winds down, she's shocked by her own reaction to the crows. Her emotions are too raw to withstand the sensory onslaught, too tender for the intensity of nature on such astonishing and grotesque display. When Joe's fingertips brush her skin, she feels it in every cell of her body, but permits no release of the tension save the involuntary pooling in her eyes.

When he catches her wiping the tear, she looks away embarrassed. "Visceral enough for you?" she says in a feeble attempt to distract them both. She stifles a bitter laugh to herself at the irony.

Joe nods, so stunned he doesn't seem to notice the tremor in her voice. "And this happens every night? It's reproducible?"

"Every night at sunset from spring to fall," she says. "Of course, you've got to time it right, but yeah."

He marvels at the crows, shakes his head incredulously, and laughs. "How did you manage this?"

"Manage what?"

"It's like you read my mind. This is perfect. Thank you."

He grabs her in a bear hug, and she locks up. She hugs back, happily, greedily, but frightened she may not be able to let go when he does. As if he understands this, he takes his time, lingers in the hug, unrushed. He lets her find her way to the release, and they both let go at the same time.

They watch the beautiful, terrible display as it winds down, the birds finally settling into their places for the night. Sarah rests her hands on the railing, and after a moment, Joes places his hand on hers. He squeezes gently.

Her first instinct is to pull away. To run away as fast as she can. Not because she wants to. Not because she has even the slightest desire to be anywhere else in the world. But because she should. And "should" and "should not" are virtually all she has to cling to now. But she doesn't move. She can't.

Her eyes flicker up at him, and he smiles warmly at her. She reassures herself. He's grateful. They're friends. It doesn't mean anything. They turn and watch together. It doesn't mean anything.

PART TWO

GOD

WHERE FATE IS THE instigator and Destiny sets the long-term vision, it's God who makes it all happen – and only when He wills it so. He may let Fate light the flame with Her clever tricks and allow Destiny to shine with Her top-notch planning skills, but make no mistake, God remains the world's first and best influencer, with an unmatched ground team. And God's true messengers – from thousands of years of priests, rabbis, prophets, and saints to friendly neighborhood pastors and not a few moms and best friends – are always the ones who point folks toward the things that make their hearts sing.

CHAPTER FIFTEEN

PERSEIDS (AUGUST, 2011)

SARAH TOSSED AND TURNED in the brutal heat as the nightmare took hold. She was running for her life, terrified and praying for someone to save her. She woke in a panic, heart racing, pumping fear and adrenaline through her arteries. Just another anxiety dream, but she couldn't shake it.

She tried to comfort herself by cuddling up next to Josh, her boyfriend. No, scratch that. Her fiancé. After a rocky few months, he had proposed on the spur of the moment earlier that night and was now sound asleep next to her. She hoped he'd stir, wrap his arm around her, and make her feel safe again. Instead, he rolled away and offered only his unsupportive back. She sensed a metaphor, but was too bleary-eyed to see it clearly. She laid there awhile longer, attempting to meditate to the sound of the fan on full blast, but couldn't shake her memories of the dream.

She got up. It was only 11:30 and the Perseid meteor shower was peaking that night. They'd talked about going out to watch, but got distracted with post-proposal sex and post-sex sleep. It was sweltering inside, the hot August days piling layer upon layer of heat until the rooms were so densely packed nothing short of an indoor snowfall could cool it. But outside, the temperature had dropped nearly 30 degrees, so she wrapped up in a blanket and went out to the patio.

Sarah hadn't seen the Perseids in years, and the last time was out in the country. But the moon was barely a crescent, and the surrounding porchlights were off, so she hoped maybe she'd spot a few meteors. The darkness summoned her nightmare again and she hesitated, but pushed through. The anxiety from her dream clung to her more tightly than the blanket. As if something inside her sensed danger ahead.

She curled up on the patio sofa and leaned back, eyes on the sky. She spotted her first meteor streaking through the darkness. Then another. And another. Each a magical shooting star. If only she had a wish ready. As she looked to the stars, she drifted to sleep.

And then, a new dream. Her favorite actor Joe stood in front of her, surrounded by blackness and radiant stars. He smiled tenderly at her. He took her hands in his own large, warm hands. She looked down at them, her hands clasped together, his hands enveloping hers, and felt a surge of energy flowing from him to her and back again through their connection. Slowly, she raised her eyes to his face. He nodded at her, lifted his hands to her arms, and pulled her into a close embrace. His long arms wrapped around her, and somehow she knew that he needed her as much as she needed him. He held her tightly, and she felt his warmth and strength pulsing through her. She felt absolutely safe.

When she jolted awake, she was disoriented by her surroundings. The stars in the dark sky were right, but everything else was wrong. It took her several moments to settle back into the real world. The dream felt so real. It was almost alarming how real it felt. Almost as if he was summoning her.

Celebrity dreams were not unfamiliar to Sarah. She'd once dreamt of having lunch with Dolly Parton, and another time of riding a roller coaster with Emily Blunt. But why this one? Why now? Joe wasn't fresh in her mind. She hadn't even seen him in anything since his sexy stockbroker soap ended three years earlier. But there he was. Exactly when she needed him. Maybe she summoned him.

The dream had been so lovely, so reassuring and right, she wished it hadn't ended so quickly. If only the nice dreams went on as long as the bad ones. But at least that warm, safe feeling persisted. She watched the night sky a little longer, now relaxed and content as more meteors crashed through the sky making dreams come true. She thought of Joe among the stars, his hands on hers, an image thankfully more compelling and more lingering than its dark predecessor.

Eventually, her fear gone, she headed back to bed and fell easily, happily asleep. The next day, she broke up with Josh.

***

Roughly 1,100 miles away, a different drama was unfolding that very same day. At age 28, Joe was terrified of being out on the street with a wife and two young children. He was hustling as hard as he could, but work had dried up for too long after "Safe as Houses," and they were way behind on the mortgage. A painful irony.

Melanie had quit acting after Nathan was born, unilaterally rewriting the marriage contract without consulting Joe. He did his best to carry the weight with grace, but that had been the first time he noticed the ache, a quiet emptiness he managed to ignore or deflect most of the time with work and family devotion. But in truth, with erratic work and four mouths to feed, the only emptiness he had time to worry about was in their stomachs.

Now, with the erratic jobs turned nonexistent, they briefly discussed the possibility of her getting some temporary work to help them get through. Doting dad Joe would love to share the burden of childcare. If they shared the load across the board, as a team, they could make it work. Just a couple months until he got some momentum going again.

But Melanie suggested that would confuse the kids and why didn't Joe just pick up some shifts at a nearby restaurant. She didn't seem to understand how being spotted waiting tables after such a high-profile launch and failure would be tantamount to career suicide in an industry where image was everything.

No, he couldn't go back to waiting tables. But an office gig – where he only had to see a few people, only had to acknowledge his failure a handful of times and then it would be over – maybe he could live with that. It's what Melanie wanted. She wouldn't say it, but he could tell. She supported his career in theory, but she craved security more. She'd drop hints and mention office jobs she'd heard about through the grapevine. "I mean, only if you think you'd want to do that."

Joe worried even a "temporary" plan B would become permanent. He'd been acting more than half his life. How could he give it up now? It was the only thing he could imagine doing the rest of his life. Still, the bills were piling up fast and the choices were drying up even faster. Ignoring the emptiness in his chest, he told Mel he would give her friend a call and find out more about a customer service opening in their office.

That night the Perseid meteor shower was expected to peak. They talked about letting the kids stay up and taking them out to watch the show, but they were zonked after a sweltering day at a neighborhood party. Then Melanie lost interest and decided to head to bed early herself. Leaving Joe very much alone.

Joe sat reading a book and trying not to feel abandoned and lost as he wrestled with the prospect of surrendering his dream. The emptiness swelled. When he noticed the time, 11:30, he switched off the lights and headed outside. His loneliness seized him as he stepped into the darkness, a darkness he feared might engulf him. Then he looked up.

The neighborhood was dark, the stars bright, and Joe gazed in amazement as he spotted first one, then another shooting star. The Perseids were indeed in view and the magnitude of the beauty was wondrous. When a third meteor shot across the sky, he closed his eyes and made a wish for guidance and hope.

That's when the vision came. Another soul, somewhere in the darkness, sharing his same sky, his same stars. He didn't see them, but he felt them. He felt *her*. Another lonely soul staring up, somehow connecting through the stars. Maybe it was just his imagination, but the thought of that one special *someone* made him feel less alone. He prayed that she, wherever she was, felt him as well.

***

The next morning, he tagged along with Mel and the kids to church for the first time in a month. He often preferred the Sunday paper to the Sunday service, but every so often, he needed the certainty and clarity that Pastor Ted's sermons provided. He warmly greeted friends, then settled in for a message he hoped would help him make peace with what he knew he needed to do. Because whenever Joe was lost, Pastor Ted always had exactly the right lesson for him at exactly the right time. Gratitude. Humility. Patience. Surrender. Sacrifice.

But when Pastor Ted took the pulpit, he preached not about sacrifice, nor about duty and responsibility. Instead, Pastor Ted talked about God's wish for you to fulfill your every dream. He spoke rousingly about staying true to your path, knowing God put you here for a reason and never to stray from or doubt that path. And he finished with Matthew 5:14-16.

"You are the light of the world. A city set on a hill cannot be hidden. Nor do people light a lamp and put it under a bushel, but on a stand, and it gives light to all in the house. In the same way, let your light shine before others, so that they may see your good works and give glory to your Father who is in heaven."

It was as if God Himself had spoken directly to Joe. The right words at the right time, and his faith was renewed. He wouldn't give up. Not ever.

Chapter Sixteen

Dinner and Dancing

The hotel's restaurant, glowing with candlelight and dimmed art deco chandeliers, is nearly empty at the late hour. Over shared caprese salad and Paolo's famous bruschetta, they clink glasses of pinot as Joe toasts to the best tour guide Seattle has ever known. He means it kindly, but Sarah smarts at the words. A reminder of her ancillary role in his life. A service provider. Valued, to be sure. Appreciated, no question. But ultimately, just a means to an end. *Fantasies can be dangerous* she reminds herself for the twentieth time.

After two days plumbing the depths, they mostly skim breezily over the surface at dinner, flitting and flirting through a host of topics from her friend Gabi to his first play to their shared love of candy corn, though Sarah insists it must be eaten with salted peanuts. He talks about the tour of old nightclubs a local music guy is taking him on tomorrow, the only part of the original plan to stick. "You could come!"

Sarah considers the prospect, rejoicing at the notion of more time. *Please God, more time.* Her heart flutters at the hopeful glint in his eyes. Still, she demurs. "I don't want to get in the way."

"I'd like it if you came." His gaze stays on her too long.

It's so tempting to say yes. The word nearly escapes her lips. Then she imagines that time spent with a stranger intruding on the space between them, their duet suddenly a trio, and she can't do it. Besides, if she's this attached now, how would she survive another day? She shakes her head. "I probably shouldn't."

Joe nods his understanding, and Sarah senses perhaps he does truly understand. The rest of the meal, they're quieter than usual. Lost in their thoughts and each other. The restaurant is undeniably romantic. The wine flows freely, as does the conversation when they talk, but only between bouts of thoughtful silence. The fleeting touch when they both reach for the bread shimmers through her. Attraction hangs thick and heavy in the air, fills in the gaps where words stop, yet the mood grows sadder. Their time together is coming to an end. Although neither can admit it, they're both grieving.

"Do you want dessert?" Joe asks hopefully when the time comes.

Sarah would like nothing more than to prolong this dinner until time itself stops, but shakes her head again. Despite her sweet tooth, she declines dessert, no longer hungry for food. Not food.

And more than that, it's the clock. Knowing it's ticking down, knowing only minutes remain for them, each tick becomes unbearable. When she had days to go, hours to go, she wished they would last forever. Now that she has mere minutes, she can't get through them quickly enough. The anticipation of what lies ahead too painful to prolong. "I don't think I could eat another bite."

"Okay." Joe almost whispers his surrender, his voice coated with disappointment. "I guess I'll get the check."

Sarah excuses herself for the restroom, drowning in a sudden wave of sadness. She picks up speed through the hotel lobby to the bathroom door, then runs to a stall for toilet paper. At the mirror, she holds the tissue to her eyes attempting to hold back the flood and not wash away what makeup remains after a full day out and about. She alternates eyes, catching the tears before they fall, and takes slow, deep breaths to calm her emotions.

Under no circumstance can she allow herself to slip into full ugly cry, but it pushes at her from every side hunting for a way in. If she lets go, if the flood comes, there will be no disguising it. She'd have to hide in the bathroom until they close. So she summons every bit of strength and determination she has and pours it into the task at hand, crushing her emotions into a teeny, tiny box she can successfully fit onto a mental shelf, tucked away at the back, unseen, unheard, and most importantly, under control.

Grasping for something to hold onto, anything to get her through these last minutes, she finds herself whispering the Serenity Prayer. "God grant me the serenity to accept the things I cannot change, the courage to change the things I can, and the wisdom to know the difference." Deep breath. Take it in.

She grants herself sixty seconds of grace, then dabs away her remaining tears and exhales the last of her breakdown. She blows her nose and stares at herself. Her nose is notably red, so she dabs some makeup on it. The pink still pokes through, but hopefully he won't notice in the dim light of the restaurant. One last deep breath and she returns to the table.

Joe signs the check, drops the pen, and closes the folio.

"Ready?" Sarah says without sitting down. May as well get this over with. The odds are high she'll lose it again, and when she does, she wants to be very far away.

Joe stutters out an answer. "Um, yeah, don't... don't you want to finish your wine?"

Sarah grabs her glass and gulps it down. She sets it on the table and forces a smile through a mask of joviality. *God grant me the serenity to accept the things I cannot change.*

Joe nods at the empty glass, looks helplessly around the restaurant, and gets up. He presses his hand lightly on Sarah's back as he walks her out of the restaurant, the pressure a gentle reminder of what will soon be lost, both of them relishing and regretting what they know will be their final moments together.

Sarah's mind reels with all the things she wants to say. She wants to tell him the last two days have meant everything to her. That she can't stop thinking about him. To beg him to stay, or let her run away with him. She wants to throw caution to the wind and wrap her arms around him and kiss him. And she wants him to *want* to kiss her, though she knows how wrong it is. And how ridiculous. How absurd to even imagine he could feel the same way. When the reality is that Joe will soon return home to his beautiful wife and perfect family, and she will return to her life of quiet desperation with a man who no longer sees her. Guilt stings her conscience, but this desperate longing stings more. Fantasies can break your heart.

Yet, still she wants. She wants to say the words, even the ones that most defy logic and sense and reality, the three words she can't possibly really feel, but aches with every fiber of her being to say. But all that's impossible.

Instead, she says, "Thank you. For dinner."

"Can I walk you to your car?"

Sarah agrees, but after a few steps she stops, her head spinning. Whether it's the wine or the emotion, she's in no shape to drive. "Actually, I think I'll call an Uber instead. I think I might have had a little too much to drink."

She pulls out her phone and opens the app. A couple clicks and she announces, "Tristan B. will be here in four minutes."

"Okay."

They stare silently at the street, feeling the breeze channeling down the wind tunnel between high rises. "It's been fun," she says, doing her best impression of someone who isn't dying on the inside.

"It's been amazing." The street is empty at this late hour. Joe casts his eyes in each direction, looking both for the car and for something to say. "What kind of car is it?"

"Silver Nissan Altima. Coming from that way, I think."

He nods and they go silent once again. Sarah checks her phone repeatedly, as if the app might deliver both her car and her salvation. "Two minutes."

"Two minutes," he echoes, tapping his foot and gnawing at his thumb, subtle hints at a violent battle raging within. Suddenly, Joe grabs Sarah's hand, covering her screen. "Or..."

"Or?"

His words gush out. "The thing is. If you Uber home tonight, you're going to have to take another back downtown tomorrow to get your car, right?"

"Probably."

"And is your car even okay where it's parked overnight?"

"I don't know, actually."

"It seems silly," he says, "to Uber all the way home and back again when you don't have to. You didn't have that much to drink. You could just wait it out."

"Wait it out?" Sarah parrots.

"Hang out a while longer. I'm not terrible company, am I?"

Sarah laughs despite herself. "I've had worse."

"You could come up."

"Come up?"

"If you want. Nothing untoward. I have a whole living room situation kind of thing." Joe is uncharacteristically frenetic, rambling. "We could sing some more. Or, I don't know, watch a movie. Whatever."

"Whatever?"

"I mean, not whatever. Definitely not *whatever*. Just..."

"I don't know," Sarah says, her own mind rapid cycling between desperation and desire.

Joe expels the last of his frenzy in slow breath, his panic subsiding. "Just come up. Hang out a little while longer. No funny business."

Of course there would be no funny business. She's embarrassed he would even feel the need to say that. Think she would need to be told. Embarrassed her feelings – which she shouldn't even be having – could possibly be on such vivid display to him.

"Just don't go. Not yet."

Or is there another interpretation? A subtle kindness? A kind of flattery perhaps. The courtesy of implying she could ever be in his league enough to consider it a possibility.

Sarah glances down at her phone then back at Joe. "No funny business, you say?" She says the words with a touch of irony, a reassurance to him. She's in on the joke.

"Scout's honor."

The courage to change the things I can. Sarah hits the cancel button on the car. Together they walk back toward the hotel doors. As he holds the door for her, Sarah asks, "Were you even a scout?"

"Don't ask," he laughs.

Joe gives a wave to the guy at the desk and steers Sarah toward the elevators. He hits the button and waits. When the door opens, he pauses and his eyes fix on nothing at all for a moment. He looks first to the elevator, then back to the front desk, processing a thought Sarah can't interpret. "Hold on one sec. I want to get some water for the room."

She waits by the elevator as he runs over to the desk. The elevator door closes behind her. She pulls out her phone and opens her texts. She stares at it a moment, thinking what to write to Ben. A little white lie to keep him from worrying.

They're headed to a jazz club that's a possible location for the film. They invited me to tag along.

She stops herself mid-text. It's almost true, on a technicality. Joe did invite her... tomorrow. Two more "theys," however. No getting around that one. But that damage is already done. Deep inhale for courage and she hits send before adding, *Means I'll be even later.*

Ben's response comes quickly. *Still working anyway. Have fun. But I want to hear all about it.*

She winces, racked with guilt at the lie, and simultaneously relieved he's working as usual. "Hear all about it" will likely translate to 60 seconds or less of passing conversation. She can muddle through. She looks up when she hears Joe's voice.

"Thank you, bro! Appreciate it," Joe calls back to the clerk as he hustles toward her, one hand in his pocket, the other balancing two bottles of water. As he approaches, he slides his hand out of his pocket and hands her a bottle. "Ready?" -

She camouflages her trembling with a nod. He pushes the button again and the door pops open. He places a hand gently on her back as they walk in. This time his hand feels very different.

Upstairs, Joe extends his arm in an "after you" gesture and lets Sarah walk in first, giving her a chance to change her mind if she wants to. And if she doesn't, reassuring her she's in control. But Sarah doesn't feel in control. She trusts Joe implicitly. But herself? Who does she become when she walks into that room? Even if nothing happens. *When* nothing happens. Is it someone she can live with? Does she even have it in her to walk away now?

She walks in.

Unlike the grand, dramatic lobby, Joe's suite is warm and intimate. And not just because of the unspoken insinuation of the giant bed with its glamorous tufted headboard commanding attention through the wide, open doorway to the bedroom. Every corner and crevice is carefully dressed in soft shades of cream and teal to create little self-contained moments designed to be remembered. Reading nook, workspace, bar, living area, bedroom.

Sarah settles at the far end of the sofa and angles herself sideways against the arm with her leg pulled in front of her. A strategically placed bumper to protect her as she nears port after years at sea, battered and beaten by the wind and the waves, but terrified of even more damage if someone finally pulls her in.

In the beginning, after almost no time, their ease together had been so natural it was unnatural. Within hours, it was as if they'd known each other forever. Both of them marked it in their own way. And both of them attempted to resist it, too, unsuccessfully. Sometimes Sarah felt so completely comfortable with Joe she actually forgot to worry. About her fractured marriage on life support. About her complete lack of direction or even hope. About how she's wasting her life in a meaningless haze because she can't seem to make herself do anything else. Even about the guilt that courses through her whenever she dares admit to herself what she's really feeling for Joe. The anxiety would always return, of course, but the relief of such respites revealed a version of herself to Sarah that she had nearly forgotten.

But now, in this room, after two days of laying themselves bare, the conversation stalls. They revert to the moment they first met, when words escaped them, nothing made sense, and everything suddenly came into very clear focus. Once again, they're silenced by the force of something they don't understand, but can't deny.

Joe attempts to offer Sarah a drink from the bar, then remembers she's there to sober up, not drink. "Never mind." He stands by the bar a moment longer and folds his arms. "Well, this is weird."

Sarah exhales relieved laughter. "Yeah. It is." And with that, the weirdness is gone.

Joe lights up with a memory. "Oh, I want to play you something." He pulls his phone out and plugs it into the speaker on the desk. "It's Gregory Porter. Do you know him?"

"I don't think so."

"I think you'll like him." Joe hits play and the room fills with a funky bass and backbeat, followed by burst of horns and a soulful, jazzy voice singing to someone named "Mister Holland." The song summons the sweet softness of a warm summer night under the fading sun. Sarah fills with nostalgia like she's known the song all her life. Joe grooves in place, serving his cheesiest white man's overbite for Sarah's amusement, daring her to join him. The sight fills her. When the song ends, Joe grins. "Huh?"

"Fantastic."

"Told you." He plops onto other end of the sofa. "Now it's your turn."

"My turn?"

"Play something for me."

"What?"

"Anything. Whatever you want me to hear."

Sarah scrolls through her phone for something that feels right. What's safe enough? And what could follow such a great song? Inspiration strikes. She plugs in her phone and hits play, smirking with anticipation.

The song begins with a woman's nasal voice wishing for a guardian angel before the vocals begin. Joe recognizes the lyrics and grimaces. "'Beauty School Dropout'?"

"Not just any 'Beauty School Dropout,'" she says. "You gave me Gregory Porter. I give you Billy Porter."

"Okay, sure, Billy Porter's a legend. But why 'Beauty School Dropout' of all things?"

"Spoken like someone who's never heard it." She resumes her position on the sofa. "Give it time." Joe shrugs gamely, along for the ride.

They sway and snap to the gentle doo wop for the first couple minutes, but when the gospel choir kicks in, Billy's belt goes into overdrive. Joe erupts with laughter and claps his hands in delight. Billy's leading a full-on gospel revival now, his voice ascending heights only achieved by the angels, hilarious and brilliant all at once. Sarah waves her arms in the air, swings her head back and forth, and sings, a full-fledged member of the choir. Joe joins in as best he can. When Billy finishes his final, showiest riff and the choir intones the big finish, Joe has no choice but leap to his feet and applaud. Sarah follows suit, always ready with a standing O for the performance.

"So?"

"Only the single best vocal performance I've ever heard in my life," Joe says dryly.

"That's all I'm saying," Sarah replies. They collapse next to each other in a happy heap on the couch. "Are we making too much noise?"

"These walls are like five feet thick. You can't hear a thing."

Sarah nods at him, making eye contact a moment too long before catching herself, now keenly aware how close they are. "Hold on." She hurries off the sofa to put on a new song.

Joe listens as the music begins. "Brandi Carlile?"

"Local hero," she sings. She skips the couch and plants herself safely in one of the armchairs while they listen wordlessly, allowing Brandi to do the talking. They steal occasional glances, lock eyes, then dutifully look away. Each of them aware of the danger, though they perceive it differently. Like blind men holding opposite ends of the elephant. One terrified because she's sure the fantasy can't be real. The other terrified because he knows it is. They fill the space with talk of Brandi's performances on the Grammy Awards and SNL and the time Sarah saw her live with Gabi.

When "Broken Horses" plays automatically next, Joe jumps up. "Oh, this song is too good. Get up."

"Get up what? Get up why?"

"I want to see your rock star."

Sarah grips the arms of the chair. "I don't have a rock star."

"I know for a fact that's not true. I've heard it. Now I want to see it. Get up!"

Sarah drags herself from the chair, aware Joe will not be denied. In truth, she has no desire to deny him anything. Joe hits the button to restart the song and cranks it. He grabs the TV remote, a ready microphone, and shoves it into her hand. "Sing."

"This is silly."

"Of course, it is. That's the point." Joe strums at his newly donned air guitar.

Sarah holds the remote up to her mouth, but feels too absurd and drops her hand to her side. "I can't do this," she says through a plaintive laugh of embarrassment. For Joe, this comes easily. He's an actor. Joe can play. Hell, he gets paid to play. But Sarah left play behind decades ago. Except, somehow, with Joe.

"Yes, you can. Come on, rock star!"

With a heavy air of resignation, she brings the makeshift mic back to her mouth. "I can't believe I'm doing this." She phones it in at first, but Joe's enthusiasm is contagious. He's aggressively strumming his air guitar and nodding rhythmically at her like a lead guitarist egging her on. She loosens up, slowly, as both Joe and Brandi work their magic on her, and before she knows it, Sarah's singing full voice and strutting around like she's born to the stage.

Joe harmonizes with her at the chorus, and she sings to him like her onstage paramour. They are Stevie Nicks and Lindsay Buckingham, making love through their music in a haze of rock stardom. By the second verse, she's screeching out her best belt to mimic the singer's scratchy perfection. She's no Brandi Carlile, but she's equal to the moment and dazzles her audience of one, the only one who matters. Joe rocks out on his air guitar, riveted on Sarah as she owns her place in the spotlight. Sarah blasts the last verse with all the power she can muster, singing directly to Joe as she shimmies her shoulders to the beat in her best rock chick move through the hard driving crescendo.

An undeniable heat rises off them. As the song winds down, Joe leans in to sing with her, sharing the same "microphone" – classic rock move – and their foreheads touch as they harmonize the final line together. The song ends, and they are still there.

***

Joe flops in the armchair across from Sarah's, gazing at her, exhausted and content after their antics. The music now plays softly in the background. Sarah returns his gaze briefly, until her self-consciousness pushes her eyes off Joe to a print of the Seattle skyline on the wall. A quiet contemplation settles over them as they descend from their frenzied high, heavy with things unsaid.

"Sarah, can I tell you something I probably shouldn't?"

Sarah hears the weight in his voice and replies, "Of course." Her voice an octave too high as she tries to convey an easy lightness she does not feel. She braces herself for whatever he's about to say.

His expression is serious. "When I first saw you yesterday. Out on the street..." He pauses, finding either the words or the courage to continue. "I recognized you, too."

Sarah's heart seizes. Her eyes dart back to the skyline. The words are oblique, a cipher whose meaning is intentionally obscured. But she doesn't ask what he means, as any normal person would. Too afraid of the answer. Even more afraid she already knows. The notion anything she's feeling could be either real or reciprocated sends waves of terror through her.

The one thing that's gotten her through this beautiful dream without a complete emotional breakdown and paralyzing guilt was the certainty it was all just a one-sided fantasy. A sweet, impossible fantasy fueled by twenty years of fangirling. Yes, that's all she is, after all. Of course, she is. A fangirl letting her imagination run wild. She was a fool to imagine otherwise. And there could be no transgression if it wasn't real. She reminds herself not to get carried away, not to read into anything. This will all be over soon.

Sarah smiles breezily as if Joe's made a quip about the weather instead of a life-altering confession. "That's a nice picture," she says, still staring at the print. "I wonder if I can get a copy somehow. It would be perfect for our office."

Our office. A little reminder of home. Of reality. Of the place she should be heading now.

"Sarah," Joe says. He stops himself from saying more, but it's enough to pull her back in.

She flashes a sad smile, then glues her eyes to the floor. Joe braces his arm on the chair and rests his head against a tripod of his thumb and two fingers. He studies her while she studies the pattern on the carpet, until finally she summons the courage to speak.

"I want to thank you," she says before taking a gulp from her water bottle. "These last two days have been really..." She considers her options. Unforgettable. Magical. Life changing. Heartbreaking. "Great. Really great."

"For me, too."

"Well, I hope some of the spots end up working for you."

"That's not what I mean."

"The thing is...." She steadies herself. "I don't think I could ever tell you how much this time has meant to me."

"It's meant a lot to me, too," Joe says, ducking his head to catch her eye.

"But it's not the same," she says.

"You sure about that?"

Sarah crosses her arms over her chest and scrutinizes the carpet pattern once again. The music has been playing through her Brandi Carlile mix and now she hears the too painful, too raw piano chords opening "Right on Time."

Joe's eyes bore into her as he rasps, "You really have no idea, do you?"

Sarah says nothing, scouring the room for something to distract her. She glimpses the clock glowing green on the desk. "I should go."

Joe gets up from his seat and crosses to her, extending his hand. "Dance with me."

"It's late."

"But not too late," he says, anticipating the song. He holds his hand out insistently, until she takes it and stands slowly. He pulls her into him, clasping her right hand while placing her left hand on his shoulder. As he wraps his arm around her back, her body floods with a sensation so intense she's certain she will drown.

They sway to the chorus of a song too potent and heart-wrenching to bear. The vocals so raw and beautiful. The lyrics so vulnerable and heartfelt. The music is an arrow piercing her soul. In normal times, the slow, haunting melody nearly drives Sarah to tears. Now she thinks it might drive her mad.

In Joe's arms, the second verse of this song about healing takes on an indelible new meaning with this man who has never hurt her. A musical narration of everything she's feeling in a moment that has truly arrived right on time.

Joe gently folds Sarah's hand in and presses it against his heart. Instinctively she rests her cheek against his chest, her ear close enough to hear his heart beating. They rock back and forth in perfect unison, Sarah held up only by the strength in Joe's arms and the sheer will not to let go.

As the soaring vocal climbs through the chorus, Sarah feels what's next. Knows it with every bone in her body. The thing she's been denying for two days. The thing she has denied for twenty years. Maybe her whole life. If she looks up...

She shouldn't look up. She should keep her head down and keep dancing. The song will be over soon enough. Too soon.

She feels Joe's hand on her head. A ghost of a touch grazes her hair, covering her head in tingles that race through the rest of her before his fingertips glide down her cheek to her jawline. She knows she shouldn't look up. And she knows she will. His fingertips reach her chin and with the lightest of touch, barely more than a caress, he nudges her chin upward toward him.

In a flash, she sees it all. Each moment that led her here, all connected by an invisible thread she couldn't see, but always felt. Diorama scenes floating in black space, suddenly lit by a floodlight, the line running through them now illuminated at last. She looks back at each moment, glowing in the darkness, the only things in all of time and space to catch the light. A backwards timeline of her life extending almost infinitely into the distance, yet all in view.

The moment he placed his hand on hers at the crow lookout. Singing in the car. When he told her about his mother. The first moment she saw him on the corner. Was that just yesterday?

Then she travels further back, further down the line to two years earlier when Synergy shut down and only Joe could comfort her. Then even further, more than a decade, to the moment when a mere dream of Joe on a starry night saved her from a terrible match. And then the line goes on and she follows it. Nearly twenty years back to an otherwise forgettable cable movie that somehow changed her. Then way, way back to one crazy New Year's Eve in college, when she *didn't* meet a guy – and never forgot him. And then, somehow, the line continues.

All the way back to the very moment she was born.

Every bit of it connected by a single, invisible thread that leads directly to Joe. An inseverable tether. A three-dimensional timeline of her life, demarcated not by birthdays and graduations, not by jobs or even her marriage. But by the only moments that matter. It's her life measured in Joe. All leading inexorably to this beautiful, impossible, inevitable moment.

She looks up.

Chapter Seventeen

Surrender

THEIR FIRST KISS IS not gentle. It's not tentative. It's the passion of a lifetime unleashed, exploding through their lips, tongues, hands, fingertips. Everything they've felt, everything they've withheld, even from themselves, pouring out in broken gasps and urgent sighs as their lips collide and their hands explore with a frightening ferocity. They cling to each other as fervently as life preservers in an unexpected storm.

Finally, as the song ends, they slow the pace of their kisses and ease back a few inches. A moment to take in the magnitude of what's just happened. They dive deep into each other's eyes. Joe asks the question wordlessly as he holds her face close. Sarah gives the faintest nod. Barely perceptible, but it's enough.

He drops a hand to hers, leading her to the couch. He fleetingly considers the bed, where he really wants her, but it's too soon for that. Despite this eruption, and because of it, they need to slow down.

Leaning back on the couch, their tongues brush each other's lips and discover each other. She tastes the wine on his breath – bitter, sweet, and intoxicating all at once. She panics about her own breath. What did she have for dinner? What you eat for dinner when you know you're not having sex is entirely different than when you think you are. She had the chicken with all that garlic. Dammit.

He kisses her neck and down to her chest. She's fixated on that chicken. That garlic. As he makes his way back up to her mouth, she pulls away a little.

"You okay?"

She covers her mouth, embarrassed. "I had garlic for dinner."

"Are you kidding me?" Heat flushes her cheeks at his laugh, but it's clearly affectionate. "We both did. And you need to get out of your head." He kisses her softly. "Forget dinner. Be here now. Right now. With me."

She smiles with relief and kisses him back. She allows his tongue more deeply into her mouth, now willing to let him in fully. He braces his arm against the cushion as he caresses her face. His free hand skates from her neck down her arm and back again. She lets out a tiny moan as he flicks his tongue along her earlobe.

But when he grazes her breasts, she tenses. He doesn't notice and continues to slide his hand over her body. As he brushes along her stomach, she freezes and grabs his hand to stop him.

"Wait! Wait!" She catches her breath and pulls out from under him. Not all the way, but enough to break the spell.

He pulls back, breathless. "Do you want me to stop?" His eyes glimmer with need. With hunger. But he's patient. Kind.

"No." She gasps for breath, her head spinning. "I don't know. Not exactly."

"Then what is it? What's wrong?"

"It's just..." She trails off, unable to say it.

"What?" He squeezes her hand. "Tell me."

"I've seen pictures of your wife."

Joe leans back at this sober reminder. He remembers showing her the family photos. It feels like a million years ago. He assumes she's feeling guilty. Now he is, too. But he's still in the moment, unwilling to surrender this feeling.

She goes on, "I've seen her in a bikini. I know what she looks like." Sarah gestures at her own body. "And it's not this."

As her meaning sinks in, Joe's guilt fades, overwritten by an almost suffocating compassion. She's so fragile, a desiccated flower long neglected, still beautiful, but ready to shatter into dust with the slightest touch. He sees it so clearly now, yet remains puzzled. Her meaning both apparent and utterly incomprehensible to him.

She gestures again over her abdomen, over everything she hides beneath her clothes. "All of this. It's not what you're used to. It doesn't look like that. It doesn't feel like that."

A sharp pang slices through Joe's heart. Hearing this glorious, sexy woman say these things about herself is more than he can bear. "Hey, listen to me. I see all those insecurities swirling around in that busy head of yours." She avoids his eyes. "But you obviously don't see what I see," he continues. "You couldn't, or you wouldn't be able to say the things you're saying."

She still won't meet his gaze. He takes her chin and nudges her face back so he can look her in the eyes. "Sarah, I see you. I see you clearly. And I want you." His voice is low, almost a whisper, a gruff rumble of desire. His words are hypnotic – and terrifying. Her eyes fill. "You don't have to be afraid." He kisses her gently. "You're safe with me." He wipes a tear from her cheek. "You're safe."

She searches for the truth in his eyes. He nods at her, and she knows it's true. This is the man who listened to her stories and self-recriminations not with judgment, but with compassion, and maybe even admiration. Who immediately understood not just the professional impact, but the emotional heartbreak of losing Synergy. The man who trusted her enough to share a story about his mom he's never told anyone. She's safe with him. He kisses her again, and this time she surrenders. He runs his hand down her body, slowly caressing every curve to reassure her. There is no part of her he doesn't want.

He eases his hand to her leg and slips it to her inner thigh, perilously close. She lets out a quiet sigh. He lightly brushes his fingers between her legs, sending shivers through her and down to her toes. He slips his fingers underneath the waistband of her slacks, caressing her stomach and easing downward.

She moans at the feel of his fingertips making contact with her belly as they kiss. Her ugliest part now feels beautiful. He finds the zipper, pulls, and inches her slacks down. Sarah's hips lift reflexively at his touch.

He reaches for her blouse to unbutton it. She panics again. Let him *feel* her, she thinks. That's enough. He doesn't have to *see* her.

He kneels on the floor in front of the couch and pushes the coffee table away. He spreads her legs and places himself between them. He kisses her thighs while he reaches up and continues unbuttoning her blouse.

Terror and desire whirl around in a frenzied dance within her. She wants this so much, but she almost stops him again. Before she can, he pulls open her blouse and kisses her stomach. She remembers his words. *You're safe.*

He finds a scar on her right side and catches her eye.

"Appendix," she says.

He kisses the scar lovingly. He pulls his shirt off and leans down to wrap his arms around her as he kisses his way back down. The feeling of his warm skin on hers, his bare chest, electrifies her.

His lips reach their final destination. He presses them against her, through her underwear. She feels his hot breath and wet tongue pressing through the fabric and a shock goes through her body. He kisses gently around her thighs and then back again. He flicks his tongue around the edges of her underwear, slipping under here and there. Ever closer.

Finally, he tugs them down to the floor, catching her eye as he does. Reassuring her. Reassuring himself that she wants this as much as he does.

He presses his mouth against her, his fingers working in tandem. She writhes with pleasure. His fingers and his tongue take turns, responding to her every movement as he learns what she likes, what she wants. With each step, he awaits her response, reading her body and breath for directions, determined to give her everything she wants while never abandoning the spot he knows will bring her to the edge.

The feeling of his mouth, warm and wet, in her most private place sends Sarah into paroxysms of desire, more uninhibited than she's been in years. She tosses back her head and closes her eyes. Her body quivers uncontrollably as he relentlessly pursues her satisfaction.

He revels in the beauty of Sarah lost in passion. He delves deeper. He continues to watch her as he slides his free hand back up her body to her breasts, kneading them hungrily through her bra before he slips his fingers in to squeeze a nipple. She moans again.

After a moment, he glides from her breast to her shoulder and down her arm. He reaches for her hand and takes it, never slowing his pace, his fingers and tongue in perfect rhythm.

The feel of his hand squeezing hers pulls her out of her throes of passion enough to open her eyes and look at him. They lock eyes and clasp hands tightly as he quickens his pace. Within moments, their eyes fixed firmly on each other, she climaxes. He relishes every moment as her body explodes with pleasure.

***

He stays where he is, kissing her thighs gently while she recovers herself. Then he climbs up to her, and kisses her deeply, traces of her pleasure still on his lips. He stands and offers her his hand. "Come with me."

As they walk to the bed, she pulls her blouse closed self-consciously. He chuckles affectionately and shakes his head at her. He pulls her blouse off, then reaches around and removes her bra. She's completely exposed now. No hiding. He holds her in another embrace and they kiss. Their bare torsos pressed together for the first time, his long arms wrap around her. Fully enveloped by him. Warm. Safe. He whispers, "You are so beautiful."

He pulls down the covers, exposing the sheets. He sits her on the bed and steps back to remove his jeans. She pulls the sheet over herself, unable to remain so exposed. He smiles reassuringly at her as he unbuckles his belt and unzips his jeans. She watches him intently. Studies his body for the first time. Marvels at how beautiful he is.

Of course, she always thought that. Tall, dark, and handsome had always been her thing. But she could never imagine seeing him like this. Now as he reveals himself in all his glory, she's stunned by the perfection of his lean body. Not obscenely muscular, thank goodness. Not an overdeveloped beefcake angling for a superhero gig, but strong, defined, athletic. And limbs so long she thinks he could probably touch the sky if he stood on his toes.

He's down to his boxer briefs now, leaving little to the imagination in the moment. He's ready for her. Then he pulls his briefs down and she sees him fully. She's stunned anew. He reaches for his jeans on the ground and pulls something from his pocket. It's a condom. He quickly unwraps it and slides it on. She falters a moment, thrown by the condom. It's good he has a condom. Thank God he has a condom. She hadn't even been thinking clearly enough to think of it. But it throws her nonetheless. Why would he have it?

Yet here is this man, this beautiful man who takes her breath away. He's Adonis looking at her like she's Aphrodite, a literal aphrodisiac if ever there were one. She trembles as he leans her back onto the bed. He pulls back the sheet and lies next to her, his body pressing against her. He captures her lips between his and she gives them willingly.

She reaches for him and finds him instantly hard with her touch. They spend fleeting moments touching each other, readying each other, their need growing. She is still so wet, so he quickly rolls on top of her. He pushes against her as he slides up and down her body, his lips and erection hard against her. He slips his legs between hers and she opens like a flower, welcoming him.

He finds his way between her legs, sliding through her wetness as he does. And suddenly he's there, about to enter her.

Desire swirls around and through them, but after this moment, there's no going back. He pushes himself up, bracing himself with his hands. She feels him there, between her legs, throbbing, ready. He stares into her eyes a moment longer, awaiting her signal, to know absolutely that she wants this.

She breathes heavily as she looks up at him. She struggles to say it out loud, to give him the word he wants. The word she longs to say, the word she thinks again and again. *Yes.* Instead, she lifts her hips and presses herself firmly against him, an unspoken invitation.

It's all he needs. He thrusts into her and falls onto her body, kissing her hard. He holds her close, needily, as he strokes in and out, feeling her body rock with his. She wraps her legs around him and takes him in.

More than his body. She's feeling him. His heart. His soul. The connection is so deep she feels her edges disappear, bleeding into his, merging into something entirely new and perfect. He feels it, too, consumed by this woman who has so beguiled him that she's all he sees, all he feels, all he is.

They thrust and rock together, lost in each other. Their lips seldom part, moans escaping around the edges of their kisses as they hold each other tightly. Together, they find a rhythm as urgent as their passion and they never falter, even for a moment, until he finally pulls his face away and cries out in ecstasy.

She feels him spasm and shake, feels his warmth as he collapses against her once again. She wraps her arms around him as they both pant, trying to catch their breath. He clings to her, utterly hers in that moment.

Now he's the one surrendering.

Chapter Eighteen

Aftermath

SARAH'S HEAD RESTS ON Joe's chest, his arms tightly around her, anchoring her from floating away. Both naked, sheets kicked off, completely at ease.

"That was...," Sarah says.

"Yeah, it was," Joe agrees, kissing Sarah's head. "You doing okay?"

She glows inwardly at the realization that for the first time in longer than she can remember, she can answer unequivocally. "I am. You?"

"I'm great."

"Yes, you are pretty great," she giggles.

Joe laughs at the innuendo. "Just pretty great?"

"Well, I don't want you to get a big head."

"Oh, so many things I could say to that," he laughs again. Joe grazes his fingertips up and down Sarah's arm and back, and her skin erupts with goosebumps. "God, Sarah. You're something else."

"Yes, but what exactly?" she says slyly.

"I've been wondering that for two days," he says as his eyes wander over every inch of her body, drinking her in. In the silence, he formulates a question. "What were you like as a little girl?"

"As a little girl? Jeez, I don't know."

"I bet you were a force to be reckoned with," he says.

Was she? A force to be reckoned with? She can barely remember that little girl anymore. "Why do you say that?"

"I have a theory about you."

Sarah mock frowns. "That sounds frightening."

He holds back a small smile before saying, "It's still formulating."

"Give me a hint." Her amusement dances in her voice. His ridiculous out-of-left-field questions can't panic her now.

"Well, the way I see it, you're hiding your light under a bushel. But—"

She pushes up onto her elbow and gives him her most defiant scoff. "I don't hide my light under a bushel! I don't know what you mean. There are no bushels."

"Oh, there's a bushel, alright. A big one, too." Joe follows the words with a proud grin.

"Maybe there's no bushel," Sarah laughs. "Maybe I just don't have a light. Ever think of that?"

He brushes a strand of hair behind her ear and grazes his fingertips down her cheek. "No, I've seen it. And it's too bright to hide forever."

Sarah rolls her eyes. "I'd like to hide this metaphor under a bushel."

"But I know you didn't always hide it. And I think it's just about time to let it shine again."

"I'm not sure how I feel about being the subject of your theory," Sarah grumbles. "I think I'd rather be untheorized."

"Oh, too late for that, baby!" He squeezes her.

Sarah rests her head back on Joe's chest. "Too late for a lot of things."

He gazes at her adoringly. "Way too late," he says.

She sighs happily, but the words unleash something new in her. Or rather, something old. Something too familiar. Something relentless and fearful that never stays away long. She runs her hand down his chest, feeling the rise and fall of his lean muscles before settling at his belly button and tracing a small circle around it as she prepares herself to speak. The moment is bliss, but a tiny shadow looms at the back of her mind now. "Can I ask you a question?"

"Anything."

"Only, I'm not sure I actually want to hear the answer."

He caresses her arm. "It can't be that bad. Go ahead. I'll tell you anything."

She hesitates and braces herself. She can't make eye contact or she'll lose her nerve, so she continues circling his navel. "Why did you have a condom with you?"

Joe freezes. "What?"

"You had a condom," she says. "Why? I mean, I'm glad you had it. I guess. Under the circumstances. But I thought you were this nice family man."

Joe's arms grow tense around Sarah, like he's afraid she'll escape. "I've been totally honest with you about who I am, Sarah."

She pushes away and sits up to look at him directly. She pulls the sheet to her, once again unwilling to be so exposed. "Then why did you have a condom with you? Do you do this a lot? Do you have, like, a girl in every port?" She says it jovially, a hint of finger quotes in her voice, almost like she's teasing. But her tone's unmistakably sharp.

"I've never done this before. Ever. I swear."

"Then why did you have a condom?"

"It's not what you think. Really." Joe is pleading now. "Can we just drop it?"

His attempts to reassure her have the opposite effect. Sarah's working herself up. "I'm sorry, but I don't think I can. Because this felt like one thing to me... before. I mean, it felt special."

"It was special. It *is* special."

Sarah's wired now, her body rigid as steel. "But now I'm thinking more clearly, it's starting to feel like something else."

"Something else?"

"I mean, don't get me wrong. It's good you had one, since, you know." She gestures at the bed they're still in. Her guilt and doubt are stirring up a dangerous brew. "But I've never done anything like this before and I certainly wasn't walking around with a condom. But you were. So, I'm kind of spinning out right now."

"You don't have to spin out. I promise you."

She pulls further away to the edge of the bed, the sheet pulled in a protective cocoon around her chest. "Am I a groupie? Is that what this is?"

"A groupie? Jeez, you *are* spinning out. You're definitely not a groupie to me."

"I just need to understand what this was. And if this is just something *you do*."

"I don't. Ever."

She stares at him as she mentally erects a Berlin wall around herself. "You just did."

"Come on. Is there anything I've said or done in the past two days that makes you think I *just do* this kind of thing?"

The logic of this seeps in. The man she's spent the past two days with isn't a womanizer. Is he? "Then why does a married man carry around a condom?"

"I don't." Joe croaks his reply, his own emotions slipping through the cracks as he speaks.

"You had it ready." She stares at him. Hard.

"Please don't make me say it."

That was the wrong thing to say. Sarah jumps up, pulling the sheet around her and leaving Joe completely exposed as she searches frantically for her underwear. She darts around the room in search, and finally drops to her knees to pull them out from under the coffee table. She pulls them on lightning speed beneath her sheet.

Joe takes a deep breath before speaking. "I got it from the guy at the desk."

Sarah stops short and lets out a half-choked laugh. "You mean, on the way up tonight?"

"Yes."

"With the water?"

"The water was a cover, yes."

Her brow furrows as she assesses. He points to the bar where there are already two large bottles of water mixed in with the other drinks and goodies. She takes this in, uncertain what to think. She grabs her bra from the bedside, turns her back to him, and drops the sheet to put it on.

"Sarah, I'm telling you. This is the first time in nineteen years I've either had, or needed, a condom."

She grabs the sheet and pulls it back up in front of her, now wearing her bra behind the sheet. "So you planned this?"

"I don't know how to answer that. I didn't plan it. No. I didn't know it would happen."

"Seems like you did." She avoids his eyes, determined to stay on top, and yanks her slacks up.

Joe throws his hands up. "I can't win here. I give up."

This stops her dead, uncertain whether she wants him to give up or not. But no, of course she doesn't. She looks at him, then averts her eyes as he grabs his briefs and slips them on. She's nearly in tears. On the cusp. Walls up and running out, or walls down and accepting the truth.

Joe decides to go all in on the truth. "Okay, look. I thought it might happen. I admit it. I mean, I felt guilty for thinking it, but I don't know. I was feeling something I've never felt before." He speaks slowly and pointedly. "It felt to me like *something* was happening here. Some kind of connection I couldn't ignore."

Sarah still won't look at him, but she's listening at last. Starving for validation that what she thought and felt, what she gave into, wasn't just in her imagination after all.

"I thought I should be prepared, just in case. But I didn't know. And I didn't plan it. I certainly didn't set a trap or anything."

She scoffs in a showy display of incredulity, but seems to soften. "Wow." He's uncertain how to interpret her response. Anger? Hurt? Relief?

"Come on. You thought it was a possibility, too."

"We agreed no funny business," Sarah insists, eyes fixed firmly on the black TV screen.

"Why did we even need to say that, Sarah? If there was no possibility of it?"

"I thought you were letting me down gently. Or teasing."

"Who are you lying to right now?" he says. "Yourself or me?"

It's a valid question. To which she doesn't know the answer. She harrumphs, but says nothing.

"So yeah, I figured, better safe than sorry." He pauses to make sure she's really listening. "And guess what? I'm not sorry."

She turns to him again. "You're not?"

He shakes his head slowly. "Nope." He crosses to her and places a hand on each of her arms, peering straight into her eyes as her frenzy leaks slowly away. "I didn't plan this. Neither of us planned this. It just happened. And it was amazing. *You* are amazing."

"No, I'm not." Her eyes dart away again. He pulls her chin back toward him and nods. Her face melts into a sad smile as she relents, then shakes her head. "Oh God, what are we doing?"

He shrugs in response. "You got me."

She pulls away, eager to escape the intimacy. "I should go."

"Hey, slow down."

"It's really late."

"Alright! Okay, you can go. But don't leave like this." He takes her arm gently as she reaches for her top. "Sarah, I want you to know this *has* been truly special."

That word again.

"I didn't see it coming. And I swear I've never done this before." Sarah softens and he goes on. "Not ever. And I know we shouldn't have let it happen. But I don't regret it. And I hope you don't either."

"I probably should." She brushes his cheek with her hand, confirming that he's real, that this is all real. "But I don't."

"Well, then," Joe says softly, pressing his lips to her hand, "that's good." He smiles contentedly, and she can't help but smile back.

"But I really should go."

***

Joe clasps Sarah's hand as they walk through the lobby, but steps outside the door, they both instinctively pause. They look at each other. It's the exact spot where they met only yesterday. They feel the heat and the vibration of the spot, as if a ley line beneath the earth has marked the site forever. They say nothing, but smile at each other before walking on.

The night is cool and breezy, a sign rain is preparing its return. Despite the chill, they walk leisurely hand in hand, in no rush to reach the car and end the night. He caresses her hand with his thumb as they walk. She responds in kind. They say little, letting their fingertips do the talking, exactly as Joe had imagined earlier in the day. Fantasy turned prophecy.

As they near her car, Joe says, "You should come with me tomorrow. On the tour."

"I think we should say goodbye tonight."

"What if I'm not ready to say goodbye?"

"I'm not sure I'll ever be ready," Sarah says. "But what are we gonna do anyway? You're flying home tomorrow night and I've got to get back to normal life."

"It won't be any fun without you."

"You're not supposed to be having fun. You're supposed to be working."

"We managed to do both pretty well the last couple days." He squeezes her hand for emphasis.

She contains her smile as she scrolls back through two extraordinary days. "Try to have a little less fun with the dude tomorrow. As a favor to me."

"Well, if he's as gorgeous as you are, I make no promises," he teases.

She rolls her eyes, but wavers inside. Leaving is getting harder by the minute. Her resolve weakening, she pushes on. "I think it's better this way. Let tonight live in its own magical, little bubble."

Joe exhales his acceptance. She clicks her car lock open. He rubs his hands up and down her arms, warming her while filling his own well for the last time. "You're a hell of a girl, Sarah." She blushes and drops her gaze. Normally she hates being called "girl." But in Joe's mouth, the word makes her feel young. And beautiful. She leans back against the car and Joe presses in close. "You know, I'll be back to shoot in a couple months," he says.

Their faces are only inches apart. "I heard that somewhere, yeah." He raises his brows at her. Asking. Offering. Entreating. She shakes her head.

"But what if—"

Sarah doesn't let him finish. "I have to get back to real life. So do you." Joe winces, but pushes himself back a few inches following her cue. "I wish you all the luck in the world with this film. You know I'll be watching."

He sighs his understanding. "And I hope you find your next great thing soon. I already know it's waiting for you."

Sarah shrugs. "We'll see, I guess."

Joe pulls back and shakes his head in disbelief before thrusting his fists downward like he's casting off a demon. "God, I can't believe how fast you got under my skin."

"Like a parasite," she giggles.

Joe groans. "Enough. Come here." Sarah sinks into his arms and loses herself for one final moment. She inhales deeply to lock his earthy scent into her memory before he cups her face and kisses her. She takes one more deep breath of Joe and exhales slowly, clinging to his shirt. She climbs into her car and turns the ignition, but before she can go, he knocks on the window and she rolls it down.

"Will you text me when you get home?" he says. "So I know you're safe?"

She shakes her head. "I'll be fine."

"You'll text me," he grins.

"I'm not gonna text you. I'll be fine. Goodnight, Joe."

Joe reaches in through the window and runs the back of his fingers across Sarah's cheek, one last touch. "Goodnight, Sarah."

Sarah avoids his eyes, but takes his hand, kisses it, and releases it. He taps the roof twice, and she pulls out without looking back. Joe smiles to himself. "She'll text me."

***

Joe lies on his bed, a notepad abandoned beside him as he flips through pictures from the day's adventures. A text from Sarah pops in.

Home now. Safe and sound.

Joe grins before typing his response. *Thank you.*

Sarah's dot dot dot appears awhile. Then goes away. Joe stares at the phone, waiting. The dot dot dot returns.

Goodnight.

***

Sarah sits in her car in the garage, staring at her phone, awaiting Joe's reply. After a moment, it appears.

Goodnight. Followed by the sleeping emoji.

A safe choice. Neither of them dares text anything more as they each return to real lives with real consequences. But the sleeping emoji is enough. Harmless, innocent, perfectly appropriate when saying goodnight. Yet the tiniest hint of intimacy. Those three floating z's just enough to float into her sleep that night and for many nights to come, summoning the most beautiful dream she's ever had – over and over again.

She smiles dreamily and clutches the phone to her chest – until her surroundings sink in. She frowns and braces herself for re-entry, for the violence of thrusting through the atmosphere and crashing down to earth after waltzing with the stars. She flips away from Joe's text and back to Ben's, which popped in while she was driving.

Heading to bed. Early morning. Tell me about it tomorrow?

Sarah drops the phone and buries her face in her hands. Guilt, commingled with relief, washes over her. "Thank you, God," she whispers.

When she's ready, she creeps quietly into the house and detours to the guest bathroom for a quick shower. She stashes the wet towel in her hamper, slides into bed as gently as possible, careful not to wake Ben, and stares at the ceiling for hours.

Chapter Nineteen

Day Three

Yesterday morning, Sarah made a promise. To tell Gabi everything today. But oh-so-much has changed since then. Can she really tell her everything now? What can she say when she hasn't made sense of it herself? And what will Gabi think? Especially after Max's cheating hurt Gabi so badly once upon a time. How many nights did Gabi cry on Sarah's shoulder after it all came out? Of course, Max was a serial philanderer with more women than they knew, but still. Ben isn't the only one Sarah stands to lose from her stupidity.

"Dear God! What have I done?" Sarah mutters to the bedroom walls. Still groggy, she pushes herself off the bed. She slept hard once she finally fell asleep and it's already eleven o'clock. At least she missed Ben this morning, but she needs to get moving if she wants to catch Gabi for her lunch break.

One quick change and ponytail later, Sarah heads for the door. Her text whistles. She expects Gabi haranguing her for an update, but no. It's Joe. She glimpses his name and freezes without reading the preview. The prospect of what could be within both tantalizing and terrifying in equal measure. She flirts with the idea of deleting it unread. After all, what good can come of it?

If he's adoring and sweet, that will only fill her with longing and regret, and then she'll have no choice but to delete it. What if Joe expresses his own regrets, perhaps seeks her reassurance she'll never bother him again or interfere with his real life? That would break her heart. Obviously, that's the right course of action, the only possibility she would even consider, but she wants to believe he trusts her. Or what if he's all business and matter-of-fact about a location or something, like it never happened? That might be worst of all, to think it meant so little to him, or that maybe she'd made it all up after all. Fantasies can be brutal.

She holds off exactly as long as it takes to collect the Space Noodles and Seattle Chocolates from the mudroom and settle herself into her car before her strength gives out.

Swam this morning. Many, many laps. Didn't help. Nice pool though.

The text is accompanied by a picture of the pool. Sarah giggles despite herself. She stares at the photo awhile, envisioning Joe's long, slender body stretching through the shimmering blue, elongated further by the reach of his arms with each stroke, gliding effortlessly through the water. Beautiful and sleek. He's right. It's a very nice pool.

***

Sarah can barely see Gabi, who's almost entirely hidden by shipping cartons of Chex cereal stacked four high, her poof of tight black curls popping out at the top, as if the top box has dolled itself up with a new 'do.

"Run out of room in dry storage again?"

"Why do they always deliver too much of some things and not enough of others?" Gabi replies without a glance. Sarah plops herself at the empty desk, her usual workspace. "At least it'll be gone by tomorrow." Gabi holds up one finger as she finishes lining through something on her desk, before looking up. "Okay. Where's my stuff and what's going on?"

"Jeez, buy a girl a meal first."

"Sorry. I'm slammed getting stuff done before my trip. But you can tell me here!" Sarah hands Gabi her bag of goodies. Gabi slides out the Space Noodles and examines them. Sure enough, they are little noodles shaped like the Space Needle. "Space Noodles. I get it now."

"Willy Wonka has nothing on you in the imagination department."

"Enough about me. Your turn." Gabi grins expectantly.

Sarah takes a deep breath and begins to talk, almost as curious as Gabi to hear what will come out of her mouth. She reports on the first day as faithfully as possible. She omits only her feelings, though she does acknowledge how handsome Joe is, how he's her favorite actor, and how the whole thing felt like a dream. But before she can get into the details of the second day, Gabi interrupts.

"Wait, who is he again?"

"Joseph Robert Parker. You know him. Remember that guy in Doc Hope?"

"Ohhhhh yeah," Gabi replies, convincing no one. "Well, I'd dump your ass to spend two days with some hot actor, too."

Sarah smiles and feigns lightheartedness. A subterfuge that would normally never fool Gabi, but a co-worker runs in at that precise moment with an emergency. A client's in crisis and they need to de-escalate. Gabi bolts out, and Sarah remains, stewing in her own juices, pondering how much more to say.

Gabi was so broken after Max. Nausea swells as Sarah contemplates confessing to basically the same thing he did. Sarah cannot lose Gabi. She's already on the cusp of a breakdown. Life without Gabi would be untenable. But she can't imagine lying to her either. It's always been much easier to lie to herself than to Gabi. Gabi always knows, always offers a safe landing place for Sarah's truth, even when it's ugly. But this truth is uglier than any before, especially given what Gabi's been through. The fact that it's also more beautiful is beside the point. At least it likely would be to Gabi.

She can't tell her, even though it breaks her heart to hide it. She'll have to carry this alone. She peeks out and spots Gabi embroiled in an intense conversation with a still fraught client. Sarah sneaks out the back door and texts from her car.

You have a lot to do so I'm leaving you to it. Have the best time. Text me every day and call as soon as you get back. Love you!

Before she pulls out, her phone whistles a text notification. She pulls it up, again assuming it will be Gabi and again surprised to see Joe's name instead. No words, just a photo of Joe in front of a club called The Blue Note. He gestures up to the sign, pointing directly to the word "Blue" with an exaggerated pout on his face. She stares at his silly expression and his eyes that are bluer than the sign above, giggles, then tucks away the phone.

Sarah spends the rest of the afternoon daydreaming about Joe and planning an elaborate dinner, both to assuage her guilt and, she hopes, to distract Ben from talk of the prior two days. She gives him a heads-up she's "making dinner" in a way that leaves no doubt he should definitely not eat out tonight, then contemplates what she can safely say to him without digging the hole deeper than she already has. Guilt already torments her. Every new lie can only compound the damage.

Joe interrupts her musings twice more with two more photos. One is inside a club, brightly lit with the daytime house lights. Joe sits at a table for two with a red glass candleholder at its center and two glasses, one in front of him and one across from him. He's looking at the empty chair, his face a portrait of heartbreak. It isn't exaggerated like the sillier first picture. It feels real. Of course, Joe's an actor. He knows how to summon emotions on cue. Still, it feels real.

The last photo is in yet another club. This one darker, more ambient. The camera points toward the stage with the piano and drum set illuminated, and pin lights scattered around the dance floor. Standing alone in one of the lights on the dance floor is Joe, his arms out, slow dancing with an invisible partner.

Each time, the photos draw her back to the freedom and hope she felt only yesterday. To the joy that Joe reminded her how to feel. To the deep intimacy and inexplicable, lifelong connection she felt with a man she only just met and will never see again. And each time, her thoughts of Joe are chased with both guilt and longing. Sarah stares at the last photo for several minutes, then closes her phone and sobs.

***

She sets the table with extra care – a roast with fingerling potatoes, pearl onions, and carrots, a nice green salad, plus Ben's favorite coconut cream pie from Dahlia Bakery for dessert – and puts on quiet music, some innocuous jazz. Overcompensating.

Ben gasps when he walks in. "Wow, what's the occasion?" He looks at her with furrowed brow.

"No occasion." Sarah says as she places a freshly acquired floral centerpiece in the middle of the table. Definitely overcompensating. "But we haven't sat down to a nice dinner together in a while, so I thought I'd make an effort."

"So tell me about the movie people," he says as he takes his seat. "How did it go yesterday?"

Sarah startles at the question. For all her fear of facing this moment, she also halfway imagined he might just forget. Such a gift wasn't beyond the realm of possibility given Ben's absences both mental and physical these days. But not this time. Apparently close encounters with Hollywood are too tantalizing for even Ben to forget. Just so long as he doesn't know quite how close the encounters were.

"It was fun." Sarah parses her words carefully to minimize the damage. "They need some scenic outdoor locations in the movie, so we mostly went to parks yesterday." All true. *They* do need scenic outdoor locations. She can do it. She can get through this.

"Yeah, Wendy said she ran into you at Luther Burbank."

Of course she did. "Oh?"

"Said you were with some hot dude." He says it lightly, but she hears the weight beneath the words.

Sarah attempts to laugh it off. "Wendy's given to exaggeration."

He stops slicing his meat to challenge her. "So, he wasn't hot?"

"I don't know," she sputters. "I mean, aren't all actors at least hottish?"

"Hmmm," Ben says, his face expressionless. "And the others?"

Sarah blanches. Time to go all in. "The crew? Yeah, they got lost, so we met up with them at the next stop."

"That's what Wendy said," he says, finally taking a bite of his roast beef. "She was pretty excited actually. She said they really seemed to appreciate you. Well, he did." Ben chews slowly, watching Sarah's response more closely than he's watched anything she's done in months.

This is a disaster waiting to happen. Sarah decides to change tack before this spinout ends in a fiery crash. She giggles flirtatiously. "You sound jealous."

He gives her a sharp look. "Should I be?"

Sarah's heart races her brain through possible responses. Nothing seems right, but an answer spills out. "Of some Hollywood actor? Come on." The words cut, but she says them anyway. "You know I only have eyes for you." She's going to hell. God help her, she's definitely going to hell. He stares at her and says nothing, but she clocks the tension in his jaw relaxing. The lines around his mouth soften. He just needs a little more reassurance. She swallows hard and adds, "Besides, what Hollywood actor is going to be interested in me?"

Ben studies her, analyzing her answer, then returns to his food. "Sorry. I suppose I'm overreacting. You did mention him the other night."

"Yeah," she says as she sucks in a breath and holds it.

His tension melts away at last as he takes a bite of his potatoes and smiles. "This is delicious, hon."

Sarah winces at the jagged edges inside her, annihilating her one slash at a time. Her lies. Her self-flagellating words. The way Ben's jealousy evaporated the moment she said what she said. *What Hollywood actor is going to be interested in me?* Her brain nearly short circuits processing the implications of Ben's about-face in that moment.

Ben picks up the conversation, now lighthearted and downright cheerful. "It sounds like you've put your stamp on this movie."

For better or worse – okay, clearly worse – Ben is more interested in this movie than in anything she's done in months. He's barely offered more than a drive-by greeting in ages. Now suddenly he's full of questions. The dinner was a mistake. Face-to-face conversation is riddled with danger. A definite miscalculation, but then, she hasn't exactly been thinking clearly.

"Kinda. Maybe," she says. "We'll see, I guess. If it even gets released."

"When are they shooting?" Ben asks, his mouth stuffed with buttered dinner roll.

"In a couple months, I think."

"Maybe they'll let you come watch."

"I don't know. I think this was kind of a one-time thing." Yes, this has to be a one-time thing. "They'll be busy during the shoot, I'm sure."

"But it would be fun though, right? To watch them make a movie?"

Sarah's getting emotional whiplash. Who is this man? He's almost unrecognizable. Or more accurately, he's like a memory. A walking, talking hologram of a previous iteration of Ben. A version who spent time with her and switched off his work for more than five minutes in a row. Where did he come from and why has he chosen now to return?

Sarah agrees blandly. "Yeah. That would be fun."

"Well, I'm glad you had a good time. You deserve an adventure."

An adventure. Is that what it was? Yes, that's it. Just an action-packed escape from daily life. Nothing more. Like zip-lining in Costa Rica or sailing to Antartica. A brief, but exciting break from life filled with sights and sounds you'll never experience again. And never forget. But when it's over, it's over, and normal life resumes. Just as it should.

Guilt and longing surge through her once again and turn her stomach. Sarah half smiles, but says nothing.

***

The best thing about Zilko, the spindly, local musician who's giving Joe his jazz club tour, is his gameness. He's so delighted to have even a tangential role in the movie industry that he doesn't think twice about an actor's eccentric photo requests. He's shot a few album covers in his time, so moody scenes devoid of context are totally his jam. When Joe hands him the phone and takes up one sad pose or another, Zilko figures he's getting into the character and rolls with it. When Joe tries to explain the photos, Zilko shrugs and says, "Actors act," while absentmindedly fingering an invisible trumpet at his side.

Of course, Joe isn't acting. He's declaring his truth in the only way he can. The fact that it will read to the rest of the world like play-acting is a bonus. But for Joe, there's nothing pretend about those pictures.

Joe himself takes the last three photos at the airport that night. As he rolls in the door, he shoots a photo of his 8:45 Seattle to Los Angeles flight on the departures board. When he settles into his seat in first class, he grabs a shot of the empty seat next to him before a large, bald dude in a polo shirt fills it and pulls out his laptop. And the last photo he takes is a screenshot of his phone playing "Right on Time," the song that started it all. Their song.

He clicks through the three photos, which he intends to send all at once, a triptych of images telling Sarah everything left to say. He's leaving. He'll miss her. He won't forget her. He stares at his phone, preparing to send, but hesitates. Sarah hasn't responded all day. He knows why, of course, but maybe it's best if he stops. Especially now that it's evening. She's probably home with her husband. The thought makes him sick, but maybe the photos are only making it harder. The flight attendant interrupts his trance to offer him a drink. He orders a beer, looks back at his phone, and closes it without sending.

He sips his beer and stares out the window at the baggage truck getting loaded from a shoot while passengers file in. He pulls out his phone and texts Melanie. *On the plane. Home in a few hours. Everything okay?*

Melanie doesn't answer. The plane's nearly full now. He should probably shut his phone off and get some sleep. He stares at the dark screen while the flight attendant announces they'll be closing the door in a moment. In a flash, Joe clicks on his phone and sends all three photos in a single text.

No changing his mind now. He waits a moment, mired in self-inflicted consternation and mild regret. He imagines Sarah sitting at home with her husband, maybe watching TV together, when the text pops in. Ben – why does he have to have a name? – would notice Sarah looking at pictures, perhaps notice Sarah's reaction, and ask about them. How could he expose her like that? He can't text again. This has to be the end.

A message pops back from Sarah. *Have a safe flight.*

Joe smiles with relief, both to hear from her, and to know she wasn't too compromised by his message to respond. It will be okay. She will be okay.

Then one more message appears. *And...*

Joe studies the screen, contemplating the promise and the power of those three little letters, and those three tiny ellipses that follow. He gnaws on the tip of his thumb while he reads and rereads everything they say, before shutting down his phone. There won't be anything more.

Chapter Twenty

Running

Sarah hadn't thought she could get much lower than those first few months after Synergy closed. She was wrong.

Joe is gone. Gone from Seattle and from her life. And though he didn't mean to, he's taken everything he gave her with him. Joy, freedom, hope. She'd come to life for two glorious days with him, but when he left, he took that, too.

Then there's Ben. She loops round and round the painful truth. She cheated, and she feeds on her guilt like a feast. She could never have imagined doing what she did, no matter how bad things were between them. Still can't understand how she let it happen. Or why. Now the lies hang on her like a manacle, weighing down every step with bottomless shame.

And to make matters worse, she's lost her best friend – at least for the moment. She goes into the office for her regular Friday shift, but everything's different without Gabi. The office is grayer. The tasks more tedious. The cartons of cereal are already gone, as Gabi predicted, and still the walls close in. She'll have to muddle through the next two weeks all on her own. And even once Gabi returns, she can't tell her the truth. Ever. Gabi's the one person Sarah can tell absolutely everything, yet she will never be able to tell Gabi what might be the most important thing that's ever happened to her. A tiny fissure Sarah fears will fester and grow.

That's the price. It's all the price. For her foolishness. For her betrayal. And she might well be paying it the rest of her life. She can only hope it will get easier someday.

Yet, despite it all, Sarah can't bring herself to regret what happened. Those two days have become part of her, permanently embedded in her flesh, in her muscles and sinews, in the breath she takes and the blood pumping through her veins. She could no more wish them away than she could her bicep or kneecap. She could no more regret them than her heart or lungs. Those two days live on in her, and she would pay any price to protect them as a simple act of self-preservation. The pain is merely proof it was real.

When a reminder pops up on her phone that night, she cringes. She's volunteered for a fun run for diabetes the next day, but she's so not in the mood for either fun or running. A high-speed marathon session with her pantry sounds more appealing, but a commitment is a commitment. So she sets her alarm, crawls out of bed, and drags herself to the race check-in promptly at 6:30 as directed.

Plopped at the 3k checkpoint, Sarah muddles through the dreaded small talk with fellow volunteers. She hates having to justify her existence to fulltime working women and busy stay-at-home mothers, all of whom have more purpose and structure to their lives than she does. Men seldom think anything of it, maybe because they aren't really paying attention, but women definitely judge. Sarah meanders through her days in a way that bores even her, but feels positively shameful when spoken aloud to women mired in meetings, deadlines, and clients, or diapers, carpools, and homework.

And so the chit-chat at these things always gets her hackles up, and she wears her inferiority complex like a brightly colored fun run t-shirt. As the runners trickle in, however, the cheers grow louder and Sarah relaxes into the flow that soon becomes a flood. She joins in out of obligation, aware that claps and shout-outs are part of the job, but finds the good cheer contagious. Buoyed by the enthusiasm of those around her, she's no longer faking it.

Joe's never far away, of course. But since she's not in a position to give into her sadness, she instead imagines him by her side. She sees him laughing with other volunteers, making everyone feel special, high fiving runners who need an extra boost. She imagines him watching her and tries to be the person she was with him. Fully present, ready to laugh, excited for the success of others.

In the midst of all the lively chaos, she strikes up a conversation with a spikey pink-haired volunteer named Dana. A successful realtor who uses her edgy style to stand out in a crowded field, Dana lost her wife unexpectedly a year ago and has buried herself in work ever since. She's only starting to come out of her haze and reengage with real life over real estate now. This race is one of her first activities since she decided she was ready to have fun again, but like Sarah, Dana took comfort in movies for a long time after her loss. Dana holds out two tiny paper cups of water to passing runners, issues a loud hoot, then turns to Sarah, "Okay, who's your favorite actress? Go!"

Sarah claps and yells, "Let's gooo!" before pausing to think. "Emma Stone maybe? Or Hannah Waddingham?"

"Hannah Waddingham, yessss! Be still my heart!" Dana dramatically clutches her chest before grabbing more water cups. She hands them to more runners, then gestures with two fingers from her own eyes to Sarah's eyes and back again. Sympatico. "And favorite actor?"

At this, Sarah freezes. Normally, she wouldn't hesitate to say Joe without a second thought. Then when the other person said they didn't know him – because hardly anyone ever knows him by name – she'd proceed to cite his entire filmography, and failing that, announce gleefully, "I'll just have you over and show you."

That visit would never happen, of course, because no one else was ever as interested to see Joe, an actor they didn't know, as Sarah was to show him off, but the mere idea of introducing others to her favorite actor made her giddy. Normally. But now, the prospect of saying his name out loud at all feels like an existential threat. And admitting she likes him, even as an actor, nothing less than a portal to oblivion.

Sarah thrusts a cup of water into passing hands. "Probably Ryan Gosling, I guess."

"Ryan Gosling. Now there is a beautiful man."

Sarah dodges runners to pick up crushed cups. "Yeah? Ryan Gosling gets your motor running?"

"I'm a lesbian. I'm not dead," Dana laughs.

After a while, Sarah and Dana are reassigned to the end of the race to hand out power bars and bananas. They roam the crowd distributing snacks and congratulating folks on finishing, then wrap the day dancing to a steel drum band trying desperately to evoke a warm summer breeze despite the grey skies and sprinkles.

Against all odds, Sarah has a good day. She and Dana exchange numbers and agree to have lunch soon. It's no replacement for Gabi's 25 years of daily sustenance, but it's a relief not to feel quite so alone as she drives home.

***

When Sunday rolls around, Sarah shuffles her nieces into her car and heads for the movie theater. While the constant presence of Joe's absence still haunts her, and her guilt still pokes her like a cactus, it's hard to be too miserable with the girls. They spend the drive singing with the radio, a bittersweet reminder of Joe, then debating all the candy they want at the movies.

"I want M&Ms," nine-year-old Lexi announces.

"Milk Duds," Emma corrects.

"No, M&Ms," Lexi says.

"Skittles," Emma giggles.

Lexi rolls her eyes and reaches out to cover Emma's mouth, laughing. "I don't care what you get. I want M&Ms." Emma tugs at Lexi's hand, but Lexi won't budge until suddenly she jerks her hand away and screeches, "Ew, she licked me!" Both girls erupt in laughter as Lexi wipes her hand on Emma's shirt.

Sarah can't help but laugh, too, as she listens to the banter behind her. Her nieces are about the best medicine she can imagine at the moment.

"Sour Patch Kids!" Emma shouts.

"You're so gross," Lexi says as she crosses her arm and looks at Sarah in the rearview mirror. "Aunt Sarah, I hate to break the news, but your other niece is mentally unwell. She may need professional help."

"I'll take it under advisement," Sarah says with a chuckle. "But I like Sour Patch Kids, too."

Emma throws her hands in the air and yells, "Yes! Ha!"

Lexi looks at them both with exaggerated horror. "You're both hopeless."

***

Sarah texts Dana and sets-up lunch for Wednesday. She worries Dana will be scared off by her eagerness, but being alone with her thoughts is so much worse. To her delight, Dana jumps at Sarah's invitation, and before long, they're chatting like longtime besties. When they discover they're both dying to see the same chick flick, they make a plan to go the following Sunday, and Sarah leaves feeling, above all, grateful.

When she gets home, she texts Gabi, who's been sending daily photos and updates from her trip. *I think I made a friend.*

Gabi replies almost immediately with *How dare you!* and a gif of a woman clutching her pearls.

Sarah smiles. *A bird in the hand, baby!*

I've been gone less than a week and you've already replaced me?

Sarah shakes her head. *I wouldn't say "replaced"... Yet.* She follows this with three laughing sideways emojis, hits send, then adds, *Besides aren't you cheating on me at this very moment in Amsterdam?*

As her finger lifts from the send button, her words catch up with her. *Cheating.* Her stomach drops at the Freudian slip, her insides churning, but within moments Gabi brings her back with a series of sobbing emojis followed by the prayer hands, and finally, *So what's this bimbo's name?*

Sarah laughs, her well of gratitude filling for the second time today. Even from thousands of miles away, Gabi's constancy and humor always keep Sarah afloat.

***

Joe waves frantically at Nathan from the bleachers, a mini bullhorn in his hands. He has no plans to use it, of course, but he makes darn sure Nathan sees it. Nathan catches sight of Joe with the bullhorn and hangs his head in dismay, before giving his father a slow, stern "don't you dare" shake of his head.

Joe grins and laughs before pressing his lips firmly together and nodding enthusiastically at Nathan, the wordless dad equivalent of "Heck yeah, I'm gonna use it, buddy!" Nathan chuckles and returns to his stretching.

"I don't know why you torture him like that," Melanie says from the bench next to Joe, shielding her eyes with her hand.

Joe takes his seat and repositions his Dodgers cap to better block the sun. "He loves it." Joe smirks as he slides on his sunglasses.

The field and stands teem with activity. There are ten schools at the invitationals and everyone's ramping up for what's likely be a long day. Nathan's running in four events and Joe beams with pride. "Come on, Nate!" he belts, a guttural boom of a cheer.

"He's not even running until the third heat," Melanie huffs.

"Don't worry, I didn't use it all up on the first take. I can do this all day."

She rolls her eyes. "So, do you want the first shift or the second?"

For long meets, they switch off time in the stands between events, so they can get a break from the sun and go for lunch or snacks. What originated solely as a matter of practicality in deference to the wilting heat, which even in May could be dire in the Valley, the plan now offers the added benefit of limiting their time together.

The tension's so thick he could take a bite out of it. Ever since he told Mel he wanted to put in the last, small piece of financing for his film. He'd come so far he couldn't imagine stopping just short of the finish line. Especially when they have far more money in the bank than they've ever had. The young Melanie would have been all-in without hesitation, cheering him on with complete conviction that he could only succeed. But time and hardship have weathered both their spirits and their relationship. Today's Mel values security more than "a pipe dream," as she calls it.

A pipe dream?

"I'm flexible. Which would you prefer?" Joe says as amiably as possible.

Melanie heaves a sigh of exasperation. "I don't care, Joe. Just pick."

Joe internalizes the wince that nearly crosses his face, but lightly taps his chest where the ache is thrumming more loudly than usual. They used to feel like real partners in life. Now they're just partners in parenting – which is no small thing. It's more important than anything, really. Still, for years, Joe clung to the hope that if he could get his career on solid footing, he and Mel could get back on solid footing, too. But it seems even with genuine financial security now, it's never enough. *He's* never enough.

Except with Sarah. With Sarah he was enough just standing there.

Joe bites his lip and forces a smile. "Okay, I'll go first, after his 300 heat." He takes the early break as a courtesy, so Mel can take hers during the hotter midday hours, but if she notices, she doesn't acknowledge it.

"Fine," she says. "I'm going to get a drink. Want anything?"

Joe holds up his water bottle and shakes his head with a smile. He watches Melanie work her way down the bleachers and thinks about the Dodgers games they went to in the early days. How cute she was with her bright red ponytail poking out of her baseball cap and how much fun they had cheering and sharing beer and kettle corn. She's still beautiful, obviously. That much hasn't changed. But all the joy has gone out of her. At least when she's with Joe.

Sarah drifts into his mind again. He smiles at the thought of her hooting and cheering next to him, despite her complete lack of interest. And she'd laugh at the bullhorn. No doubt about it.

A text pops in from his agent Clark. *Call me when you're free. It's important.*

Joe takes a deep breath hoping it's an audition or offer for something good, but when Clark picks up, he dispenses with the small talk and gets to the point. "So, who is she, Joe?"

Joe chokes on the water he's drinking. He coughs it out, then milks it a moment longer steadying himself for whatever this conversation is about to be. This is the last thing he needs right now. "Who is who?" he finally says.

"The woman in the picture."

Fuck.

"What picture? Where?" Terror strikes. Since when are there paparazzi in Seattle? And since when is he paparazzi worthy anyway? He gets recognized so infrequently. In any case, he and Sarah hadn't done anything compromising in public, right? Right?

Well, they did hold hands at the end of the night, walking to the car. And there was the hotel lobby. Security footage maybe? Footage of Joe walking Sarah to the elevators would be damaging enough. Did the desk clerk give him away? Did the desk clerk even know who he was? Didn't seem like it. He holds his breath awaiting Clark's explanation.

"On Instagram."

Joe exhales. Not paparazzi then. Not TMZ. Okay, that's good news. Maybe whatever it is hasn't spread too far yet. "I didn't post anything on Instagram," he says.

"Of course, you didn't. Somebody tagged you. Didn't you see it?"

"Clark, you pay much closer attention to my socials than I do, I can assure you."

"Well, go check your mentions and tell me who it is. We need to get ahead of this."

"Ahead of what exactly?" Joe pulls up the app and clicks to his profile, praying there will be an innocent explanation. Praying it's anyone but Sarah. He meets people all the time. It could be literally anyone. He clicks to his mentions and there it is. There she is. Sarah.

It's not so bad actually. They were at lunch at the Armory. Joe's leaning in and laughing, but all you can see of Sarah is her back and blonde waves. The caption reads: "Ahhhhhhh, #garrettbarnes in Seattle!!!!!!!!! I might be dying. Actually I think I'm already DEAD! Save me Doc Hope #riversrun #dochope #zaddy #joeparker @thejrparker"

"Find it?" Clark says.

"Yeah."

"And?"

"It's nothing." Joe steels himself. Lying about Sarah is the absolute last thing he wants to do. He'd rather be shouting about her from the rooftops. "She's just the woman who showed me around town and helped me find locations."

"Does this woman have a name?"

Joe closes his eyes, swaying into her name, summoning the courage to speak it out loud. Her name. Here. Now. In his world. "Sarah."

"Looks like you were having a good time with Sarah."

Joe pinches the bridge of his nose as he says, "Sure, she was very nice. She really got me out of a bind."

"Just be careful she doesn't get you into a bind."

"What's that supposed to mean?"

"You look happy is all."

He does look happy. Really fucking happy. And he'd only just met her then. Joe resists the temptation to respond to Clark's implication, that seeing Joe happy is somehow noteworthy. "There's nothing to this photo. We were just having lunch."

Clark pauses, then says, "Well, that's good to hear. Because if there were anything to this photo, it could be a problem. You can't afford for this movie to get tainted with scandal, buddy. Can't spook the investors or it might be over before it's begun."

Joe grits his teeth and replies, "There's no scandal. There will be no scandal."

"Great. I knew you wouldn't do anything stupid. But you might consider untagging yourself anyway. Optics, you know."

"Yeah, optics," Joe says miserably.

After he hangs up, he looks at his tag options on the photo. "Remove me from post" or "Hide from my profile." There's nothing wrong with this picture. He's just having lunch. God forbid he look amused while eating. Really, there are only two people in the world who would ever question who the woman in the photo is. One has already asked. If he removes it, maybe the other one never will. Then again, what if she's already seen it? If Joe removes it after Mel's seen it, does that look more suspicious?

Joe thinks of Sarah. He looks at the photo, at her back, at her golden halo as her hair catches the sun from the skylight. He considers removing it, one of very few pieces of photographic evidence from their time together. Well, he has loads of pictures. But not of them together. He leaves the photo.

"Shit," he grumbles. He needs to shake this off. Fast. It's time to go to church.

When his kids were sick, when his shows failed, when he nearly lost both his house and his hope, Pastor Ted has always gotten him through it. If only he weren't headed to Georgia to play Jessica Chastain's soon-to-be-dead husband, gruesomely killed by a mysterious bacteria at the end of Act One. Church will have to wait.

***

Joe's on Zoom with his director Celeste and locations manager Luke, reviewing the photos Joe uploaded before he left home. Joe was careful to scrub Sarah from the photos before he uploaded them. And ten days later, immersed as he's been in a rigorous, lively shoot, he's made his best effort to scrub her from his mind, too. But as he watches Luke click through the images onscreen, it all rushes back.

The Monorail. The labyrinth. The music museum. The selfies at Kerry Park. The troll photo is a tough one, coming as it does, right after the selfies he knows he removed. Their absence leaving a fingerprint only he can see. And also because Sarah took the picture of him on the troll's shoulder, inserting herself invisibly, but irrevocably into the photo. Then again, it turns out she's in all the photos.

Joe discusses each location calmly and professionally, betraying no emotional attachment to the locations, but he delights at how pleased Luke is with what they found. They keep clicking. The record stores. The Wheel. The docks. The narrow path through the woods. He catches his breath at that one, remembering how hard Sarah tried to be brave, squeezing all her emotions so tightly they leaked out involuntarily from her eyes while she thrust her chin forward to prove she was fine. A parade of green and blue and perfect lakeside vistas. Each sandwiched in his mind by the music they shared along the way.

And the crows. After all the pictures he took, Joe was shortsighted at the end. Too caught up in the moment, he only shot one video of the crows – the one that ends with him brushing Sarah's goosebumps with his fingertips. He wisely edited the end, but kept the first glimpse of Sarah as he panned to get the full sweep of the crows' entrance. Now, as Luke hits play and the camera swings around to Sarah grinning and shouting with glee, it's Joe who gets the goosebumps.

Chapter Twenty-One

Moving Forward

Sarah sets her laptop decisively on the kitchen island and flips it open. This is it. Today she will look for a job. And properly, too. No more half-assing it. She pours herself an iced tea, digs out a pen and notepad, and climbs onto the stool.

She's still reeling from everything that happened, of course, but at least the dust has settled. Ben's unprecedented interest in the movie people passed as quickly as it came. Sarah breathes a literal sigh of relief each time he breezes through with a quick, absentminded peck on the cheek before disappearing into his laptop, cell, or bathroom. At least the lying is over. And Gabi has come home, blissfully occupied with tales of foreign lands and pictures galore, Sarah's celebrity run-in long forgotten. No questions will be asked, thank goodness. The whole thing now safely packed away.

Of course, Sarah can't pack her emotions away quite so easily. But gradually, she substitutes sweetness for sadness until her joy at Joe's memory far outweighs her grief. Joe drifts in and out of her days like a wonderful dream she's woken from and tried to recapture by going back to sleep, with no luck. A dream she can't forget and knows she can't get back. But with the benefit of time and distance, it feels safer. Less an existential threat, more an idyll now lost.

Meanwhile, she continues to act as if she's the person she was with Joe. Fake it 'til you make it, dammit. So it's officially time to get her shit together. She starts by reviewing her materials. They're not bad, but she hasn't really touched them since her half-hearted efforts just after Synergy, so she spends two full hours punching them up for her new, improved job searching extravaganza.

She makes a list of her skills – she must have some, right? – and her areas of expertise. It's all harder than she expects, digging into her intentionally obfuscated memory banks and talking herself up, but she pushes through. No pain, no gain, they say. If that's true, then she hopes the corollary is true as well. She's had plenty of pain, so now does she get the gain?

Once she's finished making herself look as dazzling on paper as she thinks she once might have actually been in person, she logs into three different job sites and transfers her updates across all of them. She surfs through actual job posts for a while. Nothing's a fit at the moment, but she's undeterred. On the job notifications page, she sets herself a series of keyword alerts. Operations. Management. Manager. Logistics. Marketing. Director. Chief Operating Officer. C-Level. Executive.

There, now she doesn't have to find the job. The job will come to her. She's on fire. Maybe she'll even reboot her LinkedIn account. That's what professionals do, right?

Little by little, Sarah realizes she's inching her way toward a real, pre-meltdown normal. At last. She can't see it yet, but she feels it pressing in around the edges of her hazy world, as if the mists might actually lift one day and reveal land that's been there all along, waiting for her.

She reviews her afternoon's work and sits up straight with approval. She's proud of herself. But also drained. Being hopeful is positively exhausting. Perhaps she's had enough for the moment. And that's okay. This is an excellent start.

A week later, and only three short days after she applied, Sarah receives an email scheduling a phone screening call. It's only the second job she's applied for since her newfound determination kicked in. This is encouraging! The HR person told her it would just be a short conversation to address some basics, so it should be easy enough. Sarah readies herself to sound chipper and awaits the call.

When the screen lights up with an unknown number at the appointed hour, she takes a quick sip of water, a big gulp of air, and picks up. The woman somehow manages a surprising mix of friendly and curt at the same time. She peppers Sarah with a quick array of very straightforward questions about her availability, her comfort with the expected work schedule and setting, and her experience with social media. Sarah admits her social media skills are limited, but that's not a primary function of the job, so she doesn't panic. But the next question does send her into a panic.

"So, tell me about the break you've taken since your last job."

Every ounce of blood in Sarah's body drains instantly from her brain into her extremities where it does her absolutely no good. She can't think of a single good answer to this question, despite the fact that she knew it was coming. After two years of relative unemployment, it's the single most predictable question possible, and yet, she's not ready. Her words tumble out in an unfortunate mess. "Well, I, uh... that's a... it's been an interesting couple of years, you see... when I left— well, I didn't exactly leave. You see, the company was sold and I... I mean, I did do some work. I helped my friend at her job..."

The words continue in an excruciating stream of humiliation for an interminable three minutes more. When Sarah hangs up, she's more confident than ever – that she won't be getting another call from them.

***

After two weeks filming in Georgia, followed by a week of family and friends for Avery's graduation, Joe's left alone at last with his thoughts. Sarah looms larger than ever. Two days. That's all it took to feel more connected to Sarah than anyone he's ever met. Two days to quell the ache he'd felt for as long as he could remember. It was Fate. Or God. Or something. That's the only thing that can explain it. How can he just walk away?

Locations manager Luke reschedules his scouting trip for the following week, a few days before Joe heads to a glacier in Norway to rejoin the on-location phase two of the Jessica Chastain shoot. He should stay home, study his lines, and prep. But the temptation to join Luke in Seattle is enormous. He needs guidance.

That Sunday, he walks into church determined, preparing himself for whatever Pastor Ted has in store. Because whatever Joe needs to hear, whether he knows it or not, Pastor Ted will deliver. There's no crevice too deep he can't climb out, no despair too great to find hope, no moral conflict for which he can't find clarity with the right message from Pastor Ted.

He holds his breath for the inevitable, yet somehow uplifting sermon on sin or faithfulness or duty. Something to help him make peace with settling back into his old life and never seeing Sarah again. But that's not what he gets.

Instead Pastor Ted preaches on appreciation for all of God's gifts, on the importance of embracing that which God puts before you because if it has come to you, then surely it is God's intention for you. He pauses, looks down at the scripture at his fingertips, then looks back up to the congregation and continues, "Thessalonians 5:18 tells us 'give thanks in all circumstances; for this is God's will for you in Christ Jesus.' And give thanks we must. No matter the circumstances. Because giving thanks when everything's good is easy, right? 'I've got a healthy family and a good job and a big steak for dinner and I am grateful!' Sure, we can all give thanks for the easy stuff. The obvious stuff.

"But when it's hard, when it's complicated, messy, and maybe painful, when there's pain mixed with the joy, it gets tougher. Less clear. But that's when we have to double down and know that if God has put this in our path, it is a gift and we must embrace it with gratitude. For *this is God's will* for you...."

Joe bows his head and prays with the congregation at the end of the lesson, then adds a "thank you" before he says "Amen." On his way out, he texts Luke, *I'm in.*

Chapter Twenty-Two

The Return

SARAH AND GABI TAP on their respective computers, cartons of diapers forming an almost impassable wall around them.

"Who was processing gifts last?" Sarah asks, exasperated.

"Michelle."

"These donor files are a mess. Someone should train her properly."

"You mean you?" Gabi raises a brow pointedly, but keeps working.

"I'm a volunteer. I shouldn't be training people."

Gabi pouts at Sarah. "But you're the only one who knows how to do it right."

Sarah relents. "Fine, I'll set something up with her."

Gabi smiles with triumph as a knock jolts their attention to the door. Joe walks in and Sarah freezes. Gabi's eyes light up at the handsome stranger. "Hi, can I help you?" she chirps.

"Yes, hello. I was actually looking for Sarah here." Joe glances a split second at Gabi as a courtesy, but rivets instantly back to Sarah, a slow smile creeping onto her face.

Gabi's jaw drops as her head swivels to Sarah who's fallen silent with a dumb, shocked grin. Joe responds with his own dumb grin. The room grows several suns brighter from their collective shine.

"Hi," Sarah says.

"Hi," Joe replies.

The wordless smiles continue until Sarah recovers herself. Slightly. "You're here."

"I'm here."

Sarah stares in stunned silence half a beat too long. Gabi's eyes dart back and forth, absorbing everything, including the ring on Joe's finger.

"Don't I get a hug?" Joe says, arms out.

"Of course!" Sarah pops up. "Sorry."

Gabi watches, fascinated, as Sarah and Joe sink into each other like home. For several beats too long. Sarah self-consciously pulls away, aware of Gabi's scrutiny. Gabi sticks out her hand and breaks the tension, "Hi, I'm Gabi."

"Sorry, yes." Sarah shakes her head, trying to catch her breath. "Gabi, this is Joe. Joe, this is Gabi, my best friend."

"And her boss," Gabi says.

"You're not my boss."

"You report to me, so I'm your boss."

"I'm a volunteer, so I don't have a boss."

Gabi turns to Joe. "You just can't get good help these days."

Joe chuckles as Sarah steps back to the protection of her desk. The room falls uncomfortably quiet. Sarah speaks first. "So, what are you doing here?"

"Yes, Joe, what are you doing here?" Gabi echoes.

"Well, I'm in town for some meetings, and I thought I'd surprise you and say hello."

"Well, hello," Sarah says.

"Hi," Joe repeats.

"That's so nice of you, Joe," Gabi chimes in, nodding pointedly at Sarah. "Wasn't that nice of him, Sarah? To stop in and surprise you? While he's in town?"

Sarah ignores Gabi's rambling insinuations.

"I wondered if maybe we could get dinner," Joe says. He glances at Gabi before continuing. "And catch up a bit?"

"Um..." She considers Gabi, who is studying every moment with rapt attention. "Sure, yeah. I still have some work to do. Maybe another half hour? I hate to make you wait."

"I don't mind," Joe says.

"He doesn't mind," Gabi offers helpfully with a sickening smile.

"And I'll just need to let Ben know," Sarah adds.

"Of course." Joe pauses, remembers their audience, and forces himself to ask, "How is he?"

"He's good. Yeah. Busy as always."

Gabi tips her head inquisitively. "Oh, you know Ben?"

Sarah cuts her off. "Gabi, didn't you want to go check that delivery that came in today?"

"I already did it," Gabi snaps.

"No, you didn't," Sarah snaps back.

"Yes. I did." Gabi nods her head emphatically. "All done. I'm good," she says with a smile pointed enough to poke out eyes.

Sarah sighs and turns back to Joe. "Well, I guess I better finish up."

"Sure, I'll let you work. I'll just wait out there?" He aims his thumb over his shoulder.

"There's a great bookstore down the block to the left," Sarah says.

"Perfect. I'll go keep myself busy awhile and be back in about half an hour."

"Great," Sarah replies.

"Great," Joe says.

"Great," Gabi joins in.

Joe heads for the door. "Gabi, it was very nice to meet you." He flashes his sunshine smile at her.

"It was very nice to meet you, Joe," she says with too much emphasis on the word *you*.

As he walks out, Gabi's jaw drops again. She stares at Sarah who avoids her gaze and dives back onto her computer. Gabi checks to be sure Joe's gone, then closes the door.

"What was that?" Gabi demands.

Sarah flushes. "What was what?"

"What do mean, what was what? What was *that*? *Who* was *that*?"

"That was Joe," Sarah says, pounding at her keyboard. "I told you about him. I showed him around town, remember?"

"Wait, that was your movie star?"

"He's not a movie star. He's just an actor," Sarah says before adding emphatically, "And he's not mine."

"Oh my God, he's gorgeous! And that voice! Did you hear that voice?"

"I've heard the voice," Sarah snips, her frustration growing. She thought she'd dodged this bullet, but now it's made a full rotation of the earth and circled back to take another shot. She has to shut this down. Now. Sarah musters what she hopes is an even keel of mild disinterest and goes on. "You've seen him before. We've watched him together."

"Yeah, but you know I'm no good with actors. I had no idea who you were talking about."

"Well, now you do." She tries to dig back into her work and end the conversation.

"So?" Gabi prods.

"So what?" Sarah stares hard at her monitor, seeing nothing.

"What just happened here?" Gabi knocks on Sarah's desk to make her look up.

This is spinning out already and she hasn't even said anything. "Nothing. I don't know what you mean. I told you about it."

Gabi contorts her face into an exaggerated mask of incredulity. "So, you told me the whole story?"

"More or less."

"Uh-huh. Okay," Gabi says. "Then what was with the fuck vibes?"

"The what? You're crazy," Sarah laughs the laugh of the wrongly accused.

"Those were serious fuck vibes."

"You're delusional."

"Maybe *you're* delusional because there were mad fuck vibes up in here."

Sarah returns to her monitor. "I have to get my work done."

Gabi reaches across the desk and pushes the laptop closed. "Don't think you're changing the subject."

"The imaginary subject you just made up?"

"Okay, if nothing's going on, then fine," Gabi says. "But those were the fuckiest fuck vibes I've ever seen. So if nothing's happened yet, then he definitely wants it to."

"No!"

"Sarah, he came here to surprise you. He didn't just text. He didn't just email. He didn't even call. He showed up. In person. He remembered where you work – that's first of all – and he drove his fine ass all the way *to a fucking foodbank in Renton*. Just to surprise you. That's thirsty as hell. He definitely wants to fuck you."

Sarah winces and drops her eyes, afraid Gabi will know everything from one millisecond of direct eye contact.

"What's going on?"

Sarah stares down at her knees, suddenly fascinated by the striations of her jeans. She scratches at the ridged texture of the denim with her fingernail as Gabi's eyes burrow into the top of her head. "Okay, fine. Yes, something happened."

"I knew it. You fucked him!"

"Not exactly."

"What do you mean, not exactly?"

"I mean, it didn't feel like fucking," Sarah says, the word feeling dirty and wrong in her mouth in this context. "It felt like... more than that."

"More than fucking?" Gabi stares at Sarah, head cocked at an incredulous, demanding angle, mouth open in breathless anticipation.

"It kind of felt like..." Sarah searches the void for words that won't sound trite and ridiculous. "I don't want to say it." Sarah collapses into the words as she says them, knowing nothing will stop the next words now.

"What?"

Sarah cringes. "Making love," she confesses, then buries her face in her hands.

Gabi shakes her head in disbelief. "Oh, sis. You're in serious trouble."

Sarah drops her elbows to her knees, face still covered. "I know. I can't believe I let this happen."

"I can't either."

"This is all your fault!"

"My fault?"

"If you knew how to get your ass to the airport on time, none of this would have happened."

Gabi nods. "That's fair, actually."

Sarah hangs her head again. "Do you hate me? After everything you went through with Max?"

"Please."

"Do you think I'm a terrible person?"

"Babe, you're probably the best person I know." Gabi pauses a moment, then lightly sings her words. "Maybe you shouldn't have done it... but–"

"Maybe?"

"But anyone would have trouble saying no to that dude. I mean, holy fuck!"

"And he's such a good guy, too, Gab." Now the secret is out, Sarah's dying to gush. The dam has broken. There may be untold wreckage ahead, but the torrent will flow. "He's lovely and kind and fun. I've never had so much fun. And he listens. He *really* listens."

"Yeah, he's a gem. Except for the part where he cheated on his wife."

Sarah flinches at Gabi's wounds gaping anew. This is everything she feared. But Sarah's as guilty as Joe and would gladly lay herself across the sacrificial altar in defense of his character. "I cheated, too."

"Touché."

"If you blame him, blame me. But neither of us planned it. It just happened. And it was... I don't even know how to describe it."

Gabi holds Sarah's gaze. "Try."

"It was like it was meant to be," Sarah confesses, dismayed to speak the fantasy into reality. "I felt so connected to him, like nothing I've ever felt before. And he made me feel so safe, and it just felt..."

"What?"

"Perfect."

"Perfect..." Gabi expels a deep breath as she absorbs. "Crikey!"

"What do I do?"

Gabi studies Sarah's face, painted with desperation, before deciding on the only course of action. "Well, you start by having dinner with him."

"What!"

"I mean, when 'perfect' walks in the door, you don't say no to dinner, right?" Gabi's matter-of-fact logic makes the proclamation seem almost sound.

"I can't believe you, of all people, are telling me to go out with him. What about Ben?"

"I'm not telling you to sleep with him. It's just dinner."

"Seriously? After everything Max put you through?"

Gabi shudders at another mention of her ex. "Max was a giant slut screwing every woman in town and completely unrepentant. But you've never slept around and you've certainly never cheated. Whatever you're feeling, it's obviously real or you wouldn't be this conflicted."

"But what about Ben?" Sarah repeats.

"Jeez, I don't know. This is hurting my brain."

"He wasn't supposed to come back. It was supposed to be over," Sarah says, as much to herself as to Gabi.

"But he did come back. And he's going to walk back in that door soon. So you have a decision to make." They silently ponder as the wall clock ticks loudly through a half rotation. Finally, Gabi sits up straight, a determined look in her eye, decision made. "Okay, clearly the right answer is to send him away, go home to Ben, and put this whole thing in the past."

"Right. You're right," Sarah says. "I should put on my big girl pants and send him away." She nods vigorously, working hard to convince herself.

"On the other hand..."

"On the other hand?" Sarah hangs on Gabi's every word, desperate for both absolution and permission.

"I don't want to talk you into something you'll regret." Gabi doles out her words slowly, aware of their weight. "And I don't want to see either you or Ben hurt. You know I love you both."

"God, I would never want to hurt Ben."

"But when push comes to shove, *you're* my ride-or-die. Not Ben." Gabi reaches for Sarah's hand across the desk. "And what if *not* going is the thing you'll regret? Perfect doesn't come along very often."

"No kidding."

"And he's only here for a minute, right? It's not like this is something that can go on and on, right?"

"Right," Sarah agrees, sitting up straight.

"And if I'm being honest, him showing up here like this says volumes about how he feels about you. 'Cuz that dude could legit have anyone."

"I'm aware."

"And if all he wanted was a booty call, he would have just texted."

"A booty call, please!" Sarah laughs at the absurdity. She hasn't been anybody's booty call since... well, never.

"That's my point. He's clearly got feelings for you. I saw the way he looked at you."

Sarah's heart flutters hopefully. "Really?"

"Big time," Gabi says before rubbing her own face. This is all very personal now. "Okay, I think you should go."

"You do?" Sarah's face washes over in blissful terror.

"It's a fucked up situation, I'm not gonna lie." Gabi stares at Sarah a moment longer. "But life only gives us so many chances. And almost none of them are perfect. At least, I haven't had perfect yet. Not even for a night. So when something perfect comes along, I think you owe it to yourself to find out what it is."

"But if this were actually perfect, neither of us would be married."

Gabi frowns. "You don't always get to choose where or how love comes into your life."

Sarah startles at the word. "Who said anything about love?"

Gabi offers a motherly smile. "You did, babydoll. You just didn't know it." Gabi's words hit Sarah's heart like a freight train. "Now you have to decide what to do about it."

CHAPTER TWENTY-THREE

JUST DINNER

ON THE DRIVE TO dinner, they speak little, each of them attempting to triangulate the correct position. Joe's all in, of course. He's known it from the moment Pastor Ted's sermon ended. He still has things to figure out, like where it's going and how to reconcile with the moral complexity of it all. How something so wrong can also be absolutely right. But he knows without a shred of doubt this is where he's meant to be right now. He's more certain of it than anything in his entire life. *For this is God's will for you.*

He's sprung himself on Sarah, however, and she needs time. That much is clear as he watches a physiological process in action. Warm, gooey Sarah – stunned, but delighted at his arrival – ices over before his eyes into a hard, crystallized avatar who can withstand any assault to come. When he picked her up, he sensed her ambivalence – heartfelt joy laced with abject terror – and that she was debating which way the scales would tip. In the space of a few minutes, she settles on her position and it isn't the one he hoped for. He understands Sarah too well to be surprised, though. He's witnessed firsthand how fear is Sarah's default setting – until she finds the courage to push through it. She'll get there.

At the restaurant, faux candlelight from the wall of electric tea lights flickering next to their table casts a warm glow over Joe as he hands the menu back to the waitress. "There," he says with a triumphant smile. "Now

I'll be the one with garlic breath." Sarah ignores the reference to their past indiscretion.

Joe smiles as he watches her fiddle with her water glass, wiping the condensation away and gulping it like a castaway. Her nerves dance in every twitch and eye dart as she avoids his gaze. He fights the urge to grab her hand, to calm her with a gentle squeeze. She's not ready for that. She needs to find her own way to Joe. So, he waits for her. He'll wait forever if he has to.

"How's the film going?" Sarah says.

Joe lights up. "Great! Pre-production is going well and principle photography starts in just over a month." He's almost giddy, eyes bright with anticipation. "It's finally happening."

"I'm happy for you." Sarah fights to hold the wall, but Joe's joy breaches her defenses and floods her senses. She fiddles with her napkin a moment as she steels herself again and searches for safe topics.

"It's really good to see you."

She smooths her ponytail, realizing she probably looks like exactly what she is, someone who spent the afternoon at a foodbank. "Oh God, I must look awful."

"You look perfect."

She presses her lips together in a tense smile, then grabs a sour-dough roll. "Oh my gosh, it's still warm." She shreds the roll and makes a whole production out of buttering half a dozen tiny pieces before finally stuffing one in her mouth.

Joe plops his elbow on the table, chin resting on his thumb while his fingers curl against his lips, stifling a laugh. "Are you done?"

"I'm not allowed to eat a roll?"

"Of course you are."

Sarah hurls the piece in her hand onto the plate, unable to control her frenetic energy any longer. "What are you doing here, Joe?" A quiet fury laces through her words.

And there it is. The first tumbler in her lock has clicked and Sarah's alarm sounds its first siren.

"What do you think I'm doing here, Sarah? I wanted to see you."

Another tumbler clicks into place. "So the alleged meetings? Was that bullshit?"

"Ouch!' Joe raises his hands in surrender. "No, they're real meetings. I've got back-to-back meetings and a site visit all afternoon tomorrow. And the rest of the team is doing more site visits before and after. But I've already seen those locations, so..."

"You came all this way for an afternoon of meetings?" Anger drips from her voice, coating over the fear, her need to lash out growing. Because anger is so much safer than vulnerability. "You could have Zoomed in and saved yourself a lot of time and money."

Joe leans in and forces her to look him in the eye. "No, I came all this way to see you. The meetings were just an excuse." Click. Tumbler number three.

Sarah's a ticking bomb now. A human defense system whose final safeguard is self-destruct mode. And the explosion won't be pretty. "So, how's your family? How's your wife?" she asks. And there's the blast.

Joe flinches, but sits back in his chair, unwilling to take her bait. "Don't do that," he says softly.

"Don't do what?"

"Don't make this about them."

He's so calm it angers Sarah even more. "It is about them. How is this not about them? And about Ben?"

Joe winces at Ben's name, but doesn't falter. "Whatever this is – and I admit I don't know what that is – but it's just between you and me. I'm not saying they don't matter. Of course they do. But right now, Sarah, I swear to God, all I want is to be with you."

She bristles. Why does he say things like that? How is she supposed to keep her head when this man – with that face and those hands and that voice – sits across from her and says things like that?

"So this is like a booty call or something?" Forty-five minutes ago, Sarah scoffed at Gabi for suggesting such a thing. Now she's hurling it like a grenade at Joe.

His face drops. "Are you kidding? How can you look me in the eye and say that? You know that's not what this is."

"I don't know anything. How would I know?"

"Because you were there with me that night. I felt you," he says. "Not the Fort Knox Sarah sitting across from me right now. But the real you."

"This is the real me. It ain't pretty, but it's as real as it gets." Her words reveal the truth Joe already knows. He may be taking the brunt of her anger in the moment, but she's saving plenty for herself as well.

Joe breathes in Sarah's sadness slowly. He lets it diffuse through his system and calmly exhales compassion. "You can't scare me off. I'm not going anywhere. But you can go home anytime. If that's what you want. I'll understand." He watches her teetering on a knife-edge, terrified to fall in either direction. "*Is* that what you want?" She stares at the table and says nothing. "Or do you want to be here with me?" Sarah raises her eyes to face him and he knows. Joe smiles and Sarah distracts herself with another piece of her roll. "Whatever this is, it's about you... and me... and no one else."

"I don't think it works like that. It can't just be you and me."

"Why not?" he asks quietly.

"Because it's not just you and me."

Joe gestures at the room as he says, "I don't see anyone else here."

"We're literally surrounded by people."

"You're all I see."

"This is pointless." She leans back and folds her arms across her chest.

"Boy, you're a lot of work!"

"So sorry!" She huffs the words out angrily. "What, did you think I would just fall into your arms?"

"Well, I hoped."

"Well, I'm not that easy."

"Well, I see that!"

She laughs despite herself. It's the crack in the armor Joe's been seeking. "Aren't you at all happy to see me? Because you sure seemed happy when I first came in."

"You caught me off guard is all," she says. "That was before I had a chance to think. Or gird my loins."

He knows the real Sarah is in there somewhere, but reaching her behind all her fortifications is exhausting. "Do your loins really need girding against me?"

"Oh, they are well girded. Don't you worry."

"Well, thank God for that! Sarah, look—"

The waitress interrupts. "Crispy fried Brussel sprouts with bacon and a balsamic reduction. Enjoy."

Sarah jumps at the distraction. "Ooh, don't these look good!"

"I'm not giving up," Joe says as the waitress walks away.

"Eat your Brussel sprouts."

***

Throughout dinner, they talk around the subject. Sarah actively avoids it while Joe follows her lead. She tells him about the race and her "New Friend Dana" (her now official nickname) and that they've finally posted the vacant position at the foodbank.

He tells her about the movie he's been filming and how he's headed to Norway to rejoin the shoot in a couple of days. He mentions Avery's graduation and how proud he is of her, but doesn't linger on the topic. He's in the middle of an anecdote about a costar flubbing her lines because someone (no one would confess) farted, when Sarah bursts in midstream.

"I can't do this, Joe."

"Well, fart humor's not for everyone."

"What's the point?" she says. "What exactly is this supposed to be?"

Joe squeezes his mouth into a pursed lip smile of frustration. "You know, for such a smart woman, you can be incredibly stupid sometimes."

"Interesting seduction technique."

"I'm not trying to seduce you, Sarah. Don't cast me in the role of your corruptor. I'm not a villain in this story."

"Of course, you're not a villain," she says, exhaling her own frustration. It's all going horribly wrong, but she can't stop herself. She can't stop fighting, despite the fact that all she wants to do is kiss him. *Because* all she wants to do is kiss him.

"Do you really want me to leave you alone?" he says. "Because if that's what you want, I'll do it. But you're going to have to say it."

She says nothing.

"Sarah, do you want me to leave you alone?"

Sarah floats above her body, watching a tragedy unfold. She sees herself peering into Joe's sapphire eyes and her heart breaks at how vulnerable he is before her. At how sad he seems. But most of all, at the thought of never seeing him again. She can't bear that. She slips back into her body just in time to feel that selfsame heart pounding through her chest as she shakes her head "no."

His face alights with hope. "Then come with me! Be with me tonight."

"There's no way. I can't."

"Then meet me tomorrow. I have the whole morning free."

"I don't know."

Joe reaches across the table and squeezes her hand. "Don't you?"

She looks into his pleading eyes, but can't bring herself to say yes. Her already immeasurable pit of guilt growing by the minute, now pouring more into the reservoir from a new source, the River Joe. There's no right answer. Only wrong answers. How did she let herself get into this mess?

Sarah slowly pulls her hand back and frowns with a silent shake of her head. Joe has lost her. He slumps back and waves for the check.

***

They drive in silence back to his car. She pulls in and they sit, unwilling to say goodnight, unable to say anything else.

"I'll try," Sarah says at last, barely squeaking out the words.

A tentative smile creeps onto Joe's face. "You'll try or you'll do it?"

"I'll try." It's the best she can do right now.

"What time?"

"I could probably get there seven-thirty, maybe eight."

"I'll see you at seven-thirty," he says.

Sarah squeezes her eyes tight in denial of what's happening.

"This is a good thing," he says. When she opens her eyes, he looks the happiest he's looked since the moment he walked into the office that afternoon. He repeats, "It's a good thing."

Joe leans in to give Sarah a kiss goodnight. She flinches and pulls back, avoiding his eyes. All night she's been a terrified stray dog trapped in a well of her own despair, snarling defensively at the hand that would set her free, if only she would allow it. Now, as he draws close, the snarls have stopped at last, but she's still trembling with fear and maybe, just maybe, the tiniest glimmer of hope.

He leans in gently, an inch closer, waiting for her to relax. Waiting for her to trust him. Waiting for her.

Her body's still tense, back rigid, hands clenched around the steering wheel, but she summons the courage to catch his eyes. And there, she sees... no, she won't name it. But she holds his gaze.

He gives her the slightest nod, then places a warm, slow, chaste kiss on her cheek. "Goodnight, Sarah," he nearly whispers. "I'll see you in the morning."

CHAPTER TWENTY-FOUR

FLING

JOE PACES THE ROOM straightening and fidgeting. An early morning swim did nothing to burn off his nervous energy. A well-worn track in the carpet from the bed to the sofa to the bathroom and back again charts his anxiety as he waits.

Last night Joe was gifted the patience of a saint to sit with Sarah and be the calm in her storm until she could expend every ounce of her fury and fear – and with her whirlwind exhausted at last, come to rest next to him. God granted him exactly what he needed to be exactly what she needed.

But today, his patience spent, he's near bursting with excitement. She said yes, she would come to him. Well, almost. He's both sure she will come and terrified she won't. And the inner battle of these warring factions causes such desperate friction that he must keep moving or die.

It's 7:30. No Sarah.

7:31. No Sarah.

7:32. Joe forces himself to take a seat at the desk because he's driving himself crazy.

7:33. He bounces back up. If madness is the price, he'll pay it.

At 7:34, she knocks. His heart skips a beat before picking up a double-time rhythm as he reaches for the door. But the moment he sees Sarah, a calm washes over him so peaceful he sinks into it like a cloud of cotton.

They match smile for smile. Hers shy. His effusive. His nose twitches an involuntary crinkle of delight. "You came."

"I came."

"Come in. Can I get you something? I have orange juice and coffee." He points to a room service tray with two settings. Sarah shakes her head. "Or if you're hungry, I can order food."

"No. Thank you."

Joe shrugs, desperate to make her comfortable. Sarah gazes around the room, awash in shades of golden tan with gray curtains, the only pop of color the red-orange leather desk chair. "Nice room," she says matter-of-factly.

"Little smaller than the last one. Still has a couch, though." He gestures to the plush brown sofa by the window. Their previous encounter on a couch flashes through his mind while she blushes more brightly than the desk chair. He shouldn't have said that. He backpedals with a grin. "So... do you want to sit at all? Or shall we make this a standing visit?" Joe tracks her line of sight as Sarah scans the room assessing her seating options. Couch? Bed? Desk chair? Finally, she settles on the arm chair adjacent to the sofa. Joe sits on the couch near her and leans in. "Any problems finding the place?"

"Nope. Easy-peasy."

They're back to small talk? She comments that it's a nice day for the team to visit the locations. Sunny and warm. He replies it's a good thing because she did promise him sun in the summertime. *Are they really going to talk about the weather?* She says they got lucky coming when they did because there are no guarantees in June. But by July, they should be golden. He says he's holding her to that.

She launches into a story about a sudden downpour a couple weeks ago as they were unloading all these boxes in a delivery at the foodbank. And it rained so hard so fast that a bunch of boxes got soaked through and food spilled everywhere and some of it was ruined and not only that, but Gabi's shirt got soaked and super see-through and she totally freaked and luckily Sarah had a sweater in the office, which she didn't need anymore because it's obviously warm now, but she hadn't taken it home yet, so she was able to give it to Gabi and... and... and...

She's rambling, but she can't stop. Normally a sea of calm by nature, Joe's own panic creeps in. Their time together is precious. He doesn't want to waste a moment of it. At the same time, he's enamored of every nervous, verbal twist and turn Sarah takes. He can almost see her mind churning as she delves deeper into a story that's barely a story, doing full-blown narrative somersaults to avoid talking about anything real.

Her nerves are on vivid display. Her every attempt to cover them revealing her vulnerability more. His heart swells, desperate to kiss her, to hold her, to say things he knows he shouldn't even feel, let alone speak aloud. Finally, as she begins to wind down one thread and ramp up a new one, he cuts her off.

"So the Fruit Loops were—"

"I have a confession to make," he says.

Sarah stops mid-sentence, then laughs at herself and closes her mouth, relieved to finally stop her rant. She raises a brow at him curiously.

"I was terrified you wouldn't come."

She rolls her tongue around in her mouth before responding. "That's funny. I was terrified I *would* come."

"Two sides of the same coin."

"I guess you won that coin toss."

"I'm so glad you came," he offers. She smiles, but says nothing. Finally, he speaks again, "Sarah, I do want to talk to you. I want to hear every story you want to tell me. God help me, I even want to hear about the Fruit Loops. I want to know everything. And I want to tell you everything. But right now, all I really want is to kiss you."

She inhales deeply and holds it. He gets up and approaches her.

"Would that be alright?" he says softly.

She slowly releases her breath. He extends his hand to her. The hand that is always his invitation – the labyrinth, the troll, the wheel, the dance – always there to pull her in.

"You don't have to be nervous. It's just me." His voice is serene, reassuring.

"Why do you think I'm nervous?" She laughs weakly, then takes his hand and allows him to pull her up. He cradles her face and kisses her gently. For a fleeting moment, she remains passive, allowing herself simply to be kissed without responding in kind, a flicker of hesitation. But within seconds, the heat of his breath and the softness of his lips override her final defenses. She surrenders and kisses him back.

"Finally, there you are," he says in a low growl of desire and relief. "Oh, God, there you are!"

The fire ignited at last, he kisses her hard and their hands grab for each other. As Joe clutches her ass and presses her to him, Sarah struggles to regain her senses once again. "Slow down. I don't know what I'm doing here."

"Yes, you do." His mouth trails down her neck, erasing her doubts with each brush of his lips. Together they find their way to the bed, kissing, touching, and slowly pulling away bits of intrusive fabric.

He revels in the feel of her skin and the way she responds to his touch. The way she looks as she loses herself in the passion. He thrills at the goosebumps on her skin as he runs his fingertips over the inside of her elbow. He studies every part of her, making notes in his mind, like breaking down a script, filling the pages with subtext, backstory, meaning – eager to know everything, to delve into the inner life and soul beneath the surface of a character he already adores.

Her bra removed, he kisses her breast. Sarah sighs with desire, but panic sneaks back in. Panic about what she's doing. Panic that if he sees her in the full light of day, he'll change his mind about her.

She's right about one thing. Women in Hollywood, both on-set and at home, look and feel different. Their bodies are perfectly flat, toned and firm, their breasts defy gravity. Every one of them, without fail. They split their time evenly between the gym, the nutritionist, and the cosmetic surgeon's office. They pursue some manufactured idea of perfection as if their lives and livelihoods depend on it – and in some cases, they do. No, she's not what he's used to.

But what she cannot see is how captivated he is by her very realness. He marvels at the sensual pleasure of feeling every inch of her fleshy, warm body. The erotic way her soft curves give way to his touch and invite him in with the slightest pressure. He delights in the freckles on her arms from years in the sun. The striations of her skin, the telltale signs of her weight gain that she so bemoans, he wouldn't trade them for the world. Her body is a revelation under his touch. Her flesh against his lips ignites him. And he could watch her writhe like this, head tossed back, eyes closed, forever.

If only she could see what he sees. But she's still panicking. "I shouldn't do this. This is wrong. I—"

"Hey," he says quietly, "stop spinning."

"What?"

He pulls himself up and finds her eyes. "I know how your mind spins, but I want you here with me. Be here with me," he implores her.

The tenderness in his eyes relaxes her. "I'm here."

"Only here," he says.

"Only here," she repeats.

"With me." He kisses her chest again.

She closes her eyes with pleasure. "Yes."

"Sarah, open your eyes and look at me." She does. "Say my name," he whispers. And while his voice is commanding, it's not a command. It's not a power play. It's a plea. An invitation.

"Joe."

He pulls a nipple into his mouth. "Say it again."

"Joe," she gasps. And it's more than a name. It's a prayer.

He kisses his way down further. "Keep saying it."

"Joe...

"Joe...

"Joe..."

As they make love, Sarah surrenders entirely. All her doubts, all her fears, all her inhibitions finally given over to this man who somehow reaches past them and straight to the gooey, molten core of her being, who sees the worst and miraculously still wants to be with her. With his every touch, he magically transforms a black morass of scars and insecurities into something glowing and limitless. How does he do that?

She calls out his name again. He feels her surrender and shudders. She *is* his. This is all he wants.

***

They lie together in post-coital bliss, their limbs intertwined like roots of a tree grown and merged into one. Sarah sighs happily. "How did this happen?"

"I don't know. But I'm glad it did." She responds by lightly biting his chest. "Don't make me change my mind," he says.

She giggles. "I noticed you had a condom again."

"I can't lie. I totally planned it this time." Joe laughs at the confession, only slightly embarrassed. Sarah winces and laughs, too, before they slip back into silence. Caressing each other in the quiet, eyes closed, lost in the warmth, scent, and feel of their skin on skin. The minutes drift by slowly, a beautiful eternity in each other's arms that still ends too soon. "I hate to say it, but I should probably get ready to go," Joe finally says.

"Well, it was nice while it lasted."

He rolls on top of her and kisses her. "Hey, come on, it's not over. Wait for me. I only have a couple meetings, I can be back by four o'clock." He kisses her again.

"You want me to sit and wait for you for, what, five hours?"

He grazes his hand down her body and slides his fingers between her legs. "No?"

"No. I have a life. I have things to do."

"Are you saying…" He glides his fingers to her sweet spot. "That you don't want to see me this afternoon?"

Sarah gasps at the pressure from Joe's hand. "Well, I didn't say that."

He grins. "Good. Great! Then go do your things and come back and meet me." He feels her hesitation, the doubts sneaking back in. "Don't think so hard. Just say yes."

"Okay, yes." Their mouths connect in happy agreement, rebooting for another round until Joe remembers the time and forces himself to stop. "Four o'clock," he confirms climbing out of bed.

She eyes him with a carnal smile. "Four o'clock."

***

Sarah bounds off the lobby sofa the moment she spots Joe approaching the entrance. His site visits must have gone well because he's grinning ear to ear. He glows in the summer sun, wearing his golden tan, dark glasses, and easy movie star style perfectly. His lanky frame radiates heat with every step. She'd tried to ignore it before, but now it's all she sees. She pinches herself as he strides through the door. "How were your meetings?"

Joe scans the lobby. Not even a desk clerk in sight. "Hell with the meetings." He grabs her and greets her with a ravenous kiss.

"Someone could see," she says, scanning the completely empty lobby.

"No one is here. They're all headed to another site visit. Come on."

They walk arm in arm to the elevator. When the doors close behind them, he nudges her against the wall and presses himself against her as their mouths collide hungrily.

"I'm so happy to see you," he says.

"I can tell." She leers downward toward his rapidly growing hardness.

Joe kisses her again, enchanted by her naughtiness. "I like this Sexy Time Sarah."

The elevator dings and opens. After an entire afternoon of anticipation, they practically run to the room. Inside, they throw their things down and undress. Her inhibitions with Joe are gone. He yanks off his t-shirt and throws it across the room. He pulls Sarah's blouse over her head and hastily lays it aside on the couch. He kicks his shoes off, she follows suit. They pull off their jeans and within sixty seconds they're on the bed in nothing but underwear.

He kneads her flesh and thrusts against her as they kiss. She reaches down and feels how ready he is for her. When she strokes him, he grunts loudly, and she takes this as a cue. She pushes him onto his back and glides down his body.

She reaches into his briefs and frees his erection, her fingers eliciting a deep moan before she places her lips on it. He breathes heavily in anticipation. As she goes to work in earnest, his moans reach a new level.

"Oh, God!" he gasps.

She pauses a moment to pull his briefs off and quickly goes back to work, eager to maintain his excitement.

"Oh my God, Sarah! That feels so good."

His groans become more intense as he buries his hands in her hair. As much as she wants him right now, she wants to give him this pleasure and keeps going. After several more minutes, he's on the verge. It feels too good. He grabs her.

"Stop, stop! That's enough," he says breathlessly.

"I want to make you feel as good as you make me feel."

"You have. You will. Get up here."

He reaches for a condom and quickly puts it on as she adjusts her position to lie by his side. She rolls away from him for a moment to pull a pair of jeans out from under her. Whose, she has no idea, but she tosses them off the bed. He seizes the moment as she is facing away to grab her from behind.

He slides a hand under her and holds her tight, their bodies in perfect alignment. He kisses her neck as he presses against her from behind. She lets out a tiny moan, almost a gasp, so quiet, but so arousing he nearly loses it. He needs her so badly.

He reaches around and fondles her breasts. He roughly pushes her bra down and frees her breast, massaging the nipple which hardens under his fingers. She twists her face toward him and their mouths fuse together.

His hand skates down her body and pushes down her panties. He's already between her legs, brushing against her. He glides his fingers over her and touches her where she wants it most. Within moments, she reaches down and nudges him toward the point of no return. He thrusts inside.

Ferocious at first, they rock together, a single being, completely united, completely uninhibited. They both moan loudly, unable to hold themselves back. He moves his hand back between her legs. His need to please her as boundless as his need to feel her.

As their passion grows, the carnality gives way to something even deeper, more tender. Together they find a new rhythm, still desperate and intense, but more intentional, each thrust a restatement of their feelings. This is not just animal instinct. They are one.

***

Joe sits on the edge of the bed, naked. Sarah's wrapped in a blanket in the desk chair, his laptop open in front of her. She spins from the laptop back to him.

"It's great," she says.

"The crows work, right?"

"Oh my God, I can't believe how you translated them to the story. I couldn't even have imagined it. It's amazing."

He beams at her. "You're amazing."

She blushes. "You changed other things, too. There are new scenes. About Jack and his girlfriend."

"Yeah. I realized we needed more about why he did what he did," Joe says. "So Sean could respond to the affair more compassionately when he finally learns the whole story."

"I wonder what brought on that change," Sarah replies slyly.

"I wonder."

"It's really powerful," she says. "I mean, it was already so good, but now. Wow!"

"You think?" He's bubbling over from her praise.

They gaze at each other contentedly for a long time. She looks him up and down admiring his long limbs, toned, athletic. He reminds her of those classic Greek or Roman sculptures of beautiful, heroic men. He's perfect.

Except maybe for the pose. His legs crossed, ankle over knee, ostensibly for modesty, but the leg hides nothing. In ancient antiquity, the sculptors had the good sense to strategically place a fig leaf for modesty. But not Joe. And a fig leaf wouldn't do the job anyway. She can't help but giggle in the moment as he sits there, letting it all hang out. "You have no shame, do you?"

"Nope. Not with you." He shakes his head proudly. "Besides, the human body is a beautiful thing."

She suppresses a laugh at his ridiculousness. "Some more than others."

They stare awhile longer, so happy to just gaze at each other that words aren't necessary. Eventually a shadow floats through her thoughts and she sobers. "Don't you feel guilty?"

"What?" Joe stalls, crossing his legs more tightly.

"About this? Because I have to be honest, I love being here with you, more than I care to admit, but I'm feeling super guilty, too."

He drops his eyes. "Of course, I feel guilty."

"You don't act like it."

"Look, when you left that night, I was too high to let guilt seep in. I had pangs, but I distracted myself with sorting through all the pictures of the places we'd gone together. I couldn't let myself think about anything else.

So, I didn't. And the next day, too. I spent the whole day thinking about you."

"You did?" The confession touches her.

"Why do you think I sent you all those pictures? Weren't you thinking of me?" Joe laughs pathetically. "Please tell me you were thinking of me."

"Duh," Sarah says. "But you're you. And I'm just... me."

He rolls his eyes, not dignifying the comment with a response. "But on the flight home, I started feeling guilty as hell. Like, the highest I've ever been, and the lowest at the same time. I even thought about telling Mel."

She gasps. "Did you?"

"No. Part of me desperately wanted to relieve myself of the burden. But Melanie was asleep when I got home, and by the time I got up, she'd gone to work out. Then I went out and we kept missing each other... I was probably dodging her, to be honest. Then the kids got home from school and we had Avery's concert, then Nate's track meet, and I knew I couldn't do it. I couldn't blow up their lives for something that—" Joe cuts himself off, unsure how to finish the sentence.

"Well, exactly," Sarah says. Neither of them knows where to go from here.

"But I still don't regret it," Joe finally says. "Maybe I should, but I wouldn't be here if I did."

"I do."

"You regret being with me?"

She pauses to think. How to explain the cognitive dissonance of regretting her actions could hurt someone she loves, but still having absolutely no desire to have done things differently. "I have regrets, yes. But not about being with you. Why is that?"

Joe leans in and puts on his thoughtful face. "I've given that a lot of thought. I've even prayed about it. Why I don't feel guiltier. Why I'm here with you now. Why this feels so incredibly right, despite everything. I've always tried really hard to do the right thing, you know?"

She does know.

"Yet, here I am. Unashamed." He holds out his arms from his naked body as if to demonstrate. "And happy as hell to be with you."

Sarah stifles a quiet laugh. "And?"

"Fate. This was meant to happen. Fate brought you to me. And I don't argue with Fate."

"Fate? That's your answer?"

He quirks a brow at her. "Would you rather I say God?"

"Definitely not."

"Then Fate." Joe watches Sarah rub her face and groan. "Come on. You can't tell me you don't feel it."

"Sometimes I do."

"I knew it! You can't deny this. I mean, *you* can because you can deny water is wet," he teases. "But you shouldn't."

"But I also think maybe that's just us rationalizing our choices to ease our guilt."

"No way. The team is here right now visiting sites *you* gave me. Your fingerprints are all over this movie. The crows? That's all you," Joe points at her, driving the point home.

"But we could have said goodnight after the crows, and you still would've had your locations."

"Fate's plans are bigger than that. Fate brought us together to change *each other's* lives. You said yourself, my movie is better with the scenes I wrote *because of you*."

"So you're saying I'm your destiny?"

She's mocking him. He laughs sheepishly. "Call it whatever you want. Fate, God, Destiny. I'm saying this is bigger than either of us. No matter what you say."

She rests her elbow on the desk, her face on her hand, and gazes at him. "Well, I guess I don't have a better explanation." He smiles, until she adds, "But I also think it needs to end here. Don't you?"

"Needs to?" He screws up his face and shakes his head.

"I love being with you. And yes, this feels incredible. But just because it feels good doesn't mean it is good."

"That was you in bed with me earlier, right? That was more than good. That was God's work," Joe laughs.

Sarah can't help but laugh, too. She rubs her face again. "Well, God's got a funny sense of humor."

"In my experience, that's definitely the case."

"We're both married, Joe. To other people."

"I know," he sighs.

"Where can this possibly go? Honestly? Are we going to run away together? Are you going to leave your family behind for me? Am I going to leave my family for you?"

Joe looks at her blankly, desperate for an answer that doesn't exist. "I don't know what to say, Sarah. But I know I don't want this to end."

"I think prolonging it will just hurt more." He can't argue with her, so he says nothing. "I should probably go."

"Running out on me again, huh?" he says miserably.

"Is there another option?"

"I can think of a few."

"I can't," Sarah says, checking her watch and straightening her spine. "I'm afraid Fate has other plans for me tonight."

"I understand." Joe puts on a brave face. "I hate it. But I understand."

Sarah takes her time dressing, weighed down by her impending departure. A slow-motion choreography of goodbye. A pas de deux. She puts on her underwear, he finds his jeans furled in a ball where she threw them and pulls them on. She slides on her own jeans, he picks her blouse up from the couch where he tossed it. He turns it right side out and runs his hands over it attempting to press out the creases.

"It got a little wrinkled. Sorry."

She shrugs. "It's fine."

He watches her put it on, puffs his cheeks with the breath he's holding, and finally blows it out. She sits to put on her shoes.

"You sure you have to go?"

"I'm sure."

"Okay. Give me a minute." He goes for his shirt, but she stops him.

"You don't have to walk me. My car is right outside," she says. "Besides, what if we run into your people?" The outside world is no longer their friend.

He walks her to the door. They stand facing each other, each of them unwilling to reach for the doorknob. He scrunches his face. "I hate it when you leave."

"Me, too."

"It doesn't have to end here," he says hopefully.

"Yes," she says, "it does."

He chews on his lip a moment. "Why is this so much easier for you than for me?"

"It's not easy." She inhales deeply, exhales slowly. "But unlike you, I have someone expecting me tonight. So, I have to go."

He wraps her in his arms and holds her close, breathing her in one last time. "You're going to be damn hard to get over, Sarah Abbott."

Sarah feels her body meld to his like a latex mold, a perfect fit. His form will be imprinted on her forevermore. "Nah. I'll be lucky to rate a footnote in your big, storied life."

"You're wrong about that." He shakes his head. "You couldn't be more wrong."

PART THREE
DESTINY

IF YOU DECIDE TO ask the Big Three who's in charge, Destiny will assure you She's top dog as She's the one with the vision for each and every person on Her favorite little, blue marble. Which is why She's so content to spend Her days nudging billions of lost souls toward their small d destinies. Of course, Destiny has never promised anyone an easy "happy ending." Rather, Destiny aims to ensure people end up right where they should be, living the lives they need to be living. Whether they know it or not. Whether they like it or not.

Because big picture, if they follow Her lead, happiness will always find them. Eventually.

Chapter Twenty-Five

Asheville (October, 2018)

There were certainly perks to shooting on location and today was one of them. So far, the whole trip had been a perk, actually, as they'd shot amongst the spectacular fall foliage of Asheville, North Carolina for the past week. And today, they moved inside to the galleries of the Asheville museum, an ideal location for closet art aficionado Joe. Joe loved diving into the worlds and lives pictured in all those great paintings, sparking his imagination and empathy in ways that made him feel shockingly alive, even as the subjects he studied stayed frozen forever in their singular moments.

In truth, the location was the main reason he wanted this gig. He was playing the second fiddle detective working a case to solve an art heist and he spent most of his time nodding behind the main detective, who spent most of her time stooping to see things from a different angle and getting the runaround from the clever, debonair thief. As roles went, there wasn't much meat on those bones. But shooting on location in a town famous for its natural beauty and vibrant arts scene held more than enough appeal to sweeten the deal.

The AD called lunch and announced that the galleries were free for anyone who wanted to check them out after lunch, but Joe opted to skip the interminably long catering line that always formed when everyone descended at once. He didn't want to risk running out of time for the galleries, and this way the line would be gone by the time he went to eat.

He wandered through the American Art exhibit, unencumbered by aim or expectation, content to let the images wash over him until he found the ones that most spoke to him. First was a boy sneakily pouring a jug of milk for a kitten while his mother turned her back for a moment, then a ribald scene of red-faced, drunken men around a table. But even as he studied the brushstrokes that formed their ruddy cheeks, he felt a chill down his back and stiffened. He turned slowly and saw the painting he suddenly knew he was there to see.

It was far away, hanging on the wall opposite him two galleries down. His eyes glued to it, he approached slowly, allowing the image to come into greater focus with each step. Bit by bit, it revealed itself. It was a wide, dark landscape. A night scene. Towering evergreens against a night sky, a gentle glimmer around the trees at the center, the last of the fading light. The sky flooded with stars. There was dark water in the middle, in front of the trees, but still at some distance. In the foreground, large boulders rose to each side on opposite shores.

As he entered the gallery at last, he saw there were two figures, one on each boulder. Both together and not together. Far apart, but united by the same night sky. To the right, a tall, dark-haired man in a long dark coat stood with his leg jutting forward in a dramatic stance. His coat billowed. To the left, a luminous woman in a flowing white gown, almost a nightgown, her wavy blonde locks caught by the wind. Her gown hugged her Rubenesque figure in the wind and she seemed to glow in the starlight. They weren't looking at each other, though they must have sensed the other. Instead, they each looked up at the same shooting star, streaking through the darkness above them.

Joe's breath caught in his throat as he lowered himself to the bench in front of the massive canvas. He studied every corner of it, contemplated the thoughts in the man's head, imagined making a wish on that star, wondered if those evergreens and water were a real place or a figment of the artist's imagination. But mostly, he stared at her. Transfixed, his eyes combed over her face, her hair, her soft, womanly curves. He tried to look elsewhere, but she kept pulling him back, so he gave up trying and simply stared.

Moments later, a tap on his shoulder awoke him from his trance. A production assistant was summoning him back to set. Lunch was over. He hadn't eaten a bite, yet the hunger he felt had nothing to do with food.

As Joe walked back to the gallery where they were shooting, he passed the museum entrance just moments before two best friends strolled in and up to the ticket desk.

Gabi lured Sarah on this trip as a stand-in for her now ex, Max. Gabi had been dreaming of Autumn in Asheville for so long that she wasn't about to let a little thing like Max's chronic infidelity and recent excision from her life stop this trip. So, Sarah had dutifully scheduled time off work, bought her ticket, and showed up for Gabi, just as Gabi had always shown up for her.

At Gabi's request, they meandered through the galleries with no particular plan, which made Sarah downright itchy. Sarah never met a museum map she didn't like and always prioritized according to interests and available time. But Gabi was in charge this trip, so Sarah bit her tongue and followed. Right up until she laid eyes on that painting.

Sarah froze in front of the giant landscape, captivated by the magic she sensed flowing through it. And by the two figures gazing up at the sky. They didn't seem to see each other, though she could tell they each knew the other was there.

The placard on the wall attributed the piece called "Destiny" to a twentieth century artist named Trenton Freed, a contemporary of Maxfield Parrish who mimicked some of Parrish's style. The magical, almost fanciful setting. The intense hues like his deep, luminous blue sky at the tree line fading up to the midnight blue-black above, awash with stars and one shooting star in particular summoning wishes from its two observers. Sarah looked again at the placard. "Look, Gabi, this artist lived in Washington for years."

"Nice," Gabi replied without much interest. "Hey, the next gallery looks cool."

With her eyes still on the mysterious night scene, Sarah answered. "I'll catch up. I want to look at this one awhile longer."

Gabi told Sarah to take her time, then wandered off. Sarah took a seat on the bench and stared up at the fantastical scene that somehow felt so real it rattled through her nervous system like a memory. Her eyes landed on the man – tall, handsome, unknowable, yet somehow desperate to be known – and didn't leave again until Gabi plopped down beside her and slapped Sarah's knee.

"Wakey, wakey," Gabi said.

Sarah rolled her eyes at her friend's impatience. "I told you I'd catch up with you."

"That was an hour and a half ago, bestie."

Four galleries away, the AD called a fifteen-minute break. Joe chowed a banana from the craft services table, then made a beeline for the painting. Something about that piece was calling him back, and he needed to go now. He followed the path he took the first time, but just as he reached the turn where the landscape would appear, his phone rang. Melanie had taken Nathan to the doctor and wanted to give Joe an update. Joe paused, his back to the painting and to the two women seated on the bench in front of it.

Sarah begged Gabi for five more minutes. Gabi released an exasperated grunt, then said, "You're buying dinner tonight."

"Of course, I am," Sarah agreed. Gabi walked away and Sarah began her five-minute countdown with the picture. But as she sat there, something within her shifted and started to vibrate. Her body was ringing an alert, though she wasn't sure if it was alarm or delight.

Two galleries down, Joe glimpsed over his shoulder as Melanie talked and he noticed a blonde woman in a billowing white blouse staring up at the artwork. As if the figure in the white gown had stepped off the canvas and sat down. Her pull was enormous, though he chalked it up to his overactive imagination, triggered by the power of that remarkable piece. He forced himself to turn away to avoid distraction while he discussed Nathan's sprained ankle. But when he hung up and turned back, she was gone. He headed toward the gallery. Maybe she'd still be in the vicinity. Not that it mattered, but he was curious.

The PA from earlier called to him. "Joe, back in two." The banana and the phone call had taken longer than he thought. One last glance toward the painting, then he headed back to set.

Sarah checked the gallery to the left for Gabi, then doubled back to check the gallery on the right. As she passed the large entrance that had been at her back, she spotted someone turning the corner in the distance, a tall, dark-haired man who reminded her an awful lot of her favorite actor, Joseph Robert Parker. And of that guy in the landscape, as far as that went. But that was ridiculous.

Gabi slipped up and hooked her arm through Sarah's. "Ready?"

CHAPTER TWENTY-SIX

THE OFFER

WEEK AFTER WEEK, SARAH is becoming a new person. At least, that's what she tells herself every day. It doesn't always work, of course, but she tries. No more misery mugging. After all, if she doesn't believe in herself, who will?

Joe will. That she knows. He echoes through every corridor of her brain, reminding her. But it's time to pick herself up, so instead of grieving her loss, she uses it for fuel. Just as she did in the aftermath of their first encounter, Sarah continues to live "as if." *As if* she's with Joe. *As if* she's the person she was with Joe. *As if* he might be watching or she might stumble into him at any moment. Because even without Joe, *that Sarah* can do anything.

It's not always easy. The hardest times are the evenings when she sits home alone waiting for Ben to come home from another late night at work, or equally alone with Ben at home, sealed in his office. Sarah steeps in a brew of loneliness, resentment, and guilt that makes these evenings almost unbearable. But Gabi's constancy – even more cherished in the month since Sarah's second encounter with Joe - and the arrival of Sarah's New Friend Dana help her through. Fortunately, the two hit it off when she introduces them, and having them both in her life, together and separately, is exactly the safety net she needs.

She's even applying for jobs regularly now. She's set herself a goal of at least five applications per week, but it's an uphill climb, as she quickly discovers. Despite her highly marketable skills and great experience, she's a tough sell. She's way overqualified for the lower-level jobs, and has taken way too long a break to be considered for the executive positions. She's sure she could convince someone to give her a shot if she could just get in the room. She used to be really good at this stuff. But judging from the response rate of exactly one failed phone screening out of two dozen applications, most employers aren't even giving her a chance. Still, she's got to try. The only way out of this pit is to climb – even if she has to dig every step with her bare hands.

And then there are the kiddos. Since summer break started, she's been watching the girls two afternoons a week while Wendy takes a ceramics class, which quickly become her favorite times of the week. Whether it's Barbie, dress-up, or dodging the sprinklers in the backyard, the playful Sarah who Joe revealed finds safe harbor with her nieces. Somehow Joe instinctively knew what Sarah needed more than anything – to be seen, to be heard, and to remember how to play. He found a way from the start to tap into a lightness and joy she'd long forgotten. But if Joe reminded Sarah how to play, Lexi and Emma help keep her newfound skills sharp.

In fact, she's sharpening a pink crayon when her phone buzzes one sunny Tuesday afternoon. Sarah and the girls are embroiled in a marathon coloring session, with Emma hard at work on a purple unicorn, Lexi tackling a princess in a castle, and Sarah perfecting a truly magical fairy scene. Sarah ignores the phone, along with the second and third messages that buzz a moment later, determined to finish the pink highlights in her blue fairy's hair.

"Your phone's buzzing," Lexi says absently when the reminder intones a minute later, crushing her crayon down hard as she colors her sky.

"It can wait until we're done," Sarah says, picking out a new shade of orange for a spray of flowers in the corner. "I've got to finish my masterpiece."

"But it might be important," Lexi says without feeling or concern, in a way that stops Sarah short.

Sarah looks at her puzzled. "Why do you say that?"

Emma has been studiously coloring with her tongue sticking out in the universal sign of concentration. But at the question, she retracts her tongue long enough to chime in on Lexi's behalf. "That's what Mommy always says when she stops to get her phone. 'It might be important.'"

Sarah chuckles. "Well, I can't imagine anything more important than coloring right now. Can you?"

The girls sing "Noooo" in unison and go right on coloring. Twenty minutes later, Wendy arrives home to their finished creations, which the girls proudly show off as Sarah finally reaches for her phone. Her heart stops. The texts are from Joe.

She glimpses the preview of the last text, but quickly drops her phone, afraid to read it or even touch it while she's with the others.

"How'd it go?" Wendy says as the girls run into the next room.

Sarah barely hears her, but manages to mumble, "Great... great."

"You okay?"

Sarah snatches a response from her jumbled brain. "Yeah, fine. The coloring was... yeah."

Wendy's face scrunches with concern. "You sure you're okay?"

Sarah nods and forces out the lie. "Absolutely! How was your class?"

"I threw my first good pot today! I get to glaze it next time."

"That's awesome," Sarah says, beating her phone against her leg.

"What's wrong, hon? Do you need to talk about something?" She gestures at Sarah's self-abusing phone hand. Sweet Wendy. Always so caring. As long as she doesn't think you're cheating on her brother. That would probably be a line in the sand.

She looks down at her phone, clasped so tightly her fingertips have gone red with pooled blood. Talking about it might be a relief, but Wendy can't help with this. "No. Fine. Yeah. But I should get going."

Sarah says her goodbyes, dashes as quickly as she can to her car, and buckles up. She glances at the phone face-down on the passenger seat, then waves to Wendy who stands in the doorway, concerned. She forces a smile and backs out. She drives around the corner until she's safely out of sight and pulls over.

She stares at the phone, still afraid to touch it. She tries to practice her meditative yoga breathing. When that fails her, she grabs her tissue packet from the glove compartment as a precaution. She's doing so much better, but she's still on the two-steps-forward, one-step-back plan. After more than a month, God only knows what a message from Joe might unleash.

Her heart pounds through her chest as she reaches for the phone. With a single fingertip, she flips it over from the edge as if it might burn her if she makes too much contact for too long. She doesn't wake the screen, just stares at the black glass willing another notification to buzz in and illuminate it so she won't have to do it herself. But the phone just sits there, dark and unknowable, taunting her, until at last she's forced to press the button.

She rereads the top text on the lockscreen, the last one to come in. It's a hotel name and address. Can he really be summoning her to a hotel again? After the way they left it last time? They agreed. Or did they? She thought they did. She rapid cycles through exhilaration and terror as she summons the courage to pick up the phone and turn it on. She holds her breath and clicks Joe's thread.

The first text reads, *I'm here. Will you come meet me? Need to talk to you about something.*

Then the second, *Would 5PM work? Please? It's not what you think.*

That's followed by *lmk* and the hotel info, and that's it. Nothing else.

***

Sarah follows a large group wheeling in luggage and bulky, hard silver cases for equipment of some kind into the hotel. The space bustles with activity. At least twenty people buzzing around the modest lobby, checking in, clustering in discussions, tapping on phones. Clearly the film crew arrived en masse. She wishes she hadn't come. She tried to resist. She even called Joe to get whatever it is out in the open without having to actually see him, but he hadn't picked up and just hearing his voice had sent her mind and body alike into involuntary spasms. So, here she is.

Now standing here among people rushing around her, a fixed point in a time-lapse video, she feels conspicuous and exposed. She feels the vibration of Joe immediately, but it takes her a moment to spot him. He's across the lobby talking to a beautiful Black woman with long braids and more style than Sarah has managed in at least twenty years, if ever. An immediate twinge of jealousy ignites her already jangled nerves. Should she approach him? Wait for him to come to her? Turn around and run out before he sees her?

Just as she gives the last option serious consideration, Joe spots her from the corner of his eye. His eyes sparkle and a tiny smile hits his lips as he gives an upturned nod of hello. Sarah's feet adhere to the ground as she melts on the spot. Joe turns back to the woman he's talking with, now nodding more quickly, as if the speed of his nods might dictate the speed with which they finish their conversation. He says a few more words, nods a little more, then excuses himself and works his way over to Sarah, shuffling between crew members with a grin and a few pats on the back as he goes.

Then, finally, he's there. In front of her. The room quietens, the chaos fading into mere dancing shadows surrounding them.

"Hi."

"Hi."

Joe is the first to move, reaching out for a hug Sarah greedily, but cautiously receives. Her internal clock counts the duration and triggers her release at the precise moment she *should* let go, whether she wants to or not. Joe radiates heat, whether from the sun pouring through the window or from within. "How are you?" he asks.

Sarah feels a familiar weakness in her knees, which overcomes her each time she sees him anew, as if she's forgotten how handsome he is until he flashes that smile and it all comes rushing back. She steadies herself. "Good actually. Mostly. How are you?"

Before Joe can answer, a voice calls his name. It's the woman he was talking to previously. "Sarah, this is Celeste Walker, our director."

"Oh, wow! Hi," Sarah says, both delighted and flustered. Sarah loved the previous indie Celeste directed Joe in a few years earlier, but hadn't realized she was directing this one as well. Normally, meeting her would be an unmitigated thrill, but in the moment, all Sarah can think is, if even the directors look like Celeste, then how beautiful are the actresses in person? She suppresses the thought and smiles. "It's a pleasure to meet you."

"It's great to meet you. Joe has told me all about you," Celeste says.

Sarah washes crimson with alarm. Her eyes dart to Joe in horror, but he smiles innocently, betraying nothing. "He has?" she stutters.

"Absolutely," Celeste chimes. "How you swept in and saved the day, helped him find all those great locations. I think over half the locations in the film are ones you found for us."

"About two-thirds, actually," Joe says proudly. "Everything but the clubs and the houses."

"I had no idea." Sarah says. "That's great."

"And the crows. That was a stroke of genius," Celeste says.

"Well, Joe wrote a great script. I just happened to know where some birds hang out."

"You've read the script?"

Sarah panics. Has she revealed too much? She backtracks, "Well, yes, um, I... Joe was nice enough to let me... I mean, I was curious to know what all this was for."

"That's even better," Celeste says with glee. "Not that it's necessary, of course, but you'll totally be able to hit the ground running. If you say yes, that is."

"Hit the ground running?"

Celeste looks at Joe. "You haven't asked her?"

"I haven't had a chance," he says before turning back to Sarah. "I actually asked you to come down today because we want to ask a favor."

Celeste jumps in. "We want to offer you a job."

The words crush Sarah. She may have been determined not to let anything happen – she was, yes, she definitely was – but she still wanted Joe to *want* to see her. The notion that this is all just about a job punctures something precious in her. "Sorry, a job?"

Celeste explains, "Of course, Naomi—"

"Our line producer," Joe interrupts.

"Should be talking to you, but she's still in the air," Celeste continues. "Or at least Pete, our first AD, because you'd be reporting to him. But he's on an equipment run."

"So you get us," Joe smiles.

"And basically, we need a PA."

"A production assistant," Joe clarifies.

Celeste goes on. "Thing is, we have our first location PA Randy, and he's great. But our second bailed on us for another job."

"More money, longer shoot, bigger stars," Joe shrugs.

Sarah bristles at their easy rhythm. Jealousy flaring again.

"I can't blame him," Celeste goes on.

"But it does leave us shorthanded," Joe says.

"Very shorthanded. We were a lean crew to begin with," Celeste adds.

"And I thought," Joe says, then reconsiders his words. "I *hoped* you might consider helping us out."

Joe's eyes are wide with anticipation. She tries to interpret his expression, alight with hope, but also stiff, bracing for possible disappointment. It's a plea, but she can't decipher its source. Professional urgency? Or personal desire? Could it be both? She's not even sure which one she wants it to be.

"I know you have other things going on, but...," Joe trails off.

"We'd pay, of course. Not much, but something," Celeste offers, almost apologetically.

"But I don't know anything about film sets," Sarah finally says. "What does a PA even do?"

"It's not glamorous," Celeste says, apology still in her voice. "It's basically a glorified gopher. Running errands, shopping, shuttling cast and crew." Celeste pauses to let Sarah process before continuing. "Joe said you ran a big company or something. So obviously you're way, way over-qualified. I get it. But he also mentioned you're taking some time off?"

Sarah chokes down a laugh. *Taking time off. That's one way to put it.*

"If you're free, it might be fun? A little change of pace?" Celeste adds hopefully. "But I'll be honest. It's crappy pay, long hours—"

"Long hours?" Sarah repeats.

"Yes. There would be a lot of late nights," Joe says, nodding at her. "And some night shoots."

Late nights? Night shoots? Sarah reels. *What's happening here?*

"It's a big ask, I know." Celeste puts her hand in a Namaste prayer position to plead with Sarah. "But I hear you're a movie lover. And there's nothing like the magic of a movie set. And it won't be thankless. I promise I will say thank you."

"Me, too," Joe says. "I promise to show my appreciation every, single day." He smiles sweetly at Sarah. So sweetly it throws her again. *Is that innuendo?* Joe continues, "Don't think of it as a job. If you think of it as a job, you'll be insulted because it's way below your pay grade. Think of it as doing us a favor."

"A huge favor," Celeste says with her hands wide apart to illustrate. Then she pushes them together until they're almost touching and adds, "With a small paycheck."

"A huge favor. Yes," Joe agrees.

"Honestly, I know the budget's tight. I don't think I'd even want to be paid," Sarah says, equivocating within an inch of her life. She should focus on getting a real job, of course. But at least this could be fun. And a way to dip her toe back in the employment pool? Ben will be so excited he'll probably pack her lunch and push her out the door. A PA job might not actually make it to her professional resume, but maybe she just needs to get moving at this point. No matter the job. No matter the reason.

"Does that mean you'll do it?" Joe's voice raises in pitch with excitement.

"Umm...," Sarah stalls. If only she could understand what Joe really wants. "How long is the shoot?"

"About four weeks," Celeste says.

Sarah looks to Joe again. He's so hopeful. He's been playing it cool, but she can finally see the gleam in his eyes from the delight he's barely containing. Her doubt evaporates, her heart healed simply by the knowledge. She can't give in. Not this time. But the job is intriguing.

"I'll have to see if I can move some things around," she says, her own excitement growing. Joe unleashes his big movie star smile and claps his hands before Sarah continues, "And I need to talk to my husband." She looks pointedly at Joe, sending a message.

Chastened, his smile fades. "Of course."

"Can I let you know later tonight?"

***

Sarah and Joe stroll side-by-side down the sidewalk. He looks over his shoulder to a group of crew members smoking outside the hotel entrance. "So, it seems Fate has brought us together once again."

Sarah huffs out a good natured, but cynical giggle. "Is Fate's first name Joe, by any chance?"

"Hey, I didn't get our last PA a new job!"

They round the corner and walk a stretch down the sidewalk to her car. He checks to confirm the coast is clear, then grabs her hand and pulls her in for a hug. "I couldn't wait to be alone with you."

"This can't happen." Sarah tugs backward reluctantly, but her heart stretches toward him as her body pulls away.

"I'm just giving you a hug."

"Sure, you are." She allows her adoration to slip out in a half smile before she stiffens her resolve along with her posture. "But we agreed, remember?"

He steps back and leans against her car. "I guess I hoped, when you came tonight—" She shakes her head to stop him. "Okay. But why did you come if that's how you feel?"

"Because you said it wasn't about that." He frowns at her in disbelief. She reaches up and caresses his face. "And because I wanted to see you. Obviously."

He clutches her palm to his cheek. "Well, then...?"

She reclaims her hand. "Well, then nothing. This job is a bad idea. I should go." But if it's really a bad idea, why does it feel so right? Somehow it's always like this with Joe.

"Wait."

One word is all he says and it's nearly enough to stop her heart, but she's determined. "No, I'm serious. I have to be stronger than last time. Maybe it's easier for you because you don't have to go home to your family every day. But I do. I have to face Ben every night. And every morning."

Joe bites his lip before speaking. "I get it. I hear you. You don't want this happen. Fine. I accept that."

"Okay then. I'm gonna go," Sarah says.

"But we do need the help on the shoot. And you really would be doing us a favor." He has, as always, the air of sincerity in his words. And he's never lied to her before.

"So you're saying, just work on the film? Nothing else." She holds her breath for his response.

He looks her solemnly in the eye. "Nothing else." A cheeky smile slides onto his lips. "Unless you change your mind."

"I won't," she insists.

"Then just work on the film. That's enough. You'll get us out of a bind and at least I'll get to see you every day."

She analyzes his word choice and clarifies with raised brows. "As friends, you mean." Is there a world where this is possible? Where she and Joe can truly be just friends? Colleagues? Work buddies?

"Obviously," he says. She squints at him skeptically until he raises his hand to swear an oath.

"So if I say yes, then we agree, we're just friends?"

"Just friends. It won't be easy, but I'll do it." Joe extends his hand and they shake on it.

She studies their hands, clinging a moment too long. "I'll text you tonight and let you know for sure."

"Yes!"

Sarah clasps Joe's arm and pulls him away from her car door before climbing in. "This is such a mistake."

He shakes his head. "No way. You won't regret this."

"I already do," she smirks before shutting the door and driving off.

CHAPTER TWENTY-SEVEN

THE FIRST DAY

THE LINE PRODUCER NAOMI is a severe woman with severe cheek bones and an even more severe black bob. She leads Sarah into a large meeting room after a shockingly long marathon of paperwork, just for her to volunteer on set. Sarah suspects she might have had to sign in blood to get paid for the job. Now, paperwork done, they enter the fray.

The expansive hotel conference room is set up with a giant square of buffet tables, with chairs around the outside of the ring, and a second, larger ring of chairs along the perimeter of the room. Cast and crew shuffle around getting coffee and snacks, chatting, and settling into their seats. Everyone seems to know everyone, and to know what they're doing. Sarah's intimidation factor skyrockets, dwarfing Naomi's bitesize intimidation in its shadow.

Sarah spots Joe talking with two men who are attractive enough to be actors, but she's learning that's almost everyone here. Her inferiority complex bubbles up, but she reminds herself she's not getting paid and has made it clear she doesn't know what she's doing. She's set the bar so low, with any luck, she can simply step over it. Glamour and competence not required.

Naomi calls to Celeste – and by default, to the whole room – that she has arrived and they can get started. Joe clocks Sarah when Naomi begins shouting. He offers a smile and a friendly wave, but before he can come over, Naomi and Celeste rally everyone to take their seats.

The table has name cards for Joe, Celeste, and others whom Sarah assumes are actors and key production personnel. Sarah scans the name cards out of curiosity. She eyeballs the seat for Pete Abel, the first assistant director and her new boss, and watches a shaggy headed dude with a long, graying beard, baggy shorts, and a baseball cap claim the seat. She makes a mental note to say hello if someone doesn't introduce her first.

Others fill in the seats along the wall and Sarah joins them. She sits across the room and to the left of Joe, distant, but with a good enough angle to see him well. She's so fixated on watching him in his natural habitat, interacting with others, that she doesn't notice the woman who sits next to her.

"Hi, who are you?" A mid-thirties woman with teased brown hair and a bright purple streak smiles at her.

"Sorry?" Sarah says.

The woman laughs. She's mocking, but in a good-natured way. "Who are you? What's your name?"

"I'm Sarah. I'm the new PA, I guess."

"You guess? Interesting. Well, I'm Kayla, HMU. I guess."

"HMU? Hit me up?"

"You *are* new, aren't you? Hair and make-up unit," Kayla explains. Sarah blushes, but Kayla pats her arm. "Don't worry about it. You'll pick it up quickly. Just go where they tell you and bring what they ask. You'll be fine."

Sarah relaxes into a smile and finally remembers to breathe. "Thank you."

"So how did you get this job you guess you have?"

"Um, I know Joe a little. I helped find some locations in town. And they needed help at the last minute, so..."

"Joe...? Writer/star/producer Joe Parker, you mean?" Kayla says reassessing Sarah at the revelation.

Sarah nods. "But I have no idea what I'm doing."

"Well, stick with me, kid. You're sure to go places," Kayla says with a wink.

Celeste calls out, "Okay, let's get started!"

***

It's the first table read Sarah has ever seen and she's transfixed by Joe. His every gesture, every intonation, a marvel. While others keep their eyes mostly glued to the script, Joe's basically off book, so even sitting at the table, he fully inhabits the role. How she can know him so well and watch him become someone else before her eyes amazes her.

When others speak, she has to force herself to look away from him, to follow the action, not to be too consumed with him. Or worse, to be spotted being too consumed with him. She watches all the actors, laughs at all the appropriate times, gets lost in hearing Joe's father-son story of betrayal, forgiveness, and family devotion come to life like this. The whole thing is wonderful.

But whenever it feels safe, her eyes wander back to catch the sips of water, the chuckles at someone's delivery, the friendly elbow to Martin Somebody's side, the notes he marks in his binder, the whispered comment that makes Martin Somebody burst out laughing at an inappropriate moment and then apologize sheepishly, and the smirk that sneaks onto Joe's lips at the trouble he's caused.

He barely looks at the script. After so many years working on it, he must know every word by heart. Meanwhile, Sarah can barely remember what she had for breakfast. He's weaving his spell over her without even knowing it. But Sarah is well aware. Too well aware. This is going to be harder than she thought.

When the reading ends, Sarah's wrecked. Her face is hot with tears and humiliation until she notices she's not alone. At least half a dozen others, men and women alike, hold tissues to their noses or surreptitiously wipe their eyes. All around the room, folks sit in stunned silence or snuffle back their emotions. And this is just a read-through. She wonders if it's always like this, but hopes it isn't. She hopes this is truly as special as it feels. The room breaks out into applause and she giddily joins in, leading the cheers.

When lunch is called, Kayla tugs Sarah over to a young guy with carefully messy hair and an athletic fit t-shirt hanging loose except for one section strategically tucked into his jeans revealing a stylish belt. He's got to be at least fifteen years younger than she is, probably twenty, but he stands with so much presence that she's intimidated nonetheless.

"Sarah, have you met Randy? Randy is the first production assistant and he can totally show you the ropes." Kayla says. "Sarah is the new PA. Brand new today, in fact."

"Great," he says staring at his phone in disgust. "There's a shit ton to do and I certainly can't do it all. So, try to keep up." His lips smile, but his tone doesn't. It's not nasty exactly. It's more exasperated, like he's annoyed and exhausted already, though the shoot hasn't even begun yet.

"Hey, this is Sarah's first time on a movie, so play nice."

"First time?" he repeats. She watches his unlined face, untouched by even a hint of gravity, look up from his phone, then size her up in a sharp, assessing gaze. She imagines him thinking, *At your age?*

Sarah stutters her response. "I'm just helping out." Or maybe she's just projecting since she's already feeling woefully out of her league. She can do this, she reminds herself. She can do anything.

"So who have you met so far? Have you met Pete yet?" Randy says.

"Not yet."

"Let's go meet him, then grab some lunch," he suggests. Kayla nods her agreement. "While we can," he adds glimpsing the time on his phone.

Sarah casts a wistful eye toward Joe embroiled in a conversation with Celeste and Naomi. Kayla notices and says, "Unless you have other plans?"

Sarah shakes her head. If they're just friends, they're just friends. She needs to let Joe do his job. And she needs to learn hers.

***

By afternoon, everyone scatters, taking care of business. Kayla wishes Sarah luck before heading off and Sarah wanders uncertainly back into the rehearsal room. Randy's sage advice before going on a supply run was to stick close to Pete, listen, learn, and jump whenever Pete, Naomi, Celeste, or basically anyone else asks for something. Sarah assumes "basically anyone" includes Joe, but she decides it's best to keep her distance anyway, for good measure. No point in tempting Fate. Fate has already tempted her enough.

A much smaller group remains in the room now, clustered around one end of the ring of tables. Sarah sits by the wall, trying to stay unobtrusively available, visible and invisible at the same time. Fortunately, the feat is easily managed because most of the room is oblivious to her. All but one, that is.

Joe and she seem to have a homing beacon, constantly orienting to each other, always aware. At least, she feels it, but she hopes he doesn't and works hard to focus on everyone but him, aware that actual eye contact might throw either of them off their game when they most need to be on. Joe because it's his dream on the line. Sarah because she doesn't want to blow it before she's even begun.

She studies the binder Randy gave her – a handbook to the next four weeks of her life. She combs through the things he's given her with rapt attention: a shooting schedule, cast and crew contacts, a sample call sheet, a variety of set policies, and login credentials for some production software she assumes someone will eventually show her how to use.

The list of locations proves especially intriguing. It's her first peek at what stuck from their tour. She floods with intense memories and not a little pride as she sees spot after spot from their time together. Easy Street Records, the troll, the wheel, the library, MoPop and the fountain, two of the parks, and of course, the crows. It's a roadmap of a love affair, and it's overwhelming. Also thrilling.

Her eyes drift up to Joe as her feelings clump in her throat. Everything she's pushed down for weeks floats back to the surface as she watches him with the others, the model of calm assurance and kindness, collaborative, but commanding, and always ready with an easy laugh. Exactly the man she remembers, only amplified in this larger forum. She stares despite herself until he shifts in his seat and she darts her eyes away for fear of being caught. She has to be more careful. Back to the binder.

Uncertain whether she should listen or not, Sarah attempts to stay alert to the conversation without intruding, drifting in and out as the afternoon goes on. She's nose deep in an internet article on "How to Be a Production Assistant" when she hears a voice she realizes is directed at her.

"Hey, sorry, what's your name again?" Pete says.

Sarah goes hot, not at the slight, if it even was one, but at being caught off guard, the one thing she didn't want. Before she can answer, Joe chimes in. "It's Sarah," he says. Pete shoots Joe a look Sarah can't interpret.

"Sarah," she repeats with a smile.

"Great, Sarah, we could use some fresh coffee. Will you run over to Starbucks? I'll take a Grande Pike Place. Black, no sugar."

Sarah quickly flips open her notebook to a clean page and jots down his order. "Okay. Should I just use my own card or..."

"You don't have a production card?" Pete says.

"She just started this morning. She doesn't have anything," Naomi retorts.

Sarah feels like she's already letting down the team. "I can use my card, it's fine."

"No," Pete says gruffly. "Here." He pulls out a card and hands it to Sarah. "Just get everyone's orders and get back as fast as you can. And be sure to bring back the receipt."

Sarah smiles and works her way around the table taking orders from one distracted person after the next, each of them glued to their phones during their break. When she reaches Joe, he's looking right at her. She startles and glances awkwardly around the room, unsure how to interact with him in their new paradigm. "What would you like?" she asks with a polite waitress smile.

"You don't have to get me coffee," he says, embarrassed.

"Do you *want* coffee, Joe?"

"I'm fine."

"I'm going anyway, you know."

Joe shakes his head, "I'm all good. Wide awake, see," he says, opening his eyes extra wide to illustrate.

Sarah resists the urge to push back further. The familiarity would reveal too much. Instead, she chokes down a laugh of mild disbelief. "Okay. No coffee." She takes one last order, grabs her bag, and leaves without another word.

***

Joe chafes as he watches Sarah go. He was so excited to have her around, and he was sure she'd love being on set. His instincts told him that given a chance to invest in something fully, she'd remember how to shine even without his help. But she deserves better than to be stuck doing coffee runs. Don't they know what a gem they have in her? Then again, it's just the first day. They'll soon see how brightly she can dazzle. But still, coffee? And Pete couldn't even remember her name.

Joe's not thinking clearly, of course. He knows that. Coffee runs are the bread and butter of PA work. How many hundreds of coffee orders has he placed with PAs over the years? Always politely. Always appreciatively. But when push came to shove, he never refused a black Caffè Americano. Until today. And why? She seemed genuinely happy to get him something.

Maybe because he's terrified she's pulling away. When she first walked in, he didn't get a chance to talk to her, but her bashful smile when he waved was enough to keep him going. Those flushed, apple cheeks were irresistible. *God, she's cute!* Just having her around put air in his lungs. At the end of the reading, he noticed muffled sniffles around the room, but all he really cared about was Sarah wiping tears from her eyes. Impressing her felt important, necessary even. He snapped the image in his mind to keep forever. If the movie fails miserably, at least he'll have that.

But why wouldn't she look at him? As he'd tried and failed all day to catch her eye, something sank within him. A glittering helium balloon floating high overhead when the day started, slowly descended to the ground until it was crushed underfoot. Other than their first hello, and their awkward coffee exchange, she hasn't made eye contact once, and the lack of contact singes him. A coldness that burns. She didn't even wait for him for lunch. He agreed to just friends, but this is harder than he expected. If he has to spend the next four weeks seeing her, longing for her, but not touching her, not even really talking to her... well, the prospect isn't one he can afford to contemplate right now.

The meeting resumes, now even smaller. The remaining actors have gone and Joe does his level best to jump back in with both feet as they review the budget. It's actually a little easier with Sarah gone. But when the door opens from the outside, he jumps in anticipation. It's only Randy.

Five minutes later, Sarah does walk in and Joe's eyes bolt to her, eager to catch her in a glance that says she's still his. But she's focused on her cup carriers and looks at no one until she glimpses Randy who waves her over. One by one, she silently delivers the coffees from the carriers while the others speak, double checking the names as she goes. And the last coffee she delivers is to Joe. She sets it down in front of him and walks away to Randy without a word. Joe stares at his name on the cup, then checks to see if Sarah's watching. She's not. Randy has her focused on a laptop in the corner. Joe picks up his cup and takes a sip. Black Caffè Americano.

**

Randy clicks rapidly around the production software, giving Sarah the nickel tour. He shows her the shooting schedule and how it's integrated into the script, how to filter sides – the specific scenes to be filmed – by day or character, and how to pull call sheets. He shows her the process for printing call sheets and sides, pulls up the expense log, and on and on. Sarah does her best to keep up, jotting down keywords and reminders as he goes and praying she can retain everything.

She manages to tune out most of what's going on behind them, but before they finish, she hears the loud click of the door opening and closing several times. When she looks up, most of the remaining group has left. Only Naomi, Celeste, and Pete remain at the table. Joe's making a beeline for the exit. He glances her way before walking out. When they lock eyes, he grimaces mournfully. Then he's gone.

Sarah stares at the closed door and chokes back her pain at the realization that this is how it will be from now on. A whole day in the same room with him and barely a few words between them. And when they did speak, hiding everything real between them. Not from others. That was bad enough, but manageable. Necessary. But the real injury was hiding from Joe. Joe, who saw into her heart from the start. Joe, who seemed to know her better than she knew herself almost as soon as they met. Joe, who made her feel more alive than she'd felt in years. How can she withhold herself from Joe? And then again, what choice does she have?

"Earth to Sarah," Randy says.

Sarah blinks herself back, apologizes, and dives back into the training. Ten minutes later, Pete's voice booms across the room. "Randy, we're heading out. Get some sleep tonight. We're full throttle tomorrow."

"You bet," Randy calls back.

"Also, Joe just called. He forgot his binder. It's on the table. Can you run it up to his room?"

"I'll take care of it," Randy says with a wave. The others depart, leaving Randy and Sarah alone in the giant room. "First one in, last one out, you'll get used to it."

Sarah smiles over her ambivalence. "I don't mind. It's nice to be busy."

"Still, the days will get long quickly. I've still got things to do here, but it's only 4:30. Why don't you take advantage of the early day and get out of here."

"I don't mind helping."

Randy shakes his head. "I'm just printing stuff. It's a one-person job. No worries."

"You sure?" Sarah says.

"Absolutely," Randy says. "But could you run Joe's notebook up to him on your way out?"

CHAPTER TWENTY-EIGHT

TRUTH

JOE STARTLES AT THE sight of Sarah at his door. "Hi," he says, his voice thick with reticence.

"Hi." She holds out his binder.

"Sorry, I thought Randy would bring it up."

An odd response. Is he disappointed? Angry at her? "Randy needed to finish some things, so he asked me to drop it off on my way out."

"You're done for the day?"

"Yeah," she says, waving the binder at him.

"Sorry, thank you. Do you want to come in?"

Not angry, then. Sarah scans the room. It's large with a nonthreatening living area in sight, but she can spy the edge of a bed also in view. "I shouldn't."

"Just for a minute. Tell me about your first day."

Sarah allows herself to linger in his eyes for the first time all day. "Friends?" she says.

"Friends," he agrees. He goes on as she enters, "So, how was it? What did you think?"

"It was fun. I'm already learning a lot. I hope I can keep up."

"Nothing you can't do in your sleep, I'm sure. You're certainly capable of more than fetching coffee."

Sarah shrugs. "I was happy to get it." She pauses, deciding whether to say more. Joe busies himself tidying papers on his desk, shuffling then reshuffling, moving them back and forth from pile to pile. He spends way too much time on those papers. Finally, she goes on. "You're good at this. With them. You're so organized, so on top of everything."

"Thanks. I try."

"You're a natural leader, I can tell. Commanding, but kind." Joe clears his throat as he stares down at his desk. Sarah continues, "How did you think it went today?"

Joe moves on to hanging up a jacket and straightening his shoes by the door. He's uncharacteristically frenetic. She's only seen him like this once before, the night they were first together, when she was about to head home after dinner. An anxiousness that only ended when he invited her to come up, as if simply saying the words he couldn't contain any longer expelled his inner chaos. "Good," he says. "Overall. Honestly, it was a little harder than I expected it to be."

Sarah puzzles over the response. "But it seemed like everything went so smoothly?"

"That's not really what I meant," he says with a quick glance at Sarah. His meaning hangs heavy and clear. He takes some toiletries out of his bag and carries them to the bathroom.

Sarah contemplates her fight or flight response at the emotional truth rearing its ugly head, but opts for an attempt at proper "just friends" conversation. "You were great in the read-through."

"I was kind of phoning it in," he calls from the bathroom where he's taking an inordinately long time to organize his toiletries.

"If that was you phoning it in, I can't wait for the real thing."

He brushes past her, frantic for things to do. "Yeah?"

"Yeah. You made me cry."

He finally stops tidying and looks at her. "I don't ever want to make you cry." A stillness falls over the room. Once again, he's said the words he couldn't contain any longer, words that can't be unsaid. "Sarah..."

Flight it is. "I should go."

"Why does it feel like you're always running out on me?"

Sarah inhales deeply for strength. "I can't do this. I can't go through this again."

"Can we talk? Please?"

"You promised," she says.

"I tried. I swear to you I tried." The agony stretched across his face speaks to the truth of this. "I didn't ask for you. I specifically asked for Randy. But you knocked on my door. You. And I think there's a reason for that."

"We didn't even make it a day," she grumbles to herself, then to Joe, "What is there to talk about?"

"You know what. I know you're feeling it, too."

"Whatever I may or may not feel doesn't matter," she says, eyeing the door. "Not more than our families." Even after twenty years, she remembers too well the sting of her parents' divorce. "Not more than the people we'd hurt."

The words bring them to a screeching halt, and they retreat to their corners. He drops on the couch. She pointedly plops herself in the desk chair at a distance. Each mulls over their next move. Joe speaks first. "You're absolutely right. We both have people we love. And the last thing I want is to hurt them."

"Exactly."

"But you can't deny what's happening here," Joe says. "We both know you knocked on that door today for a reason bigger than a binder. I don't know what this thing is. I don't know how to explain it. But I know I've never felt anything like it. I know I can't stop thinking about you."

She sighs, exasperated, "I just got my life back." He waits curiously for her to go on. "For months now, ever since I met you, you've taken up residency in my brain. You've occupied my every thought, my every breath. I've tried to go on as normal, but you were always there, kissing me, smiling at me, making me feel..." She takes a deep breath before continuing, "But I finally started to shake this thing. I didn't know when you were coming back and that was fine. I finally felt like I was moving on from whatever that was. That crazy blip."

"It was more than a blip. And technically it was three blips," he smirks, trying to break the tension.

She glares. No time for levity. "It was so hard. I mean, have you seen you? You're not easy to get over. But I was doing it."

"And then I came back and screwed it all up again." He nods sadly. "I'm sorry for that."

They fall silent again as Sarah kneads her lower lip, contemplating. "I mean, the first time, fine. It was a slip. Chalk it up to the wine and a magical evening. The second time, I don't know, I guess it was a fling. Maybe that's the word? It shouldn't have happened. But still redeemable. But if we start it up now, you know what it is."

"Tell me," Joe says. "Tell me what this is."

There's only one answer Sarah can give, but she hates it. She hates the word, hates the implication, hates the possibility that what she's feeling could be so tawdry and sad. "It's an affair." The word stabs. She lets it hang there a moment before adding definitively, "I can't be a person who has an affair."

Joe doesn't miss a beat. "Okay, but what if it's more than that?"

Sarah stops in her tracks. *More than that?*

Joe repeats himself. "What if this isn't an affair? What if this is something more?"

"We both know this ends when the shoot ends. It has to. So, what else *can* it be?"

"I don't know. But I'd sure like to find out. Wouldn't you?"

The word *Yes!* screams through her nervous system. Between an unforgivable affair and a completely unrealistic future together, is there a third option? Something as destined and beautiful as every single moment she's spent with Joe has seemed? Something uniquely theirs, both fleeting and eternal, gifted by the gods just when they needed it most? Something as inevitable as it is impossible. "This is crazy," she says.

"I think that's why you're so scared. I know you don't want to hurt anyone. I know that! Neither do I. But that's not what this is really about, is it?"

"I don't know what you mean," Sarah says, staring hard at the floor.

"You're scared to death this might actually be something real. Something... *destined* for us."

Destined? She'd thought the same thing, but it's even more unnerving hearing it spoken aloud. "Well, that would be a disaster," she whispers.

"Look, I don't know what to say. I get it. I do. But you are so deep down in my system that I can't shake you. I've tried, believe me. Bottom line, I'm not ready to let you go." He lets the sentiment set in before adding emphatically, "And I don't think I'm supposed to. Not yet anyway." Sarah's eyes burn a hole through the carpet. She laughs bitterly, but still won't look up, so Joe tries again. "Sarah, I know you're scared. I'm scared, too. Hell, I'm terrified."

She eyes him cautiously. "What are *you* afraid of?"

"I'm afraid of hurting people I love, just like you." His face twitches at the thought.

"Then what are we doing here?"

"But I'm even more terrified you'll walk out of this room and out of my life. And I'm not ready for that."

She thinks hard before finally speaking. "The thing is... If I let you in, really in... you could destroy me."

"And there it is," he says with a nod.

"You could. You'd have the power to do it."

"But. I. Won't," he says calmly, definitively, compassionately. "And that's the truest thing you've said since you walked in here today." Sarah shrinks into herself as Joe goes on. "Do you remember what I said to you our first night together? When we were on the couch?"

Sarah flashes back to the feeling of his hands on her body for the first time. How thrilling it was, to feel him, to feel wanted by him. And how vulnerable she felt – until he said those words. She couldn't forget those words if she tried.

"Do you remember that?"

"Yes," she replies, expressionless.

"What did I say?"

She opens her mouth, but nothing comes out.

Joe goes on in her stead. "I said you were safe with me. And you are. And you always will be. I promise you, I will never hurt you." He pauses and waits for her. When she still doesn't speak, he adds, "And by the way, you have the same power over me."

"Oh, come on," she grumbles.

"You know, I can't decide if your skepticism is more insulting to me or to you. Don't you know? Your name is written all over this city. Monorail. Sarah. Seattle Wheel. Sarah. Every building, every park, every tree. Hell, even the crows caw your name. Sarah, Sarah, Sarah."

"Alright, stop cawing my name!"

"We have crows in LA, too, by the way. And that's not even to mention half the songs on the radio. And the thought of going through this shoot without you at my side is killing me."

"But what's the point? It's all going to end in a few weeks anyway. Then what?"

She has an undeniable point. "I don't know. You're right. I think if we're being realistic, maybe there's a clock on us. And we have to accept that."

"So isn't it better to end it now and save a lot of heartbreak?"

"Oh, baby, you've got it backwards. If the clock is ticking on whatever this is, then I don't want to waste another day. Hell, I don't want to waste another *minute* without you." Sarah buries her face in her hands as Joe crosses the room and kneels in front of her. He gently takes her hands in his, but she avoids his eyes. "This is it, Sarah. This is what we get. This may be *all* we get. But right now, this feels like everything. *Like this is our moment.*

And I'm asking you to stay." When she says nothing, he adds. "I know you want this."

She finally looks at him. "Of course I do," she says before pulling herself up and toward the door. "But I can't."

"And I want this," Joe says as he stands. "I want you."

Those words in that voice steal her breath. Feeling so wanted is intoxicating. She pivots halfway to him, unable either to walk out the door or to face him.

"I honestly wish I didn't," he goes on. "But I do. I want you, Sarah."

She folds her arms tightly across her chest. But those words. How can she resist those words?

Joe creeps up to her. "I don't want to hurt anyone either." He casts his eyes down a moment, then back to Sarah. "But I know with every fiber of my being that this moment is meant to be. It's ours." Sarah dares a glance into his eyes, but can't hold it. "Can't we just be together, here and now? Just you and me?" He pauses, then adds emphatically, "And no one else... no one else... needs to be in this room with us. Just you..." He gently pulls her arms away from her chest and takes her hands in his once again. "And me."

"Joe..."

"Sarah..." He stands in front of her, too close. Her eyes rooted to the floor, Sarah's breath escapes in a shaky tremble. A soft rumble of desire rolls through his voice as he murmurs, "I just want to be with you. I just want to touch you." He caresses her hair down to her neck and finds her eyes at last. "I just want to kiss you."

Their lips meld in a velvety, lingering kiss.

"No one can know," she finally says in quiet gasp of breath.

He kisses her again. "Just us," he whispers.

"Just us," she agrees.

Chapter Twenty-Nine

The Shoot

Sarah sees Joe little the next day. He's in costume fittings first thing, then shooting by mid-morning, while she's sent on constant errands – picking up a cast member, out for coffee, and on three different supply runs for three different people.

Although she and Joe once again barely speak the whole day, everything else is different from the day before. Whenever she enters the room he's in, the air crackles with electricity. They know before they see each other. They catch eyes, but suppress the smiles they each know are hiding behind their tightly closed lips. A secret knowing. A precious secret that illuminates them both from within. Yesterday's longing and heartbreak replaced by desire and anticipation, knowing however long and exhausting the day may be, at the end of it, they will be together.

Mid-afternoon, Sarah's sent back to the hotel to tear down their production office. They'd been using one of the hotel's conference rooms for the first couple days for the all-call and table read, but now they're downsizing and moving upstairs to one of the production's hotel rooms. She helps Randy relocate their computers and printer and a surprisingly large number of crates upstairs, bit by bit. By the time the large room is cleared, the day's nearly over.

Randy checks in with Pete when they finish. Pete calls him back to set, but passes on a message to let Sarah go for the day. Sarah suspects they're going easy on her because she's a volunteer. Or maybe because she's the newbie and still doesn't know how to do much. Either way, she needs a reason to stick around until Joe gets back, so she offers to print the next day's call sheets and sides.

Randy frowns. "You sure you're up to it? We only went over it once."

"I think so" Sarah replies, pleasantly surprised by how confident she feels. "Logistics, data, apps, stuff like this, used to be my thing. Before my glamorous movie career."

"Well, don't get too good at it," Randy says. "I still need my job." He leaves her with instructions and a room key and trills as he closes the door, "See you in the morning!"

Sarah finishes up her work, then pulls out her phone to text Joe and kill time. She hides out in the production office, praying no one else shows up before him. When she told Ben about the job, she'd warned him there would be a lot of late nights for the shoot and she didn't know when yet, which was true fortunately, so she hadn't lied. At least not yet. And as a result, he's not expecting her in time for dinner tonight or any other night for the next month. It was an easy adjustment for him to make, since he's barely home anyway, and rarely present in any real sense. In fact, he seemed happy Sarah had something to do.

Of course, the obvious truth is he probably wouldn't be quite so happy if he knew the whole story. No man wants their wife sleeping with someone else, even if only in principle. But in her darker moments, Sarah wrestles with an even uglier possibility. That he might not actually care that much if he did know. He did seem jealous at dinner that night, but maybe that was more wounded ego than anything. She used to know with absolute certainty that he adored her, but that certainty faded right along with dinners together and any semblance of a sex life. It's been a long time since she felt like she factored into his thinking much at all.

In any case, what she has with Joe has nothing to do with Ben. Joe had seen that first. While she was still clinging to her perfectly valid fear of hurting others, and of getting hurt, Joe had already embraced the strange, yet undeniable truth. Theirs is a connection unlike any other, entirely apart from anything and anyone else. But she understands at last.

The need to be careful is undeniable. No matter how shaky their marriages, neither of them could bear hurting their families. That knowledge is paramount. Sacrosanct. Plus, Joe told her about what his agent Clark said, that exposure could spook investors and put the whole film at risk. If a small production like this, with no buzz or big names, gets tainted with scandal, investors could still pull out rather than throw good money after bad, destroying Joe's dream in a devastating flash. Yes, secrecy is a must.

But Sarah finally sees and accepts what Joe saw from the beginning. There's a tiny, but infinite world that is all theirs. A moment in time, brief but everlasting, that's just for them. Their eternal tether, which has connected them for longer than either of them knew, has tugged them back together and intertwined them so tightly as to leave no air between them. In this world, in this moment, they are only each other's.

She assembles and organizes the last of the print-outs and leaves them for Randy as instructed. Then she leans back and spins the desk chair in dreamy circles, thinking of the night ahead. Her reverie is broken by the chirp of a text from Gabi. *How's it going so far?*

Sarah realizes that after her late night with Joe and all the craziness of the day today, she hasn't told Gabi what's happened. She winces as she looks for the words. Gabi will take her side no matter what, of course. When Gabi says ride-or-die, she means it. But finding the right words, especially in a text, is still a tricky prospect. Sarah thinks carefully. Their best friend code is strong, but it's like a game of Password. Sarah needs to give the clue in the fewest words possible. Finally, she answers, *It's... perfect.*

Within seconds, Gabi's response pings, *Guuurrrl, call me. I need to know everything!*

Just then, the door lock clicks and Joe walks in smiling like the cat who swallowed the canary. Sarah giggles as she feels her blood heating. She holds up a finger and returns to her phone for a final, quick message to Gabi. *Later. I promise!*

***

A disorienting clang bounces off the walls as Sarah enters. They're shooting in one of the jazz clubs and Sarah's supposed to help corral the extras who will play the denizens of the nightspot. She scans the room for the source of the clamor and spots a drum set knocked on its side by a crew member now clumsily trying to reset it. Then it hits her. Even as they're dressing the space for a 1970s vibe, the bar is unmistakable. She's never been here, but she knows that stage and dancefloor well. It's where Joe posed in his photo, dancing with Sarah's ghost, while the stage behind him stood eerily empty. She must have stared at that photo a hundred times.

A tap on her shoulder brings her back to the present. "You made it to day three. Nice! You here to help me?" Kayla says.

"I'm supposed to help with the extras."

"Great, you'll be with me and Tish, the costume designer. C'mon." Kayla leads Sarah to the makeshift costume shop at the back of the club. They're shooting a flashback scene this morning, so the tiny team has their work cut out for them with 30+ extras soon to descend on them, all needing 1970s era club wear, hair, and make-up.

Kayla and Tish are busily setting up an assembly line for the soon-to-arrive extras, with a holding pen, a screened off area for fittings, and two stations where extras will land once they're in costume. They both have extra hands for the day, local make-up artists and costumers, to assist with the glamming. Sarah's job is to check-in the extras and keep them flowing efficiently from station to station, then out to set. Sarah scans the list of extras and drums her fingers on the clipboard.

Kayla clocks her panic. "It's dead easy. When they get here, just check them in and lead them back here. We'll do the rest."

Sarah smiles her gratitude and shakes her head. "I don't know why I'm so nervous."

"It's all new. You're a fish out of water right now," Kayla says as she fluffs a wig.

"That's for sure."

Kayla sets down the wig. "But you're swimming just the same," she says with a smile and wink.

Sarah laughs in appreciation. She's never been a winker herself, but she enjoys Kayla's skillful deployment and takes heart. She heads for the front door and before she knows it, the first extras descend. She marks them off one at a time, walks them back, then returns to greet the next arrivals. Before long they're coming too quickly to make a trip for each one, so she holds them in groups, walking them back four at a time while asking the next person to wait by the door with anyone else who arrives. When the group gets too large for the waiting area, and too big to loiter in the foyer, Sarah commandeers a corner of the bar where there's no activity and stations the waiting extras there.

The work is hectic, but easy. Far easier than anything she did in her prior professional life certainly. Still, she's amazed how even this small task energizes her. She calls out across the club to the next group and waves them over. As the group of four gathers their things, Sarah grins with satisfaction. It's barely a job. She could do it in her sleep. But feeling responsible and together, taking charge of something and managing it well – these are things she used to take for granted. Now they feel foreign, and surprisingly exhilarating.

She's actually having fun.

Once everyone's checked in, Sarah has time to loiter a little longer and watch Kayla's team work. She marvels as the people who walked in as 21st century hipsters emerge from Tish's dressing area in brightly colored polyester suits, wrap dresses, and platform shoes, ready for a night on the town fifty years ago. But it only gets better when they land in the hair and make-up chairs.

The men don't need much make-up since they'll be fading into a dark background. The women's make-up is more glamorous to read on camera, but it's the hair where the real fun starts. Kayla puts a pick gently to the newly affixed afro on the extra in the chair. "For scenes like the one we're shooting today," Kayla explains, "silhouettes matter most because it'll be dark in the club." She pats the extra's shoulder to release her, then welcomes the next extra to her chair. "Faces will get lost in the background, but not hair. Hair sets the scene."

Kayla asks Sarah to take photos of the process and of the extras in full 70s drag, featuring a cavalcade of shags, wedges, pageboys, deep side parts, mutton chops, and caterpillar mustaches. Sarah complies, pleased to have an excuse to stay where she is. There's a calm Zen quality about the process as Kayla and her team apply make-up and spirit gum and affix each wig just so. Each extra enjoying the attention like a day at the spa. Yet, the Zen's also infused with an undeniable energy, which pulses and invigorates everything. They are making magic together – and Sarah's a part of it.

For the first time since Synergy, she remembers how good it feels to be part of something that truly matters to her. Sure, she's a small part, but like they say, there are no small roles, only small actors. Maybe it's time for her to stop acting, and living, so small.

***

Sarah inserts the keycard for the third time into the production office door. The tiny light clicks red again. "Dammit," she mumbles to herself as she shuffles her large bag and heavy armful of binders.

"Problem?" a voice says from behind her.

The director Celeste approaches. Sarah grumbles over the binders, "My key isn't working."

"Let me help." Celeste reaches for the binders and lifts them from Sarah's arm, glimpsing in Sarah's bag as she does. "Maybe it's the wrong key. Maybe it's that one."

Sarah glances down at her bag gaping open and realizes with horror what's happened. She's using Joe's room key. She had tried so hard to keep them separate and straight, but somehow in the chaos of the day, she must have mixed them up. Idiot.

"Which one?" Sarah says dumbly, scrounging for an explanation for the other key. Her mouth bone dry.

"You have another hotel key there," Celeste says pointing to the tip of the card peeking out of an inner pocket. "Maybe it's that one."

Sarah furrows her brows and reaches for the key, "Oh no! I must have picked up someone else's key by accident." Her fingertips tingle as she fumbles for the key and drops it. When she stoops to pick it up, her bag slips off her shoulder and more things pop out. She attempts to gather them all, panic making every action inefficient and frantic. "Sorry! I'm a mess."

As Sarah shuffles her stuff back into her purse, Celeste picks up the key and inserts it in the lock, which clicks green and the door opens at last. "There," Celeste says kindly.

Sarah smiles nervously, slips Joe's key into her pocket, and follows Celeste into the room. "I feel terrible, though. I hope no one's panicking about their key. I'll turn it in at the desk."

"Sarah, it's okay. Don't worry," Celeste says, a smidge too solicitously. "Everyone gets two keys." Her tone is warm, reassuring. But is it just Sarah's imagination or is she implying something more? Her face is unreadable. "Just in case," Celeste adds.

Sarah nods her appreciation, but her shoulders tighten. Surely she's just being paranoid.

CHAPTER THIRTY

MORE

THE DOOR FLINGS OPEN and before Sarah knows what's happening, Joe grabs her hand and yanks her into his room. A shriek of delighted glee escapes her mouth as he pulls her into him, slamming the door behind her and pressing his lips to hers. She falls back against the door and he pushes closer, running his hands over her body as they kiss. She wraps her arms around his neck and luxuriates in his explorations. Sheer joy.

"God, baby, you're so hot," he breathes into her neck as his tongue trails upward. And for the first time in far too long – with Joe's warm, wet breath in her ear and his hands hungrily palming her breasts, then gliding down her stomach and around to grab her ass – she feels it.

"How much time do we have?" she mutters as their lips slip apart.

"Not enough," he says, unbuttoning her blouse. "But I'll make it work."

They stumble their way to the bed, clutching and squeezing and disrobing en route. No time to waste. Joe has to leave for set in under an hour and every minute is precious. This is the first day they've spent without speaking. Sarah was busy wrangling extras most of the day and Joe was busy staying out of the way. He'd wanted to speak to her so many times, but hadn't wanted to distract her as she found her groove. Or raise suspicions. They're known to be friends, of course. No reason they can't chat. But they have to be careful.

They make love urgently, with the passion of a first love. Like lovers decades younger just discovering the incendiary nature of a true soul connection, the physical act transformed by the intensity of desire for someone who is absolutely meant for you. Every kiss is electric. Every touch burns. They move quickly, desperately at first, overwhelmed with their need for each other. They rock together to a fever pitch until they collapse. But as they gaze into each other's eyes just after, happy and exhausted, what began as fiery and fierce transmutes into a tenderness so profound it nearly brings them both to tears.

***

Joe checks his text. "Pick-up is ten minutes out." He watches Sarah zip up her jeans, straighten her top, and cross the room for her boots. "I wish you could come to set tonight," he says.

"Me, too," Sarah says. "But Pete said he didn't need me. Naomi said she didn't need me. How could I justify it?" She plops on the side of the bed and hikes up a jean leg.

"It's just..." Joe grazes his fingers down her back as he thinks. "It's not enough time. We're going to be like ships in the night. I want more than that."

Sarah zips one boot, then tugs on the other. "Meaning what?"

"I want more than stolen moments with you."

She absorbs his words with a sad smile. "But how? This is dangerous already," Sarah tells Joe about the incident with Celeste and the keycard. "I mean, it wasn't a huge deal, but still."

It's true. It is dangerous. But ever since he met her, Sarah's been Joe's saving grace, and the film's saving grace as well. How can the woman who saved his trip and gave him the crows, the woman who filled the emptiness with her very breath, be anything other than good luck? Sarah herself is the ward against danger.

"What if someone catches me coming and going around the hotel at the wrong time?" she goes on. "Or from your room?"

"Well, the good news is, I'm the only one in the production on this floor. I made sure of that."

"Why?" Sarah says, before gasping indignantly and slapping Joe's arm. "You knew!" she laughs as she hits him.

"I hoped!" he chokes out through laughter as he protects himself from Sarah's playful assault.

Sarah crosses her arms in mock anger. "Even so. That still doesn't help if I run into someone in the elevator at midnight when I was supposedly done at eight."

Joe jumps up in a sudden burst of energy. "Get a room at the hotel. We'll pay. It would make it a lot easier with the long hours you'll be working anyway. They've gone easy on you so far, probably because you're new. But trust me, the schedule's about to get real. You'll be shuttling actors at all hours and fetching God knows what. If you're staying with the crew, you'll have a reason to be here at any hour. No one will question it."

"Is that even an option? When I live here?"

"We budgeted for another PA room. You're already saving us cash on your salary. And your car. A room is literally the least we can do."

"But I wouldn't be in there at all."

"It wouldn't be the first time a room sat empty. And it's a normal operating expense. I'm sure I can make it happen."

She's unconvinced. Then again, Joe does have a knack for prophecy. "But what would I say to...?" They wince in unison at the name she can't bring herself to say.

"We're getting you a room to stay with the crew because of the schedule. All true."

Sarah gives him a hopeful, but wary look. "I don't know."

"I do," he grins. "Trust me."

***

Sarah teeters onto set with a stack three boxes high of doughnuts balanced in her arms. She was asked by craft services – or the crafties as insiders call them – to do a supply run and had offered to put a more local spin on the restocking. She's already picked up bulk supplies to refresh the cheese, crackers, hummus, veggies, fruit slices, chips, trail mix, five different drink options. And now, the piece de resistance. Top Pot Doughnuts.

She drops the boxes proudly on the table, excited for the mostly out-of-towner cast and crew to sample the deliciousness of the local institution. She cracks open a whole box of apple fritters, Top Pot's crowning glory, and inhales the sweet, cinnamon laced delirium wafting through the air. She cuts each fritter and doughnut in half, then stares happily, debating whether to take the honor of the first taste, when she hears her name.

"Sarah, there you are."

She stiffens at the voice, which she recognizes as Pete. Not a bad guy, just a tad gruff. She sighs at the realization she won't be getting any Top Pot of her own after all, at least not yet.

Pete's huddling with Celeste, the director of photography Igor, and Joe. "Can you run to Starbucks?" Pete says.

Sarah casts an involuntary glance toward the fresh pot of coffee on the crafty table before catching Joe's expression. Before she can answer, he jumps in. "You know there's coffee right there, right?" he says, his irritation evident.

"Joe," Celeste chimes in quietly, attempting to subtly keep the peace.

"I prefer Starbucks," Pete says.

"You're really going to make her make a special coffee run just for you?" Joe retorts.

"I *like* Starbucks," Pete says.

"Actually, I like Starbucks, too," Igor offers agreeably, unaware of what he's stepped into.

Joe's face twists with disgust. "That's not the point."

This is so not what Sarah needs. She just wants to keep her head down and do her job as well as she can. No small roles, only small actors and all that. But Joe is turning this into a whole thing. It's sweet of him – God, so sweet! – but way out of line. She dives in to head off the coming freight train. "It's fine! I'm happy to get the Starbucks."

"You don't have to, Sarah. We've got coffee here," Joe says.

"Actually, she does. Because I asked her to," Pete says. Pete and Joe lock eyes for a tense moment, everyone around them shifting uncomfortably. Even Igor has finally picked up on the charge in the air. Glaring at Joe, Pete adds without turning, "Sarah, Joe seems to think I'm abusing you. Do you feel abused?"

"Not at all. I'd like to get the coffee. Joe, it's fine. I'm happy to run to Starbucks. It's what I'm here for." Sarah smiles and nods in exaggerated joviality.

"What's your problem, dude?" Pete says, still in standoff mode.

Joe spots Sarah's plaintive face, begging him to let it go. He takes a deep breath and relaxes his posture, considering his next words. "She used to run a company, *dude*," he says before pivoting, trying to diffuse the situation he's created. "I just think we should play to people's strengths."

"Joe," Celeste says softly, "it is her job. At least part of it."

"I could use a Frappuccino anyway," Sarah says pleasantly, urging Joe with her eyes. He really needs to back off.

"Fine," Joe says, eyes fixed on Sarah, before nodding to Celeste. "Fair enough." He pats Pete amiably on the arm. "Sorry, Pete. I guess I'm just tired."

The whole group relaxes into tentative laughter, attempting to expel the weirdness. Celeste gives Joe's arm a supportive squeeze then glances at Sarah. They catch eyes and the director smiles awkwardly at her before quickly looking away as if she's seen something she shouldn't have.

Unnerved by Celeste's expression, Sarah inhales deeply. "Anyone else want Starbucks?"

***

Sarah folds her legs under her in the chair and leans against the cushy arm, her fourth adjustment in five minutes. Her body is wound too tightly, locked by her brain, for her to relax. She tries to read, but can't concentrate through the cloud of frustration, fear, and anger swamping her thoughts. She's spent the day avoiding Joe because she didn't know how to digest what happened and couldn't take it up with him in public anyway, but she has to say something.

The door clicks as Joe walks in and wraps his arms around her. He kisses her behind the ear and whispers, "Hi, beautiful." A thrill bounces around every corner of her body like it does every time he touches her. But she resists, straightens her back, and says nothing.

Joe can't miss the volume of her silence. He swings around and plops on the coffee table in front of her. "You okay?"

She stares at him sternly. "You can't do that, Joe."

His face falls in instant recognition. "I'm sorry. I just don't like the way he treats you, like you're just the coffee girl."

"I am the coffee girl," she says emphatically.

"You're so much more than that."

"To you. To him, I'm the production assistant. And he treats me just fine. Seriously."

"Yeah, but—"

Sarah cuts him off. "But nothing!" It's the most heated she's ever been with him. "I'm doing the job I was hired to do. The job you hired me to do, by the way. And I'm happy to do it." Joe hangs his head. "You can't do anything like that again. You have to let me do my job and trust I can take care of myself if there's a problem."

"I do trust you. Completely."

Sarah almost softens until she flashes back to the expression on Celeste's face. "Besides, you're gonna make people suspicious acting like that."

"I'm sorry." Head still low, he adds. "I just want everything for you."

The rasp in his voice scrapes over Sarah's heart, his sad puppy face almost more than she can bear. Her point made, she lifts her hand to his cheek. "I'm pretty sure I've got everything already. But I'll tell you what. If I need back-up, I promise I'll come to you. Deal?"

"Deal," he croaks mournfully.

She leans forward in her seat and Joe raises his head to meet her lips. Just before they touch, she whispers, "I love—" her voice catches in her throat. She stumbles, then continues, "—that you care enough to look out for me. Thank you."

"Oh, Sarah," Joe whispers back as their lips melt into each other, "if you only knew." They lean their heads together until the stillness is interrupted by Sarah's phone. It's Gabi.

"I should get this," she says as she moves for the door. Part of their agreement to shut out the world and keep their time together sacrosanct. Their "just us" agreement. No conversations with or about family in the room. It's a false reality, they know. A bubble that must eventually pop. But for now, it allows them to keep a holy place that is wholly theirs. A place that will always be theirs. The gift of eternity in a hotel room.

Although Gabi's the one person who knows the truth, she still counts as family, so Sarah slips into the hallway and heads for her own room. "As luck would have it" – Sarah had rolled her eyes hard when Joe smirked his way through those words – she ended up with a room on the 6th floor with Joe. The only other 6th floor room in the production. *Funny thing, that!* She spends no time to speak of there, but it's a useful retreat for occasional calls with Gabi or Ben – though Ben mostly just texts, as usual. Sarah may be in a constant state of change these days, but Ben is still Ben, after all. They don't talk when she's home. Why would they talk now?

Sarah and Gabi talk for half an hour, giggling like teenagers. Sarah flops on the bed while gossiping about everything that's happened. Gabi tells

Sarah how the new hire at the foodbank is working out and updates Sarah on *Our* New Friend Dana, since Gabi has now adopted Dana as well. "With you gone now, I have to hang out with someone," Gabi announces sullenly.

Sarah rolls her eyes. "It's barely been a week since I saw you last. And you say that like it's a punishment. Dana's awesome."

"I know," Gabi sighs. "She is. But it doesn't mean I don't miss you."

"I never thought it did." Sarah smiles hard through the line to be sure Gabi hears it.

"Just don't get any big ideas about running off to Hollywood and leaving me."

Sarah's smile fades at this. "Don't worry, for better or worse, this will all be over in a few weeks." Even as Sarah says it, she shuts her eyes to block it out, but the words float around behind her eyelids like she's stared into a bright light a moment too long. And maybe that's just what she has done.

***

Sarah unwraps a new ten-pack of notepads and plops them on the supply table before tidying the sharpies and pens into their cups. She's straightening the binders, three-ring hole punch, and stapler into a pleasant configuration when she hears Joe announce, "We have a problem." Assuming he's talking to her, she spins in terror to face him.

Celeste interrupts her conversation with Igor. "What's up?"

"The park where we're supposed to be shooting tomorrow has been double booked," Joe says.

Celeste stares at Joe blankly. "I don't understand."

"They booked a wedding there right when we're supposed to be filming," Joe says.

"Wait, back up. First, why isn't Pete telling me this?"

"That costume warehouse is way out toward the mountains. I've tried him twice, but he must not have service."

"So you got the call?" Celeste asks.

"I'm on a list of producers, I guess. I just turned on my phone during our break and the message popped in. You probably have one, too."

Celeste pulls out and switches on her phone. A message from an unknown local number pops in. "Damn," she says. The muscles on her face visibly tighten. "Where's Naomi? Can she deal with this?"

Igor chimes in, "Naomi's on her way to LA."

"Timing is everything." Celeste sets her jaw and thinks. "Luke?"

"Scouting another film," Joe says dejectedly.

Celeste drops her head and rubs her temple. "You're telling me we have no location tomorrow, two hours before the end of the business day, and absolutely no one to troubleshoot this issue who isn't supposed to be on-set again in five minutes?"

Sarah has been hanging back listening and fiddling with a pen cap to contain her anxiety, but Celeste looks so desperate, she's compelled to step forward. To stop acting small. "I can fix it," she says. "I know all the locations, I know the shooting schedule. I can figure something out."

Joe watches Celeste hopefully. Celeste smiles kindly, but shakes her head. "Thank you, Sarah. That's good of you to offer. But it's not that simple. It's not just the locations. There are budget impacts with how we schedule the cast, when they're on, when they're on hold—"

"The day out of days schedule. I know."

"You know the day out of days?" Celeste says.

The astonished director glances at Joe's gleeful expression. "I told you she's sharp," he says.

Celeste raises her hands in front of her in a gesture of combined praise and declination. "I just don't think it's realistic."

Her hesitation makes sense. Sarah should probably be more hesitant than she is, but something in her knows she can do this. A month ago, she could barely get out of bed. Now she thinks she can literally save the day for an entire film production? Yes. "Let me try. Really. Logistics are my thing. At least they used to be."

Celeste looks first at Igor who shrugs uncertainly, and then at Joe. "She ran a multi-million-dollar company, Celeste," he says.

The director laughs in dismay and shakes her head again. "I guess whatever you come up with is better than losing a whole day. Go for it. See what you can do."

Celeste returns to discussing the next shot with Igor, and Sarah dashes off to tackle her project. Joe can barely contain himself.

***

Two and a half hours later, as Celeste yells, "Cut," Sarah walks in with a binder full of papers to distribute. She announces that she identified days she could switch without throwing off the actors' work days. Then she cross-referenced those with the scheduled locations to determine which would be likely to be most flexible and easiest to reach on short notice. She made some calls, smooth talked a couple location contacts, and coordinated with the Seattle film commission to update the dates on their permit. She double checked the shot list, updated the shooting schedule, and confirmed the call list. She emailed all the decision-makers to confirm the changes in writing, waited for confirmation back in writing, and then printed all new call sheets, sides, and copies of the updated shooting schedule for everyone involved.

Boom.

Celeste stands speechless as she flips through her stack of papers. "It'll be a push for the actors."

Joe scans the schedule. "It's mostly me and I'm ready. Tad and Ellis only have a couple lines and Allie's a pro. She'll be fine."

Celeste continues scanning for problems. Finding none, she looks up in amazement. "Sarah, you are a wonder."

Sarah offers an embarrassed shrug. "Logistics are my thing." A giddy rush bubbles up in her smile. She did it. She really fucking did it.

"They certainly are," Celeste says. She spots Joe's Cheshire Cat grin and laughs. "Your girl is something else," she says before walking away. Joe bounces his brows proudly at Sarah before following Celeste back to set.

As the set buzzes back to life after their break, Celeste's words are still ringing in Sarah's head. *Your girl.* She said those words – to Joe. Why? Maybe she just meant it colloquially, like "yer man" in Ireland, and "your boy" in bro talk. Or the old, sexist term for men's secretaries? Even that would be preferable to the possibility freaking Sarah out at the moment. Moments ago, she was sailing, but the implication of those words winds her like a shot put to the chest.

Sarah's hand tingles as the world begins to shrink to a pinpoint, but before it gets there, a manically proud Joe sneaks behind her and whispers in a raspy, low growl, "I'm going to fuck you so hard tonight." The words travel straight down a vibrating nerve from her ear to her heart where they split off and hit her groin and funny bone at the same moment. She bursts out cackling so loudly she instinctively covers her mouth. But by the time anyone spots the source of the delighted outburst, Joe has dashed away and left Sarah standing all alone. In her very own spotlight.

***

Sarah leans on the reception desk at the Seattle film commission office as she waits for her contact Louise to emerge. She fiddles with the crinkly cellophane wrapper of the Seattle Chocolates she's brought as a thank you, then tugs the bow that fastens the bag a little tighter. A young woman with a pixie cut and bright red glasses walks out from the offices beyond the desk. "Sarah, hi, I'm Louise."

Sarah offers her hand as she speaks. "It's so nice to meet you in person."

"Yeah, same," Louise says with a cheerful smile.

Sarah launches in without further ado. "I know you have a lot on your plate, so I don't want to keep you. But I was running errands near here and

I just wanted to bring you this as a thank you for all your help sorting out our last-minute permit date changes the other day."

Louise makes a decidedly unladylike grunt of delight. "Salted chocolates, yum!" She clutches them with a greedy grin. "That was really sweet of you. Unnecessary, but sweet. Thank you! I was happy to help. I'm just glad you caught me when you did! Five minutes later, I would have been buried in a hiring committee meeting until the end of day."

"Hiring?" Sarah says. Her heart beats faster at the word. The thought of working somewhere like this had never occurred to her, but as she looks around the colorful, creative, but still professional offices – the workspace equivalent of a mullet – the idea sings to her. Oh yeah, this is an actual place people work. She's almost afraid to speak, but she forces the words out. "What are you hiring for?"

"We're about to start an interview process for a new Director of Operations. But when you called, it was just a preliminary meeting, so I just finished everything up for you and went a little late. No big deal."

Director of Operations? That job has Sarah written all over it. The symphony in her heart plays ever more furiously. "You're about to start as in the position is closed or...?" If it's not too late to apply, this could almost feel —

"Not yet. It closes today actually."

Like Destiny.

***

"I have news," Sarah says as she pours wine into a glass for Joe.

He walks out of the shower wrapped in a towel, takes the glass, and sips before setting it back down to dress. "What kind of news?"

Sarah takes a breath and announces, "I applied for a job."

Joe freezes, towel on the floor, naked. "What?" he grins. "What job? Where did this come from?"

Sarah eyes his privates. "Put on some pants and I'll tell you."

Joe slips on his underwear, followed by a pair of sweats, then plops himself in front of her. "Tell me."

She giddily recounts the events of the day and how perfect the job seems, at least on paper. "So I ducked into the production office and got my application in this afternoon."

"Wow!" Joe says.

"It was a little rushed, but I think my letter was pretty good. Plus, the folks at the office said they'd watch for it."

Joe stares at her in stunned enchantment, a smile almost too wide to squeeze out words. "That's amazing," he finally says.

"Well, I've just applied. It doesn't mean I'll get it."

"You'll get it. And you'll be great."

Sarah flushes red at the compliment, the wine and her own excitement adding layers of rosiness to her cheeks and chest. *Joe and his prophesies.*

"Hey, if you need a reference from a bona fide film actor who 'you may recognize as Jessica Chastain's dead husband in a sci-fi thriller coming soon to a theater near you,' I'm in."

"I was counting on that," Sarah says. "And of course, I've got Polly and Chuck from Synergy. And actually, I asked Celeste today if she would be a reference."

"You asked Celeste?" Joe says, impressed with her gumption.

"I figured film commission, film director. Might be a good connection to make. She barely knows me, but she said she'd be happy to."

"Of course. She's done nothing but sing your praises since you saved the shoot the other day. You don't need me at all." Joe pulls Sarah into a hug. "I'm really proud of you."

Sarah melts into his bare chest, the warmest, most blissful place she knows. "Thank you," she murmurs, "but I do need you."

Joe gently pulls back and shakes his head. "You did for a while. But not anymore." He reaches for his glass and holds it up, prompting Sarah to do the same. "Here's to the most incredible woman I've ever known," he says, "and a future so bright it's blinding."

***

Sarah and Joe fall into an easy, happy rhythm over the days that follow. The hours are long, the schedule unforgiving, but they sail through each day with a song in their hearts, and each night they give their songs voice. They make love, talk, watch movies, and sing.

They take turns choosing songs and artists. Sometimes they try to stump each other and other times they choose comfort tunes that evoke the sweetest nostalgia. Brandi Carlile makes frequent appearances, her special place in their story cemented forever, but night after night, an odd hodge-podge of others weave into their story as well. Adele, The Temptations, George Michael, Frank Sinatra, Taylor Swift, Al Green. And on one particularly ambitious evening, the entire Broadway cast of "Hamilton." Sometimes they rock. Sometimes they roll. Sometimes they croon. Sometimes they swoon. They dance through some songs and laugh through others. But they always sing.

Once in a while they sneak out to remote locations where they can enjoy life on the outside together. A visit to the Japanese gardens, a lakefront dinner, a drive through the mountains. But mostly they're content to dine on room service and DoorDash and harbor in the quietude of each other and their private sanctuary.

Sarah lunches whenever possible with Kayla or Randy, or both when it works out. She shares little snippets about her life, but mostly listens as they tell stories about the industry. Kayla dishes on which actors are sweet and talkative in the chair, which ones want to rock out, which ones put on their ear pods and don't say a word, and which ones are so impatient they twitch through every minute like a thoroughbred at the gate. Randy reveals secrets and intrigues from past sets and his prior job as a personal assistant to an extremely famous actor like gossip column blind items. He teases with particular relish the Hollywood hunks who've hit on him, and the only one he happily accepted. No names, but enough hints to allow motivated listeners to figure it out. The gossip is always juicy, but affectionate.

When the topic turns to Joe, they both readily agree he's definitely one of the good ones. And he's super hot. Sarah doesn't argue.

***

Back in the room one night, Joe looks up from the script pages he's reviewing and announces, "I had an interesting conversation with Igor this morning."

"Yeah? About what?" Sarah plops on the side of the bed to file her nails.

"You."

Sarah drops her file. "Excuse me?"

"Well, kind of. He said I was different this shoot, happier than he's seen me when we worked together in the past."

"Aww." The glee on Joe's face is enough to fill Sarah a dozen times over. His joy is always contagious, but the thought that she might have something to do with that joy amplifies it by a magnitude of ten.

"Then he asked me if I was getting some."

Sarah braces herself. Nothing that follows that sentence can be good. "Uh-oh. Where is this going?"

"He thought maybe it was Allie," Joe says. "'On set romances are not unheard of,' he said. I denied it vociferously, of course. I said I was just excited about getting my movie made."

Sarah releases a quiet breath of relief. That's not so bad. "Well, you are," she agrees cheerfully.

"I am indeed. But he also informed me," Joe pauses with a smirk for dramatic effect, "if I did want to hook up with someone, 'that PA Sarah' would be up for it." He tilts his head to an amused, expectant angle and awaits her reply.

"No!" She should have held onto that breath.

"Apparently he's seen her check me out and she definitely has the hots for me." He grins proudly.

Sarah laugh-cringes. It's equal parts hilarious, embarrassing, and terrifying. A couple weeks ago, this announcement would have struck pure terror in her heart, and now she's giggling. This must be what personal growth looks like. She's finally relaxing into her life – even if it's only a temporary version of life. "God, I better be more careful. What did you say?"

"I called him out for being wildly inappropriate and told him to knock it off or I'd report him." He says the words definitively as if that's the end of the story, before adding, "Then I said if that were true, I'd be very flattered because 'that PA Sarah' is a great lady."

Oof! This is worse than the humiliation of being clocked by clueless Igor of all people. "Great lady? That's how you described me? What am I, on Downton Abbey?"

"What should I have said?" Joe asks. "Great girl is infantilizing. Great woman sounds like you're Eleanor Roosevelt."

"How about *beautiful* woman? Or great person," Sarah suggests helpfully.

"Oooh, those are good words." He throws the script dramatically on the desk. "Maybe *you* should be the screenwriter."

"Maybe I should," she says with a smirk as she resumes filing her nails.

"Well, I didn't want to tip my hand. But now I think of it, you're right!" Joe crosses to the bed, tosses the file aside, and seductively pushes her down on the mattress. He straddles her, sitting up with his phone in his hand. "I'm going to call Igor right now and fix this." Sarah giggles as he switches on the phone.

"Maybe don't do that," she says, laughing harder as he pretends to dial.

Caught up in her joy, Joe nods decisively. "Oh, I'm doing it. I'm calling this minute because Igor needs to know the truth!"

"You wouldn't dare!" she shrieks through peals of laughter.

He leans down, brings his face almost to hers and his phone to his ear, and says in a giddy, frenetic gush, "Hello, Igor? I want to set the record straight. That PA Sarah is a beautiful woman! And a great person! And I am completely in love with her!"

When the words hit the air, the room goes still.

They stare into each other's eyes. "I am. It's true. I'm in love with you, Sarah."

Her eyes flood. She tries to speak, but the magnitude of the moment silences her.

"I love you so much," he says again.

Sarah quivers beneath him as she steadies herself. Grateful for the weight of his body pinning her down, anchoring her to the moment, certain that without it she would float into space. Grateful to feel his heft restraining her, containing her, sustaining her. Grateful for the heat of his body, warming her inside and out at every point of contact. And equally grateful for the warmth in his eyes.

When Joe blinks, she watches a tear glide down and pool on his cheek, threatening to dampen her own. And she utters at last the words she's longed to say since the first moment she laid eyes on him.

"I love you, Joe."

***

Sarah nearly cries before she even opens the email from Louise at the film commission. The subject line is enough to trigger tears. She sits alone in her car, clasping her phone, reading the words again and again. "Scheduling an interview." Louise had said they planned to move quickly and here it is, not even a week later.

When she finally readies herself to move past the preview, she opens the email. It's true. They want her. At least for an interview. And it's not just any job. It's a job she actually wants. In fact, she wants it more by the minute. This isn't one of the vaguely appropriate gigs she's been throwing in for because she just needed to kick herself into motion. This is a perfect fit both for her skills and her interests. And from her limited experience, the folks who work there are pretty great. Everything about it just feels so right. Perfect even.

She'll need a cute outfit for the interview, however, and nothing she's been wearing on the film will pass muster. She'll have to go home for clothes. Her stomach roils at the prospect of running into Ben, as unlikely as that is since he's always at the office. Or somewhere he claims is the office. She's never known for sure. They've been texting as often as ever, which is to say a once or twice a day, but she's only spoken to him a couple times. He's just as busy as always, of course, and for the first time in years, she's busy now, too. Guilt still knots her stomach when she thinks of Ben, but the version of Sarah she's rediscovering every day is too precious to allow her to loiter for long in those feelings, not when gratitude and hope are stationed at-the-ready so nearby.

She finds a window around dinner time after dropping off some actors who are wrapped for the day and pulls up to the house saying a quiet prayer that Ben's not home. He won't be home. He's never home this early. She clicks the garage door opener. He won't be home. The door glides open. He won't be home. She spots the other car parked in its spot. He's home.

For all her certainty that he wouldn't be there, Sarah hadn't taken the time to plan for the possibility of seeing Ben. Of pushing her way through a face-to-face conversation and a sea of conflicting and complicated feelings. Of lying to his face. She's often wondered whether he's been lying to her all these months, about his whereabouts and work. About who he's with. She has no proof, of course, just worries and doubts bubbling up where attention and affection used to be. But *if* he has been lying, he's an old pro by now. She isn't. She's not remotely prepared for this. She takes a moment to mentally arm herself, bolstered by Joe's freshly declared love, and walks in.

The first thing she sees when she steps into the kitchen from the mud-room is a huge spread of takeout food across the island, open and still steaming. Swimming Rama, Lemongrass Chicken, Basil Fried Rice, Yellow Sapphire Curry, Spring Rolls. It's a massive feast. For one?

Ben walks in, eyes on his phone, and jumps when he sees her. "Sarah, hi," he says with evident shock. He's already changed out of his suit and into a t-shirt and track pants. His glasses are nowhere in sight. When was the last time she saw that? "What are you doing here?" he adds.

Sarah checks her mental rolodex of possible responses. Comment on the food. Comment on his clothes. Comment on her reason for being there. But she's still fully entrenched in defense mode, and the best defense is a good offense. "What are *you* doing here?"

Ben's face twitches almost imperceptibly. "Um, I live here?"

"But you're never here," Sarah bursts out before she can stop herself.

His head jolts backward with surprise. "I think never is an exaggeration."

"Is it?" she says, settling into her righteous indignation. When he goes slack-jawed with non-response, she shifts tack. "Quite a spread you've got here."

"Yeah, I..." Ben eyes the food as if seeking a reasonable explanation of the meal that could feed and army. "I have a lot of work to do. Thought I'd order in."

"All this just for you? Or is someone here with you? A *work colleague* maybe?" The lady doth protest too much, methinks. Sarah is certainly being Shakespearean in her stupidity at the moment.

"Here with me? What? No, of course not," he says. "It's for leftovers." He eyes her carefully. "Sarah, what's wrong? Are you mad at me?"

Suddenly, she realizes with an ice cold flash that she is. After all those months, no years, of feeling abandoned by the man she trusted to help her through her darkest times, she realizes that she's been furious at him.

And deeply hurt, of course. But it was so much easier to accept the hurt – along with its companions, loneliness and rejection – than to confront and express the anger. So, she'd held every ounce of her fury in, until this very minute. Because for the first time, her anger isn't the most frightening thing she's feeling. It's at least partly fueled by her guilt, which is so much worse as she stares directly into Ben's eyes. She wasn't prepared for any of this.

"I don't know. Maybe I am," she finally confesses. She's not ready to cop to the guilt, which is still fresh and dangerously potent, but maybe it's time she admitted to both Ben and herself the weight she's been carrying for so much longer.

"Okay," Ben says softly. "So, stay and have dinner with me. Let's talk about it." When she says nothing, he adds with a forlorn chuckle, "I've got plenty."

The sensation of this moment is alarmingly familiar and unfamiliar at the same time. It's like that dinner they had after Joe left the first time. When Ben couldn't get enough of hearing about her adventures with "the movie people." Why does he only come back to her when she's pulling away? Why couldn't he be there for her when she really needed him? Maybe one day she'll be ready to talk to him about all of this, but not today. Still, she shouldn't take her own guilt out on him.

Sarah looks over all the food, then back to Ben. She softens and answers as gently as she can manage. "Can't. I just need to pick up some clothes. I have to get back." Ben's mouth opens as if he might try to change her mind, so she heads him off. "We have a night shoot tonight."

Besides, the man she loves is waiting for her. Well, the *other* man she loves. As she looks at Ben in this moment, present and vulnerable, looking like the man she used to know, she realizes she does still love him. But there's a whole river of hurt under the bridge and she may just be too far downstream to turn back now. And Joe is waiting.

"A night shoot," Ben says with a sad nod. "Oh."

***

Halfway through the shoot, Sarah steals away for lunch on the lake with Gabi.

"So it's good then?" Gabi asks over a half-eaten BLT.

Sarah basks in the sun as she gazes across the water to the forested green of Mercer Island in the distance. "It's better than good. It's the happiest I've ever been in my life."

Gabi smiles at her, but deep reserve strains across her face. "Cri-iii-KEY," Gabi drones slowly.

Sarah laughs. "So crikey's about done then?" The surest sign Gabi is done with her latest word is the evolution in its pronunciation. When Gabi starts stretching it or shifting emphasis to enjoy it, its days are numbered. It's only been a couple months – some words could last as long as six – but crikey was never a great fit.

"And Ben? How's he dealing with you being gone?"

Sarah chafes at the question, pin pricks of guilt agitating her psyche, but Gabi has always been a straight shooter and Sarah would expect no less now. She tells Gabi about her recent encounter when she stopped at home. "I know I need to talk to him at some point. Like really talk to him. But right now," she looks at her friend plaintively, "I need this, Gabi. Like I need to breathe."

Gabi takes another bite of her sandwich before continuing. "Babe, you know I'm happy for you. I want you to be happy more than anything in the world."

"I know." Sarah braces herself, sensing Gabi's reticence reverberating with her own anxieties about where it's all headed.

"But what are you going to do when it's over?" Sarah drops back against her chair, folds her arms listlessly, and says nothing, so Gabi adds, "Is it going to be over?"

Sarah closes her eyes and rubs the bridge of her nose to steel herself against a hard reality. Finally, she opens her eyes, the glow of elation replaced with a cloud of grief. "It has to be. I could never ask him to leave his family." She pauses for a moment, thinking of the photo Wendy texted that morning of the girls wearing the paper crowns they'd made. "And I'm not sure I could leave mine either." If only her husband could be the new-old Ben again for longer than a single conversation.

Gabi reaches across the table and squeezes Sarah's hand. "We'll get through it."

Sarah's heart pings gratefully. With Gabi, it's always *we*. "If you knew what it's like, though, Gab. It's like it was meant to be. Like this eternal, destined thing. How does that just end?"

Gabi shakes her head helplessly. "Maybe Destiny has other plans for you. I think you *were* destined to find each other. But maybe it's for a reason you can't see yet."

Sarah nods silently at the suggestion, the faintest glimmer of hope that perhaps she can make sense out of this whole thing when it comes to its inevitable end. Even if it's all as impossible as she thinks. Fate didn't bring Joe into her life for no reason. Destiny hasn't taken her on this whole wild ride just to deposit her back in the same pathetic ditch when it's over. It's too late for that. She's already changed so much. Healed so much. She won't go back to that ditch.

Sarah pokes at her salad and plucks a blueberry into her mouth. "Anyway, how are you?" she asks, opting to change the subject before her heart cracks in two.

"Good," Gabi says with a smile. "I'm getting used to the new hire."

"I'm glad you finally have full-time help," Sarah says. "It'll really help you dig out."

"You're probably right." Gabi reaches for her iced tea, takes a sip, and swirls it around her mouth before continuing purposefully, "And I've been hanging out with Dana a lot."

"I'm glad you two are getting along."

"Yeah, I like her," Gabi says.

"I like her, too," Sarah says breezily as she shoves a forkful of greens into her mouth.

"No," Gabi says carefully, "I mean I *like* her." A car horn in the street honks loudly, as if on cue.

Sarah stops mid-chew, eyes wide, absorbing Gabi's words. "You *like her* like her?"

Gabi nods. The news is a shock, not just because Gabi's never given so much as a hint of interest in women before. In fact, she was downright boy crazy in college. But because she's been so resolutely alone since Max. As if she had lost all interest in even the possibility of romance. Until now, apparently. Until Dana, apparently.

Sarah crinkles her brow in disbelief. "In twenty-five years I've known you, you've never *like* liked a woman before... Have you?"

Gabi shakes her head no. "What can I say? First time for everything."

"And does Dana *like* like you, too?"

Gabi nods again, this time accompanied by a tiny smile she can't quite hold in. "It's kind of..." Gabi holds herself very still, a timid, yet hopeful expression telegraphing her nerves about this announcement, even to Sarah. "Perfect."

Perfect? After a split second of processing the previously unfathomable news, Sarah's face cracks wide with glee and she starts to chant, "Gabi and Dana sitting in a tree—"

Gabi throws her napkin at Sarah to stop her and they burst into laughter. Gabi giggles, "Love is a many-splendored thing, huh?"

"Indeed," Sarah says, her eyes welling with happiness once again.

Chapter Thirty-One

What Could Be

LIKE MANY OF THE best ideas, the inspiration for the getaway strikes over pizza and beer. After listening to Sarah brag for three days about two of the best local pizza chains anywhere, Joe decides it's time to find out what all the fuss is about and orders one signature pizza each from Pagliacci and Zeeks. Both are delicious and any notion of choosing a winner is quickly dispelled, replaced by the happy stupor of a slight beer buzz and one slice too many. They slump in their chairs across from each other staring at the remnants.

"We're gonna be eating pizza for days," Sarah drones.

"You underestimate me," Joe says. "Breakfast is the most important meal of the day, after all."

"It was good, right?" Sarah says, her pride overpowering her mild desire to wretch from that last slice.

"Very good. Not as good as my pizza, mind you. But still good."

Sarah smirks incredulously. "Your pizza? Don't tell me you cook, too."

"I do. And don't look so surprised!"

"Sorry."

"I wish I could cook for you," Joe says wistfully.

Sarah conjures an image of Joe in a professional kitchen with a chef hat, clogs, and an apron, serving up beef bourguignon and a chocolate soufflé. "I'd like that," she says with a twinkle. "I'd like to cook for you, too."

As sweet as the notion is, it makes them unexpectedly sad. For all the wonder of their time together, there are so many normal things they want to do, too. So many simple joys that feel so impossible. Joe stares back at the pizza, and Sarah takes the looming sadness as her cue to start tidying. Joe watches her combine the leftovers into a single box and consider her options for fitting it in the fridge.

"What if we went away somewhere?" he says.

"When? Where?"

"I have a couple days off coming up."

"I don't."

"But you have one. I bet you could swing another one if you tried," Joe says. They had been talking about a day trip somewhere for their shared day off. Snoqualmie Falls maybe. Or Bainbridge or Camano Island. But this would be so much better. "I could help, pull some strings maybe," he adds hopefully.

"You absolutely cannot do that," Sarah says with a pointed edge. "It would be way too suspicious. You have to stay a million miles away from it."

Joe throws his hands up in surrender. "Okay, I swear. But I do think you could get the day if you ask. You're volunteering. What are they going to do? Fire you?"

"You know, this is your movie I'm working on," Sarah reminds him. "Your movie that will suffer if balls get dropped."

"We're talking about one day. An easy one. Small cast, no extras, no public to keep at bay. It's a cakewalk."

A cautious smile creeps onto Sarah's face. "It would be fun... but I don't want to let anyone down. Least of all you."

"Trust me," Joe says with his patented smile. "The crew can live without extra granola bars for one day."

Sarah contributes more than food to the project, of course, but she takes his point. And as usual, his enthusiasm is too infectious to resist. They spend the rest of the evening plotting their getaway. After two hours on the rentals site, they've booked a waterfront escape with a "modern, well-equipped kitchen including all your cooking essentials." They take turns reading bits of description.

"The large, tree-lined lot ensures a tranquil retreat and complete privacy from neighbors."

"The spacious main bathroom includes a clawfoot tub and a walk-in shower to wash away the stress of the world."

"Includes 60 feet of private beach including a private dock and boat launch for all your watersports, fishing, and boating needs."

Sarah turns to Joe. "Do we have a boat?"

"I don't think we have a boat, no," Joe says with a solemn shake of his head. "But it sounds good anyway."

"Are you kidding? Our very own house. Just for you and me? It sounds perfect." Sarah sets down the laptop and heads for the bathroom, but Joe grabs her.

"I can't wait to play house with you," he says, wrapping his arms around her.

Sarah gasps, "Wait, we already booked! What if I don't get the day off?"

"Then I guess I'll just have to go on my own," Joe says with a squeeze that makes it clear that's enough talking for now.

***

As luck would have it, Sarah's job interview is scheduled for the same morning she's supposed to head out of town with Joe. She's virtually catatonic. It's her first real interview in thirteen years, since she originally interviewed for Synergy back in the day. She interviewed informally over the years as she climbed the ranks at Synergy, but those had always felt more like friendly conversations than stress tests.

Joe helps her prepare. He teaches her his techniques for calming his nerves, then searches popular interview questions to roleplay the interview with her. The trend toward modern, experiential "tell me about a time when..." questions sends her into a frenzy initially, but becomes a gift as it forces her to remember all the things she's overcome and accomplished professionally. She delves into her memory banks and unearths a bevy of achievements she'd managed to paper over with despair and guilt when the company folded.

With Joe's help she comes up with a plausible explanation for not working the past two years – needing a break to heal after the grief of the company she loved closed and helping with her friend's organization. The answer involves a minimum of spin and at least some truth. An answer she can live with.

She manages to get the 8:00 slot, so she's done and out the door by 9:30. Joe waits for her outside, leaning on the car with an expectant smile. "How'd it go?"

Sarah nods happily. "Good, I think. At least it felt good."

Joe lifts her in a bear hug. "I knew you could do it!"

"I haven't done anything yet," she says, tamping down expectations. "But even if I don't get it, this is progress."

"You're getting it," Joe says. "I have a feeling about this, and my feelings are never wrong." Always the prophet.

They hit the road, singing all the way, and catch the ten-thirty ferry from Mukilteo. They stand on the deck for the full ride over to Whidbey Island, soaking up the sunshine and view despite the battering wind. The sky is vibrant blue and clear, the water almost blinding from the sun, and the deep greens of the island enchant them as they sail ever closer. Joe envelopes Sarah from behind, his head resting on hers, protecting her from the bluster. Their seagull escort calls noisily to them and announces their arrival before the announcement chimes to return to their car. They drive off the ferry and reach the house, where they'd arranged an early check-in, before noon.

The house is nearly hidden by mature landscaping and a tall fence, but the path is invitingly lined with colorfully painted stones. The reclaimed wood door with arched top and fused glass seascape window opens into a charming interior with bright white walls, wood beams, and just enough beachy décor to set the scene without tipping into kitsch. As they roam from room to room, Joe makes pronouncements about all the new places they can fool around. "Look, babe! A new bed," he says gleefully.

"Ooh, a new bed," Sarah echoes, amused.

"Look, babe, a new couch!"

"Ooh, a new couch," she laughs.

"Look, babe, a new shower! With a bench!"

"I see that."

"Look, babe, a kitchen island!" he says with relish.

Sarah rolls her eyes. "You're really having fun with this, aren't you?"

Joe takes her hand and leads her out to the back deck, gesturing in a broad sweep across the vista down to the water. "Look, babe, a whole backyard!"

"You know we're only here two days, right?"

Joe smiles and answers with a kiss.

After a quick walk through the stone beach of a backyard, dappled with more cheerfully painted stones, and back to the house to christen the new bed, it's time for food. To emulate regular life as much as possible, they agree there will be no restaurant food for the next two days. They plan carefully, not wanting to waste food. For breakfasts, they keep it simple, fruit and cereal. They will make lunches together and one dinner each. One shot to impress. They plan their menus down to the last detail before wending their way through curvy backroads to a local grocery store charmingly named The Happy Hen.

They grab a cart and dreamily stroll through the store, orienting themselves to the location of various foods and checking them off the list on Joe's phone as they go. They could speed up the process by splitting up, but they have no interest in hurrying, or splitting up. The simple leisure of pushing a cart up and down the aisles together, discussing the ripeness of bananas or whether asparagus is still in season, finding out what kind of cereal they each like – it's everything they want. They're falling in love again and again, one Happy Hen aisle at a time.

When they finally reach the checkout, they look down at their cart and realize despite their best efforts, they've ended up with far too much food. They'll definitely be leaving some things behind. They catch eyes and shrug, then reach into the cart from opposite sides – Joe in front, Sarah in back – and start unloading items onto the belt in unison. A team.

As the clerk runs through the last item, she says to Joe, "Do you have a Cluck Card?"

Joe looks up at her in amusement. "No, I don't have a Cluck Card." He glances at Sarah, who's still behind the cart, and they smile at each other as if the Cluck Card is somehow the most special, most precious secret any two people have ever shared.

***

Sarah makes one of her few specialties, Tuscan chicken on a bed of angel hair pasta, for dinner. It's delicious. After two years of mostly staying home, she cooks much better than she used to, but only a handful of selections from her repertoire make her really proud. This is one of them. It's loaded with garlic, of course, but she's long past worrying about that. And as Joe so rightly points out, garlic doesn't matter if they both eat it.

Joe moans rapturously over his first bite, "Oh my God, this is so good!"

Sarah smiles appreciatively and thanks him, but when the moans continue, she adds, "Okay, actor dude. You're overacting a little."

"I'm not acting. This is unbelievable." He shovels another giant bite into his mouth. "Is everything you cook this good?"

"Not even close. But I'm glad you like it."

Joe hums happily over his next few bites, smiling at her as he chews. Sarah eats slowly, mostly enjoying the show Joe's putting on. When he finally slows down a bit, she looks at him thoughtfully. "I have a question for you."

"Oh?"

"Why me?"

Joe puzzles over her question, then registers what she's asking. "I can't believe you still don't know the answer to that."

"Come on. You could have any woman in the world." Earlier in their relationship, this question might have been rooted in insecurity stemming from Sarah's inability to believe that someone like Joe could fall for someone like her. Fortunately, those days are long gone. She is deeply rooted in her certainty of Joe's love, and just as certain that she is worthy. Now what drives her is a need to understand this beautiful, impossible gift dropped from the heavens just for them. A gift with an expiration date.

"Well, first of all, as you well know, I wasn't in the market. Not even a little. And second, I wanted you. Only you. Baby, we were destined for this. I told you, it was Fate."

"Yeah, but why?"

"Why Fate? You may as well ask 'why the oceans?' or 'why the sun?'"

She gives his arm a playful tap of annoyance. For some reason, she needs to hear this. "You know what I mean."

Joe shakes his head at Sarah. "I could give you about fifty reasons, and they'd all be equally true. But I don't think you'd believe any of them. So why don't you tell me why you fell for me first?"

Sarah laughs, "Have you seen yourself lately?"

Joe raises his brows seductively. "So, you just want me for my body?"

"Well, I don't *not* want you for your body."

"C'mon." He taps her back.

Sarah sighs. "There are more reasons than I can count. Your humor, your kindness, your intelligence." Sarah's face contorts at the effort to find the right words. "But I suppose more than anything, it's because with you, I feel seen. I feel like you really, truly see me. Maybe more clearly than anyone I've ever known."

Joe leans in pointedly. "That is exactly how I feel."

"Yeah, but you live in a spotlight. Everyone sees you."

"No, they don't. They see what I show them, or what they want to see. But you saw through all of that immediately. You saw me."

Sarah accepts this answer wordlessly, recognizing the truth. She's seen him from the start. Long before she understood or admitted it. Even before she met him, she always saw Joe. That's the bell that rang in her. Recognition. She returns to her food, smiling at her chicken.

After dinner, they clean up together. They rinse dishes and load them in the dishwasher, wash the pots, wipe down the counters, shake off the placemats. They say little, but brush closer than necessary when crossing paths and give little love taps when passing behind each other. It's all so wonderfully simple and domestic.

When the cleaning is done, they curl up on the couch under a large, soft cable knit blanket. They watch a cheesy romcom on the house's cut rate streaming service. Until they don't. Their hands roam and their lips find each other and after a while, the TV is barely even background noise.

Before bed, they stroll down to the waterfront. They plop themselves in the two chairs facing the water and reach for each other. The night is dark and clear, and the sky is full of stars. Stars you rarely see in Seattle thanks to the lights and the frequent cloud cover. But tonight, on Whidbey Island, they are in full force. A shooting star crosses the sky above them. It's magical.

They stare out at the dark water, glistening with the reflection of the moon, and listen to it quietly lapping on the beach and splashing up the sides of the dock that extends in front of them. The peaceful stillness envelopes them and permeates the thin membrane between them. They feel the energy, warm and comforting, pulsing through their hands from one to the other and back again. It is, literally, Sarah's dream come true.

Sarah catches sight of a tethered ring-shape life preserver hanging on the side of the small boathouse where the kayaks are stored. Although it's grayed out by the night, she can just make out a hint of the bright orange color she knows it must be by day. She follows the line of the white rope tether from the hook where it hangs to the ring itself, waiting to be tossed out and pulled back in. To save whoever needs saving. But it's the line, catching the light of the moon, which sparks her memory.

Her mind flashes back to her first night with Joe. Their dance. Their kiss. Her vision. The long, once invisible but now undeniable thread running through her whole life, connecting her to Joe. She sees it again, glowing in the darkness, the unbreakable filament stretching through time and space and tethering them to each other. Then. Now. Always.

Sarah's eyes fill with the joy and sadness of the vision, of everything it means. Her tears catch the moonlight. Joe notices as they escape and trail down her face. He reaches over and wipes them away. "Hey, hey, what's wrong?" His voice cracks with concern.

"It's all so perfect."

Joe nods. It is perfect. He understands the gift this is. And the cost of it, too. The sadness that must inevitably follow. "It's not over," he says. "We still have time."

"I know," Sarah replies and squeezes his hand. She forces a smile and looks back to the water, but Joe senses an ellipsis in her words.

"Is there something else?"

"It'll sound crazy," she says.

"Try me," he urges softly.

Sarah glances back at the tethered life preserver, takes a deep breath, and tells Joe the story. Of her vision, of her connection to Joe through all these pivotal moments of her life, of the tether she feels to him. An eternal tether that defies logic or reason, but she feels it nonetheless.

Joe listens quietly, his brows knitted in concentration, saying nothing as she unfurls the tall tale. When she finishes, she braces herself, prepared for the worst, sure he'll be running for the hills or ready to commit her. But Joe just kisses her hand and says, "That doesn't sound crazy to me."

***

In the morning they find a waterfront park and stroll for hours along the beach alternating with wooded paths, and then back to the beach. The hike brings back the day they spent touring parks the first time, a sweet memory. But today is so much better, peppered as it is with furtive gropes, occasional make-outs against accommodating trees, and the quiet knowing that they are each other's. They hold hands every moment. No denial, no fear. They're giddy teenagers in the throes of new romance. They're octogenarians bonded through a life-long love. They are tethered. Forever.

Back at the house, they make lunch together, chopping vegetables, mixing a lemon dill vinaigrette, and tossing it all with freshly cooked Isreali couscous. As Sarah scoops the Mediterranean concoction into bowls for them, Joe watches and says, "I want this."

"Me, too," Sarah says without asking for clarification.

Halfway through lunch, Joe sets his bowl aside, leans his elbow on the table and his face on his hand. Sarah raises her brows in amused curiosity as she takes another bite.

"I want to be bored with you," Joe says.

Sarah finishes her bite, then rests her own face on her hand, saying nothing. She waits for Joe to go on.

He speaks slowly, thoughtfully. "I want to be annoyed with you... I want to be nagged by you."

Sarah smiles at him, mostly to hold back tears.

"I want to be stressed with you... I want to be tired with you."

"We've done that one," she interjects.

Joe picks up speed. "I want to travel with you. I want to clean the house with you. I want to go to baseball games with you."

"Baseball?" Sarah scoffs in mild dismay.

"I want to watch you not enjoy yourself at baseball games with me."
They both laugh to swallow feelings that might otherwise swallow
them. "I want to adopt a dog with you."

"A dog," Sarah says dreamily.

"A pitbull. Named Daisy. With an unstoppable tail." Sarah lets slip
a little sniffle that exposes her and Joe's voice breaks as he adds, "I want
everything with you."

Sarah drops her hand from her chin to the table, palm up. He
glides his middle finger lightly over her palm and wrist. His touch
sends tingles through her body and when she twitches, he presses down
firmly to soothe her too sensitive skin. He flips their hands so hers is
on top, then leans down and kisses it gently.

"We have everything," she says. "At least for today."

Joe traces the veins on Sarah's hand with his other fingers before
sandwiching her hand between both of his. "What if it's not enough?"

"We have ten more days."

***

It's Joe's turn to make dinner, and his grilled salmon, honey glazed
carrots, and cilantro lime rice are a triumph. After dinner, they pull
out the paint kit provided by the host to paint their own stone for the
stone beach garden. Sarah looks at Joe, paintbrush poised in her hand.
"What should we paint?"

"Something easy."

Sarah thinks a moment. "Sarah+Joe?"

Joe nods. "Forever."

Joe begins by painting the surface white. They let it dry briefly, then
Sarah dips her brush in the blue paint and writes "Sarah+Joe," before
handing the brush to Joe who adds "Forever." Sarah dips another brush
into the red and adds a couple hearts to finish off their masterpiece.

When the clean-up is done, they take one last stroll down to the water before pouring more wine and settling onto the deck to watch the sunset.

***

The morning comes unbearably early since they have to catch the 6:30 ferry to make it to set on time. After a quickie in the shower, they strip the bed, throw their sheets and towels in the washing machine, run the dishwasher, clean out the fridge, put the recycling in the appointed bin. They leave the kitchen island mercifully unchristened, but Joe knocks on the granite countertop as they head for the door. "Next time."

Before they climb into their car, they take one last walk among the rocks and find a special spot for theirs. They cradle it a moment between their hands, then Joe stoops to place it on its bed of gray, the most important stone of them all among the multitudes on an endless stone beach. *Sarah+Joe Forever*. At least here, in this special place, they will remain just as they are. They clasp hands and head for the car.

On the ferry home, he plops on a bench at the back of the ferry, and she leans into his arms as they watch their dream home recede into the distance. He kisses her head and squeezes her tight, and she squeezes his arms in return. If they squeeze tightly enough, maybe they can hold onto this.

But as they return to their car to exit the ferry, Sarah finally turns on her phone. They'd had no service on the island, so she hadn't bothered to look until now. A voicemail pops in. Followed quickly by another, then another and another and another. Her phone is blowing up. Wendy's called twice and the rest are Ben. Seventeen calls in total, all since last night.

Something terrible has happened.

Chapter Thirty-Two

Family

Joe watches Sarah's face in horror as she melts into anguish. "What is it?" She holds a hand up to silence him. She listens to one voicemail, then another. He can just make out a woman's voice, then a man's voice, both pitched high with intensity. He can't hear what they're saying, but Sarah's tear-streaked cheeks as she listens tell him enough. He holds his breath and waits.

She pauses after the second message. "It's Emma," she says. Joe goes blank trying to place the name. "My niece. She's been hit by a car."

Joe jars at the words, at the reminder Sarah has a family. Another family, apart from him. But the news is too grave to allow himself to linger in his thoughts. "Oh my God! How is she?"

"I don't know. I have to listen to the rest of the messages." He pulls her in and tries his damnedest to hug away the fear and sadness. But that's impossible.

Sarah shrinks before his eyes as she adds, "She's six, Joe," then dissolves into tears. Joe thinks of the giggly little girl who clung to Sarah at the park that day. Cars around them start up their engines. Sarah starts to pace between their car and the one in front of them. "Oh God, how could I be gone like this? What was I doing?"

The words stab Joe in the gut, but he says without hesitation, "You have to go. Go be with your family. We'll get you there."

"Poor Wendy and Alec. They must be devastated. And Lexi." She's still pacing, but she pulls the phone back to her ear. "I have to listen to the rest of the messages."

A horn honks at them. Cars not too far ahead are starting to pull out. They'll be up soon. "Give me the keys," Joe says. "I'll drive, you listen."

"Ben must be wondering where the hell I am. What have I done?"

Joe fights to catch his own breath. "This isn't your fault, Sarah." But as she slides into the passenger's seat, she looks at him like it absolutely is.

***

Joe pulls into a spot near the record store where they're shooting. He stays just down the street so they're out of sight as they get out of the car. He folds her in his arms, holding her as tightly as he can. "She'll be okay. They'll take good care of her."

Behind them, Celeste walks out the door with her phone to her ear. She glimpses the scene, pauses a moment, and goes back in, unseen.

Joe kisses Sarah gently on the forehead and releases her. "She'll be alright. Have faith." She smiles bravely, but terror and guilt flicker in her eyes. "I love you," he says.

"I love you, too," she says before turning to climb into the car.

Joe chokes back a wave of grief and gasps for breath, a suffocating heaviness overtaking him as Sarah speeds away.

***

Sarah's half desperate as she runs down the hall from the nurses' station to the sitting area, reaching the small, enclosed space with so much speed she nearly plows into a terrified mom stepping out to find the restroom.

She apologizes profusely, but as they each clock the grief of the other, all is forgiven. The woman gives a pained smile and walks on.

Ben leaps to his feet when he sees Sarah. She freezes. She's only seen Ben the once since moving into the hotel, when they very nearly fought before she came to her senses and got out of there. That was a week ago. A week that feels like a lifetime. A lifetime of laughter and joy and achievement. A good life. A happy life. A life she's not ready to surrender. Yet, there's Ben.

He offers a tight grimace muted by a cultivated numbness, his default survival technique, his deep agony belied by the smile he musters at Sarah's arrival. His façade cracks and she rushes to him with arms open. They sink into each other, finding the softness of a familiar, safe place to collapse into their shared fear and worry.

He's not Joe, but he is her husband, the man she's spent eleven years of her life with. He's grieving and worried, and it's her job to be there for him, to hold him up in this moment. Whatever she may want, whatever she may need, Ben needs her in this moment, and she cannot fail him.

"How is she?" Sarah whispers into his ear.

Ben clings tightly, unwilling or unable to let go yet. "She's back in surgery. It's been an hour already." Finally, he lets go.

"Where are Alec and Wendy?"

"They went for coffee," Ben says. "I offered to go so they could stay close, but Wendy was losing her mind, so they needed to walk. They should be back any minute."

Sarah slides her hand down to Ben's. "What about you? Do you need anything?"

"Just you," he says, squeezing her hand. "Where have you been?" His initial relief at seeing Sarah tinged now with anger. No, not anger. Dismay maybe? Hurt certainly.

"I'm so sorry." She nearly sobs the words, her guilt eating at her as she speaks.

"I called you so many times."

She planned her excuse on the way, but sputtering out the lie burns. "We have to turn off our phones on set." She pauses to let her very real tears fall, then pushes forward. "Then I was so exhausted last night that I just forgot to turn it back on. I came as soon as I heard."

"Well, I'm glad you're here now. I really needed you."

"I know," she squeaks between gasps of breath.

"We all do."

Sarah senses the earth shaking beneath her, a seismic event that threatens to crack her world open and destroy everything. She's so sure everything is about to collapse that she's genuinely surprised neither Ben nor the couple sitting sullenly beneath the hanging TV notices the vibrations. She smiles, a sadness with more layers than she can count behind it. "I'm here. Of course I'm here."

When Wendy and Alec return, Sarah pleads their forgiveness. She hugs Wendy as if her own life depends on it. Wendy tells her the whole story and Sarah just keeps saying, "I'm sorry. I'm sorry. I should have been here. I'm so sorry." The women cling to each other as they take a seat, clasping hands while the men pace impatiently. The minutes drag out like hours.

Sarah's phone rings. She glimpses at the unknown number, then tucks it back in her pocket.

"Do you need to get that?" Wendy asks.

"If it's important, they'll leave a message."

Eventually, a nurse comes out to tell them Emma is out of surgery and the surgeon will come out to update them soon.

"How is she?" Wendy begs.

"She's resting comfortably in recovery. The doctor will tell you more."

***

Joe paces the room wearing a path in the carpet. He checks his phone every two minutes for missed messages, making sure his ringer is on, double checking his signal. He tries watching television, but everything is insipid and tedious. He tries reading, but can't see straight.

He decides to walk down to "her room," the room they only use for family calls, in the futile hope that maybe she came back and stopped in there for some reason. Maybe she needs some alone time after what happened, a little quiet time to digest all her worry before bringing it back to their sanctuary. Joe would understand that. Of course, he would. He will gladly leave her alone if that's what she needs. He just needs to know she's okay.

She's not there. It's clear the moment he opens the door, but he walks into the bathroom anyway to confirm. When the bathroom yields nothing, he opens the closet and stares at the few clothes she's left there for show, just in case. Maybe if he stares at them hard enough, says the right incantation, he can make her corporealize within them. And then she'll step out, kiss him, and reassure him everything is fine. He stares long and hard, but she doesn't appear.

Too wired to sit still, he goes for a swim. A large black stone has planted itself in his gut, weighing him down and making every movement heavy and painful. Joe pushes himself hard anyway, lap after lap, to the point of exhaustion. To the point where merely lifting himself out of the pool feels like it might shatter his bones. When he manages to climb up to the side of the pool, he sits with his legs dangling in the water, panting from exertion. Tears sting his eyes and he gives thanks there's no one else there to wonder whether it's tears or pool water dripping down his face.

When he gets up, he reaches for his towel and glances at his phone. At last a text. And it's just popped in. Sarah is there now, texting him at this moment. He grabs his phone and opens it, hours of torture at an end.

Emma is going to be okay. Thank God!

Joe's face melts into tearful relief. Although he met Emma only once, it always hurts to see a child harmed, or God forbid worse, especially for a parent who's lived through years of their own agony and worry. And then the more personal relief that Sarah, too, will be okay now that her niece will be. Joe felt Sarah's anguish like his own and her palpable relief washes over him like a balm.

And finally, he allows himself the most selfish celebration of all. Sarah hasn't forgotten him. He's still a part of her life even in a family emergency. In some small way, he's a part of it because somehow, maybe he's her family, too. He recognizes the absurdity of the notion. But denying it feels equally absurd.

Still, fear nags at him. Every moment since she rushed off to the hospital has been laced with sheer, unadulterated terror that this incident will insert a wedge between them, draw her away from him and back into her life from before. That this terrible incident will mark the beginning of the end.

Because as certain as he had been from the very beginning, Sarah had been equally uncertain. He had fought it, of course, because he was desperate not to hurt his family, his kids. But he always knew the truth. He sensed the hand of Fate the very moment he saw her and never doubted it. He only doubted himself and how he could manage his feelings. How he could navigate a world split in two.

But Sarah had been entirely different from the start. Like him, she'd always felt it. He knows that now. Their eternal tether she calls it. But she had fought it so much harder and for different reasons. Perhaps it was the weight of twenty years of desire and denial. Twenty years of convincing herself her feelings were imaginary, pure fantasy. Twenty years of certainty that Joe, a man she didn't even know, couldn't possibly love her.

Twenty years of being completely wrong.

What had been brand new and undeniable to Joe was buried under a lifetime of denial for Sarah. No wonder she fought it so hard. Yet, they'd found each other at last. And although they both know it must end far too soon – they only have a week left, after all – it can't end like this, with Sarah simply disappearing back into her life, sucked in by trauma and familial obligation. No, that can't happen. But the fear of it haunts Joe every moment she's away.

And so her text means the world. The fact that he's still in her heart and mind, even now, brings him immeasurable comfort and steadies him at last. But his fleeting relief is dashed by the next text to pop in.

Can't make it back tonight. Sorry. See you tomorrow.

The stone in Joe's gut grows heavier. *Back*, she wrote. Not "home."

The three little dots appear and offer hope of something more, some words of tenderness or reassurance to ease his burden. They flash at Joe, tantalizing him with the promise of Sarah, that some real piece of his Sarah will come through in the next message. Until they disappear, and the stone in his gut morphs into a boulder.

And that's it. No "I love you." No "I'll miss you tonight." No coded intimations of affection or longing or even regret.

He tells himself it doesn't mean anything. She's probably just sitting with the family and can't say more. She wouldn't dare. He knows this logically. There's no reason to worry. And yet.

She's spending the night with *him*.

The black boulder grows into a black hole, and Joe prepares to be swallowed by it.

***

Emma wakes in her room, still half delirious, but her nonsensical stream of consciousness, which is only fractionally sillier than half the things she says anyway, makes Wendy and Alec sob with relief. Sarah sobs, too, and says a quiet prayer of thanks.

After a short visit, Emma's eyes droop heavily, and Sarah hops up to dim the lights. A small light by the bed illuminates the space, enough for the family to see, but not enough to disrupt the sleep of a sedated child badly in need of rest. As everyone gazes at Emma in silent gratitude, Sarah studies each of them. Emma, Wendy, who's become a real friend over the years, Alec, and finally Ben himself. She thinks of Lexi at home with a babysitter, probably asleep already, protected from the worst of the worry and trauma. This is her family. The family who has brought her in and made her one of them. She feels so much love for them that it spills from her eyes yet again. And she remembers exactly what she's known from the start. She could never choose to hurt them. Any of them.

Then she thinks of Joe. Joe who is everything. Joe who makes her sing in every imaginable way. Joe who is literally her lifeline. And her heart aches so badly she realizes she's clutching at it when she hears Wendy say, "Sarah, are you okay?"

Sarah forces herself to draw her hand away from her heart, still aching, as she says, "I'm fine." She keeps her voice low in deference to the sleeping child and takes a deep breath. "Actually, now that we know Emma's going to be okay, I have some news." Ben's head swivels from Emma to Sarah with keen interest. "I'm interviewing for a job. I'm a finalist actually. That was the call I got earlier. They've invited me for a second interview."

"What?!" Ben's eyes go wide.

"I mean, I don't want to jinx it, but I'll know soon."

Wendy and Alec congratulate her with big smiles and excited hushed tones, flooding her with questions about what the job is, how this happened, and when she'll know.

Ben stares at her, dumbfounded. He's clearly pleased, but there's something else there, too. Guilt shoots through her. She should have told him.

His lips turn up cautiously. "That's amazing, hon. Congratulations."

***

Sarah walks into her bedroom, with Ben, for the first time in weeks. The room feels charged and foreign. Everything feels terribly wrong. Like one of those road trip movies where two people who don't like each other are forced to share a hotel room and sleep in the same bed. Except not the ones where they end up falling in love. The ones where they end up barely sleeping at all, or sleeping with one eye open, one foot on the floor, and praying no one ever finds out about it.

This should be the most natural thing in the world, climbing into bed with her own husband. Even a husband who hasn't touched her in nearly a year is still her husband. And she does love him. Tonight has reminded her of that. He's a good man. He's kind and gentle, when he's present. He loves his family. But he's not Joe.

She hesitates in the doorway, trying to think how she can change her clothes without Ben seeing her. He answers the question for her when he gestures at the bathroom. "Okay if I go first?"

"Fine," she says. As soon as he shuts the door, she runs for the closet, throws off her clothes, and as quickly as possible puts on her sweats, the least attractive and most protective of her sleepwear.

A few minutes later he emerges from the bathroom in his underwear. He plants a kiss on her head. "It's good to have you home."

"Yeah," she says noncommittally as she hops up and brushes past him toward the bathroom. "It's been a while."

He catches her arm, forcing her to look at him. "I've missed you."

"Yeah," she says again, as lightly as possible, "It's been a crazy few weeks."

"I don't just mean the last few weeks."

Sarah sucks in a breath, unsure what he's saying. "Me, too," she finally says, her body running cold all over.

He studies her a moment longer. "I'm proud of you. And this job. I think it could be really great for you. It feels like you're coming back."

Coming back? The words echo in her head. Sarah forces a smile as her brain races through the permutations of possible responses, triangulating the safest landing place.

Before she can say anything, Ben adds, "I wish you had told me about it though."

"I should have, I'm sorry," she says softly. "I've just been so busy. And you always have so much on your plate, I didn't want to bother you until I knew."

"Bother me?" he says, a raspy shock in his voice. He looks down at the floor for entirely too long. "You're right. I have been working too much. I haven't been here for you. I've realized that." The words sound careful and rehearsed, like he's been waiting for his chance to say them. "When things fell apart for you, I felt so helpless. So, I worked harder. Figured at least I could make sure we were financially secure so you didn't have to worry about anything. But you needed me and I blew it. I should have been here for you. I'm sorry."

Sarah's head spins at the discussion two people who can't possibly be she and Ben are having in this room. What is he saying? And where were these words months ago? A year ago? Why now? When she's so far gone she's barely even in the room? She struggles to reinsert herself into her body and extricate herself from the conversation. She smiles sympathetically. "It's okay. I'm better now. You don't have to worry about me." Sarah gives Ben's hand a gentle squeeze of reassurance before heading to the bathroom.

As she shuts the door, he says, "I want to be here for you, Sarah. I *will* be here for you."

***

Sarah loiters in the bathroom as long as she can reasonably justify. She sits on the toilet and groans occasionally, hoping she's pulling off a convincing rendition of the bad stomach blues. Ben's normally so tired he's out as soon as his head hits the pillow. With the added stress of Emma's accident, he's sure to crash hard. She just has to wait him out.

When at last she does emerge, she tiptoes to the bed, sets her alarm, and climbs in as slowly and carefully as she can. But as she rolls on her side away from Ben, he reaches for her.

"I've really missed you," he says in a husky whisper.

She freezes and her body tenses. His hands on her feel wrong. What once would have felt warm, welcome, familiar, now chills her. So foreign. So very wrong. She wanted this for so long. Where was he then? She doesn't move. She doesn't stir or say a word, her body as rigid as a steel post.

"What is it?" he says. "It feels like you're a million miles away."

"Sorry, I'm just tired," she says, still not looking at him. "And worried about Emma."

"You heard the doc. She'll be fine." He runs his hand up and down her back, trying to relax her.

"Ben, I just can't. Okay?"

"Sure." A note of dark resignation tinges his voice. He pulls his hands away and rolls onto his back. He stares at the ceiling, then lets out a long, slow sigh. "You're going back tomorrow? To... the shoot?" The tension and hurt in his words are unmistakable. And she's probably imagining it, but is there also a hint of suspicion?

Sarah gulps for air as she answers. "I am."

"It'll be over soon, right?" His voice cracks a little as he asks, and she feels it. His jealousy. It's not just wounded pride. There's real pain there.

Sarah's tears pool on her pillow. "Yeah. Another week."

"Good." His voice is low and tight. "That's good. Finish it. Do what you need to do. Then come home to me." Sarah squeezes her eyes shut, willing the tears to stop when Ben adds, "I'll be waiting for you."

Chapter Thirty-Three

What Is

BY THE TIME JOE arrives for his call, Sarah has already been and gone, sent on errands and a shopping trip. They spend the morning missing each other, and avoiding each other when they do cross paths in the presence of others. Actual communication is far too dangerous and loaded to attempt under the circumstances. Sarah still reeling from the night before, Joe terrified he's lost her. Each knows they should text the other in a safe moment to check-in and say something reassuring, but neither can find the words. It's torture.

At lunch, Joe turns on his phone to a text from Melanie. *Call me.*

Sensing urgency in the terse message, Joe immediately dials. "Hey, what's going on? Are the kids okay?"

"They're fine. Why?"

"You scared me. I got the feeling something was wrong from your text."

"Yeah, well..." Melanie trails off.

"What is it?" Joe says.

"Have you looked at Instagram lately?"

Not this again. This can't be happening again. He should just deactivate that account. He never uses it anyway. "No, why?"

"Someone tagged you in a picture. Says it's you."

His heart races. "And is it me?"

"Hard to say for sure. It's shot from the back. A man and a woman holding hands, on a beach."

Joe drops his head in recognition. They'd been so careful not to go anywhere crowded on their trip. And nobody ever recognizes him anyway. Except when they do, apparently. "Well, that doesn't sound like me then," he says. The phone beeps in with another call. "Hold on, let me see who's calling... Just Clark. I'll call him back."

"No, if Clark's calling, you better answer. I'll wait," she says. That's Mel in a nutshell. Nothing's ever more important than a call from Joe's agent.

Joe clicks over. "Not a good time, Clark."

"There's another photo," Clark warns.

"Yeah. I know. I'll call you back." Joe clicks back to Melanie. "Still there?"

"It does kind of look like you," she says. "Tall, dark hair, broad shoulders."

"You've just described half of Hollywood."

"Half of Hollywood's not in the Seattle area. You are."

"I am absolutely certain there are men meeting that description in Washington, too." When she says nothing, he goes on. "I'm on a shoot, Mel. Why would I be out walking on a beach with some strange woman?"

"I don't know. Why would you?"

"I wasn't!" Joe is trying his damnedest not to get defensive, but he's slipping. "What makes you think it's me?"

"See for yourself."

Joe pulls up the image. It's a glorious photo. It's unmistakably him and Sarah, and in another life, it would be absolutely frame-worthy. In this life, he's relieved to see neither of their faces is remotely visible. The caption reads, "Guyzzzzzzzzzz, I totally just saw @thejrparker on the beach!!!!!!! Omgggggg!!! I couldn't get my camera fast enough to get his face, but I swear to you it's him. God, he's so hotttttt," followed by three fire emojis, followed by three heart eyes emojis.

He brings the phone back to his ear, but before he can comment, Melanie says, "You know, she kind of looks like that other woman."

Well, this conversation just took a turn for the worse. "What other woman?"

"In that picture from a couple months ago," she says.

"I don't know what you're talking about," he says. This is hell. Joe hates lying. A little lying in his profession is necessary. Claiming to be proud and excited about projects he hopes no one sees. Pretending to love co-stars who were, in reality, complete assholes. Acting like he wouldn't rather gnaw his own foot off than play the dad in "Battle of the Pixies."

But lying to the people who actually matter hurts like hell. And of all the things he doesn't want to lie about, Sarah sits right atop that list. With the exception of Clark and that previous photo, he's mostly gotten through this thing with Sarah through careful avoidance. He's been lucky. Until now.

"Hmm. You know you really should check your socials once in a while," Mel says.

"Apparently."

"Hey, why did you shave your beard again, by the way?"

"What do you mean? I'm working. I'm usually shaved onscreen."

"No, when you were in Seattle the first time. You went with a beard and came home without one."

He didn't even think she'd noticed. Joe makes a fist and squeezes it, trying to channel all his anger, resentment, and defensiveness into his hand and away from his mouth. "You're asking me why I shaved my beard three months ago?"

"Yes, I'm asking you why you shaved your beard three months ago."

"Well, it was three months ago, Mel, so I have no fucking idea." Then again, channeling is overrated. "It was probably getting itchy. It does that sometimes. What are you trying to say?"

Maybe he should just let it out. Maybe it's time. The way she's needling him, maybe she wants it, too. Or maybe she's building her case for the divorce attorney.

Finally, she speaks. "I wouldn't have thought you'd go for someone like that, I must say."

Like that? That's a low blow. Lower than Joe would have imagined she would go. Melanie's been selfish at times, demanding, sometimes cold, but she's never been outright mean. It's been a long time since she's seemed interested in anything Joe did besides showing up for the kids and booking gigs with big paychecks, but maybe she's actually hurt. "Mel, come on. You're not that person."

"What do you care? You don't know her, right?"

She has a point. If it weren't him in the photo, he might be disgusted by the dig, but he wouldn't be hurt. So, he can't be hurt now. He takes a silent breath and says steadily. "It's not me. I'm on a shoot."

More silence. The sensation of letting her get away with saying *that* about Sarah feels like a grenade in his gut. He's so tempted to go all in. Just push a little harder and he can blow this whole thing up. The truth will come out and the lying will be over and then maybe he can actually be with the woman he loves. This is it. This is the moment. Why not go all in? Why not?

"What would the kids think, Joe?

Shit. The kids. That's why.

Maybe there's a way. Somehow. God, let there be a way. But this isn't it. He tempers his voice, strips away all the heat he feels until his performance is one hundred percent camera ready, and then he says calmly, "It's not me, Mel."

There's another long silence. When Melanie finally speaks, her voice is flat and resigned. "Okay. If you say so." She sounds unconvinced, but willing to move on. With one proviso. "You should probably untag yourself anyway. We wouldn't want the kids to get the wrong idea, now would we?"

"Of course," he says, defeated. "Consider it done."

***

In the afternoon, they're shooting at one of "their parks." The sun is bright, the trees and the grass are a hundred shades of green, and Lake Washington glimmers all around. The spectacular beauty of a Seattle summer in vivid technicolor. Yet there's a pall over the day. They're both running on fumes. And they still haven't spoken a single word to each other.

Sarah gets assigned to crowd control, blocking the public from wandering on set while they're rolling. As luck would have it, they're filming in almost exactly the spot where Joe first imagined kissing Sarah. The memory of it floods his senses and fills him with the strangest nostalgia, as if his time with Sarah was already over. He prays it's not, but the fear looms. He uses the feelings in his scene.

They're shooting one of the most critical scenes in the film, when his character has a meltdown over both the loss of his father and the discovery of his father's secret family. It's not hard for Joe to tap into feelings of profound grief and desperation. The tears come easily in take after take as he drops to his knees and sobs. His emotions are as raw as they've ever been. His performance radiates truth. He's always been a bit method, but the day takes far more out of him than most.

When Celeste calls "cut" for the last time and they wrap the scene, the crew remains silent, giving Joe a moment to compose himself, then erupts into a round of applause. There hasn't been a moment like this since the table read. That had been a heartfelt, authentic response to the story as a whole, and it was lovely. But this is so much more intense because they all know they've witnessed something truly special today. The kind of performance people don't forget. The kind of performance that wins awards.

Sarah applauds, too, and as Joe finds her through the crowd, she brushes away tears. She's not alone. Others are crying, including Celeste who is shaking her head in wonder, and Kayla who snuck onto set for the last couple takes. Even Pete ostentatiously honks into a handkerchief to expel his emotions. But Sarah's tears are all Joe sees.

***

Back in their suite, Joe stares out at the rooftops and lights, waiting for Sarah, willing her to walk in the door. With each passing minute, he spirals, increasingly convinced she's not coming. Getting home later than he does isn't unusual, of course. As a production assistant, she often works the longest hours. First in, last out. But tonight, every tick of the clock feels like a rake scraping over his skin, scratching him raw as he waits.

Finally, he hears the door click. He closes his eyes and draws a slow, deep breath preparing himself for whatever walks in. He faces Sarah as she closes the door behind her. They stand across the room from each other, still and silent, locked in their places, waiting.

"Hi."

"Hi."

They stare another moment, breathing each other in from across the room, reacclimating to the world that is just theirs.

"Sorry it's so late," she says. Joe shakes his head like it doesn't matter. "They had me running all day, making up for lost time yesterday maybe. Then I was on a long call with Gabi just now." She pauses to steady herself. "She was kind of talking me off a ledge, I guess."

"Are you okay?" His face twists with pain.

"Yeah," she nods tentatively. "I'm... okay. You?"

An eternity passes before Joe moves his head slowly from side to side. No. He's not okay. He's not remotely okay.

Sarah collapses. "Me neither," she sobs as she runs to him.

He folds her in, and they cling to each other for dear life. Her warm, soft body molds to him as he squeezes her tighter and tighter, and all his anxiety drains away. The darkness lifts like a phantasm that's been exorcised by the mere touch of Sarah's skin. All his worry, all his fear simply gone.

Because she is his. And nothing can change that.

***

They lie together, naked, uncomfortably sweaty from their reunion. Sarah listens to Joe's heartbeat as he lifts his head to plant a kiss on hers. A loud growl emanates from his stomach. "You're hungry."

"Not anymore, I'm not." He threads his fingers through her hair and twists a yellow curl around his finger. "Sarah, I think we made a mistake."

The words knock the wind clean out of her. *A mistake?* But she reminds herself she's safe with Joe. She pushes herself up to look at him. "What do you mean?"

"I think we made a mistake not to talk about our families. I don't want to know half of you. I don't want to love half of you. I want all of you. Even if some of it hurts."

Sarah looks at Joe's right forearm. At the tattoo she usually avoids. His only tattoo. Two names, two dates, in beautiful calligraphy. Avery and Nathan. His children. And what must be their birthdates. She's glimpsed it countless times, every day, but always glanced away, afraid to break their rule, afraid to reconcile with the world outside. She runs a finger gingerly over the ink at last. "I agree," she says.

They spend the rest of the evening in hotel robes picking over room service and telling stories. Joe tells Sarah about the kids when they were little, about Avery's broken arm and Nathan's tonsillitis. He tells her about Nathan killing it on the track and about Avery's beautiful singing voice, though she basically refuses to sing at home or even in the car with him. He proudly beams about Avery heading to Stanford in a few weeks and moans that Nathan will be gone before he knows it, too.

He confesses he's not sure what will be left of his marriage when Nathan goes. He talks about the Melanie he met when they were young, about the dreams they shared, and about how much things have changed over the years. How all that's left between them is the children, who will be gone soon, like it or not. He thinks she would leave him if she could –

and he would be okay with that – but she hasn't worked in almost twenty years and wouldn't know where or how to start a new life. And he admits the guilt and the obligation he feels over that knowledge.

Sarah, in turn, talks about everything that happened with Emma, and about all the adventures she's had with both her nieces this summer. She talks about Gabi and their New Friend Dana, who is apparently now more Gabi's than hers, to Sarah's great delight. She tells Joe about her parents' divorce when she was in college and how Gabi got her through the resulting breakdown.

"You survived your parents' divorce," Joe observes, too thoughtfully to be thinking only about Sarah.

"I did. Eventually. It was devastating at the time, I can't lie, but it was the right thing for them."

Joe nods and drifts off. Sarah watches him drift and gives him time to navigate whatever's inside. Finally, she pulls him back. "Want to talk about it?"

"No, it's your turn. I want to hear more. I want to hear everything."

Sarah picks up where she left off talking about Gabi. How Gabi has gotten her through everything for twenty-five years, the dearest, most ridiculous of friends. She talks about their early, wild days, their road trips in their twenties, and the bad boyfriends they supported each other though. And that leads, at last, to Ben.

So she talks about Ben. What a gentle man he is, how kind he is, how good it was with him for a long time. Until everything happened with Synergy when he seemed to check-out completely. Right when she needed him most, he started working more and showing up less. Not just physically, but mentally, too. And how deeply that hurt her. "But now I'm realizing maybe it was at least partly my fault. Because I checked out, too, when I gave up on myself. And I think he didn't know how to handle that." She pauses, reflects a moment, then adds, "In fact, he apologized about that last night."

"He apologized?"

"Yeah. He wants to make it right," she sighs. She watches Joe's face cycle through a complex set of emotions before she continues. "But now I think I owe him an apology, too. Not just for this," she says gesturing at the two of them, "but because I was the problem all along."

"You weren't a problem," Joe corrects. "You *had* a problem. And now you've worked through it." He smiles lovingly at the very present Sarah. "And you're not checked out anymore."

"No. I'm right here," she agrees. She stares down at her sandwich awhile, then back at Joe. "What are we gonna do?"

He shakes his head. "I don't know."

"They're real people, Joe. Your family. My family."

Joe gnaws at his thumb. "They sure are."

"Is there any way to a happy ending here?"

"There has to be. Because all this has happened for a reason. I know it."

Sarah offers an unconvincing smile. "Can you really see me fitting into Hollywood?"

"I would be proud as hell to have you on my arm on any red carpet. But we don't have to live there," he says hopefully. "I don't have to be there hustling anymore. I've got a great team and twenty years of contacts. I can move away. I could move here."

"But that's where the industry is."

"Hardly anything shoots in LA anymore.'

"But that's where your kids are."

Joe winces, but stiffens his jaw. "Not for long."

Eventually they decide to call it a night. They both have an early call tomorrow, and it's been an exhausting day. Plus, Sarah's got her follow-up interview at lunchtime and needs to be her best. So they brush their teeth, wash their faces, crawl into each other's arms, and their eyes fall instantly shut, as heavy as their bodies in the bed.

And yet, with the end ticking nearer, sleep takes longer than it should to arrive.

***

The moment Joe sees Sarah, he knows. He takes one look at the slow smile creeping onto her lips and knows she killed it at her interview. Her old self-doubt so entirely eradicated she can't even fake false modesty. She's utterly transformed. She has embodied at last what he always saw in her. The only difference is now everyone can see it. Even Sarah herself.

She stands as he enters the room, waiting for him to come to her – eyes so alive, lips parted in a sly smile that bespeaks both her success and her desire – and he's dumbstruck by something he didn't think possible. She's become even more beautiful, even sexier, even more magnificent. Because she knows it. He was drawn to her from the moment he saw her, of course, dazzled by the light he could see within, emanating from her core, shining just for him. So brightly he thought it was a trick of the sun. But now, this Sarah, who knows her worth again, who feels her beauty, who stands in her strength... this Sarah is blinding.

Pride and desire drive him to her. He makes love to her greedily, devouring every inch of her body and soul with his mouth, hands, and heart, knowing as he does it will never be enough. He could spend every moment of the rest of his life making love to her and it would never be enough. She's everything he wants. She's the only thing he wants.

***

Joe leans against the headboard reviewing his scenes for the next day when Sarah, who's sitting on the edge of the bed with her nose buried in her phone, suddenly asks, "Do you ever Google yourself?"

"Rarely. I mean, I'm an actor so my ego demands an occasional googling, but it's generally a bad idea."

"Actually, we're in Microsoft country here. I should have said…" she eyes him suggestively, "do you ever *Bing* yourself, Joe?" She raises a brow at him in an exaggerated attempt at sultriness.

Joe responds in kind, with a low, growling sexy time voice, "I have been known to *Bing* myself occasionally, yes. But I like it better when you *Bing* me." He sets the script down, grabs her, and pulls her toward him.

"Oooh! Maybe I'll *Bing* you right now," she says. She bites her lip seductively.

"Yes, please," he gamely agrees, hoping he's rested long enough.

Sarah leers hungrily as she climbs toward his face and kisses him deeply. He smiles in anticipation of what's next. But instead of coming in for another round, Sarah grins, flops on her back, and pulls her phone up. She leans against his chest as she searches his name on her phone.

"Denied!" he groans.

Sarah laughs as she scrolls through pictures of him. "Man, this guy's hot!" She flips to a full body shot of Joe standing on a red carpet. He wears a black suit and black shirt, long, lean, and sleek. "Look at that tall drink of water. Makin' me thirsty."

Joe makes his move, reaching for her breast. "I'm ready to quench that thirst anytime."

She jovially slaps his hand away and keeps scrolling. "Hey, it's baby you."

"Wow, look at me. That was like 15 years ago. Check out at all that hair. I was a sexy kid back then. And I knew it, too."

"Yeah, you were cute, alright," she says. "But I like grown-up Joe better." She flips to another more recent, more mature picture. Rugged with stubble and a James Dean squint. "There he is. That's my guy!" He gives her a loving squeeze. She keeps scrolling. "Boy, for a guy who claims he's not famous, there sure are a lot of pictures of you online."

"It's not how many pictures there are. It's how many people are looking at them."

She swipes to another picture on a red carpet. He's wearing a tight fitting t-shirt and jeans, perfectly groomed stubble topped with a hipster mustache. He wears light-tint sunglasses and a blue and gray striped slouchy beanie on his head. "Such a hipster you were."

"I was having a moment."

"Couldn't be bothered to dress up?"

"It wasn't my premiere. What do I care?"

"Fair," she nods amiably. She flips to a production still. "River's Run!" Her voice goes wistful. "I loooved that show."

"You did? You watched it?" He lights up.

"Of course, I did. I've seen everything. Isn't that how this all started?"

"That was my favorite project I ever worked on." Joe waxes sentimental before squeezing her again. "Until now, that is."

They kiss tenderly. When Sarah pulls away, she launches into praise for River's Run. "It was a great show. It really was. It should have run forever."

"If only they'd asked you."

"Dummies."

She happily scrolls through a couple more pictures, then reaches one that stops her cold. Joe feels her body go rigid in his arms and looks to see what's wrong.

It's a photograph of him on the red carpet. With his family. He's got one arm around his wife and the other on his daughter's shoulder in front of him. Melanie looks glamorous in a short black, one-shoulder dress and cherry red stilettos, hair sleeked back in a long ponytail. Their children gleam happily in front of them, a few years younger than they are now. Melanie's arms wrapped tightly around their son, pulling him close to her, protecting him.

The room fills with silence.

"Well, that's probably enough pictures for now," Sarah finally says. She swipes away and turns off her screen. He pulls her tightly against him and plants a kiss in her hair. She tugs herself loose and sits back up on the side of the bed.

"Want to get something to eat? I'm starved." The words gush out in a torrent. "Maybe we should go out? What do you think? Chinese? Thai? Thai sounds good, don't you think?"

Joe reaches for her hand and looks at her steadily. "Hey, just you and me in here. Right?"

She rolls the answer around her mouth solemnly, then finally says with determination, "Right."

Chapter Thirty-Four

Triumph and Tragedy

THE NEXT MORNING SARAH gets the call she's been waiting for from the film commission. She's standing in the middle of Costco when they offer her the job and she has nowhere near enough cool to play hard-to-get. She nearly shouts her yes through the phone. Shoppers with giant carts jolt in surprise as they pass.

Sarah does a silent happy dance, hopping her feet up and down in a little circle while she listens to the woman on the other side talk about start date options and paperwork. She doesn't hear much of what's said, but she hears the part about how they'll email all the details, which is good enough for now.

When she hangs up, a nearby woman in a bright red vest with a tray full of samples raises a tiny paper cup of spinach ravioli by way of a toast. Sarah walks over and takes the cup. "Congratulations," the woman says.

"Thank you," Sarah grins before tossing back the ravioli in celebration.

***

When Sarah pulls up to the house where they're shooting, she texts Joe. She has to tell him the news first. *Need you for 2 minutes when you're free.*

Even as she hits send, she sizes up the house and realizes it's impossible. The house is swarming with crew inside and out, loading in equipment and lining up for the food truck catering lunch. There's not a private spot in sight. There's literally no way she's getting him alone today. She reluctantly fishes her cartons of food out of the car and carries them into the house's kitchen where she finds Pete and Celeste talking and Randy tapping frantically on his phone.

"This is a nightmare," Celeste says.

"I've got a call in with the team in L.A.," Pete replies, "but they reckon it will take them a couple days best case scenario to find someone and get them up here. I'll call the local film commission for leads, but that'll probably take just as long."

Sarah whispers to Randy, "What's going on?"

"The sound mixer fell. He's okay, but concussed and out of commission," Randy whispers back.

"How long can we delay?" Celeste asks.

Pete grimaces. "Even if we can absorb the costs, Joe only has one buffer day before he's off to another shoot."

Celeste puffs out a long, frustrated breath. "We were so close. Just three more days."

Sarah steps forward. "I might know someone." Every head swivels to face her. "At least, I might know someone who knows someone. My brother-in-law Alec is an audio engineer. He knows every sound guy in town."

Celeste's jaw drops in wonder before closing into a hopeful smirk. "Why am I not surprised? If you think there's a chance, by all means make that call."

Twenty minutes later, Sarah marches into the room where Celeste, Joe, and other cast and crew are lunching. She announces that Alec found a friend who can start this afternoon. "Fifteen years in film and TV, he's union, on a break, and can start this afternoon," she reports.

Joe's face erupts in a blinding grin mirrored by every other face as the room fills with cheers. Celeste is the first to speak. "Someone tell Pete he can stop making calls. Our guardian angel has come through again. Sarah, we're going to have to get you a pair of wings."

As the room celebrates, Sarah blushes, then catches Joe's eye and taps her phone. Within less than a minute, he excuses himself and heads to the back of the house. Sarah returns to her car as Joe strolls to the far end of the backyard.

From the safety of her car, Sarah calls and Joe picks up instantly. "You fucking beauty," he says. "You are a miracle worker!"

Sarah giggles. "Well, that's not the first miracle today."

"No," he says, his understanding clear.

"Yeah. I got it, babe. I got the job."

Joe punches the air and cheers, attracting attention from the crew, but he doesn't care. "Fuck yeah! I knew it!" Sarah can feel the sunshine of his grin right through the phone. "I'm so fucking proud of you!"

Sarah laughs. "I've never heard you so profane before."

"You've never heard me so fucking excited before," he quickly retorts.

Sarah sighs happily. "I couldn't have done it without you."

Joe looks back at the house, at all the people buzzing around, making his dream come true. A dream that's been saved time and again by Sarah. "I couldn't have done any of this without you," he says. "And tonight, we celebrate!"

After hanging up, Sarah calls Gabi to share the news. Gabi reacts in a typically Gabi way. She runs around the foodbank with her phone in the air shouting the news to everyone. Sarah hears shouts of congratulations across the line from various folks, but none more enthusiastic than Gabi's when she finally returns to the phone. Sarah has never had a better cheerleader. Except maybe Joe.

A text pops in from Ben. *I made a reservation at Daniel's on Lake Union for Saturday. You'll be done then, right?* Done. With what, she wonders? Before she has time to contemplate the question, his follow-up comes. *I thought maybe we could start over?* It's a sweet gesture. Daniel's Broiler was where they had that delicious dinner before he walked her out on the pier and proposed by the dark, glimmering water. She remembers like it was yesterday how he knelt to one knee while the Space Needle towered above them, aglow against the unusually starry night sky. It was magical.

She should tell him about the job. Of course, she should. But how? And who is she telling? Her husband and life partner whose life will be materially impacted by her new role? Or a longtime friend with whom she shares a beautiful past, but not a future?

Sarah puts the phone back into her pocket and goes inside. She finds Kayla who is busily tidying her work station and organizing her make-up. Sarah makes her announcement, and Kayla grabs her in her first congratulatory hug.

"You're swimming with the big fish now!" Kayla says with a wink.

"I'm super excited, I have to say."

"We have to go out and celebrate. Tonight."

"Oh, no, I can't," Sarah demurs.

"You can and you will. C'mon, you've backed out of drinks every time, but not tonight," Kayla says. "I know, let's go for karaoke! I saw a bar doing it near our hotel."

Horror flashes across Sarah's face. "Karaoke is really not my style."

"We'll invite Randy and Tish, too. Invite everyone. Your husband. All your local friends. We'll make it a party!"

Sarah shuffles her feet and shrugs. "I don't hang out with a karaoke crowd." That's not entirely true. Gabi would do karaoke in a heartbeat, but Sarah couldn't very well explain inviting Gabi without inviting Ben, too. "Let's just keep it a crew thing."

"It's your party," Kayla says happily. "Ooh, I'm gonna sing Tay Tay! I'll text Randy now."

Sarah thinks of Joe, of their plans to celebrate, and says as casually as possible, "Maybe we could invite Joe?"

"Joe? Parker?" Kayla says with a screwed up face. "God, I always forget you even know him. You like never talk to him."

"I do," Sarah says, trembling on a tightrope as she speaks. "But I don't want to 'bother the talent' as they say."

"Okay, great," Kayla says without a second thought. "Let's ask Joe. What's the worst that can happen? He'll say no?"

***

"No!" Joe says. "Really? Seriously?"

"Why not? We know you can sing." Her question is disingenuous. She knows perfectly well why he doesn't want to go. For the same reason they've avoided every other non-obligatory social outing this shoot, because it's too hard to be around others acting like they're not together. And on this night of all nights, when they want to celebrate together. And when the shoot is almost over.

Yes, they've begun to discuss the possibility of a real life together – how their lives could combine, how they might tell others, how they could minimize the damage and protect the kids. There's hope ahead. The outline is still fuzzy, however, and the future uncertain. A separation of some kind looms, no matter what. This night is too precious – but Sarah has already said yes. "One drink, one song, then we'll go," she offers.

Joe mulls it over. "Are you going to sing?" he asks pointedly.

Onstage? With an audience? Absolutely not. But she knows what he wants to hear. "Maaaaybe."

"Maybe's not good enough." He stares at her, calling her bluff.

Sarah rolls her eyes in surrender. "Okay, yes. I'll sing."

Joe holds onto his smile, pinching his mouth tight around it as if he could actually deny Sarah anything. And it is, after all, the first time *she's* lured *him* out to play. That's something to celebrate in itself. "Fine," he says cracking wide. "We can go."

***

The bar is only half full, but it's more than enough people to keep the stage occupied by regulars and karaoke devotees. Tish begged off for the night, but Randy and Kayla gamely drink and alternate their renditions of Taylor Swift, Harry Styles, and a delightfully silly duet of "Single Ladies." Joe takes the stage a couple times himself, with a Hozier tune followed by "Mack the Knife."

All the while Sarah remains planted firmly in her seat. She hoots and cheers for the others, hops up for standing O's, but never so much as glances at the book of song choices. When Kayla ducks off to the bathroom and Randy heads to the stage, preparing for his next performance, Sarah leans over and whispers to Joe, "Wanna get out of here?"

Joe keeps his eyes fixed forward and whispers back, "Desperately."

"Great, we'll wait until Randy finishes his song then make our separate excuses and get out."

"Not until you sing," Joe says with mischief in his smile.

Kayla slams back into her seat with a drunken slur. "What are we talking about?"

"We're talking about why Sarah hasn't sung yet," Joe says, "and how it's her party and she really needs to sing. Don't you think?"

"Hell yeah, she does! Sarah, why haven't you sung yet? Get your ass on that stage," Kayla says.

Joe shrugs. "Your audience demands it."

"I really can't," Sarah says, downing her drink.

"Sure, you can! Here, I'll help you pick the song." Kayla pushes the songbook between them and leans in conspiratorially.

Joe nudges Sarah with his eyes and an evil smile. She reluctantly opens the book. Page after page of songs and artists of every genre and era. Classics, oldies from her youth, showtunes, songs so new she can barely pronounce the artists' names. She searches for something she can even imagine getting onstage and singing without wanting the ground to swallow her whole.

Then she sees it. The song she needs to sing. The only song she can imagine singing tonight. It's perfect. She orders another drink, and as Randy returns to the table, she jots her pick down on a tiny slip of paper. Kayla and Randy watch with giggles of approval.

Joe leans over to peek. "What are you singing?"

Sarah pushes him away and folds the slip of paper secretively. "I'm singing Nunya."

"Nunya?" he says.

"Nunya Bizness!" she proclaims proudly. Kayla and Randy howl with laughter. They're definitely drunk, but Sarah's catching up. "It's a surprise. Wait and see like everyone else." She mime-zips her lips closed, locks them, and throws away the key.

Joe purses his lips and leans back, nodding his head in mock offense. "Oh, it's like that?"

"It's like that," she grins.

Sarah's next drink arrives, and she has just enough time to gulp it down before she's called to the stage. She whispers giddily to Kayla and Randy before she goes up and their heads bob in happy agreement. Joe watches it all unfold with amused interest and a sudden, keen awareness he's the only sober one in the bunch.

As Sarah takes the stage, her cheering section gets loud, her three fans hooting and clapping like their team just won the World Series. She fills her lungs and holds it until the music begins, eyes on the floor, not yet ready to face her audience.

Joe recognizes "The Story" right away, and the singer, Brandi Carlile. Who else? He smiles to himself as Sarah sings the first line of a song they've sung many times over the past weeks, the definitive love song for soulmates. As much as he wants to take in every moment, he closes his eyes for a fleeting second to steel himself. When he reopens them, she's still singing shyly to the floor, but when she reaches the first chorus, her eyes float up and cross the room, landing on Joe at the word "you" before moving on.

She swings into the second verse with more force, just as the song does, now playing the whole room with more confidence. When the verse demands, she bursts into full voice to blast out the words that are undeniably her truth. And although her gaze glides all over the crowd, Joe's under no illusions to whom she's singing.

She works the crowd, all those nights "performing" with Joe paying off at last. She's a new Sarah, one unafraid to shine and bask in the applause, at least for this moment. But with every line, as she works the room, she manages to sweep past Joe on the word "you." Every time. Too fast for anyone else to notice, but it's a beacon to Joe who feels her pouring love directly into him. Her secret message laced through the lyrics, hidden in plain sight. Every line they've crossed, every rule they've broken, it's all been worth it. It will always be worth it. Because they were made for each other.

Perhaps Randy and Kayla might have noticed if they were a little less drunk, but they're far too distracted with their synchronized table dancing to track Sarah's line of sight. During the musical break, Sarah prances around, then busts out her air guitar and mimics her first night with Joe when they sang and danced to another Brandi Carlile song. And then another. Sarah rhythmically rocks back and forth on her invisible guitar like the goddess she is and Joe's heart swells with the exultation of the moment.

Halfway through the last verse, Sarah waves Kayla and Randy to the stage. They take their places behind her, dancing in unison with the same moves they were rehearsing at the table. Sarah glides into the final refrain of the chorus and they back her with the most enthusiastic "ahhhhs-ahhhhhs" imaginable. Glee erupts across Joe's face. His fist hits the air in triumph while Sarah belts the final chorus for all she's worth. With Kayla and Randy now safely behind her, she sings directly to Joe. Every word.

And on the final line of the song, Joe mouths the words right back to her, their declaration to each other. Because it will always be true that they were made for each other. The song over, Kayla and Randy swamp Sarah with hugs and laughter, but over their shoulders, she locks eyes with Joe who simply beams.

***

Joe walks Sarah into their room, his arm around her waist to steady her. She stops inside the door and attempts to push her shoes off her feet, but is too uncoordinated in her condition to manage it.

"You're drunk. I like you drunk," Joe chuckles. He sits her down in the chair nearest the door and kneels to pull her shoes off.

"I'm not drunk. I'm squiffy," she says, wrapping her fingers in his hair as he fiddles with her shoes.

"Okay, I like you squiffy," he smiles. He lifts her back up to move her toward the bedroom, but she stops and spins a little.

"I might be drunk," she announces with particularly unfocused eyes. Joe stifles a laugh. He pulls her arm over his shoulder and leads her to the bed to help her undress. "I'm a good drunk."

"Yes, you are," he says as he slides her top over her head.

"Not maudlin like some people. Or grumpy." She squishes her features into a drunk grumpy face as she plops down on the edge of the bed.

"No, you're neither one." He pulls her back to standing so he can slide her jeans down. "You're a very good drunk," he agrees.

She throws her arms around Joe's shoulders and kisses him. "And now I would like to have drunk sex with my hot man." She drops back onto the bed and attempts to pull him with her.

"Well, that sounds like fun," he says sweetly. "But maybe let's wait until tomorrow."

"Noooo, I wanna fool around now!" She throws herself flat back on the bed, arms splayed. "You have my permission to ravish me."

Joe laughs again as a warm river of tenderness rushes through him. He shakes his head. "Remember that part about how you're drunk?"

"I know. It'll be fun!" she says giddily. "Besides, you have an open invitation."

"I'll ravish you tomorrow, I promise." He gently scoots her up the bed toward the pillows. He rolls her one way to pull out the blankets from under her body and rolls her back the other to cover her. "Stay here," he whispers. He walks into the next room and comes back with a glass of water. "Drink this." He helps her sit up and take a few sips, then he holds out two ibuprofen pills. "Take these." She does as she's told and drinks another half a glass of water. He eases her back down onto the pillow, then slides onto the bed next to her and watches her fading in and out.

"You take such good care of me," she says dreamily.

"The feeling is mutual."

Sarah's eyes are heavy. She's close to drifting off. "Why are you such a good guy? You make it very hard not to love you."

"Why would I want you not to love me?" he asks softly, grazing her cheek with his fingertips.

Sarah lets out a sleepy mini-moan like she's trying to speak but can't quite master the skills to do it, before half opening her eyes and looking into his. "It would be so much easier if I didn't," she says. And then she's out.

He lies beside her, kisses her forehead, and caresses her hair as he watches her sleep. "That would be easier, wouldn't it?" he whispers.

***

The next day is tough for Sarah who's still weathering the effects of her liquid courage the night before. By the time evening rolls around, she's perfectly happy to curl in her favorite armchair reading. But when Joe flops on the sofa, he brings a gray cloud with him. He's been talking to Nathan and he's somber. He stares into space, deep in thought, until he feels her eyes on him. She's watching him with concern. "You okay?"

"I'm fine." He offers a tired, pensive smile by way of reassurance. "Nate's having girl problems. Nothing serious," he says with a light eye roll, but he slips quickly back into his ruminations.

These last few days, they've dared dream about their life together, dared to plan it. They've thought through the painful decisions. Agreed they should take their time, for the sake of the kids. They can each get a new place. Joe's a temporary place in LA where Nathan and Avery can stay with him sometimes. Sarah's the home they'll share one day, hopefully soon. He'll come up as often as he can. She'll visit him in LA, or maybe even on location.

The conversations haven't been easy. The decision to walk away from their lives and their families weighs heavily on each of them. For Joe, his kids are the obvious glue, but he's shared a lifetime with Melanie as well. So much of what they've shared is gone, but not everything. Not their partnership as parents, or the bond of getting through leanest imaginable times together. Not the home they've built together. Admittedly, it's been years since they've been truly connected, and just as long since he's felt supported. And yet, there was a glimmer – when she called about the photo of him and Sarah on the beach. An unexpected hint that she still cared, that perhaps at the other end of all that distance there was still a woman who wanted to try. The very fact that Melanie could feel hurt suggested there could be something left to preserve. Maybe they just lost sight of each other across the distance. Maybe.

And Sarah has Ben waiting at home for her. Seeming more like the old Ben every day. Ready to work at it. Eager to start over. Why did she have to fall in love with someone else for that to happen? Plus, walking away means losing Wendy, Alec, and the girls as well. Her whole family, lost in one fell swoop. Again. Just like her parents' divorce. Just like Synergy. At least this time, she'd be the one leaving, but it still hurts.

That's the cold, hard reality. No matter what they choose, there will be hurt. That's the price Fate and Destiny demand for the gift of finding each other.

Now Joe wears his sacrifice on his face. He's giving up so much. For her. Talking to Nathan tonight has reminded Joe of the cost. It's reminded Sarah as well. Nathan's pain. Avery's pain. Memories swirl of how she fell apart senior year when her parents announced their divorce. How angry she was at them, how quickly she shut out her then boyfriend and nearly destroyed her entire academic career. She recalls the anguish of losing faith in love and marriage for all those years. Then she thinks of Ben, who once upon a time helped her believe again, and even of Melanie. She tries to read again, but the words blur and her attention fades. The cost is so high.

She closes the book.

"Remember when I told you about my parents' divorce?" she finally says. Joe nods. "Well, like I told you, it was the right thing for them. It was time. Their marriage didn't work anymore. It did at one time, when I was younger. But sometimes that happens, and it's nobody's fault. And they were both so much happier after the divorce."

Joe devours every word, thirsting for the reassurance only Sarah can give him.

"And it's true, a lot of kids come through divorce just fine."

Joe gazes gratefully at Sarah. His hope. His saving grace. His angel in the marble. She's right. They'll be okay. It will be painful, but in the long run, it will be better for everyone.

"The thing is," she continues with a lump in her throat, "eventually I was okay, but it did tear my life apart at the time. I spun out. I blew up a relationship with a guy I thought I might marry one day. I came this close to flunking out. If Gabi hadn't been there…" She shakes her head at the unfinished thought.

"Ah." The clipped grunt escapes Joe's gut as if he's been punched.

"I mean, maybe it'll be different for them." She's twisting herself in circles, desperate to avoid the words she has to say. She swallows hard, voice trembling as she pushes forward. "But I was a senior in college when it happened, and if I'm being honest, if I'd been younger and more dependent on my parents… Or still living at home when my father moved out. I think... it might have felt... like he was leaving me, too. Even if I knew that wasn't true intellectually. I think that's how I would've felt." Joe winces, holding his breath. "I mean, I already felt abandoned, and if there had been someone else involved – an affair – I can't even imagine how betrayed I would've felt."

Joe's face melts into a grimace. "So, they don't have to know... yet."

"You want to lie to them then? For how long?" A lightning flash of agony crosses Joe's face. "How do you explain coming to Seattle all the time? Me coming to LA? How many *years* do we have to spend lying? And hiding to make it okay? And is that really what you want?"

Her words pierce Joe's heart as cleanly as an archer's arrow as he accepts what she's really saying. She's not – as he first thought – helping him make peace with splitting up his family. She's giving him permission to let her go.

Grief drains the color from his face. "Baby, no! We can—"

"No, baby... we can't. We can't take our happiness at the expense of someone else's." Sarah wrings her hands as if conjuring the words through a spell. "We can't do that to them. To any of them. And we've both known it from the start. We just let ourselves forget for a while because pretending felt so good."

Joe grasps desperately for words. "They always say don't stay together for the kids. Don't they?"

"Maybe. But were you going to leave Melanie before me?" He says nothing, but she knows the answer. "I can't be the reason, Joe. I'm not willing to be." And there it is. The bottom line. The card that trumps all others. Her wound, long sealed shut, no longer painful, but leaving impenetrable scar tissue.

Without saying a word, Joe gets up and heads for the fridge. He pulls out a beer, cracks it open, and takes a long swig while staring at nothing. Then another. It's bitter and heavy and sludges through his system like a darkness descending. Finally, he speaks. "What about me? Don't I get a say in all this?"

"Yes. You get a say in what you choose in your marriage, with your kids. But whatever you choose, it can't be because of me. It has to be about you."

"But..."

Whatever argument he's preparing, Sarah needs to head it off. Because for the first time, she's absolutely sure. "Anyway, it's not just that. It's about Ben, too. He's changed. I can tell."

Joe takes another long draft of beer, finding an equilibrium with the darkness, and rubs his temple. Suddenly, his head is splitting. "Are you choosing this because you want it?" he says. "Or just because you think it's the right thing to do?"

"I want it." She pauses thoughtfully. "*Because* it's the right thing to do. And because I think Ben and I can be happy again. Like we used to be. He loves me."

"*I* love you!" Joe insists as he bolts back to her side, attempting to reclaim his place in her life.

"And I love you. God, so much!" She raises a hand and palms his cheek, trailing her fingertips up to his temple. She rubs gently, soothing his head by instinct.

He takes her hand in his, presses his lips to it, and studies her mournfully. "Do you still love him?"

"Yes," she admits with a nod. She hesitates to say the words out loud here, to admit that she loves her husband, of all people. How strange. Words that should flow out like air. But in this room, in their precious bubble, Joe is her oxygen. Joe breathed new life into her. And yet. "I love him, too. Not like you, but..."

"No, it's okay." He squeezes her hand. "It's good. I'm glad you love him. I couldn't be happy if I didn't believe that." Unable to stay still, Joe drops to his knees in front of her, an act of supplication. A reminder that he remains hers, will always be hers. Abandonment has haunted her again and again for all her adult life, but he won't abandon her. "Sarah, all I've wanted since the first day I met you – well, not *all* I've wanted, but the most important thing – has been for you to be happy."

"And now I am. And I will be. And you made that possible." She reaches for his head again and this time runs her hand through the softness of his hair until it comes to rest cupping the back of his neck. Both giving and drawing strength through the touch. Her heart swells with gratitude. "You walked into my life at the very moment I needed you most and you pulled me in. I'd been adrift so long I didn't even remember what land looked like. And you saved me. At least until I could save myself."

Joe considers this. The beautiful, brilliant, healed woman in front of him can do anything. Handle anything. Yet, the urge to protect her is still so strong. "But he hurt you."

"He did. He made some huge mistakes. I blamed him for checking out on me," she shrugs at the truth before she goes on. "But I was too deep in my fog to see how checked out I was. I basically let everything go, including my marriage. Until you came along and you *wouldn't* let go. No matter how I tried to push you away."

"I couldn't. I tried," he says, "but something kept pulling me back to you."

"Our tether," she says and Joe nods his agreement. "You were right. This was meant to be. You and I are knitted together. Forever. No matter what happens."

"No matter what." Joe contemplates the undeniable truth. He felt from the start they were meant to be, but what a complicated, improbable journey. He dutifully resisted at first, but in his heart, he always knew there was no fighting Fate. So, he went into it knowing it could never last. Knowing that this wild, miraculous odyssey would eventually have to end. Even Odysseus himself eventually returns home, a man changed by the winds of Fate, interfering gods, and unimaginable adventures. Yet, somehow in these recent days, he's allowed himself the dream of staying in the intoxicating presence of this magical woman. He might think Sarah, a goddess in her own right, bewitched him just as Circe once hoped to entrance Odysseus. But Sarah is true and guileless, and he will always love her. No enchantments required.

"Because of you, I found the courage to live again. You helped me find the old Sarah."

The light in Sarah's eyes nearly melts him, while simultaneously igniting him. How can there be so much hope and joy and heartbreak in a single look? He knows the answer to his next question, but he asks anyway. "And that Sarah doesn't see a future with me?"

"I can see a million futures with you. But all of them have the haze of fantasy. A wonderful fantasy, but not my real life. Not now." Sarah smiles wistfully. Three months ago, when she first met Joe, she desperately fought off her fantasies of where things could go with him for fear they would break her. Ironic, then, that giving into those fantasies is what saved her. Yes, fantasies can be beautiful, too.

"My life is here, Joe," she continues. "With my work and my family. It's a good life." They lean into each other, their foreheads pressed together, feeling their connection. She kisses him softly and he welcomes her lips like water in a desert. He soaks her up until at last she pulls back and looks into his eyes. "And you have your own family and life in L.A."

Tears come to Sarah's eyes as the import of what she's just said sinks in. Fate brought them together, no question. But as surely as they were destined to be together in this moment – to heal and love each other through the darkness – now they're also destined to part.

Joe lifts himself from the floor and takes her hand, leading her once again from her chair to a spot together on the couch. She curls into him and he cradles her in his arms as they reconcile themselves with what is to come.

CHAPTER THIRTY-FIVE

THAT'S A WRAP

THERE'S A ROOM SERVICE tray full of mostly uneaten food shoved on the desk. No appetite. They sit in silence across from each other at the table. Tomorrow's the last day of the shoot. Sarah checks out in the morning. The end is near.

Joe picks up his phone, taps a couple times, and a Tony Bennett and Lady Gaga duet starts. "Sing with me," he says.

"Joe... I can't."

"Sing with me," he insists. He starts singing the Tony Bennett part, nodding to her, encouraging her to get ready to chime in. Sure enough, when Gaga sings, so does Sarah.

They sing to each other, feeling both silly and sad, but in the moment, also so grateful. They laugh, make eyes, and flirt like performers onstage as they croon. This moment is a gift, a much-needed grace note in their otherwise heartbreaking swan song.

When the song ends, they fall quiet again. Sarah stares thoughtfully at the nearly empty bottle of wine between them. "You know, I've just realized. This is the last bottle of wine we'll ever share."

"Well, we better enjoy it then," he says with a determined smile. He drains the remains of the bottle equally into their two glasses, then holds his up to toast. "To us!"

Sarah raises her glass and repeats the toast with her own smile. So much better to celebrate their time together than grieve its ending. If only it were that simple and feelings came with an on/off switch. After a long sip, she leans her elbow on the table and rests her head on her hand. Joe mirrors her position as they gaze at each other. "So this is it?" she says. "We just... go home and never see each other again?"

"I don't know. I think so. Yeah." Joe picks at the plate of fries still on the table, dips one in ketchup, and eats it. It's grown cold, leaden, and entirely appropriate for how he's now feeling. When he speaks again, his words burst out like he's made a terrible discovery. "Jesus! Never is a long fucking time."

"Never is forever," Sarah says. It's the sort of oddly obvious observation that somehow renders the truth even more jarring than before.

Pain shoots across Joe's face like an electric shock. His eyes dart around the room, searching for the answer in some corner, under the couch, or on a bedside table. Finding none, his eyes land back on Sarah's face. She is resolute, but bittersweet emotions well in her eyes.

"And I promised I would never hurt you," Joe laments.

"You didn't. You couldn't. I chose this," she says. "I chose it because this hurt is a hell of a lot better than never feeling what I've felt with you. I chose it because it's worth it." She reaches across the table for Joe's hand. "Every minute of this is worth every minute of hurt that comes after. And I'm so grateful that you came into my life."

"No regrets then?"

"Not ever." Her face goes warm with the tears now falling. "But what about you?"

Joe swallows his own emotions. "I'll be fine."

"Can you and Melanie...?"

He's given the question she's trying to ask a lot of thought since their discussion last night. Imagining what his homecoming might be like. How he could walk in the door with a more open, more hopeful heart. Would it be enough to make a start? Could things really change? "I don't know. Maybe? For the first time, I think maybe there's something there to hold onto. At least to try." Joe troubles his lip in thought. "I know that's not much, but it's more than I could say a couple months ago." He shrugs. "In any case, we're good co-parents. The kids feel safe and loved. That's what matters most."

"Is that enough?"

He's thought about this, too. He taps thoughtfully at the base of his throat, connecting with something deep within. He was right when he said this all had to happen for a reason – and at last he understands that reason. The reason they were brought together, the reason they will always be tethered. Like the two babies who once slept side-by-side, drawing comfort to ready them for an unpredictable life ahead, Joe and Sarah have been given *this moment* to fortify each other, just when they needed it most. To love so deeply that their unbreakable bond strengthens them enough to face – and embrace – whatever comes next. Galvanized by their love.

As bittersweet as their looming goodbye may be, it's not the end. It's the beginning of better lives for both of them. Because they're ready for it. They've made each other ready. Sarah's come back to life, ready to dazzle the world with her brilliance that she forgot, but he saw from the start. And as for Joe, Sarah's made him whole – and made his dream possible.

"Sarah, before I met you, there was a hole. I didn't know what it was, I just knew something was missing. Something has always been missing. So, I lived with a constant ache. A pain I couldn't place, but couldn't shut out. But the instant I saw you, I knew. It was a Sarah-shaped hole. And now it's full."

"But if we're not together..."

Joe glimpses at the tablet on his nightstand, thinking of the book he's been rereading this week. "You ever hear of the hero's journey?"

"Sure. A bit."

"Well, you know how I love mythology, right? Roughly speaking, Joseph Campbell says that at the end of every journey, the hero returns home with a newfound balance between the inner and outer worlds. And he's able to live in the present because of it."

"I take it you're the hero in this scenario?" She grins with the playful jab, a flicker of silliness to stave off the sadness.

"You got a problem with that?" he chuckles in return, happy for the gift of levity reminding them both that there is joy alongside the sadness tonight.

"Nope!" she responds with a giggle. "Perfect casting."

"All I'm trying to say is, I used to live with that ache, and it was always fueled by worry about the next gig, how I'd pay the bills, whether my movie would get made, or distributed. And also by sadness at a past with Melanie that I couldn't seem to recapture, no matter what I tried."

"And now?"

"Now, I just feel whole. Like, one way or another, it's all going to be okay." He chokes up as he presses his hand against his heart. "The ache is gone. I can't explain it better than that. But just knowing you're in the world fills me up. Whether you're in my arms or on the other side of the planet."

"Joe..."

"I'll have my work, my kids... and you. It's *so much more* than most people get." As he speaks, an unexpected smile erupts across his face. "More than I ever dreamed." His eyes shine and he radiates a joy that seems impossible in this moment. It's almost disconcerting. And heartening. If it's true.

"Are you just acting for me right now? To make me feel better? Is this acting?"

"I've never once acted with you."

"Then you have to promise," she says.

He pulls his hand from his heart and extends it. Sarah shakes it, but despite Joe's sincerity, the tears roll. Joe fights to keep it together, wavering between his newfound certainty and his still very tangible grief.

"Maybe we don't say never," Sarah says, circling back to where they started. "Maybe it's true, but maybe we don't need to say it?"

Joe scrunches up his face. "How about... instead, we just say *not now*?" Joe reaches for the hand he was just shaking and clings to it. "Listen to me. You and I, this isn't over. Okay? This is forever." Sarah presses her free hand to her face to wipe away the tears trailing down her cheeks, but she smiles as he continues. "You and I are going to walk out of this room and back into our lives and we are going to be happy. You hear me?"

Even as the promise sears her heart, Sarah nods her agreement. She already knows it's true, but if she had any lingering doubts, Joe erases them. Because his words have an air of prophecy. Like they always do. And he's always been right before.

Joe goes on, "And you're going to be happy for me and I'm going to be happy for you. And you are going to shine so brightly. I only wish I could be here to see it." His voice cracks, his composure fading once again. "But no one and nothing can ever take this away from us. You've changed me." He taps twice on his heart. "You're a permanent fixture. Nothing will ever change that."

"Nothing," Sarah agrees.

He stands and pulls her up into his arms. They meld into one, cool water on hot sand, soothing and utterly inseparable. For now. A blissful relief, even as it breaks their hearts because it's only a matter of time before it evaporates. Her face pressed hard into his chest, she whispers under her breath, so quietly he can't possibly hear, "Tethered."

And as if he's heard her through his heart, "Tethered," he says softly into her ear.

They're locked in their own universe, surrounded by the vast blackness of space, in a silent vacuum with no sounds but their own, each a sun for the other providing all the light and heat they need. A universe that is still and beautiful and eternal. All theirs.

Sarah's weak in Joe's arms. He tugs her gently toward the bed.

"Babe, I can't. I'm not in the—"

"Shhh, I know. Just come on." He leads her to the bed, they kiss tenderly, and he wraps her safe in his arms. They hold each other. They hold each other and hold their story. They hold every kiss, every laugh, every tear, every time they made love, every place they went, and every song they sang together. Singing together would always be their first love language.

They fall asleep in each other's arms.

***

Sarah wakes with Joe spooning her, his long body curved against every inch of hers and his arm tightly around her. She listens to him breathing slow and steady in her ear, feels the rhythmic tickle to her hair with each breath. She carefully rolls over to face him. He stirs. They gaze sleepily into each other's eyes.

"Hi," he says.

"Hi," she smiles at him.

"Last day."

"Last day," she echoes, wiping crusty sleep from her eyes. Her hair is matted into a wavy, golden knot of a halo around her head, her eyes barely open, and she has a long crease running the length of her face from her forehead, over her eye, and down her cheek, the temporary scarring of a pillow imprint.

Joe beams at her. "God, you're beautiful."

He leans in to kiss her, but she covers her mouth. "I have morning breath."

"Shut up and kiss me," he says. And she does.

They take their time, studying each other, memorizing. Sarah combs his body for mental souvenirs she can lock in her heart and keep forever. The hair on his chest trailing down to his belly button, his beautiful hands, long fingers, the firmness of his lean muscles, the way his chest expands and contracts with each slow, deep breath. His only tattoo, the one on his arm, which she avoided for so long, but now seems so perfectly him. She examines his three tiny imperfections, the scars of a life that leaves no one unmarked. The chicken pox scar between his eyebrows, the scar on his knee from a fall on a cement basketball court, and the one on his inner wrist from the time the wind blew the storm door he was knocking on so hard it shattered around his hand.

She memorizes his hairline and the perfectly rugged lines on his face. They will change over time, of course, but not for her. For her, he will always be exactly as he is now. She runs her fingertips over those lips that kiss her so deeply she feels it in her soul, and he catches them with kisses as they pass. She records every inch of him in her mind. She knows she'll see him again and again, on TV or in movies, forever. But this is her movie she will replay the rest of her life, and she wants to remember everything.

He does the same, tracing the geography of her body as he's done countless times before. He feels every gentle curve, runs his eyes and fingers in tandem across every peak and valley. The bend of her elbow, the curve of her hip, the slope of her calf. He revels as if it's the first time at the fleshy softness of her breasts, her nipples as they harden, the stomach she once hid from him, and the warm center of her sex, all irresistibly soft and yielding to his touch.

A thrill goes through him watching the goosebumps that still rise when he runs his fingertips over her inner arm. He goes over every beautiful bit, every perfect imperfection, locking her in his mind and sealing her in his heart. He kisses her all the places he loves, and all the places he knows she loves.

They make love for the last time. Reminiscent of the first, not a millimeter of space between them. Tender, connected, unrushed. As if maybe they can make it last forever.

***

It's time for Sarah to check out. Although Joe doesn't leave until tomorrow, she made the mistake of letting it slip to Ben that the shoot ends today, so she has no excuse to stay for Joe's last night. If they had a future together it would be different. She could stay. But that's not possible now. *Not now.*

She collects her stuff from the other room, packs her bags, and sets everything by the door. Each moment carries the weight of the end. The last time she puts on her watch from the desk. The last time she unplugs her phone from the bedside table. The last time they hug in the room that is only theirs. They whisper "I love you" and cling to each other for as long as they can before the clock demands more of them.

Joe pulls her luggage as they walk into the hallway. For the first time, they weave their hands together as they trudge down the hall. Despite being the only ones staying on their floor, they've always been too careful to risk contact outside the room. They've rarely walked down the hall at the same time. When they have, they've kept their distance as much as possible, Sarah's drunken escort notwithstanding. Just in case. But today they are unafraid of being seen. Or more accurately, they are more afraid of letting go than being seen. They take the risk because they cannot let go. Not yet.

They pause at the elevator bank and stare at the button staring back at them. The last barrier between them and the end. They exchange pained smiles before Sarah pushes out her breath and presses the button.

They walk into the elevator, still clasping hands as tightly as possible. They ride silently, knowing everything that needs to be said has been said. These are their last moments together and they won't ruin them with words. A sadness swells within them as the floor numbers descend, a countdown to the end.

6...

5...

4...

Sarah swipes away a tear. Joe does the same a moment later, but screws up his face to hold it in. "Not now," he whispers, reminding them both of an imaginary someday.

3...

2...

In the split second the bell dings for the lobby, Sarah takes a deep breath, releases Joe's hand, grabs her bags, and walks out of the elevator ahead of him without a word, head high as she approaches the front desk.

Joe pauses a moment, then walks out behind her and straight out the front door.

***

Sarah's last official duty is to drop off some dry-cleaned costumes to Tish. Her volunteer stint is over. There's more to do to wrap-up the shoot, but Randy will take care of it. Sarah hooks the clothes on the rack, then she finds HMU and plops herself into Kayla's chair.

"Want me to make you up?" Kayla says as she shuffles around, packing things up.

"No, I just want to sit here and mope."

"Ugh, God, I know. The endings are the worst. You get to know people, you care about them..."

"Yeah."

"You *drink* together," Kayla adds with a wink. Sarah will miss those winks. "And then poof, they're just gone."

"Poof," Sarah says sadly.

"Nobody warns you about that part. The end."

"Nobody needed to warn me," Sarah says. "I saw it coming from the start."

Kayla clicks closed a case. "Hey, we've got our group chat. We'll keep in touch."

Sarah smiles. "I'd like that."

"You sure you don't want me to give you a little zhuzh? I could hot you up for the wrap party tonight, make you extra glamorous for that husband of yours, who must be missing you by now."

Sarah grimaces. "I don't think I'm going."

"What?! You literally have to go. It's not optional."

"So, like, compelled by armed guard?"

"It's the one time everyone gets to celebrate together. As a family. And say their goodbyes."

"I just don't think I have it in me," Sarah says. "Besides, I've already said my goodbyes."

***

Joe scans the bar, watching for Sarah's blonde waves to pop out in the crowd, listening for an echo of her laugh. But she's nowhere. He texts her *U here?*, attempting to be casual enough to avert suspicion should Ben see the message on her lockscreen. Half an hour later, he texts again, but gets no reply.

The bar where they shot at the beginning is now packed with giddy cast and crew members drinking, hugging, telling stories, and announcing what's next for them. A critical mass has been reached. It's time for speeches.

With Celeste and Naomi's approval, Joe goes first. He can only muster so much false joviality and the sooner he says his thanks, the sooner he can escape the mob of good cheer. When he steps onto the small stage and looks at the crowd, however, he's buoyed by their smiling faces. He floods with gratitude for all these beautiful people who have helped make his dream come true, and he tells them exactly that. He calls out Celeste, Pete, Igor, and Naomi by name, then he calls out his co-stars for their performances and for helping him go where he needed to go. And he shouts out Randy and Kayla for their superlative karaoke chops.

Then he shares his long-held philosophy that being an actor is, on some level, getting paid to say goodbye to people you care about, or even love. Because no matter how long the show goes on, whether it's a film or a TV show or a play, it always ends eventually and you have to say goodbye. So, you have to learn to embrace every moment while it lasts.

"I have enjoyed every single minute," Joe says. "I promise you that." He slowly scans the faces of the smart, talented, insane people who have worked so hard together for the past month, many months in some cases, and chokes back tears as the crowd hoots and claps for him. "And if it doesn't hurt to say goodbye, then you didn't care enough, right?" The crowd erupts in cheers and applause. He raises his beer by way of toast and shouts, "Thanks, everybody!" before hopping down from the stage.

Cast and crew pat him on the back and come in for hugs as he pushes through the crowd, but they refocus on the stage as Celeste goes up to speak. Joe is grateful for the reprieve. He stands by the buffet table and swivels his head between Celeste and the door, still hoping for a miracle who will not come.

Celeste finishes her remarks and Joe applauds, though he hasn't heard a word. The door opens – a flash of hope – but it's just a grip returning from a smoke. Her speech finished, Celeste sidles up next to Joe reaching for a plate. She considers him a moment as he watches the door.

"It's a shame Sarah couldn't make it tonight," Celeste says, studying Joe's response.

"Yeah," Joe agrees, avoiding her eye. "Yeah, it is."

"She did a great job. She was a good call."

"Thanks, yeah, she's great," Joe says. Tears well in his eyes for what feels like the hundredth time.

Celeste furrows her brows and frowns sympathetically at Joe. "The movie wouldn't have been the same without her." Her voice is kind.

"Noooo, it would not have," Joe agrees, still attempting to dodge eye contact. He turns and quickly flicks a tear away, hoping she didn't see. But when he glances back at her, he knows she did. And that she understands. She smiles warmly and gives him a reassuring pat on the back. His secret is safe with her.

Joe pulls himself together. "Hey, thank you for everything. It's been an honor to watch you work."

"I had great material and a great cast," she smiles. "That made it easy."

"What you do is not easy. I know that."

Celeste shrugs in agreement and begins to fill her plate.

"You know, I'm not really in the mood for a party," Joe says. "Plus, I've got a lot of packing to do. I'm going to head out."

"You don't want to say goodbye?"

"Nah. We're all flying out together. I'll see everyone in the morning." He gives Celeste a quick, heartfelt hug and heads back to the hotel. To his room. Alone.

***

The next morning. Sarah settles into her bedroom window seat, but it feels different now. This has always been one of her favorite spots in the house, especially since Synergy. Her little corner to watch the world go by. It's still a sweet spot to pass a few minutes, but watching the world isn't as appealing as it used to be. She's ready to go out and live in it again.

It's early yet. Ben left for work a few minutes ago and now Sarah watches a parade of kids marching down the road behind a single leashed dog. Her phone chirps at her. It's Joe.

Moved my flight back. Flying out alone. Drive me to the airport?

***

Joe waves from the sidewalk as Sarah pulls up. Instead of just popping the lock for him, she climbs out and walks slowly around the car into his arms. Her body pulses with the magnetic pull of him. He is her North. And she is his.

Joe drops his bags in the trunk, and they get into the car without words. What's even left to say? Being together is enough.

As they pull onto the highway, he reaches for the radio. A last song or two maybe? But the radio doesn't cooperate. As one song ends and the next begins, they freeze. The piano chords are unmistakable. The song that started it all. The dance that changed their lives.

"It's our song," Joe says tentatively, scanning Sarah's face for her reaction. She's stoic, but the moment they first kissed floods into each of their minds simultaneously. She grabs the button and switches it off. Someday, yes. Not today.

Joe threads his fingers through Sarah's on her knee. They drive in silence a long while like that, his thumb gliding lightly over her skin, their only communication. His mind wanders through all the things he would say to her if they had forever. The stories he would tell. The ideas he would share. The bad jokes he would dole out when she needed a laugh. But those are words for a life they don't get.

Not now.

Not yet.

***

Joe hands off his luggage to a skycap with a tip and turns back to Sarah. They melt into each other as the world honks, shouts, and waves around them. A cop yells to keep it moving, but still they do not move until he whistles nearly in their ears, making his point.

Joe takes a step back and grazes the sides of her breasts and waist before landing on her hips. Sarah feels the same bolt of electricity that shocked her the very first time he touched her. "Whoever said it's better to have loved and lost—" she says.

He cuts her off. "Was talking about us." She nods with a contented smile. He taps twice on his heart. "Don't forget."

"I couldn't forget you if I tried, Joe Parker," she says with a chuckle. "I'll have reminders everywhere."

"I won't need reminders, Sarah Abbott," Joe says as he squeezes her hips. He holds her in his gaze, smiles softy, and says in his prophet voice, "You're ready, baby. And the future is so bright."

Sarah glows with the warmth of the sun and her love for him as she replies. "Back at ya."

And they both know the words are true. They've made each other ready, each of them a key for the other. Together they've opened the portal to all the good to come. And there's so much good to come. He pulls her in one last time. She buries her face in his chest as he burrows into her hair, taking in the sweet jasmine scent as deeply as possible. He whispers in her ear, "I will love you every single day for the rest of my life."

She squeaks out her words, barely a breath. "Every day."

They let go. He slides his hands through her soft hair and brings them to her face. He pulls her in for a final kiss – long, slow, almost chaste. A kiss they will remember to their dying day. Their faces linger a breath apart, then he looks into her eyes for the last time. There are no tears. They're done with tears. Sadness remains, but it's blended now with the profound joy of all they've given, and all they've found in each other.

"Forever," he says.

She nods. "And ever."

Chapter Thirty-Six

Hopeful Ever After

Sarah takes her place in the sun on the patio of her new office overlooking Elliott Bay. She's lunched with new colleagues every day and this is her first meal alone since she started. The team is gracious and fun and has worked hard to make her feel welcome and supported. But now she's grateful for a quiet lunch to herself to read her book.

Joe's been gone a month and life has taken on an entirely new shape. The job's barely two weeks old, but already she feels the excitement and passion of real work that challenges her. She gets up every day energized by what's to come. Supporting the creative work of artists in Seattle is more fulfilling than she ever imagined, especially now she's seen it up close and personal.

Things are better with Ben, too. He meant what he said. He was waiting for her. If she's honest, he's still waiting because she's not all the way back yet. Back to herself, yes. No longer at sea. But she's still coming back from Joe.

However, Ben is patient and present. For some strange reason, he's willing to keep holding on. Perhaps because he's remembered how good it can be between them. Sarah remembers, too, and despite all that's happened, she finds herself grateful every day for him. He comes home every night now. They take turns cooking, and some nights they cook dinner together. They binge TV shows and tell each other about work. They double-date with Gabi and Dana and Wendy and Alec. It will take time to find their way all the way back to each other again. To release what's past – all of it – and find their future together. But she promised Joe she would be happy, and she's finding her way there with Ben.

Sarah takes a bite of her egg salad sandwich and cracks open her book. The fountain next to her gurgles so loudly she almost doesn't hear the text pop in. She checks the phone, unsure whether she imagined the chirp, but there it is. Another photo worth a thousand words from Joe.

It's a new tattoo on his left inner forearm. The mirror location of his other tattoo, but on the arm that leads to his heart. The image is of two beautifully rendered cartoon crows, one obviously a "boy crow" and one obviously a "girl crow." They're flying on opposite sides of a globe, but they have a beautiful, golden cord in each of their beaks that floats and twists its way around the globe and keeps them tethered.

Wanted to show you my new ink, he writes.

She taps back, *I thought you said you didn't need any reminders.*

Joe's reply comes quickly. *I didn't need it. I wanted it.*

Sarah stares at it a moment longer, falling in love with the image. It's whimsical and charming and perfect. She types, *What did you tell M?*

She watches the three dots as Joe writes back, *I told her it was a souvenir of my movie. She didn't seem to give it much thought.*

Sarah holds her breath a moment, holding in all the feelings. Not suppressing them, but sitting with them. Simply allowing them to be. Then she types, *I love it.*

She pauses a moment, writes *I love you,* then erases it before she hits send. His dot, dot, dot reveals he's doing the same. There's no need to say it. They know.

***

When they start editing back in LA, it's clear they really have something. Word spreads and they show footage to a few folks who kick start the buzz.

By the time they have a rough cut of the whole film, several distributors are interested, and after a mini-bidding war, Joe's film gets picked up by a major indie distributor. It's everything Joe dreamed of and more.

It will premiere at Sundance, with a wide theatrical release date shortly thereafter, followed by an aggressive video-on-demand plan, and they put real marketing dollars behind it. People will actually see Joe's movie, which was by no means guaranteed from the start. There will be awards and open doors and opportunities that will change Joe's life. They'll see his performance and cry. And whether they know it or not, they'll see Sarah in virtually every frame of the film. At least, that's what Joe sees.

He sends Sarah and Ben an invitation to the premiere through official channels, but isn't surprised when she declines. Probably just as well. But he's so proud of the film. She needs to see it.

***

Sarah plugs away at a budget spreadsheet on her computer, trying to massage the numbers into harmony, when the FedEx guy taps on her office door. She'd found a FedEx note at home the prior day and rerouted it to her office since she wouldn't be home to receive it. An unexpected package requiring her signature was too intriguing to leave unattended on her front step.

"Sarah Abbott?" The dude marches in without confirmation or invitation and thrusts the clunky signature tablet in front of her to sign. She uses the attached stylus pen to scribble an approximation of her signature, then trades it for a small white, purple, and orange FedEx box. No hints of what's within. Until she sees the sender's name, J. Parker.

Sarah walks to the door and gently closes it, hoping not to attract attention. She sits at her desk and stares at the box. It's been seven months since they said goodbye, six since he sent the photo, their last contact until now. She studies the name and the return address, the little piece of him he's sent with this box. His home. His life. Handwritten on an address label right next to her name and address. Her home. Her life.

She carefully edges her finger under the cardboard lip and pulls it open, then slides the contents out. It's a slim, flat, beautifully fabric-wrapped gift box with a perfect bow only slightly compressed by the shipping box. She fluffs the bow and smiles, then lifts the lid.

Inside is a special screener copy of Joe's film. There's a note on top, written in Joe's hand, that reads:

I'm sorry you couldn't make it to the premiere, but I understand. I hope you watch this with someone you love. And that it makes you proud.

J.

P.S. I'm doing a musical next.

***

Sarah and Ben watch the movie together. He puts out his arm and she folds into him, bracing herself against a torrent of emotion she knows will come. He knows it will come, too, and he holds her close as the film starts.

They watch the same film, but see different things. For Ben, who knew little of the story or the players, it's an abstraction made real. It's everything Sarah talked about and everything she omitted. He feels her twitch and catches her downcast eyes when Joe first comes onscreen and he knows at last what – and who – nearly took her from him. And who brought her back to him, too. Despite a perfectly natural desire to hate the film, he finds he can't. It's actually very good. And in a strange way, he's grateful for it. Because no matter what happened in the past, she's in his arms again.

Sarah allows herself to experience as much as she can as she watches, knowing she will need time to process alone later. There's too much. Too many memories. Too many feelings. But it's good. It's all so good. The film is so good. No, it's great. The ending is powerful and Joe is extraordinary. She's always known that, of course. Now the world will finally see it, too.

Just before the final scene fades to black, Sarah hears the song, quietly at first, in the background as a camera pulls back on Joe walking through the park along the lake. Their song.

Tears stream down her face as the credits roll and the lyrics fade in louder. All the emotions she held at bay throughout the movie rush in at last, the dam broken by the song that started it all, that opened the door to a love that may not have been right, but was certainly right on time. They sit through the credits, Sarah weeping, Ben holding her and gently kissing her hair. They ride it out together.

Sarah cries, but she smiles, too. She's proud. And content. And happy.

Near the end of the credits, a long list of "Thank Yous" filled with names Sarah recognizes and some she doesn't. That's followed by a shorter list of "Special Thanks" with individual messages. And at the very end...

"To Sarah, who makes everything possible"

Makes. Not made.

The copyrights and logos scroll by and then the last words roll onto the screen.

"A Tethered Production"

Sarah and Ben sit quietly a moment before she finally sits up and takes a deep breath to center herself.

"How are you doing?" Ben asks.

"Good. I'm good."

He considers a moment. "It was a great movie. I can see why it meant so much to you." Sarah reaches for his hand and squeezes it, but says nothing. Ben pushes himself off the sofa, still holding her hand, and kisses her gently on the forehead. "I'm proud of you, Sarah. I'm going to get ready for bed." As he walks, she holds his hand until he steps out of reach and lets her hand float back to her lap.

Sarah sits with her thoughts for she's not sure how long and stares at the paused screen, still showing "A Tethered Production" in stark white against the black background. She smiles. Then she hears Ben's voice. Has it been a minute or an hour?

"Sarah?"

She angles to his voice behind her. For a moment the smile drops, her reverie broken.

"Sweetie?" he says.

Sarah smiles again, this time at the sound of Ben's voice. They've found each other again. She's kept her promise to Joe. She clicks off the TV, nods to herself, and answers as she gets up. "Coming, hon."

ALSO BY AJ WHITTIER

Good news!
Sarah & Joe will return very soon for a second chance at love.

———◆◇◆———

Until then, enjoy
Magical Seattle Book 2: The God in 3B
(published Summer 2025)

———◆◇◆———

Sign up for my newsletter for news, updates, and a special, same-universe
bonus story at AJWhittier.com

PLAYLIST

Music is an incredibly important part of Sarah & Joe's journey together. Many additional songs and artists made their way into my writing playlist for them, but here are the songs that were mentioned by name or direct reference in *Always Never Meant To Be.*

———◆◇◆———

You Are My Sunshine, Johnny Cash
Everybody (Backstreet's Back), Backstreet Boys
Kiss Me, Sixpence None the Richer
My Lovin' (You're Never Gonna Get It), En Vogue
Tell Her This, Del Amitri
Mister Holland, Gregory Porter
Beauty School Dropout, Billy Porter, Jessica Stone, & Grease Ensemble
Broken Horses, Brandi Carlile
Right on Time, Brandi Carlile
Alexander Hamilton, Original Broadway Cast of Hamilton
Single Ladies (Put a Ring on It), Beyoncé
Mack the Knife, Bobby Darin
The Story, Brandi Carlile
I've Got You Under My Skin, Tony Bennett and Lady Gaga

———◆◇◆———

Look up Always Never Meant To Be on Spotify to listen!